THE DEMON'S DOMAIN

Octobre 23 1811

Madame France

Doit

THE DEMON'S DOMAIN

THE DEMON PRINCES
BOOK FOUR

L. ALEXANDER

ALSO BY L. ALEXANDER

THE DEMON PRINCES SERIES:
The Demon's Deal
The Demon's Discovery
The Demon's Delight

THE GARGOYLE KNIGHTS SERIES:
The Gargoyle's Grace
The Gargoyle's Gift
The Gargoyle's Glade

SUGGESTED READING ORDER:
The Demon's Deal
The Gargoyle's Grace
The Demon's Discovery
The Gargoyle's Gift
The Demon's Delight
The Gargoyle's Glade
The Demon's Domain

NOTE:

**This matches publication order as the two series intertwine, have overarching plot threads and recurring characters throughout.*

*However, each book can be read as a standalone as well, each book is a new couple getting their happily ever after.**

*This one is for my friends who crave the deep,
steady love of a man like Zayne, Percy or Sebastian.*

May that kind of love find and attack you. <3

The most

BEAUTIFUL

part is,

I wasn't even

LOOKING

when I found you

— Blindsided by Forever

AUTHOR'S NOTE

While each book in this series is new fated mates finding their happily ever after, there are story arcs that continue through every book in the series and some are also expanded on in the connected Gargoyle Knights series. To help keep things clear, I've assembled a family tree, glossary and maps sections for authorlilyalexander.com.

This is not a dark romance, but there are some potentially heavy or triggering themes that come up throughout the book. You can find a list of tropes and content warnings below as well as on my website.

Please reach out to me directly for specifics if needed, I'm more than happy to give details, page numbers—whatever helps you best decide if your mental wellbeing and this story are compatible.

Tropes: fated mates, angels, gargoyles and demons, pseudo-medieval European setting, affection through caretaking, disguised identity, magical power discovery, found family

Content: explicit violence, mention of imprisonment, gore & death, mention of injuries, on page body modifications (tattoos), discussion of additional tattoos and piercings, mention of rape / forced impregnation / eugenics (none on page), explicit sexual content, heat-like estrus cycle & some omega characteristics in the FMC, reference to Christian-based mythos for angels / demons / gargoyles

CHAPTER 1
PHIN

"GO ON NOW. They're expecting you." Father Morton ushered me through the vestibule of the church, pulling together the sides of my too large, secondhand coat as we walked. He shoved the basket full of burned candle remnants at me as he opened the church doors, the cold air momentarily stalling my ability to breathe. "Georgina said she could trim your hair while you're there. She'll have more of the tonic for you as well, no need to continue using fireplace ash. Isn't that something to look forward to?"

"Some men have long hair," I argued, but there was no strength in it. I'd long since adapted to speaking in a low whisper that wouldn't betray my identity or bother my damaged throat. Having to carefully select my words from the often nonsensical jumble that crowded my thoughts didn't help, either. "And I wear my hood when I go out. Would it be so bad to let it grow a little? Just this once?"

"We've been through this, my child." He looked down his nose at me, shaking his head. "I empathize, truly I do, but it's necessary." Father Morton sagged and dropped into a whisper, even glancing around to be sure there was nobody else around to hear him. His hands lay heavy on my shoulders as he looked me firmly in the eye and spoke so low his voice was very nearly carried away by the echoes of the hallway. "They'll *never* stop searching for you, Seraphina—"

"Phin," I insisted. That was the one piece of me that had never changed, no matter how else my appearance was disguised. Never had I been a Sera, and Seraphina was a name only those that hunted me used.

"Of course. My apologies. We need to keep up this appearance for now, even if it's just clothes and a haircut. It's the best way to keep you hidden. I know this is difficult, but I promise it's necessary." His dark-brown eyes pleaded with me, and I softened.

This man had watched over me for more years than I cared to count, and he wasn't asking anything outlandish. I was just … tired.

Tired of pretending. Tired of living half a life in this tiny village where I couldn't even make a friend because I was a danger to myself and those around me simply by existing. My desire to *be* a friend, to participate in the community parts of village life, to have a simple, aimless conversation, to even laugh freely, was starting to feel too big to contain.

"I understand." The words left a sour ache in my throat.

"When you get back, we can spend some time working in the library, perhaps? Copying the holy texts is a productive and fulfilling task for us both. The apothecary finally got in some of the blue ink you are so fond of, as well as the gold."

I brightened. Being among the books soothed me like nothing else. I loved the smell of the old parchment and leather, the ink. It reminded me of the many hours I spent at my father's feet in the archives he kept.

My penmanship was somewhat lacking in grace but legible enough, and I took great joy in creating the artistic swirls, scrolls and flourishes around the edges of the pages. The act of copying the letters, the scratching sound of the quill on parchment, it was all deeply meditational.

Father must have truly felt awful about things if he was dangling my favorite reward.

"Yes, please."

"Good. Be sure she actually counts. We're returning—"

"Thirty-six, I know." I marched down the steps, chin tucked, as a gust of wind threaded its icy tendrils into every gap in my oversize clothes.

The walk to the chandler's wasn't far—nothing in town was—but I had to take the extra-long route that passed all the shop windows on the side of the street facing the square only to circle around to the back alley. It didn't even matter that I was there on actual business; I was the village's invisible resident and rarely got to use the front door.

I tapped the designated knock, and Georgina hustled me in like she'd been standing right there waiting for me.

"About time, young man!" she huffed. "I haven't got all day, you know. Not even for Father Morton's special requests." She assessed the contents of basket. "What've you got for me? Looks like maybe twenty or so?"

"Thirty-six."

"What's that? Speak up."

"Thirty-six," I said as loudly as I could, which was still barely above the hushed voice one would use in church. Anything louder strained my throat, and even that volume was pushing it. I held the basket out so she could get a closer look.

Her eyes narrowed, but she proceeded to count as I stared back at her. She seemed annoyed to be caught in her usual attempt to short us. It fascinated me that Georgina was constantly trying to cheat the church of all places out of candles. I couldn't imagine what she thought she had to gain by doing so. "Alright, as you say then." The matronly woman assessed me, her eyes sweeping up and down. "Go sit. We'll get you looking presentable again."

I walked past the two helpers she had dipping tapers in a large tub and a third that was setting wicks in glass containers then pouring in ladles of the thick, faintly yellow wax mix. One gave me a quick smile and nodded in greeting but none of them dared do any more than that. I lifted my hand in a brief wave, thrilled to have been acknowledged. People were mostly indifferent, and all kept their distance. It was for my safety, as well as theirs, but still stung.

I took a seat on the tall stool in the corner of the room, and Georgina approached with her shears, wearing a worn apron she'd only half tied. Her motions were brutally efficient as she removed perhaps an inch of growth. My natural pale color made the strands sparkle as they filtered through the sunlight coming in through the windows on their way to the floor.

"This new mix is better," she muttered, using her comb and scissors together to further shorten the cut along the back of my head. "You'll only have to use a bit and spread it through instead of applying powder."

"Thank you," I muttered. We'd tried just about everything over the years to color my light hair dark. Ashes, soot, charcoal. Nothing stayed very long, and it was tiresome to keep reapplying. "Face too?"

Georgina nodded, eyes squinted as she evened out a section. "Yes, just put a little on your finger and wipe it on your lashes and brows." She assessed her work. "There. All done."

I slid off the stool and reached for the broom resting against the wall, cleaning up the mess. The bell on the front door rang, announcing the arrival of a customer.

"Three at once, mercy me," she muttered. "Be right with you!" Georgina called, removing the broom from my hands and ushering me away from the front of the shop while bundling me into my coat.

"I'll have the new candles delivered to Father later on. They're not set yet." There was urgency in her face as she pressed a jar full of an oily black substance into my hands and opened the back door. She all but shoved me by the shoulder over the threshold.

"I'll tell him. Thank y—" I stumbled into the cold alley, barely fast enough to keep from getting caught in the door as it slammed behind me. Reaching up, I grazed the back of my head with my fingers, dismayed to find the strands even shorter than she normally trimmed them. I quickly pulled up my hood, the jar of colorant for my hair sloshing around as I slid it into my pocket.

My steps were heavy as I moved down the alley. I didn't want to stay out in the cold, but I longed to do something other than return straight to the church, to have somewhere to go other than the places I ran my normal errands for Father Morton. At least in the warmer months I could spend some time in the woods foraging or collecting flowers and pretty rocks.

Though being warm in the cozy vault below the pews, surrounded by the glow of oil lamps, parchment, and ink was definitely preferable to remaining outside in the bitter winter wind alone.

I glanced at the alley-facing window of the apothecary as I passed, surprised to find someone looking back at me. Silver eyes held mine from behind round wire-rimmed spectacles, an unfamiliar handsome face with sharp features and tidily cut dark hair staring back at me.

My heart thudded too hard, too fast, and everything in my body felt prickly, like when my leg fell asleep because I'd been sitting too long. I forced my feet to keep moving, my expression to remain neutral. Heat washed over my skin followed by ice, panic taking hold as I rounded the corner and doubled back along the front of the building toward the church. I walked as fast as I could without outright running, careful not to bring any additional attention to myself.

I was absolutely certain that the beautiful man in the apothecary window had never been to this village before. I also knew that he'd seen me clearly; he'd looked directly into my eyes. I'd even felt his gaze follow me all the way down the alley.

The thing I was most sure of, was that he was no man at all. He was a demon.

And I had no idea whether that meant I was in more danger than usual or not.

"THIS IS NOT what we agreed to, Seir." Anxiety over being so far from home gnawed at my nerves.

"You need a little adventure now and then," my brother replied, an irritatingly excited grin on his mouth as he tugged me along by the hand like we were children. His breath puffed out in front of him as he spoke, and the cold air bit at my cheeks. I burrowed my hands farther into the pockets of my coat, which unfortunately was not meant for this kind of deep chill. "So do I, for that matter," he added. "Come on! What harm could it do? Coltor is watching the gates, and we won't be gone that long. Besides, I was sent on a very specific mission to find some of these plants for Hailon. You know I can't stand to disappoint her."

I sighed. There was no arguing with that. The Fates had chosen well in his wonderful mate Hailon, and if she'd actually made a request, it was worth my brother pursuing.

"What are we searching for in Vincara then?" I asked, looking around at the small village he'd brought us to. "Have we come to visit the monastery? Shouldn't we have brought Vassago along, if so? Or taken the closer portal? The only thing nearby is a small village."

"So where in Vincara are we then, brother?"

I frowned at him. "This doorway lies in the forest on the outskirts of Aymonroux."

His head turned my direction as we made our way toward the center of town, a devious grin on his mouth. "Here I thought I might be able to surprise you with our destination. Clearly, you've wandered further from the crossroads than I thought."

I scoffed. "You were trying to stump me? Did you not think I could identify the specific doorway we traveled through?" I frowned, confused by why he hadn't seen the flaw in his plans. "I would recognize any of them, even if I don't visit what lies on the other side even a single time." His eyebrow raised as though in challenge, and I dug in, frustration brewing. I couldn't tell if he was just trying to get a reaction out of me or being serious. "I know *all* of them. It's my *job*. Has been for centuries. You know that, right? It's very important to me that you know that, brother."

Seir laughed, the sound free and easy, a plume of breath hanging on the air in front of him. In many ways, I envied the lightness he'd always carried. He dipped his head in friendly greeting to one of the townsfolk who glanced our way while my skin tingled at the sudden attention.

"I might have my moments, but I'm not a *complete* idiot, Tap. Of course I know that. There's just so many now, I thought I might be able to surprise you, is all."

"Imagine my relief." I pushed my glasses back up my nose and glanced around as Seir paused at a storefront window, the painted golden lettering scuffed and faded. "An apothecary? Rylan couldn't procure what she needed?"

He shrugged. "Hailon came to me with her list, so I assumed not. Maybe she didn't ask him." A broad smile reappeared on his mouth; clearly Seir liked the idea that she'd skipped asking our very well connected archmage brother in favor of him. "I tried all the places in Revalia and Emankor I could think of, but none had what she wants. One of the merchants recommended I come here." He pulled a scrap of parchment from his pocket, a list of several items in clear script upon it. I followed my brother into the store, the scent of herbs and earth heavy on the warm air.

"Be with you in just a moment," a gruff voice called from the back of the store.

Seir waited at the counter, reading over his list with a pensive expression. I was drawn to the back wall, where bouquets of flowers rested in baskets, tied up and wrapped, ready for gifting. As it was barely past the turn of the new year, I couldn't help but wonder how they managed to keep such a variety of fresh blossoms for sale.

"Interesting place," I muttered to myself, pausing with a fingertip on the petal of a light-blue hydrangea as movement outside the dirty windows caught my attention. Across the alley, someone quickly exited through a shop's back door, fingers feeling along the back of their head before they pulled up their hood. I couldn't tell if I was looking at a man or a woman; the simple trousers and heavy coat gave no sense of figure away. They walked toward the apothecary, hands stuffed in their pockets, frowning. My breath caught when bright lavender eyes rimmed with smudgy lashes met mine through the glass, but they didn't slow their stride. I stared as long as I could see them, transfixed, blood rushing loudly in my ears and a strange crushing sensation gripping my chest. In response to the increase in stress, I turned the ring on my index finger around and around with my thumb. My heart had jumped to a fierce, rib-pounding beat, and I rubbed my hand over my coat in a useless effort to slow it.

It seemed it really was best I remain at the crossroads unless leaving was absolutely necessary.

"Sorry to keep you waiting. Can I help you?" the gruff voice said, breaking me out of my reflection. I turned to find Seir stiffly reciting the names of several plants. I slowly walked over to join him at the counter. The portly, aged shop owner diverted his attention from my brother to me as I approached. "Sure, I can get those for you." He glanced between us, gaze calculating. "Won't be cheap though. Several of those items are rather rare. I'll need guarantee of payment up front, I'm sure you understand."

Seir set a single silver coin on the counter, making a point to jingle the pouch he kept in his pocket. "We're good for it. But I'm afraid I must insist that we see the items before I pay the balance."

The shopkeeper's eyes bulged, and he choked on his words. "Of course, sir. Apologies, it's just not often we see such ... *particular* requests. Especially not from out-of-town visitors. Excuse me." One leg betrayed a bit of a limp as he scuttled through the door to the back room, mumbling words that made it seem like he was already mentally spending the money Seir was ready to trade for Hailon's list of herbs.

"That single coin alone is worth far more than what you asked for, and I'm certain you know that."

"I do." Seir nodded. "He needed some motivation, so I provided it. Now, if he tries to take advantage ... that will be a whole other conversation." His set of three sharp canines appeared, his normally jovial grin having taken on an edge. My brother's duality was often a source of both amusement and terror.

"Mmm." While the shopkeeper gathered Seir's order, we perused the other wares. Between us, we selected a few trinkets, a tin of assorted teas, and several unique sweets. Seir found nail lacquer on the shelf with cosmetics and whooped in excitement before choosing a bottle of black for me and three new colors for himself. I picked up a sizable puzzle box that looked like an oversize book. I was sure it would keep me amused for a time as I turned it over to examine the fine details. I took great joy in replicating such clever items once I'd solved the puzzle and disassembled the contraption so I could work out the specifics of the design.

Between the collection of cosmetics, the inks and quills I found off in a corner, and the fresh out-of-season flowers, I was intrigued by the apothecary's selections to say the least. For such a small village, the shop certainly catered to some very expensive and niche needs.

I stared out the window again as Seir selected several bouquets. An enigmatic smile and violet eyes flashed through my mind, and I mused about why the person I'd seen earlier had been leaving through the back door of the shop across the way.

"Here you are," the man said by way of announcing himself. He unloaded bundles of dried herbs, packets of seeds, and even a few live plants onto the counter.

Seir looked them over, and when I nodded that it all looked to be in order to me, we set the rest of our items on the bench as well, much to the shopkeeper's delight. Several coins passed from our hands to his, and he bounced on his surprisingly nimble toes as he logged our transaction in his ledger.

"Pleasure doing business with you gentlemen. We also do special orders," he enthused. "Have yet to get a request we couldn't fulfill. Though a couple of these"—he gestured to the herbs—"are exceptionally limited until next growing season, and therefore will be very hard to get and increasingly costly."

"Good to know," I muttered, glancing back at the inks.

"Thank you." Seir gathered his bundle of packages, and I took mine, bracing for the cold that awaited us outside.

"Come on." My brother bumped my shoulder with his. "Let's get an ale to keep us warm and see what the local cuisine is like." My brother tugged on my sleeve, his boundless energy returning.

"Seir. Not what we agreed," I reminded him.

"Another hour, Tap. Please? Humor me. The gates are well watched in your absence." It was the sadness in his eyes that got me, the way he begged like a sad pup while somehow making it seem like he was doing what was best for me. It had always been like that between us.

"One glass."

His smile broadened. "You won't regret it, I promise."

"Bold of you to assume I don't already."

His laughter lit up the space between us as we strode off to find the tavern.

AFTER A HEARTY meal, two tankards of ale instead of the one we'd agreed upon, and a double coat of black nail lacquer for us both, we made our way through the quaint town square back toward the portal. In truth, I'd gotten a bit too comfortable at our table, as it was right next to the hearth, and was dreading even the short journey back in the cold. Unfortunately for me, Seir was also dragging the return walk through town out longer than I'd expected, so my bones were already chilled again.

I'd become spoiled by the consistently comfortable climate at the crossroads.

My brother's focus had been only on the apothecary on the way in, and he was struggling with the desire to gaze through every other shop window we passed now.

"We really do need to get back," I urged, Seir's attention drawn by what looked like a studio for pottery and glassware.

"I *have* to go in here. I promise I'll be quick," he said with urgency, not waiting for me before stuffing his parcels into my arms and throwing himself through the door.

"I'll be waiting here, I guess," I called after him, shaking my head and gesturing with full arms to a stone fountain. Across the square, clusters of patrons hustled into the tavern we'd just left.

The door opened and closed as people huddled under their cloaks, going in. As I prepared to take a seat on the edge, the church bells began to chime the hour. Two bells, after a quaint little melody. A group of three, the last of the rush to get into the tavern, paused before disappearing behind the heavy wooden door.

I clenched my jaw and my fists, sagging into myself as the resonance of the iron made my teeth ache and turned my thoughts into a tangled web of nonsense. The tone in the iron was familiar, but not in a pleasant way. I was thankful to have missed the chime for midday. Twelve would have been torturous.

When the ringing stopped, I turned toward the church and found myself stunned once again.

The person I'd seen in the alley was just standing there in the churchyard, and they weren't even wearing a coat. Their breath puffed out in quick, measured clouds, and, even from a distance I could see their body shaking from chill. Without making a sound, they sagged nearly in half, one hand fisted over their breastbone.

My whole body screamed, urging me to take action. My heart squeezed like it was in a vice. And my own breathing was stilted and raw as I panted through the pain, unable to look away from them for even a moment.

Just as I took a step, a priest hustled across the churchyard, blanket in his hands. He wrapped it around their shoulders and shepherded them back inside. I stared at the closed door longer than I cared to admit, warring with the urge to run across the square and go inside myself.

Movement drew my eye to the steeply pitched roof. A statue shifted from a crouch to fully standing and spread his wings out wide, staring me down the whole time.

An explanation for my odd reaction to the whole situation percolated through my thoughts as I wondered whether or not the stone kin protecting the church was friend or foe.

Seir emerged, another package in his hands. "All set!"

I shifted my focus to my brother for a second, and when I looked back at the church, the stone kin was gone. "What was so important in there?"

Seir squeezed his parcels to his chest, broad smile on his mouth. "Wind chimes." His face fell as he got a good look at me. "Are you well?"

"Indigestion." I rubbed at the burn behind my ribs with the heel of my hand, but it would not be soothed.

He nodded, a knowing look in his eyes. "Probably the tavern food, you're not used to anything so rich. You eat the same few things all the time when you bother to eat at all."

I muttered a vague agreement as I followed him back to the portal, my thoughts elsewhere. Thankfully, he carried the conversation on without realizing I was distracted, content to chatter all by himself.

My only focus was on the disturbing notion that I needed to return to Vincara. Soon.

I needed to speak with the stone kin who guarded the church.

I was now certain that those entrancing violet eyes belonged to my mate.

CHAPTER 3
PHIN

SEVEN DOSES. THAT was all that was left.

I stared at the little bottle, willing the liquid inside to multiply. It did not.

Carefully, I placed a single drop of my daily tincture onto my tongue, grimacing at the potent bitter taste, the way it burned all the way down my throat and into my stomach. Hands trembling, I resecured the cork and set the vial on my little bedside table, nervously clutching at the oval amethyst pendant of my mother's necklace.

The apothecary had promised Father they'd have a fresh batch ready by the end of the week, but that was far too close to me running out completely for my comfort. I hadn't gone a single day without it in years, and I didn't want to know what would happen if I did. I was already struggling with the formula needing to be changed—my freezing episodes were becoming much more frequent and at times were fully debilitating. And that didn't even account for the main reason I took it. To run out completely would surely be catastrophic.

Father called from the main room of the library. "Are you ready to get started?"

I stepped out of my small room and joined him, relieved to find that my frayed nerves were somewhat settled. Whether that was a real side effect of having taken the tincture or just my imagination, I wasn't sure.

Silently, he set out our quills and ink, then spread parchment over the two workstations. When his eyes caught mine and held, a frown tugged at his mouth. "Are you feeling better?"

"Yes. Sorry about before. I thought I had more time." I'd gone out into the churchyard to fetch some of the few remaining fresh herbs to cook with and had gotten caught by the bells. I'd never even made it to the garden.

"That's alright, my child. It's not your fault."

He settled a leather-bound tome in front of me, and I turned to the pages where I'd left off the last time. Words became nothing more than curves and lines as I copied them letter by letter to a fresh sheet of parchment. I absorbed no meaning from the writing like this, my focus distilled down to nothing more complicated than the way my quill rasped against the fibers in the paper.

I was setting aside my seventh page when I looked up to find Father Morton dozing in one of the comfortable armchairs. His workstation was clean, and the oil in the lamps was running low.

Once I stopped, my body's aches began to make themselves known. My shoulder was tight and sore, my eyes tired and starting to blur. My stomach growled and my throat was painfully dry. Sad that the pleasant activity had come to an end, I set to cleaning up my station as well. The new pages were laid flat on one of the shelves to dry, the book I was working from reshelved. The pots of ink and quills went in a little nook so they wouldn't be somewhere they could get bumped or spill.

Yawning so big my jaw cracked, I reached above my head,

indulging in a powerful stretch. Joints popped and muscles creaked as everything loosened back up.

"Father?" I leaned close to his ear, one hand gently shaking his shoulder.

He blinked awake. "Are you all finished?" I nodded, and he got to his feet, giving my work a cursory glance. "Nicely done. Come. Let's get some supper, yes? We've been down here for hours. I abandoned my labors quite a while ago, but I was loath to interrupt you. You always look so peaceful when you are deeply focused like that." His heavy hand patted my shoulder, and I reveled in the praise.

I followed him up the stairs, admiring the smears of ink on my fingers, already regretting that I'd have to wash it away.

Just as we went into the small kitchen, the telltale creak of the door opening stopped us.

"I'll go," I offered.

"No, no. You're not in your robes and your hair coloring is wearing off. I'll greet them." He slipped on his own robe and went into the main vestibule. I glanced around him, but I couldn't see much. "Hopefully they're just here to light a candle or take a moment of prayer."

I began assembling a quick meal of soup and bread, Father's voice rising and falling a few times while I stirred.

Father rushed through the small kitchen and into his room. On his way back, he made strong eye contact and said, "Do not leave this room."

Stunned by his gruff tone, I just nodded.

As everything simmered, I washed up the few dishes left from lunch. Out the small, wavy window over the sink, I caught a glimpse of three people walking across the yard back toward the tavern. They were all huddled together, wearing hoods over their heads and scarves across their faces. It was impossible to tell anything about them, but they didn't seem to be from the village based on the shabby condition of their clothing. Nobody would survive the winter very well here without a decent coat.

Father came back in, expression blank and his mouth tight.

"Everything alright, Father?" I asked.

"Fine, fine," he answered hastily. "I'll just wash up so we can eat." He wrung his hands together, and my stomach churned. He was lying. "Would you mind bringing it into my rooms?" he asked. "I have evening service to prepare for."

"Of course." I dished up the soup, carried his to the small table in his room, and ate mine standing at the counter, wishing I'd been able to get a better look at whoever had visited and left Father in such a state.

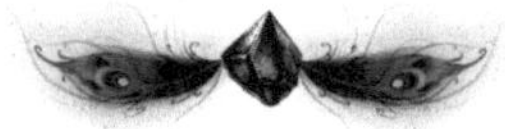

FATHER MORTON ALMOST never sent me to the apothecary, but he was too busy preparing for service to go himself, and I was desperate for my tincture.

Unable to stop fixating, I had pilfered the library to find possible suggestions for an alternative in case the worst happened and I had to take emergency measures. The books were laid out on one of the small tables, mocking me every time I walked in or out of my little room. Several of the suggestions were more familiar to me than I cared to think about, but I'd survived them once; I could do it again. Especially if they bought me time until I got my hands on more tincture. Finding the plants, however, given the season, might prove a significant challenge.

And I was out of time.

I'd used my last dose of tincture before breakfast, and it was nearly dark. Father had become exasperated with me peering into his room over and over again, hopeful they'd sent word that it was ready. He shooed me out the door with an extra scarf wrapped around my neck, coin in my pocket, and a muttered prayer that they'd done what he asked.

Things had been a little extra tense between us since the night the strange visitors had upset him, but we were mostly pretending everything was fine. It was a welcome relief to have a moment away from the church if I was being honest.

I hustled across the square toward the alley behind the shops, through the noise from the dinner crowd at the tavern spilling out into the street, and in and out of the light from shop windows.

The rear door of the apothecary was almost directly across from the one at the chandler. I rapped the knock I'd been instructed to give and waited, my breath hanging in plumes of steam in front of me. Sunset had come and gone, and full, frigid darkness was rapidly approaching, the soft slush and snow already icy under my boots.

The old proprietor peered through the small crack he'd opened the door. "Can I help you?

"Father Morton sent me." His blank stare made my heart skip. I forced out the words I'd practiced over and over in my head on the way over. "His tincture, it's supposed to be ready today." My quiet voice was muffled by the heavy air.

With a grunt, he disappeared. My throat closed further the longer he was gone, worry that he still didn't have it or had just left me standing there in the cold setting in deep. I only breathed fully again when he finally returned with a slender glass bottle. I offered the coin Father had given me, but he refused it with the wave of a hand.

"Keep your coin." He frowned. Then he cleared his throat. My heart began to pound louder and faster the longer he delayed. "Please give our apologies to Father. We can't make this anymore."

Panic raced through me, icy in my veins. "Why not?"

"The ingredients. Perhaps you could try another apothecary."

"But there is no other." He just shrugged as I stuttered out the frantic argument. "I'll pay extra," I rushed to say, though I didn't have any money to speak of. Maybe I could help Georgina at the chandler, or perhaps he needed someone to clean or stock shelves, and I could trade? Surely there had to be something I could do to earn some coin.

"Not about the money." He moved to close the door, and I shifted in my panic, blocking it with my foot. His eyes traveled from the scuffed toe of my boot back to my eyes.

"Where's the rest?"

"That's all there is. We can't help him anymore." There was pity on his face as he looked me over. He straightened, glanced both directions as though making sure we weren't being watched, and tugged on the door again. My foot slipped from the little space, and I heard him latch the lock as soon as it clicked closed.

"No. Please."

I stepped back, shock leaving me numb as I stared down at the precious little bottle. Less than half what it should be. Six weeks' worth, perhaps less. Not much time at all.

My throat burned from all the words I couldn't say, all the screams I kept locked inside. Frantic thoughts bounced around inside my head; panic clouded my ability to think or speak coherently.

Fingertips numb, I shoved my hands down into my pockets and walked as fast as I could back to the church, panic gripping my chest and tears threatening to fall the whole way.

CHAPTER 4
TAP

FROST-DUSTED LEAVES CRUNCHED softly under my feet as I traversed the forest toward the little village.

I'd managed to keep myself away from the apothecary in Vincara for over a week, but my patience had found its limit. Besides, I needed more ink. Some hollow needles as well. Perhaps a new quill, or a more complicated puzzle box as I'd already solved the one that looked like a book and had disassembled it to make my own version. Anything to help distract me from my fixation on the person with violet eyes and the crushing, fiery sensation lingering in my chest would do.

The temperature was somehow even lower than it had been when Seir and I visited, and very few people were out because of it. Smoke plumed from chimneys, everything too quiet under of the heavy weight of the cold. The snowcapped mountain range loomed behind the town, silent and seemingly endless. Somewhere up there was the stone monastery my brother had used to learn how to manage his bloodlust. I had long thought I should visit but never managed to go.

The bells on the apothecary doors chimed, announcing my entry. I was instantly grateful for the warmth of the shop.

"Welcome back, good sir!" The proprietor brightened, straightening up behind the counter. He was clad in what looked like a new vest, and a pair of shiny spectacles was perched on the top of his head. "What can I do for you today?"

I gestured toward the small area where the ink and quills were. "What type are these?"

He puffed up proudly. "Iron gall."

To his credit, iron was more expensive but also more stable than carbon or botanical varieties.

"The blue, what is the pigment?" The depth of the sapphire color was striking. I preferred black, but the blue would certainly be lovely to use. There were several new colors on the shelf since my last visit as well—yellow, green, red, and even gold. The cost seemed prohibitive for such a rural village but there must have been buyers for such a thing or it wouldn't be stocked.

"The broker guessed they used lapis for the color, but I'm more inclined to believe azurite or even true cobalt."

The shopkeeper was clearly well learned about all his products. Perhaps my earlier impression of him as only interested in profits had been misplaced. His clientele must be quite pleased with his eye for detail and be willing to travel for his unique offerings. I was here, after all.

"I'll take two of the black, and one of the blue. Should I just ..." I plucked one of the bottles off the shelf.

"Yes, please take your pick."

I chose the bottles I wanted and approached the counter, going back quickly for one of the fancier inkpots and quills on a whim. "Do you carry medical supplies?" I asked, setting those with my inks.

His head tilted to the side. "What would you be needing, sir?"

"Needles. Both with a solid core and hollow, if you have them."

The shopkeeper rubbed at his chin. "I might have something." He turned and started pulling open drawers. The whole wall behind the counter was made up of different sizes and shapes, it was a wonder of construction and likely filled with untold treasures. I added building one along the large wall in my workshop at the crossroads to my endless list of potential projects. "Ah!" he exclaimed, climbing down off the step stool he'd mounted to get to one of the higher levels. "These, perhaps?"

I was presented with a felt cloth displaying several silver needles in varying lengths and circumference. They looked more suited to sewing or other tapestry crafts than my purposes, but they would do with some minor modifications.

"I'll take the lot."

The gruff little man smiled and set to packaging up my purchases. Coin exchanged, I gathered the parcels and left the shop, oddly in no rush to return to the crossroads.

Seir would have been proud, I thought, as I casually made my way to the tavern and actually found myself enjoying the relative peace that came with my hearty meal and ale next to the fireplace. I did wonder if he was unreasonably busy in my absence or if he'd had to call in some assistance, but the notion didn't make me as itchy as it normally would. The villagers were very good about ignoring my presence as well, which led me to believe they got a reasonable amount of people passing through. It was nice not having inquisitive eyes following my every move.

As I was paying out the barmaid, she glanced over my shoulder and frowned. "It's best if you wait outside."

I turned too late to see who she'd addressed, but my gut churned and my chest felt less heavy as I collected my change.

Violet eyes seared into me as I exited the tavern. "You." The word was barely a whisper as it left their lips, but I could still feel the accusation in it.

"Hello." I lifted a hand in greeting, immediately feeling awkward. I cleared my throat and pushed my glasses up, heart pounding.

The barmaid arrived then, shoving a corked ale jug as well as a wrapped basket at them. "Tell Father Sunday roast is chicken this week, not lamb." She glanced between us, one eyebrow raised. "Don't go causing trouble now," she warned, disappearing back into the tavern. I wasn't entirely sure which one of us she was addressing.

Eyes wide, they shifted the items around to carry comfortably and turned away, walking toward the church as fast as they could go.

"Wait," I called, taking several fast steps to catch up. "Would you like some help?"

"I'm fine, thanks."

"Really, it's no trouble—" I reached out and grabbed for the ale, which had slipped from their grip and tilted as it made its way toward the frozen ground.

"What do you want?" They stopped, stance defensive. Their quiet voice had an edge of desperation, and I realized that the sheen in their eyes was not just extra moisture from blinking back the frigid air.

I raised my hands up, the ale jug thumping against my chest at the swift motion. Frustration roared through me, the need to soothe them nearly overwhelming. "I'm sorry. I was just trying to help." The stunning violet eyes pierced me with a glare. "I'm here getting some things from the apothecary." I dug in my pocket with my free hand and produced the little parcels.

"You were here before."

"Yes." We came to a stalemate, just staring at one another's faces. Theirs was a study in opposites—sharp cheekbones and soft jawline. Pale skin highlighting their dark eyebrows and eyelashes, but the color didn't seem natural for some reason. "I'm Tap. Pleased to meet you ...?"

They turned and dashed off again without responding. I should have let them be, but I couldn't leave without knowing more. "Please, allow me to apologize!" I broke the silence between us as my feet hit the dead grass of the churchyard. "I feel as though I've gone about this all wrong somehow."

There was not even a single glance spared for me as they mounted the stairs and disappeared into the church.

I stood there for several long moments, debating what exactly the correct thing to do would be.

"Bold of you to come back here, demon. I thought we understood one another despite not actually speaking the last time you visited this village."

I turned the direction the voice had come from, and my breath puffed out in front of me as I looked up to the roof. "Hello."

The stone kin man shook his head and leaped from the roof, heavy wings stretching wide to slow his fall as he landed near the rear of the church. I walked toward him, trying to still keep my eye on the church door, but he took several steps into the cover of trees beyond the property line, and I lost my sightline.

"I'm Tap," I said, putting my hand out. I recognized his features, the scowl in particular. "You must be another of Magnus's sons."

Surprise pulled at his dense black eyebrows. "Another?" He made no move to shake my hand, his arms crossed tightly over his chest. He was taller than me by just a small margin, broad in the shoulder like Coltor, and he had Magnus's eyes.

"Yes, I'm well acquainted with Coltor. Your father and my brother Rylan are quite close." His expression remained unchanged, and I found myself scrambling to offer some tidbit of information that would convince him we were not enemies. "I've met your sisters as well. Lovette is a gifted healer, and Imogen is a marvel at the forge."

He tucked and hid his wings, reverting to his fully human form. This seemed positive, like he didn't deem me enough of a threat to remain in his larger, more formidable gargoyle skin. "Do you live in Revalia then?"

I shook my head. "No. Two of my brothers do, though. I reside at the crossroads."

His stance relaxed, and he finally extended his own arm. His grip was brutally firm as he shook my hand. "Well met then, demon, and my apologies. I'm Tormund."

"Pleased to meet you."

"What brings you all the way out here?"

"Your apothecary. They have a selection of things I can't find anywhere else." It wasn't entirely a fabrication, though not the whole truth either.

"And your interest in the church?" he gestured vaguely at the ale jug in my grasp.

My chest tightened. "Personal." His eyebrow raised. "Curiosity then. Is this your post?"

"Yes. I've been stationed here for quite some time. Speak plainly, what is it that interests you here?"

"The person that was in the churchyard, the one that dropped this. I'm … drawn to them."

Tormund grunted and rubbed at the dark-brown beard covering his chin. "Elaborate."

I decided there was nothing to be lost with honesty and blurted, "I believe them to be my mate."

He froze, and a gruff laugh rumbled out of his chest. "Unexpected, indeed." His head ticked to the side, but he said nothing further.

"Why are you posted here?" I asked, though I already suspected I knew the answer.

"There are secrets kept in that church that require protection."

Simple and direct, but still incredibly vague. I could appreciate that, honestly. "I mean no trouble."

"But still, you bring it." The large gargoyle let out a heavy breath.

"I'm only meant to protect the dwelling and those deserving of such protection inside it. To misdirect threats. Are you a threat, demon?"

"Of course, I am. But not to them."

Tormund nodded, one corner of his mouth ticked into a smile. "Fair enough. You're welcome here, so long as you keep it that way."

"You have my word."

"Good." He shook my hand again and turned to go. "I should warn you, Father has a Heavenly visitor at the moment."

"Someone other than the person I'm interested in?"

"Indeed. High rank by the looks of him."

"Mmm." That complicated things. "You'd allow me in there with him, knowing what I am?"

He shrugged. "I suspect you to be less of a threat than him, if I'm being honest. He feels ... darker than you."

I wasn't sure whether I should be offended by that or not. "Can I pass along any message to your family, should I see them before you?"

He smirked. "Tell them I hope to join them at the conclave soon. Good luck to you, Tap. I'll be close by, so make sure you and the angel in there behave yourselves."

His wings deployed, and he was airborne in the space of a breath, disappearing into the low-hanging clouds, leaving me standing in the cold alone.

I gathered myself and crossed the yard again, unsure whether I should just knock on the church door, not feeling as though I had a right to just walk in. I was rescued from my internal panic by the appearance of the priest, though the dark expression on his face as he crossed the short distance between us argued that I might not be saved at all.

"Inside. Quickly, if you please. Our humble church is as solid as the mountain itself, but quite a challenge to keep heated." He eyed me warily from under bushy gray eyebrows as he stiffly gestured toward the door. "And the neighbors do like to gossip." The priest relieved me of the ale with a quick grab, eyes darting every direction as though ensuring we weren't being watched.

To be fair, we were. Just not from the directions he was looking. Tormund peered down on us from the roof, his dark laughter reaching my ears just as the door closed behind us.

I lingered in the vestibule alone, their conversation of harsh whispers echoing back at me from somewhere past one of the side doors. Just beyond the little entryway where I stood was a lovely grotto with memoria candles, their flames flickering in the draft of the open chapel. I leaned closer, curious about the intricate carvings inside small alcoves in the heavy stones of the walls.

One was a bust, made for one of the previous priests, Father Aymon. The very one the village was now named after.

The priest reappeared. "What is your business here?" he demanded. There were suspicious new lumps under the sides of his robes.

"Have you ... *armed* yourself? Has the clergy started training with weapons again? I thought that was long since done." I was teasing, but my amusement was clearly not shared. I sobered. "Apologies, Father. I assure you, I'm no threat."

"One shouldn't tell lies in the house of God." The priest shakily removed a sword that was likely nothing more than wall decoration, still in full sheath, and a broom from either side of his robe, holding them defensively.

I raised an eyebrow. "Is He home, Father? Should I speak with Him directly? Perhaps I should, it would put centuries' worth of questions about where He's been to rest." The priest inhaled in surprise, adjusting his stance. This was not the right tack to take, and I knew it, though at present I did have several pressing questions for the Fates, and including Him in my inquiry would have been welcome. I showed the priest my hands, doing my best to appear contrite. "I'm no danger to you, I promise. Nor your other company or acolyte. I don't even have a blade on me."

"Your kind has no need of such things to be dangerous." The priest chuffed. I inclined my head in deference. He wasn't wrong, but I was not a brawler like some of my brothers were.

"I'm not an acolyte," the soft voice came from just beyond the door.

My mouth twitched with the threat of a smile. The fact that they were speaking to me at all soothed the raging pull of the bond. "Be that as it may, my point stands. I'm happy to prove it, though I'm not sure how. I haven't burst into flames or anything similarly terrible since coming onto the grounds. Surely that's a worthy argument in my favor?"

"What do you want with us?" the priest asked, looking at me with heavy suspicion. I wondered if he finally realized I hadn't even so much as raised the volume of my voice. "Whose orders bring a demon to Aymonroux?"

"Orders?" I frowned. "I haven't taken orders from anyone in quite some time. My assignment is permanent, and I am dedicated to it." The priest shifted his weight from one foot to the other, his frown deepening. "I came to your village to buy ink and needles." I presented the parcels I was keeping in my pockets once again, seeing no need to include the other much more pressing reason I'd ventured back. "I have no command sending me on missions to places such as this."

"Then why not just make your purchase and be on your way? Why follow Phin here?"

I rolled the name around in my mind, committing it to memory, enjoying the way it glowed around the edges as I repeated it to myself. "They dropped your ale, so I brought it. I was only trying to help."

"I said I was fine." Phin came out of the shadows in full earth-colored serving robes, complete with golden ropes tied around the waist and a hood that covered most of their face. Only a sliver of chin and mouth was visible, and even that disappeared when they bowed their head slightly. "But thank you for bringing it."

"Make your intentions known," the priest grumbled, clearly frustrated with me, or perhaps both of us. "I have other company and am pressed for time. Are you here for something in particular?"

A flash of violet eyes met mine from under heavy shadows.

I wasn't sure how to answer the question for a moment, because I absolutely was, but not quite how they likely thought I was. "No. Yes." My face heated as I became flustered. Seir would have absolutely been rolling with laughter if he were there to witness me floundering over my words, and *inside* a church, no less. "I saw you through the apothecary window last time I visited ..." I broke off, sure that sharing how their eyes had haunted me day and night since I'd first seen them was a step too far at this point in our acquaintance.

Their head snapped up and for a second, I had an excellent view of them, despite the hood. The longer I looked, the more certain I was that the person before me was not presenting as their true self.

"I saw you in the yard when the bells rang the hour." Both of them straightened. "In truth, I simply couldn't escape my curiosity. And apologies for being trite, but I fear I have the same question you do. What exactly is an angel doing in Vincara?"

Phin's eyes widened a bit further before they turned to the priest. I immediately regretted having made them uncomfortable with my blunt question.

While I was distracted by Phin, the priest jerked forward, and something wet hit my cheek.

"Holy water?" I surmised. Seeing no reaction other than for me to dab at the moisture with my sleeve, the priest sagged. I wasn't sure if it in was disappointment or relief. "Would you like me to touch an idol as well? See if it burns my flesh?"

"No, no. You've proven yourself well enough I suppose." He waved a hand and grumbled several words under his breath. Father clucked his tongue and leaned the sword and broom against the nearest wall, clearly having decided I offered no imminent bodily threat.

"Morton, is there a key for this little room? It's locked," a deep voice asked, floating in from another room.

Phin dashed to a corner, chin dropping to their chest as their arms linked inside the sleeves of the robe.

"No need to open it, it's just storage for … damaged or discarded things," the priest rushed to say. "Did you find what you were looking for?" he asked, eyes on me but clearly asking the other man.

"Unfortunately, no. You have many tomes but not the one I need."

Phin's whole body sank into the shadows of the corner they'd gone to as the man stepped out from the hallway. I could feel the way they tried to sink into the very plaster, make themselves invisible to him.

Already on edge from their response, I blinked, stunned into silence as I recognized the angel's face.

The tall silver-blond man paused for a beat, took me in, and laughed. "Father, are you in the habit of letting just *anyone* into your church?" Father Morton began to babble, but the angel just patted him heavily on the shoulder. "I jest. Greetings to you, Tap. What are the odds we'd both end up in a place like this on the same day?"

"Hello, Armaros. Incalculable, I'm sure." I forced my tone to stay light, despite the way just being near him made me uncomfortable.

"Are you also here for a lost relic?"

"Something like that," I muttered. I glanced at the priest who looked as though his heart might stop at any moment.

"No fighting," he ordered.

Armaros laughed. "We can be civil, can't we Tap?"

"Of course."

Father Morton stared between us, then finally let out a breath. "Come, then. My supper is getting cold, and it's much warmer in my chambers."

"After you." The angel gestured with his arm, sending Phin scuttling quickly after the priest at as much of a distance as they could manage between either of us.

I couldn't help wondering what exactly I'd walked in on, but I was thankful to be there … if only for Phin.

CHAPTER 5
PHIN

T WAS LIKE I was standing and watching things happen from somewhere outside my body. I was very sure I was awake and had all my faculties about me, but being stuck in a room with both an angel and a demon wasn't unlike the sensation I got during one of my freezing episodes. I was hot under the heavy robe but thankful the weft of the fabric allowed me to see through it fairly clearly while remaining hidden.

We adjourned to Father's small living quarters, the angel doing a poor job at disguising his wrinkled nose as he took in the small room that only hosted a single bed, small desk, fireplace, and table. The shelf behind the desk held several books and a set of scrolls, and there was a window over the bed, but nothing that would indicate a man had spent most of his adult life living there. Decorations were sparse, and everything from the furniture to the curtains and the hand-braided rug on the floor looked like it had seen better days, just like most things in the church.

"Please, have a seat." Father gestured to the little table. "It isn't much, but you are both welcome to share in my meal." Armaros took the chair on the opposite side from the demon, leaving one between them for Father.

Holding my breath, hood as far down as I could tug it, I came forward and poured ale into their cups. I made the mistake of looking away from the food as I dished out stew from the big tub the Spruce and Axe had provided. Both the angel's violet eyes and the demon's silver ones tracked my every movement, but the weight of them felt vastly different. The angel's felt predatory, the demon's merely curious.

My hands trembled, giving away the fact that the rolls we'd bought were day-old as they struck the edge of the bowls with a solid sound. I hastily retreated to the corner of the room the moment I was finished, thankful it hadn't been my day to prepare dinner on top of everything else. I certainly didn't want my mediocre cooking to be the feature during such a meeting when I was already drawing so much unwanted attention. Though he'd barely twitched, I had been braced for the angel to snatch at my sleeve or tug off my hood every time I got within his reach. He was the embodiment of everything I was being hidden here from.

"So, Tap," the angel said, blotting his face on the edge of Father's stained tablecloth like it was a napkin after a single sniff of the stew and delicate bite of a roll, "what is it you're here for? Never seen a demon so eagerly visit a church before."

The scholarly demon set his spoon down. "I actually came for the well-stocked apothecary," he said. "But one of my brothers once found a rare book here. As I was nearby …" He shrugged.

The angel grimaced as he sampled the ale. It seemed none of our offerings met his approval. "I see." He looked at Tap as though trying to tell if he was being truthful.

"And you, Armaros? What is it you seek here? It's not often angels venture to the earthly plane. At least, not without violent intentions."

Father gasped, choking on his food.

"Very straightforward. I like it," the angel laughed. There was a flash in his eyes as he glanced in my direction that made me feel like there were bugs crawling all over my skin. "Not many are bold enough to address me so, though I suppose I should have expected such from a fallen." His laugh made my stomach turn. "A relic, as I said, though it seems it is not here as I'd hoped."

"I'll keep looking, though many have been lost to time. It may be a fruitless search, unfortunately," Father mumbled.

"Is there anything else I should know about your recent visitors, Father?"

Father Morton shook his head. I held my breath, not wanting to miss a word. "No. I've recounted the whole conversation we had."

"Other visitors? You seem to have many for such a small village," Tap commented, eyes sliding to me for a brief moment.

"Indeed," Armaros agreed. "Tell me again what they said." His voice went cold.

Father Morton blustered under the hard stare of the angel. "They're looking for a woman they say they know. I suspect based on their description, a Nephilim."

I froze, heart pounding behind my ribs. I practiced slow breathing, but my head started to feel floaty. Surely his tactic was purposeful, but I felt completely exposed. The three visitors from the other day *had* actually been looking for me. Why hadn't he told me?

The angel glanced at me again, and I willed the walls to swallow me whole. "Aren't we all?" he muttered.

"Is Heaven seeking out Nephilim now?" Tap asked. "I didn't think they held much interest to the celestial plane due to their ... varied natures."

Armaros grinned wide. "We're calling all our flock home, particularly Nephilim." He playfully gestured toward the demon. "Even the fallen could be welcome, if you're interested. You carry angel blood, after all. At least you did."

"I leapt from the celestial plane for good reason. I have no interest in returning."

Armaros spread his hands wide. "As you say, then. But yes, I'm working on an initiative. It's quite genius, really." The angel's eyes flashed in excitement, but his abrupt shift hinted at mania, like he couldn't wait to brag. Nothing about him felt right, and I'd met many angels before coming to live here. My own father was one, after all, and he was the opposite of this man despite their similar physical traits. "I've been doing research on Voices. How to select and pass down the more desirable ones. So naturally, finding those with angelic blood who can help us with the practical parts of testing my theory is necessary."

The demon's mouth dropped open, and his eyes flashed red. "You're seeking out Nephilim to use as ... *breeding stock*?" He pulled a face, clearly disgusted.

Father Morton was nervously eating his food, seemingly happy to let them carry the conversation as long as neither he nor I were the focus of attention.

"That's a rather crass way to put it, though accurate I suppose, as more babies *are* the goal. There are rewards in place, of course, not the least of which is the privilege of being matched with a full angel for the duration of one's participation in the program. We require more participants to help us create the next generation. Full angels with the ability to reproduce in such a manner are not as plentiful as we'd like, and they're doing what they can already. However, with my new method, we can ensure only the most useful and desirable talents are passed on, making all new births that much more valuable."

I fisted my hands and continued being invisible, every last one of my parents' worst fears being confirmed right in front of me. I was beyond thankful for my tincture, no matter how bitter, or how much it burned, in that moment.

The demon sat back in his chair, clearly trying to create distance between him and the angel. His voice grew louder as questions poured out of him. "The records you want—I'm assuming they have to do with this? Why is such a thing necessary at all? Are the faithful no longer being rewarded with residence and wings like in days past? Is there something other than their penchant for picking pointless fights with other species reducing the number of angels?"

Armaros laughed, the bitter sound digging into my skin as it rolled over me. "Scholar to scholar, new angels being made has become a rarity. We don't know why, but this is how we fix it. My brilliance has found a way!" He cheered for himself, making us all jump as he pounded a fist into the table. "And somewhere, there's a ledger with record of all Voice talents to ever exist. I want it. Imagine, knowing which family line had the ability to freeze time for a moment, or see into the future. Who could Voice an object into being or move one at will, or manipulate the thoughts of others. Such information would help immeasurably with my efforts. As would a few dozen Nephilim," he muttered the last bit of his diatribe, glancing at me yet again. "Your servant, Morton. Is there something … unusual about them?"

I did my best to breathe, but staying upright was becoming a bigger concern. My heart pounded against my ribs, and the same numb feeling had started to creep into my fingertips like when I had an episode.

"Nothing of note. He's just a village boy I keep on to do chores." Father Morton's words were measured, but I worried he'd spoken too quickly, that the angel would be suspicious.

"Mmm." Armaros narrowed his gaze and looked away again. "You're sure there's nothing else I should know about?"

"I've told you everything," Father Morton assured him.

"That's a disappointment. I expected my visit to yield more … tangible results." The angel looked at the demon with a smirk. "Perhaps you know where I could find some Nephilim?"

"No. And this is a deplorable mission, Armaros. Do you not see that?" The demon shifted in his chair, eyes red and teeth elongated. It should have frightened me. Instead, that odd tightness I'd experienced when I first saw him through the apothecary window squeezed along my ribs. It was Armaros that had my jaw clenched and a shiver running along my spine.

He sighed. "I shouldn't have expected a *fallen* to understand or support any sort of plan to expand the population of Heaven." Armaros chuckled darkly as he gathered his belongings and stood. "Send word immediately if you get any other visitors I should know about or if they return. It's important I find them."

"Of course." Father scrambled to his feet.

"Tap."

"Armaros." The demon had his arms crossed, eyes blazing red as he stood.

The angel laughed as Father Morton escorted him back through the church. "See you around, Tap. Always a pleasure."

The demon only looked my direction once Armaros was out of sight. "Are you alright?"

I exhaled and breathed fully for the first time since he stepped into the church. "Yes."

Odd that, how an angel leaving and a demon staring at me brought nothing but ease.

"ARE YOU SURE you're not hungry, Phin? There's plenty left," Father offered for the third time. I shook my head, stomach still too knotted up to even consider food.

Once Armaros was gone, I'd slumped into a seat at the table and removed my hood, thoughts spinning wildly as I recounted what I'd heard.

"I don't mean to rush you, but I should be getting back soon," Tap said, eyes back to silver behind his spectacles.

"Back to where?" Father asked.

"Shall we make a gentleman's agreement to be honest with one another, Father? Or do I need to keep secrets for my safety? I've seen the company you keep." The demon held his hand out, his elegant fingers capped with nails coated in a slick black lacquer.

The words bristled against my skin as his eyes skimmed over my face, too close to my own burden, too familiar.

"A truth for a truth?" Father prompted. "No deception?"

"I have no reason or desire to lie."

"No blood required?"

"Of course not. We're not signing contracts or making deals. Just having a friendly conversation."

Father wiped his hand on his robe, measuring the demon with his eyes but reaching out to shake his hand, nonetheless. Then Tap offered his hand to me.

"Oh, I ..."

"I do not wish there to be mistrust between us, Phin." He bent his head slightly, earnestness in his stoic expression.

"Alright." I put my hand out tentatively, and his much larger one engulfed it, his grip warm and firm as he gently pumped my arm up and down a few times. A hot shock passed between us, and when his eyebrow raised the same time my eyes widened, I knew he felt it too.

Father eyed our hands suspiciously as they separated. "Friendly conversation, indeed," he muttered. "Let's start again. Where are you so anxious to return to?"

"The crossroads."

Father blustered and pushed his dish aside. "That's no answer at all."

"And yet, it is the truth." Tap turned his hands palm up on the table. "And you? What are you doing with them, here in this remote village? They're clearly being sought out by the angel you just hosted at your table." His gaze pierced into me, but it was not threatening. It was as though he were looking past all the cosmetics, all the layers, and studying what was underneath. I fidgeted under the weight of such a stare.

"What do you know of Heaven, in recent times?" Father asked. He waved a hand to signal I should stay seated as he rose to fetch the bottle of spirits he kept in the drawer of his small desk. He poured himself a healthy measure and consumed it in one swallow before offering the bottle to us. At our mutual refusal, he buried it back in the drawer and returned to the little table.

Tap's head tilted, and he pushed his glasses up the bridge of his aquiline nose. "Not much. I've not walked there in centuries."

My fingers twitched, the casual revelation of his age a surprise. I was nearing my seventy-fifth year, though with much of that time spent split between Earth and the celestial plane, my true age was closer to thirty very sheltered human years.

"Are you of the original fallen?" I asked, interest piqued. Their names were all recorded in the archives, but only those with special privileges ever got to read the histories kept there. My father had been one of the few with access, and I'd done my best to remember every lesson he ever taught me during our time together in those rooms, but many of my memories were fragmented or lost altogether now.

Tap gave a single, shallow nod. "Yes, my brothers and I leapt long, long ago." He turned back to Father Morton. "I can only assume things are not as perfect as your brethren would have the faithful believe?" His mouth twitched at the corner when Father didn't respond. "Imagine that."

"What will you do with the information you've learned here?" Father asked, urgency in his tone. Tap shrugged. "I am trusting you, demon, not to use any of this to harm us."

"I have no quarrel with you, Father. Friendly conversation, remember?"

"Yes, so you said." He glanced between us, then took a deep breath. He filled his empty glass with ale, though his sigh indicated he would have preferred another serving of spirits instead.

Tap sat back in the skinny wooden chair. "Is Phin your given name?"

"Yes," I said immediately.

Father shook his head. "They know her as Seraphina."

Tap's mouth twitched into a brief smile, expression softening. "Your parents either had a marvelous sense of humor or were trying to hide you in plain sight."

"Both, perhaps," Father confirmed.

"I prefer Phin."

He nodded once. "Understood." The demon's silver eyes thoughtfully caressed my face once again before he turned his attention to Father. "What is your plan should he return and see through your misdirection about who she is? If he decides to do something as simple as lift her hood? What if others continue coming here looking for her?"

"Like you?" Father asked, an edge to his tone.

"No," Tap shook his head, eyebrows pinched together in confusion rather than offense. He absently pushed at his glasses again, moving them up his nose. "Not at all like me. You heard what he wants her for. He spoke plainly."

"He's an angel, revered, beloved by Him—"

"*He* hasn't been seen in at least a century, probably closer to two." Father blustered, but the demon continued, "And you are wise to be afraid of them." The statement hung on the air. Finally, the demon sat back again. "Have you considered taking her to the monks? Surely the monastery is more secure than here?"

"The monks are no more trained to fight than I am. It would be unfair to ask them to defend against such powerful beings on her behalf." I looked away. I'd visited the stone-walled monastery high in the mountains several times with my parents over the years.

The monks were always very kind and welcoming. The last thing I wanted was to put them at any risk. "He would take her." Father said it as though still unsure, despite it being our most consistent fear, as if Armaros hadn't clearly spoken his intentions.

"Yes. Without remorse. To be used as he pleases, no matter what is best for Phin, with no consideration for what she wants." He turned to me, jaw flexing in his agitation. "Are you in communication with your parents?"

The remaining warmth drained from my face. I missed them desperately. "Not since I came here."

"As I suspected. You fear the Heavenly for good reason." His face pinched again, gaze far away as he glanced toward the door, one hand twisting the rings in his earlobe.

Father sighed. "I promised I would watch over her. Swore to keep her safe. We've been lucky so far, very lucky—"

"It seems to me your luck has run out." His voice grew loud and he tilted his head, one eyebrow raised as he appraised Father Morton.

"Father?" My chest was tight, heartbeat throbbing in my ears, several terrible scenarios playing out in my mind and words piling up in my throat. "Who were the three visitors?"

He hesitated, swallowing and opening his mouth several times without actually committing to saying something.

"This is important, Father," Tap insisted. "Wouldn't you agree?"

The priest sagged, gaze shifting between us, shame in his eyes. "Travelers. Angels. Two men and a woman." I swallowed a gasp. "They stopped by the tavern, here, several shops. Asked some ... unusual questions. Brother Frohman from the Spruce informed me of their visit as soon as he was able, as did Georgina. She said they stopped into the chandler while you were there." Georgina hustling me out the back door floated into my memory. I reached up to touch my hair out of reflex. Tap's silver eyes were fixed on mine, and I blushed under their intense scrutiny.

The demon, mouth tight, changed subjects. "What is it you do here, Phin?"

"Sorry?"

"Do you have talents? Skills?"

Nervousness crept in, making my fingers tingle and my cheeks burn. "I help care for the grounds. I cook some." I shrugged. None of my daily tasks were that impressive.

Father's features softened as he looked at me. "Modesty is one of her many virtues. In truth, I am able to focus on my sermons without interruption because of her. She is always running my errands, making sure I eat. The candles, the cleaning, the changing of ceremonials for services." He smiled proudly. "Even the vault benefits from her skill." As though realizing he'd let a secret slip, Father straightened. Perhaps the single glass of spirits had packed more of a punch than I'd thought. "As you heard, we keep a collection of texts here." Father shifted around and cleared his throat, redirecting the subject. "Phin's well educated. Though I fear she's seen little of the world beyond this village. Safety has taken priority over exploration."

"Naturally." He turned that intense silver gaze back on me. "You were taught reading, writing and sums, yes? Perhaps it is not the same now, but I recall the celestial gardens were particularly well appointed for botanical studies. And they instructed on strategy and the basics of swordsmanship and battle, I presume?"

"Yes, that sounds right." I was not half as strong physically as most of my classmates, and I had done poorly in my weapons classes as well as math. As a Nephilim, I'd only been invited to take the beginner levels. My parents had done what they could to make sure I kept up, but my mind had not been of nearly as much value to the Heavenly council then as my body was now.

"My favorite was animal care. In my time, they had quite a menagerie on the grounds. There were more of them than there were of us. I took quite easily to speaking with them all. I suspect my affinity for creatures is in part how I ended up with the station I did once I left."

"That sounds nice." I inhaled deeply, trying to ensure I spoke clearly. Not being able to increase my volume often worked against me. "I was only allowed to observe the creatures, but they were all very beautiful. I spent as much time as I could watching them."

His smile dropped away. "You were only allowed to observe?" Tap's tone was soft, sincere.

I nodded. "Interacting was strictly reserved for full-blooded students."

His face scrunched up as though he'd tasted something rotten. "Well. It's been a very long time since I was a student myself, I apologize if I let myself get carried away. Things are clearly different now than they once were. Too often, things don't change for the better. I rarely reminisce about such ancient history, perhaps it's best if I stop altogether." I bobbed my head, a little confused by his mood swing. He continued, "I realize it's brazen of me given our recent acquaintance, but what if I told you I could offer a solution?"

Then everything stopped, my thoughts grinding to a halt as the chiming of the bells rendered me speechless and frozen.

CHAPTER 6
TAP

PHIN'S GAZE WENT blank, and she sagged in her seat as the bells tolled. My own jaw ached, the same itchiness in my teeth and skull from the tone of the metal returning. I shrank into myself, shoulders hunched and thoughts unfocused, though nothing felt as intensely as when I was outside and they'd gone off during my last visit to the village.

"Isn't that something," Father murmured, looking between us.

I recovered once the bells stopped, but Phin sat dazed in her seat still, one hand clutched around the pendant that hung over her breastbone.

"Is she well?" I shifted so I could get to my feet quickly, worried she needed a healer. My hands itched to touch her, the bond flaring in panic for her well-being.

"It may take her a little bit to get back to herself, but she can hear us fine." He patted her shoulder gently.

I relaxed back into my seat but was not comforted. Phin's gaze was unfocused and distant, the violet in her eyes nearly eclipsed by the black center. Her breathing seemed shallow, and her fingers clenched and released in a consistent cadence.

"Is there something unique about the bells?" I asked.

His eyes were shifty as he glanced between us. "The bells have been here as long as the church, there's really no telling—"

"I thought we agreed to honesty, Father?" I reminded him.

His gaze fell to his hands on the tabletop. "There are some traditions that resist change."

"Forged with blood then." My voice dropped low. He was absolutely right; some things never changed, no matter how much they needed to. He gave the slightest nod. "Given freely? Some kind of dedication ceremony? A blessing?" He said nothing, but the way his cheek twitched gave me my answer. "Ah. So the blood of those injured or lost in so-called holy battle, then." Father Morton's head bowed and I clenched a fist. It was possible that my own blood was present in the iron, or that of my brothers. Others of our kind who had fallen while fighting Heavenly adversaries. My brother Rylan had a collection of blades forged in much the same manner in order to be more deadly to certain foes. "Who?"

"I don't have details, only vague notes written in code from my predecessors. The translation key has been lost to time."

I puffed out a breath, nerves on fire. Rage crept back into my veins, burning me from the inside out. "So, keeping her safe here involves a certain amount of torture?"

He winced, cheeks turning pink as he looked at Phin, who seemed to be coming around. "Unfortunately, yes. But it was never my intention to harm her."

"You never told me about the bells," she groused at the priest, speech slow and stilted, her quiet voice full of shock.

"You have my apologies, but there was nothing to be done about it. And in fairness, it does give a certain amount of protection. Once I realized, I moved your room to the lower level to provide more distance from the sound." Her frown was rivaled in intensity by the hurt in her eyes. The priest blushed deeper, guilt etched into his features. "Forgive me, my child, I've done the best I could with the tools and resources available to me. Even if that was only a closet in the nave or a storage room in the cellar."

I wasn't so sure I believed that. Phin looked terribly betrayed over his choices now that a stranger was examining them with her. My demon, normally still and quiet, was riled on her behalf. My anger had gotten quite a chance to lash out today.

"What is your suggestion?" she asked, attention turned to me.

It was rash, what I was doing, entirely unlike my normal, methodical approach to things. But it didn't feel wrong. In fact, I was experiencing the strongest sense of rightness I'd felt in years.

"The crossroads is a place between all places. One could argue it's a virtually impossible location to find at all. Not to mention, it's very well guarded," I explained. "There's always at least one demon on duty"—I gestured to myself—"often two. There are more within reasonable travel distance. Sometimes there's a member of the stone kin present as well."

"Stone kin?" Father asked on a gasp. "I thought that was just a fable, a clever history for some ugly statues."

"That's unkind, Father."

He blanched. "I mean no disrespect. One must admit they aren't carved to be particularly attractive."

"You mean gargoyles?" she asked, eyes wide as though she found the notion of an animated statue fascinating. "Like the statues on the roof?"

"The ones that channel water are grotesques, but yes, exactly like that. The ones that live and breathe when not in their statue form are called stone kin. There are some that are just carvings, however. You've never met one?" My heart thudded at a rapid pace behind my ribs. Despite the odd circumstances, I was deeply enjoying this conversation if only to see her face transform with wonder.

"No."

"Perhaps you have and just didn't realize. They're not terribly unlike you or me."

"Wouldn't it be funny if the ones on the roof woke up at night and we never knew?" she mused, a spark dancing in her eyes.

"Indeed." I looked forward to the day she either realized or I could tell her that at least one of the carvings here was, in fact, hiding a secret life, one dedicated to her benefit and protection.

"I could swear one of them moves a little day to day." She ducked her head, clearly embarrassed to have said so out loud.

"I thought demons and stone kin were mortal enemies?" Father Morton interrupted, eyebrows drawn together. "That they were created to keep holy buildings safe from your kind."

Phin's face fell. "If that's true, they would have attacked you, right? If they were alive? To keep you from coming inside?" I didn't begrudge her the disappointment that crossed her face but craved telling her the truth all the more.

"Perhaps. Though it would seem that many of the old beliefs and hierarchies are changing," I answered vaguely. "In any case, it would be very difficult for anyone, angels included, to find you at the crossroads." This, at least, was indisputably true. One would have to stumble upon a portal and have enough knowledge of the doorways to correctly access the right one.

"You're suggesting I go there with you? To stay?" The little space between her eyes wrinkled in confusion.

My pulse pounded in my ears. Phin saying it out loud made my half-thought out plans real. The ache in my chest intensified, clearly in approval of the idea that I'd have my mate close at all times. It took immense effort to remain calm on the outside, to say the words that were truth but also remained neutral.

"Only if you'd like to, though it does seem a logical option. For your safety."

"Why? You don't even know me." Her mouth curved into a

perplexed grin. She was clearly more stunned than amused, but her lightness couldn't be fully dampened, it seemed.

"My offer is not purely philanthropic." That was understating things, but still honest. "I need help. I have a library that would benefit greatly from an attendant."

She blinked three times in rapid succession, her attention thoroughly captured.

"You would just … keep her there?" Father asked, his interest also piqued, though he was disguising it a little better than she under a layer of concern.

"If she wants to come, yes. Though I'm afraid that would leave you without your helper, Father."

He frowned at me. She looked between us. I could feel both of them genuinely considering the suggestion that had come to me on a whim, and even I was surprised it would suit everyone's needs so well.

It was impulsive and potentially disastrous, but I was already committed and couldn't bring myself to regret having made the offer. In fact, the idea of having unlimited time with her was attractive for reasons that had nothing to do with my freshly awakened mate bond.

"There's no rush to decide," I said after several long moments of silence, despite the screaming in my head to the contrary. "I can return another time." My chest ached and burned at the suggestion, but there was no part of this I could hurry along or simply foist upon her. She needed to have a choice, in all things.

Phin shifted. "Father, it was angels here that day? You're sure?"

He grimaced. "Yes. And they were looking for you, my child."

Her face transformed, a momentary flinch, one that made my thoughts go blurry around the edges with anger. "Could I leave, if I wanted?" she asked, eyes wide and round. "Come back here? Or go elsewhere? Is there a village nearby? Other people?" The more she spoke, the raspier her voice got.

"Yes. Everything one could need is easily accessible, and you would be able to go where you like, though I cannot guarantee true secrecy or safety anywhere but the crossroads itself. I could draw up a contract if it would make you more comfortable? We could negotiate all the details. List them out plainly before you decide." A vice tightened around my ribs, but I forced my breath and voice to remain even. "But be assured Armaros *will* return. He was too interested not to."

"My parents. If—*when*—they come back, could they get a message to me there?" Phin asked.

"Yes, there are methods of communication that could be used in such an instance."

She nodded slowly, a whole conversation held between her and the priest with just their eyes.

"It is a better option than we've been presented with so far." Father Morton reached across the table and covered her hand with his.

"Is it wrong to trust him?" she asked. They both pinned me with a stare.

"I can step out for a moment if you like?" I suggested, feeling awkward that they were discussing me while I was still present.

"No, stay," Phin said quietly. "I mean no insult. I'm just not always the best judge of things. I'd like Father's opinion."

"As you wish." I leaned back in the chair, hands folded in my lap as they continued.

"No, I don't think it's wrong. He's been truthful," Father Morton said sincerely. I appreciated his words, despite the covert insult.

"What about the chores?"

"I can find some members from within the congregation to help me, don't worry about that." He patted her hand.

I felt it then, the subtle shifting of my entire world.

Phin looked at me, violet eyes bravely holding my gaze even as her voice wobbled. "I ... Yes, okay. I'll go with you."

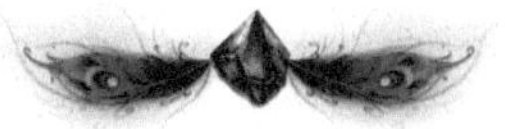

AFTER A BIT more discussion about logistics, Father led us all down a steep stone stairwell to the lower level of the church. There were marks on the walls, traces left behind from the fingertips that had dragged along the stones for balance and comfort up and down through many decades. I added mine, unable to ignore the pull of participating in such rich, tangible history.

At the bottom of the curving stairs sat thick wooden doors that stretched from floor to ceiling. They would certainly serve as a mighty blockade if not propped open, but they seemed out of place in a humble village church. Through them was a room perhaps double the size of Father Morton's modest living quarters. The walls were lined with shelving, the air was heavier and scented with the unique smell of old books.

Phin walked straight to one of the shelves and ran a finger down the spine of a wide leather-bound tome. Her eyes lingered on it as she continued on to the single doorway at the far end of the library that Father had gone ahead to unlock. She disappeared into the dark room, leaving the door halfway open behind herself.

"Does she scribe for you?" I asked, noticing the works in progress on a shelf.

Father clasped his hands at his waist. "She does." After a moment's deliberation, he pulled a stack of single sheets from a shelf. "Most of these are hers."

The form was tidy, the flourishes clearly made with care. They were also proof that the apothecary had at least one customer for the gold and blue inks I'd admired. "I will not allow her talents to be neglected. She'll be able to practice whenever she likes."

"She'll be very happy to hear that, I'm sure."

I scanned the shelves, finding many old tomes. Surprise lifted my eyebrows as a few stored near the floor were obviously ancient and beyond any monetary value. I wondered if these were the secrets Tormund was protecting or if he'd been referring to Phin. Glancing over, I realized that the massive, heavy doors did make sense after all, if this was what was kept behind them.

A much more sinister thought crossed my mind. He'd locked her bedroom door to keep the angel out. And the bigger ones ...

"These doors—you lock her behind them?" He bowed his head and my anger flared. "How often?"

"Only at night," he said quickly, hands raised. "After dark, once she comes down. I lock her in. For her safety. And to block the sound of the bells."

I simply stared at him, communicating how displeased I was with that information until he turned away from me.

He sighed and hunted along the shelves until he pulled out the book he wanted. He cracked it open on the little desk and flipped pages, stopping about three quarters of the way through. When he spoke again, it was in the old language, a tongue I would never forget but had not used in centuries. Father had selected a vow to read, and I understood immediately what he was doing.

As he spoke, my demon was brought to the surface. I rarely shifted anymore, but the old tongue triggered an almost instant response. My black bat-like wings unfurled from my back and spread wide, taking up most of the free space in the room. The tip of my thin, whiplike tail came to rest by my foot and tapped restlessly on the floor. I could feel my canines elongate and my tongue split at the tip. My scalp ached where my crescent-shaped horns had slid out, the points facing the wall behind me. Father Morton, to his credit, didn't stop speaking, though he'd taken a step backwards as he surveyed the changes.

He stopped talking, and I completed the phrase I'd committed to memory centuries before, the old language rolling off my lips like I'd never stopped speaking it. Sparks flew as I spoke, the priest's eyes widening when he realized he'd invoked the magic built into the language itself.

He nodded solemnly, and looked in the direction of Phin's room, then back to me. "She is not for you, my son." Father Morton frowned, leaving me curious what he'd seen in my face that concerned him.

"You would claim me?" I joked, a bit shocked that he'd addressed me in such a way. "Even after seeing the ancient words burn in the air between us? After seeing my true nature?" I gestured to my body, intentionally shifting all my features back to their human form, thankful my clothing hadn't suffered any damage.

He shook his head, but a half-hearted smile crossed his face. "You're very strange. Not at all what I expected of a demon."

"I'll take that as a compliment, Father."

"You should. And I would welcome you into my flock, if not for the obvious reasons that's not possible, of course."

I smiled back at him, genuinely amused. "Thank you for that."

"Still, Phin is opposite you in the most vital of ways. She is *not for you*. Understand?"

I did. But given the circumstances, I wasn't sure his assertion or my agreement even mattered. Never mind that he was entirely, fundamentally, wrong.

"I was very much like her once," I said earnestly. "Not so different now, all things considered. Rest assured I have no interest in seeing her harmed." Nothing could have been truer.

His gaze went somber. "I am entrusting you with her care," he pleaded with me, hands pressed together in front of his chest. "I made a vow to keep her safe. If this is how I fulfill that promise, so be it, who am I to question the will of the divine?"

"You believe the *divine* brought me here?"

"How else could this have come to pass? A demon in my church? There's no other explanation." I didn't dispute his assertion, because there certainly were forces beyond either of us that had brought me to this place.

"Then the divine also brought you an angel. One who is hunting her quite literally for her body. One you seem quite friendly with, all things considered."

Father grimaced. "Sometimes my business is messy, I'll admit. But I send her with you with my blessing. To ensure she's valued, and not reduced to a ... a function."

"She will be safe with me," I swore, a flare of heat going off behind my ribs.

Father Morton took my hand between his and held on tight, releasing me only when Phin returned with a small bag full of her worldly possessions and a tentative smile on her face.

And so, a covenant was struck between a man of the cloth and a demon over a Nephilim with violet eyes, and the demon absconded with her back to his domain to watch over and keep safe, for as long as she would allow it.

Amen.

CHAPTER 7
PHIN

I WAS NO STRANGER to traveling by portal, but it had been quite some time since I'd experienced it.

The last journey I'd taken through one had been with my father, our arrival back earth-side from Heaven. We'd been scheduled to return again in just a few short weeks, but instead, our earthly home had been destroyed, my parents had left me with Father Morton, and I hadn't seen either of them since.

My stomach lurched as we stepped out of the device and into a vast hallway of doors.

"Welcome to the crossroads," Tap said politely.

My eyes bounced from one doorway to another, and I couldn't help marveling at the sheer number of them. Each was different than the one before it, if only by a tiny detail on the frame or the hue of the space within the passage itself. They seemed to go on forever down the corridor, rows upon rows of them side by side.

Another voice greeted us back from a short distance away, getting closer as it spoke. "No need for formalities, I'm not—"

A man—another demon, this one with shoulder-length auburn

hair, tan skin, and an abundance of freckles—came to an abrupt stop in front of us, eyes widening as he took me in. He finished his thought slowly. "A stranger." He reached out a hand, an easy smile brightening his expression as he took me in. It was kind despite the fact that he had three sharp canines instead of just one on each side of his mouth. "But *you* are. Hello. I'm Seir."

Tap shifted his stance as I accepted Seir's offered hand and received a firm grip and solid shake in return. I simply stared at him, already regrettably beyond my daily capacity for responding to surprises with even a modicum of grace.

"Seir, this is Phin. She's going to help get the deals library sorted."

"Wonderful! Another assistant." He hadn't let go of my hand, and I struggled to keep steady as he pumped my arm up and down excitedly. "You'll be well organized and able to actually relax in no time, Tap. This is excellent news."

"That's the hope." Tap gestured for me to come forward after patting his brother's shoulder, asking him wordlessly to release me.

"Sorry." Seir laced his fingers together at his waist as though restraining himself, his friendly smile still in place.

"Phin, this is my brother, Seir. He's actually around quite a lot lately. He's the second demon I mentioned before."

I tensed, and to my surprise, they both noticed straightaway.

"I don't have to be," Seir jumped in, eyes shifting between us. "If that's a problem."

I froze, unsure whether to trust how they were both being so accommodating.

"We can take it a day at a time. Should you find yourself over-whelmed, just say so." After I processed Tap's words enough to nod, we walked toward what looked like an open living room at the end of the massive corridor.

"Are we inside?" I asked, not finding a ceiling when I looked up, but also not finding sky. It was warm and there was no wind, but the space felt too vast and open to be a typical structure. Now that I'd noticed, it was slightly disorienting.

"In a manner of speaking, yes, but also no. As I said before, the crossroads is a place between all places. This hall, these libraries and my—*our*—living quarters are neither inside nor out. I have given walls and even ceilings to some of the rooms for comfort, though that's not strictly necessary. It will become less noticeable over time. Would you like to sit?" Tap gestured to a new-looking leather sofa.

As I settled onto the first cushion, I noticed Seir hesitating at the far end of the furniture arrangement.

"I'll go on home, unless you need me? Hailon is due back from the city soon."

"That's fine. Phin, is it alright if he returns tomorrow? Or would you like a few days to adjust without any other ... personalities to maneuver?"

I opened my mouth and closed it again just as fast, floundering for a response. Was I being tested? What if I gave the wrong answer?

"If you don't like my company, I'll leave, no questions, though I can't guarantee no hurt feelings. How about that?" Seir offered, his expression gentled and oddly familiar for reasons I couldn't quite figure out.

Still, I struggled to formulate words. There was no disingenuousness in either of them that I could tell. It was wholly confusing to have my preferences considered at all, let alone catered to. "Okay."

"Good. I'll see you tomorrow then. Nice to meet you!" He bounced away, waving his hand as he went. I could somehow feel that he'd gone, like when a beam of sunlight goes behind a cloud.

Tap, on the other hand, exuded a sense of calm. He felt like the gentle ripples in a lake. It would definitely be a mistake to under-estimate the power there, but they could also be very soothing if you relaxed into their embrace.

I flinched from my own thoughts, wondering where such a strange comparison had come from. A burst of heat stung behind my ribs, reminding me that I had passed on eating supper with Father Morton and that it had been a great while since I'd traveled to a plane beyond Earth.

"I was not expecting to return with a long-term guest when I left here this morning." He adjusted his glasses, then fidgeted a bit, picking along the edge of the nail bed on his thumb with his forefinger. His black lacquer had chipped away from where he was rubbing. "Excuse me for just a few moments? I'll prepare your room."

"I can help," I suggested, not keen on being left alone in this strange place. "I'm very skilled at changing linens."

His mouth flattened into a thoughtful straight line and after a beat, he gave a short nod. "Yes, alright. Perhaps a tour then? So you can learn the lay of things?" Tap stood and I followed him through a set of double doors off to one side of the living room area.

"This is the familiar contracts library." His mouth ticked into a gentle smile as I looked around. The scale of the room took a moment to comprehend. It wasn't a particularly long or wide space, but the shelves climbed up the walls for what seemed like an incredible distance. There was a large table and chairs at the center of the room, aligned with the oversize fireplace.

I blinked. "Familiars? Like animals and witches?"

"Yes, like that." One corner of his mouth tipped up. "Creature and mage pairings require formal contracts. They're drawn up, approved by me—well, they were—and kept here. Temporarily, at least. Long-term temporary." His eyes narrowed and he opened his mouth as if to say something but then seemed to change his mind. "In any case, organizing and shelving the contracts had gotten away from me, and I had to enlist help, much like I have with you, to get it sorted out. Merry has made great strides here in very little time."

I stumbled over his words. Another woman? Was she also part angel? My skin prickled. Was he also … collecting us?

"Does she come here like Seir does?" Another thought made my throat dry. "Or does she live here too?"

Tap shook his head. "No, she resides earth-side. Her visits are not frequent." That simultaneously brought relief and an odd sense of regret. If someone else were here at least I might have a chance at making a real friend. "There's something about the dust here." His mouth quirked thoughtfully and his eyebrows pinched together as he ran a fingertip along a shelf and looked at it before rubbing it away with his thumb. "It bothers her, so it's best she not linger. Seir often takes her some documents to be sorted or approved. She's in charge of all this now, unless there's a problem. She has other duties topside as well."

"There's a ceiling in here," I muttered, finally realizing why the room felt somewhat cozy despite its size. The fireplace wasn't lit, but I imagined when it was going the room was quite comfortable to work in.

"Yes. If you find that the rooms without one are bothersome, I can set an enchantment to give them one."

"It's not a real ceiling?" I asked, suddenly eager to climb the rolling ladder that circled the room and check for myself.

"Real enough." On that cryptic note, he continued through another set of double doors with glass in them as I stared at his back. "And this is where I need your help most, Phin."

I gasped, realizing that the size of the first library had not at all prepared me for this one. It was maybe twice as wide but many, many times longer. Shelves lined all four walls with only the massive fireplace on the far long wall interrupting them. They climbed to the same unnerving height as the other room if not a bit higher, all filled with scrolls, envelopes and ledgers. Everything upon the shelves was arranged haphazardly at best and perilously at worst. There was a stout, broad table in the center that might seat twenty or more, if one could locate the table's surface or a single chair through the piles of documents. A rolling ladder sat off in one corner, blocked in by stacks of boxes, paperwork spilling out of them all. Another look revealed that the track for the ladder went all the way around the room, just like in the smaller library.

Tap sighed and glanced over at me. "Do you regret agreeing to this yet?" I shook my head. I didn't mind a challenge and I enjoyed setting order to messy things. "Good. A decent portion of what's here can be sent off to the archives. That will grant some open space and limit the number of documents to be sorted through."

"I can handle this," I said, and meant it. I thought of the library in the church basement, how I'd lovingly catalogued and shelved each volume, even if I wasn't allowed to read them all.

Tap smiled, backing us out of the libraries and taking us through an open doorway behind the living area.

To the immediate right was a well appointed kitchen and dining area.

"Are you hungry at all? Thirsty?"

"I'm fine, thanks." The thought of food might appeal soon, but my stomach would have to finish unknotting first.

"I'm due a thorough restocking, but there should be something worthwhile to eat in there. Please help yourself to anything you'd like." He gestured to a door across from the open kitchen. "Through there is the washing tub and a drying line, as well as an extra bath and toilet." A bit further down he paused at another set of doors directly across from one another. He gestured to the one on the left. "This is my room. Down the hall are the workshops and..." He shook his head. "No matter. We can discuss those another time. This one will be yours." He opened the door to the right, and we stepped inside.

The room was impressively large compared to the tiny space I'd kept at the church and included a private bathroom. The walls were bare, and the furniture was limited to a bed and a small dresser, but it was clean and warm.

Tap was frowning again. "We'll need to get you some things."

"This is fine," I insisted, a blush heating my cheeks, uncomfortable making any requests or continuing to take. Over the last several years, I'd become used to living in similar simplicity. Additionally, it not only felt like an abuse of his generosity, but also as though payment would be required at some point. I had no money to trade with, which left me feeling as though suspended above a pit, waiting to see whether the rope would get pulled one direction or the other, or simply let go of. I blinked and forced myself to shove such thoughts aside. "Where are the linens?"

"Just here." He slid a small trunk out from under the bed and pulled sheets, a pillow, and blankets from it. We worked in silence, movements oddly coordinated as we tucked and straightened.

"Thank you," I said, suddenly feeling overwhelmed. Urgency flooded my veins as my heart pounded impossibly fast and my fingertips went numb. I needed him to leave. I didn't want him to see me have another attack. "I think I might clean up and maybe rest for a bit, if that's alright?" I could only hope he ignored the tremor in my voice, how breathless I sounded. My shoulders began to ache as I silently pleaded for him to go.

"Certainly." He ducked his head and backed toward the door. "Please move about freely. The portals excepted, of course." Tap hesitated in the doorway, and I forced myself to breathe through my nose instead of panting like my body wanted to. "It should be mentioned that time moves differently here than it does on Earth. Every hour here is about half again what one there is. I'd imagine that you've become well acclimated to that cadence. No need to push yourself if you're tired."

I nodded that I understood, my tongue too heavy to use. Once his footsteps moved down the hall, I slid to the floor, limbs like lead and mind too full to function.

My last thought before I lost the ability to think straight or speak was that it wasn't fair; I should have had longer between episodes. There weren't even any church bells here.

CHAPTER 8
PHIN

ONCE THE NUMBNESS passed, I got shakily to my feet, determined to make good use of the bath. The thought of languishing in hot water to chase away the chill that lingered in my bones after living in the drafty church for so long was a temptation I couldn't resist. If nothing else, I could wash the fake colorants from my hair and face.

The bathroom itself was just as plainly decorated as the bed-chamber. A small water closet for the toilet was set off in one corner, and the shortest wall hosted a length of countertop and sink with a plain mirror over it. The tub was oversized, and the main attraction of the room. It sat under a four-paned window with a plain curtain, the windowsill extra deep and serving as a shelf for the cake of soap and shampoo bottles. To my absolute delight, water ran steamy directly from the faucet, and the towel I'd been left was plush and soft. The soap and shampoos smelled like lavender. Tears sprang to my eyes as I took stock of the space, moving from one thing to the next with an odd sense of wonder.

Father Morton had done his best, but luxury was not in his vocabulary. Old, scratchy towels and the cheapest of soaps had left my hair dry and skin itchy and raw more often than not. My clothes were all second- or third hand. Not that he was living any differently—everything the church had was old and worn. The new items presented to me here were a much-appreciated novelty, one that reminded me of the comfortable life I'd had before my parents had left me at the church.

As I settled into the hot water, I shoved away all thought; it could wait for a little while. I soaked and scrubbed, emerging only once the water had cooled and my fingertips were wrinkled.

After dressing in my most comfortable tunic and the one pair of soft woolen leggings I'd managed to keep in good repair, I emptied the contents of my bag onto the bed. There wasn't much to put away, but I methodically stored my meager collection of clothing in the dresser and lined up my collection of pretty rocks on the nightstand by color.

My stomach finally decided to come around, growling loudly as I returned to the bathroom, hanging my towel to dry and making sure that the tub had emptied. The one in the church had a habit of draining very slowly, then stopping with an inch or so left in the basin. This one, on the other hand, worked perfectly.

Finding everything in order and with no other tasks to distract me, I cautiously went back down the hall toward the kitchen.

Despite the quiet, there was an ambient hum, like the whole of the crossroads was breathing. It likely had something to do with the energy flowing to and from all the portals, but it reminded me of the way Heaven had always sounded, just lower, softer. I found it comforting.

As I peered into the kitchen, I stiffened at finding Tap standing at the counter. His broad shoulders moved with precision as he worked, barely wrinkling the sleeves of his shirt. He turned, sensing me staring. His quick glance turned into a longer one, and I blushed as he scanned me up and down. The corner of his mouth ticked before he turned back to his preparations.

"I thought you might still be resting, I was going to bring this to your room. Did you find everything you needed?"

I stepped closer, unsure what to do with myself. "Yes, thank you."

"Good. It's just sandwiches, but I thought I should make an attempt at a proper meal." He turned, two plates in hand, and gestured with his elbow toward the table. "I don't often have guests, at least not ones aside from my brother, so I'm afraid my hospitality skills are a little rusty."

I sat in one of the four mismatched chairs, and he selected the one across from me, setting a plate in front of us both. "You're doing just fine."

He visibly brightened at my compliment and turned back to get a pitcher of water and cups, along with a bowl of cut fruit. "That's kind of you to say."

Everything looked fresh and delicious. While the offerings were plentiful in Vincara, particularly through the merchants that brought things to the apothecary, Father and I had mostly survived on bread, stews, and whatever root vegetables were either in season or kept well.

My stomach rumbled again, and as I blushed, he smiled and took a hearty bite. Encouraged, I sampled some of the fruit and was pleasantly rewarded with a burst of flavor I hadn't tasted since before coming to Earth the last time.

I gasped, nostalgic tears suddenly burning my eyes. "Starberries." I inhaled slowly, trying to regulate the surge of emotion that had hit me from the sight of the fruit. "It's been a very long time since I had these." I picked one of the little coin-sized golden fruits out, pleased to find he'd cut them in half to better show their five-pointed shape.

"My brother has taken an interest in specialty plants recently. Between his gardens and Merry's greenhouse, there's quite a number of things growing I haven't seen in an age. I think we all remembered a fondness for these."

"The brother that I met? Seir?"

He shook his head, half of a berry impaled on the tine of his fork. "No, another. Rylan."

"How many do you have?"

Tap's head tilted. "You recognized that I was of the original fallen. Do you also know how many of us there were?"

I considered, but that part of my memory was fuzzy. There was no recognition like there had been connecting his name and that he'd leapt from the heavens. "No, sorry."

"No need for apologies. I was curious what you'd been taught, is all. I have seven brothers. We all left with Lucifer."

"Oh. That's quite a few."

"Indeed." His eyebrows dropped and he frowned. "Do you have any siblings? Are there other Nephilim like you out there we should be worried for? It might be possible to arrange something for them as well. I should notify my brothers of what Armaros is up to, regardless."

My fork halted halfway back to my plate. It was such an odd thing for him to say, and yet, it didn't seem as though it was an unusual question for him to ask at all. Of all the things in the world for him to want to know, he was most curious whether or not I had a loved one we should be seeking out to protect? We'd barely met, and he thought there was a *we*?

"Why?"

His eyes widened slightly as he absorbed my confused tone. "Why not? Shouldn't they also be saved from such a cruel fate?"

"But ..." I found myself unable to disguise my shock. "You don't even know me."

"I wouldn't know them either, but if you thought they were worthy of being spared, family or not, I would use my resources to find a way." His head tilted to the side, eyes narrowed and mouth tight in confusion. "Is that so different from what you would do, if our roles were reversed?"

It took me several moments to gather my wits enough to respond. Everything about him threw me off balance. "No. I suppose not." I stared at him, waiting for a change in attitude, some indication of humor or anger that would expose him as the devious, trickster creature I'd been taught a demon might be. But nothing happened. He radiated only sincerity and gentle strength, and I had no idea how to reconcile that. "I'm an only child," I admitted. "Though I'm sure there are others out there, they are not relations of mine."

Tap nodded and conversation fell off as we both worked through our meals. My stomach was pleasantly full and my mind tired from over analyzing everything that had happened since I'd woken that morning by the time we finished. I reached for the plates, but he waved me off.

"I can manage the dishes if you'd like to return to your room to rest." When I didn't move, he continued, "If not ... I have several hobbies. Most are not what I would consider good choices for entertainment, but I'm sure we could come up with something."

My body was definitely tired, but I was certain my thoughts would continue to spin for quite a while.

"What time is it?"

"Something comparable to nine bells or so, probably."

Torn between my desire to explore my new temporary home, to stay and study this fascinating demon, and my fatigue, I hesitated. In the end, much like my stomach had decided for me, a yawn betrayed my exhaustion and made the choice for me.

Tap smiled softly. "There's no sunrise here, but you'll find that the windows brighten and darken with the passing of time." It wasn't until then that I even realized I hadn't thought twice about the fact that there were windows here at all. "Sleep as much as you like, there's no rush. When you're up and ready in the morning, come find me. We'll go over what needs done in the library then."

"Okay. Good night."

"Sleep well, Phin. If you need anything, I'll be in the great hall." I turned to go but paused at his next words. "It looks nice, by the way."

"Sorry?"

"Your hair. There was something in it before, yes? This color, it suits you much better."

I blushed hot, fingers straying to the short strands at the back as I left the kitchen on another mumbling of gratitude and returned to my room. I went through the motions of preparing for bed, making sure the door was open enough that I could see a sliver of light from the hallway before I slid between the sheets. The mattress was far softer than I was used to, the blanket warmer. As I sank into the pillow and my eyes grew heavy, I silently listed off the things I was grateful for out of long ingrained habit.

My new residence was unexpected to say the least, but I didn't feel as uncomfortable as I'd worried I might, in any sense. I nestled down and blinked heavily up at the vast darkness that was neither ceiling nor sky, but somehow felt like both, oddly optimistic for the first time in years.

CHAPTER 9
TAP

SEIR AND I were discussing my shopping order when Phin wandered out into the hall, her clothing fresh and eyes bright.

"Good morning," I greeted her. "Did you sleep well?"

She dipped her head. "I did. The bed is very comfortable."

"I left breakfast on the table for you if you're hungry."

Her cheeks pinked. "I found it, thank you."

"Good."

Seir's mouth dropped open, and he stared at her, then looked at me. "Tap?" We'd gotten straight to business, and I hadn't had a chance to discuss the finer details regarding Phin's employment yet.

"That hair color suits her far better than the black, don't you think?" I teased him, keeping my voice level as I played ignorant to his clear concern.

"Sure, it's nice." He gestured to me that we should step off to the side while flashing her an awkwardly big smile, one where all his sharp teeth showed.

As much as I enjoyed watching him silently panic, I didn't want to make Phin any more uncomfortable than she already seemed to be.

"Phin, it appears that my brother has recognized your true nature. I promise he'll keep it to himself. Seir," I drew my brother's wide-eyed attention back from my new librarian, "nobody can know that Phin is here."

"Oh. Yes, of course." He swallowed thickly. "Though I did mention to Hailon that you had found a new assistant when I got home last night."

"That's fine."

"And Merry happened to be dropping off some things, so she may have also heard, and she perhaps went home and told Coltor, I have no way to know for sure."

I fought a twitch at the corner of my mouth. Word may have spread quickly in the glade where they all lived, but knowledge of Phin was safe between my brother, his mate, and our friends. There were no other residents there to find out. Though ... that likely would mean the rest of our family would know soon as well. I sighed, realizing that I'd failed already.

"Understandable. The important part is that nobody outside of our circle knows she's a Nephilim, alright? This is important. There are some angels trying to find her, and we don't want that to happen."

He straightened, panic ebbing away as I acknowledged the key piece of concern for him. "Of course. She'll be safe with us, you know that." He smirked. "Only you would find an angel to set order to your library full of demons' deals, brother." He chuckled, but the sounds stopped the moment Phin's gasp echoed around us. "Sorry, sorry. Ignore me," he stepped back, slowly making his way toward the portal that would carry him to Revalia, my shopping list in his hand. "Let me see what I can do about all this, yeah? Sorry, Phin. I have a bad habit of speaking without thinking things through. It's nice to see you again." At that, he disappeared into the portal and was gone.

I sighed, forcing my shoulders to relax. "You get used to him."

"Deals?" she inquired, cheeks pink and violet eyes wide. "That whole library is deals?"

My heart sank, worried I might have lost her before she'd even had a chance to get started. "Yes. Will that be a problem?"

Her lips parted slightly, confusion wrinkling the space between her eyebrows. "No. I just ... wasn't expecting that, I guess. You took me in there yesterday, I saw what was on the shelves. I just didn't think ..." She trailed off, glancing around. "Are there other books here as well?"

Feeling returned to my fingertips as I relaxed the grip I had on them behind my back. "Yes, I also have a small leisure library. Perhaps you could help there as well, if you're so inclined. It, like most things here, suffers from a lack of attention. You'd be welcome to read from my collection, of course." Relief flooded my veins as she nodded and gestured vaguely toward the double doors that led to the libraries.

"Would you please show me where to start?"

"Of course."

I allowed her to lead us through to the library and just stood aside while she gazed around in wonder. I envied her in that regard. The only thing I felt when I came into the room was a paralyzing sense of failure.

"I didn't realize there was so much paperwork involved in making a deal," she muttered, picking up several documents one at a time from the table before letting them fall again. "I thought it was some negotiation, a bit of blood, a handshake, that's that."

I chuckled. "Sometimes, yes. But most of them are meticulously written out so that every detail, every loophole is covered. No self-respecting demon would want to be caught out by an unexamined detail." I thought of my brother Rylan, who had been the most dedicated to making deals out of us all. His contracts were truly artful, though he'd long since given up making them.

"My mother always said that those studying the law could learn a thing or two from demons."

My smile was broad and genuine, the sensation a bit foreign to my cheeks. "She wasn't wrong." I chose a handful from the table and flipped through them. "You'll be looking for markings in silver, those contracts have been fulfilled. Anything red is still an active contract and needs to be retained here, same with the gold, though they are just awaiting payment collections. We can work on the best way to organize them once some of the dead ones have been cleared out."

"Where will they go?"

"They'll be archived."

"In Hell?"

"Yes."

She frowned. "Why not just destroy them? If they're fulfilled, why do they need to be kept at all?"

Her excellent question gave me pause. "I honestly don't know. Those in charge love their files, though. Always have."

"What do they do with them in the archives?"

"Your guess is as good as mine. I can't imagine that they are referenced all that often, but they must be of some value. Otherwise, why bother?" The weight of the responsibility for keeping them was too heavy for it to be pointless. If I found out I'd worried myself sick over a process that had no value, I might lose what remained of my mind.

"Maybe it really is similar to learning law, or a legal library. They keep all the old files in case they need previous contracts to justify later cases."

"Perhaps."

"You never asked?" There was no condemnation in her voice, only wonder.

"No."

"Weren't you curious?" Her eyebrows drew together, and her head tilted to one side just slightly.

"I'm sure there was a time I was."

"Then why not ask?"

Her insistence amused me. "Because it doesn't matter. Nothing about my job would change, regardless of the answer."

Her fingertips pushed a few around, a frown creasing her face. "Are they fragile?"

It was my turn to be confused. "No. They're just parchment and ink. Some wrinkles or bending won't ruin them. As long as the marks and their color can be made out, the condition is irrelevant." I recalled Merry's panic over some of the oldest disintegrating at the lightest touch. "Some may fall apart due to their age. Don't worry yourself if it happens. Just put what you can of those in one place and we'll send them back as well. Any contracts that have been languishing here that long are either almost certainly already fulfilled or simply never will be."

Phin grew thoughtful as she pushed a pile of them out of her way, unearthing a bit of bare tabletop and then a chair as contracts spilled all over the floor. After a glance at me to gauge my reaction, she continued down the table, arms extended wide as she cleared working space and unburied a second chair, then a third. She shuffled her legs as she made her way back, gently carving a walking path through the piles.

The purposeful chaos of her actions unlocked something inside me, and some of the heaviness that pressed on my shoulders when I looked at the mess my negligence had wrought lifted. I'd never considered doing such a thing, despite the fact that my disorderly piles often fell over on their own. Once I put something down, that's where it stayed, and I couldn't quite get my mind or body to move things again unless I was going to take the time to complete the whole project. Doing something like she had might have allowed me to get past being frozen in overwhelm—it might have allowed me to get started. It was so simple, yet entirely foreign. I was awed.

"Sometimes, you have to make a bigger mess to get things cleaned up," she said softly, but with great determination and a bright smile. My heart skipped a beat, then thudded an odd rhythm, trying to catch up again. "Would you mind bringing me some crates? I'd like to get started."

"Of course."

"Silver only," she confirmed, sliding into one of the available chairs and pulling over a pile of contracts, immediately creating a space to stack them by color.

Her smile was sudden and bright, and it left me breathless. My heart felt like it was being squeezed by a giant hand for several seconds, and I fought the wave of dizziness that swept over me as I rushed from the room. I saw no need to burden her with my panic—I could surely manage that in private while her attention was elsewhere.

As I collected some crates, I worried I'd greatly underestimated the possibility that it would be more difficult having her near with the bond unfulfilled than at a distance.

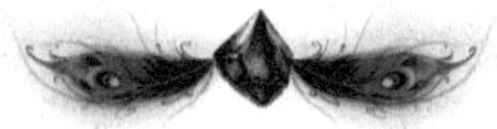

"WHERE ARE THE books kept?" Phin asked quietly as she blew on her soup to cool it down. At my delay in response, she added, "May I borrow one to read?"

"Yes, of course. I'll show you the workshops after we eat."

I was rediscovering my talent for cooking in the short time since she'd arrived, making good use of the groceries Seir routinely delivered for the first time in months. It brought an immense amount of satisfaction to prepare a meal and watch her enjoy it. I knew that was partially the mate bond, but as I mostly lived off of anything I could eat with one hand while walking the great hall, my stomach was rather pleased with the change as well.

"You mentioned hobbies?"

"Yes, I've taken on many throughout the years. Painting, woodworking, writing. They all offer their own escape."

"Do you have a favorite?" The spark in her eyes told me her interest was genuine.

"I'm not sure I could choose only one. Though perhaps it's just that whatever I chose, my answer might change if you ask again another day."

"Fair enough," she said with a smile.

"Father Morton said you scribed for him?"

Her head snapped up. "Yes. I always enjoyed my time in the library."

"Your room was right next to it. Did you not get to visit whenever you liked?" She shook her head, gaze back in her soup. I was left confused by the sudden shift in her mood.

"Most of the texts and practicing writing were off-limits unless Father could be there with me."

I balked, heat filling my veins. "Why? Surely you sitting there reading did no harm. I saw the chairs, the lamps. Were you expected to just ignore the whole room as you passed through it? To sit in your little bed closet instead of using the larger space?"

Phin set her spoon down and blotted her mouth on a napkin. I suddenly wished I'd waited until she was finished eating to inquire further. "Not entirely, but in some ways, yes." Anger, hot and vicious began to swirl in my chest. "He wasn't cruel about it, but he knew that spending time in that room, reading, scribing, was my favorite reward."

"Reward." I bit the word off, feeling all the time less and less charitable toward Father Morton.

"Yes. I sometimes needed the prospect of something pleasant to motivate me to complete my tasks."

I breathed slowly in through my nose, desperate to settle the storm of fiery discomfort that had kicked up behind my ribs. She'd already seen my temper, but I didn't want her to fear me or worry I'd have an outburst every time she was honest about something. However, the bond certainly seemed to think she'd been mistreated during her time at the church, and I was inclined to agree the more I learned.

"How ... how many workshops are there?" she asked, redirecting the uncomfortable conversation.

I breathed in and out slowly before speaking. "Many. And unfortunately, they're all a bit neglected due to my lack of time to practice anything else with regularity. You're welcome in them whenever you like, you don't need to ask permission. We'll make you your own space, and I can purchase anything you need that I don't already have." I'd never made an offer even vaguely similar to anyone else, but it felt completely natural to invite her into every part of my life, despite the newness of our acquaintance.

Phin blinked at me, eyes wide. "That's very generous."

"I want you to feel at home, Phin. I know the circumstances are odd, but there's no reason you can't enjoy your time here." I wanted nothing more than for her to be happy and to stay with me, even after organizing the library was completed.

Such an odd notion, but one I was at peace with. I'd been a solitary creature my whole life. I'd spent centuries alone, excepting infrequent visits from one of my brothers here or there, or very rare trips earthside. I wondered if I should be concerned over how easily I'd adapted to her presence.

I was pleased when she finally picked up her spoon again and continued eating, but tensed, remembering what she'd find behind the workshop doors. I'd made a very conscious effort to keep the main living areas free of clutter, but the workshops ... they were a mess. Not that it would be a surprise to her, given what she'd already seen in the library, but the thought of revealing more half-completed projects and untidy rooms to her made me squeamish. I was deeply ashamed of my inability to finish things. Even Seir, who'd visited regularly and had for many years, never saw the other rooms.

Phin was more, though. She was my mate, whether she recognized it yet or not, and I couldn't help but worry that my failings would keep her from accepting me once she figured it out.

CHAPTER 10
PHIN

DOWN THE HALL a short way from the door to Tap's bedroom was the one that led to the workshops.

"This is a bit complicated, but not difficult once you get the hang of it," he said, pointing to the symbols carved into the wood on both sides of the door frame. "Each one is a different room."

"There's more than one room behind this door?"

He nodded. "Yes. The workshops are all here. Just depends on which you'd like to call up." He pointed at a symbol that looked like the serrated teeth of a saw blade and pressed his palm to it. Briefly, it glowed gold before the latch on the doorknob clicked.

"Here's the woodworking shop." He opened the door and leaned in, gesturing for me to do the same. The room itself was about as large as the smaller library. There were shelves and tables, a small seating arrangement and tools; everything one could want to learn or practice anything and everything about woodworking along with somewhere to rest and ponder next steps. "And here"—he pulled me back into the hallway, closed the door and pressed his palm to a symbol that looked like a paintbrush—"is the painting studio."

A gasp flew from my lips when Tap pushed the door open to reveal the second room, a whole new space full of canvases and easels where the woodworking shop had been a moment before. "Saints and devils."

Tap flinched, a grimace on his face as he looked around. "I know." He adjusted both his glasses and his earrings, clearly uncomfortable. "It's just as disastrous as the deals. They all are."

"No, it's incredible," I breathed, still taking in the full scope of the space.

"Oh?" He looked around, eyes narrowed, as though trying to see what I was.

"May I?"

"Please." He gestured with his hand, and I stepped forward, pressing the original saw symbol again. Once I heard the click, I threw the door open wide and walked in, awed by the neat stacks of lumber in all sizes and wood varieties off to one side of the room, the smell of it rich and earthy in my nose.

Tap followed behind me, a silent shadow as I moved from one thing to the next. I started at the woodworking tables, running my finger over the vices attached to the sides, poking at the variety of saws and carving tools scattered across the surfaces. There was a small puzzle box on one, along with several flat panels of wood with intricate notching to one side.

"Did you make the chairs in the kitchen?"

Tap blinked, startled by my question. "I did. How did you—"

"They all complement one another as well as the table, but they don't match. Similar wood, but different styles. Seems like something that might happen if they were made one at a time with a gap in between."

He inclined his head as though congratulating me for solving a riddle.

"Can I see another?"

"Of course."

We stepped into the hallway, and I chose the paintbrush, following the order he'd started with.

Heavy cloths were laid across the floor and covered in splatters of color. They muffled my steps as I walked from one easel to the next, looking at the partially finished paintings. Canvases, finished and blank, were stacked in dozens against the wall, empty frames in piles next to them. Cups full of brushes and endless tubes of paint lay strewn across two large, worn tabletops. One easel held a portrait in progress, a family, it looked like. One of them definitely resembled Seir. Some of the faces were complete but most were nothing more than a vague bodily outline.

We went back out, and I pressed several other symbols, looking over the room as it changed each time with wonder. He had a workshop for small metalworks and jewelry making, a room dedicated to embroidery and needlework, along with a full-size loom and dress form with a half-finished suit jacket on it. There was one with a potter's wheel and kiln, another with a cauldron for wax and a rod with candlewicks ready to be dipped. Any craft one could want to practice, he had a room and all the tools required for it. They were dusty, but as many hours as he spent in the hall plus the little-to-no sleep he got, I could understand why. There simply was no time for him to do any, let alone *all* of these things.

Finally, we went back out, and he smiled at me as he pressed the symbol that looked like a book.

"I believe this one is what you originally asked for," he said, gesturing with his arm for me to enter first.

The library included a cozy sitting area with chairs and a sofa around a low table, all facing a fireplace. The hearth was cold and swept clean, a clear indication nobody had been in here in quite some time.

He crossed to the shelves with a tense expression and began

pulling things off from several different shelves. "I'll just ... make some space. Some of these can go elsewhere."

"Are fires even necessary here?" The question was out of my mouth before I had time to consider censoring it.

Tap huffed a low laugh as the stack in his arms grew taller. "No. The temperature can be altered other ways, but they do bring a certain comfort, wouldn't you say?"

"Where does the smoke go?"

"Away." He shrugged, carrying his stack over to the wall and setting them down before returning for more. I tried to see what he was taking, but none of the spines were facing out. "Don't concern yourself overmuch with details like that, Phin. The workings of this place are complex but also very simple. I've shaped the living space as rooms because it's what I'm used to, what makes me most comfortable. They didn't always look like this, either, but that's neither here nor there. The fireplaces and stove burn wood, the smoke goes up a chimney. The water in the faucets is either hot or cold depending on which handle you turn because that's how it should be, and it drains away when you let out the stopper. Nothing has to be more complicated than that. The workshops can only be visited one at a time, unless you'd like for me to put the rooms side by side down the hall, then they can all exist at once. Both things can be true. If you need more space, a ceiling ... I can requisition such a change, or perhaps do the enchantment myself."

"So it's ... magic." No other word felt as right as that one for what he was describing.

His smile was soft as he nodded. "As you say. Perhaps it is." He set down the rest of the books he'd pulled down, the stacks not insignificant, but he hadn't made a dent in the overall collection.

"But you still need supplies?"

"Yes. Food and other expendables need to be brought in. All the tools here were acquired over time as well. But shopping is far more convenient than it otherwise could be, given I have access to infinite portals."

There was no arguing that.

I went to the shelves, finding that the private book collection he claimed was small was in fact quite substantial ... and just as disorganized as he'd said. There were endless hours of reading material here, of all kinds, mixed together in piles and groups that made no logical sense. But I could fix that. I absolutely *needed* to fix that.

Seated on a heavy rug next to the library was a stout writing desk, and atop it at least a dozen different quills and inkpots, parchment sheets, and drying powder.

"This is all truly stunning."

"Each of the hobbies has brought me great joy at one point or another. You're welcome to try any that interest you."

"When was the last time you got to spend any time in here?" I asked, running my finger along the hearth, cutting a line through a decent layer of dust.

He frowned in concentration. "It's been ... a while. Inspiration has been as sparse, as has free time."

"Thank you for showing me." I glanced around, trying to decide where I wanted to start.

"My pleasure. I mean what I said, please make yourself at home in here. And not just to organize books," he looked me in the eye, expression serious. "You have leisure time, Phin, make use of it. The deals aren't going anywhere, and you don't have to spend every waking hour working. That's not the intention or the nature of this arrangement."

"What about you?"

"Me?"

"When is your leisure time?"

"I ..." His lips flattened. "My schedule is unusual. I would never ask anyone else to hold the same hours I do. That would be cruel."

"But you could take some time away if you wanted?"

He pushed at his glasses, fingers twitching at his sides. "I suppose arrangements could be made, yes."

"So, you'll join me?" I asked, flushing hot when I realized how forward that question sounded. "I mean, I don't know what half the tools do. I'd like it if you could show me or explain some of them at least."

"Hold still." He lifted a hand, reaching out to pluck something off my collar. "Yours?" He spun a small silver feather between his fingers. I groped along my back with one arm, blushing furiously. I'd felt the painful prickle of some breakthrough feathers when I had my last episode, but hadn't thought they'd come all the way in.

"Yes."

"It's a lovely color. Matches your hair." His head tilted to the side. "When was the last time you stretched your wings, Phin? I'm guessing that was not allowed while you were in disguise?"

I tensed. "No, I couldn't." For several reasons. "It's been a long time."

He frowned and nodded, still twirling the feather. To my shock, instead of handing it to me, he pulled it through the buttonhole on his vest pocket, using it as his own adornment.

My mind stuttered, wondering if demons had the same unspoken language as angels about some things. I assumed they might, as he was technically a fallen angel. But still, surely he didn't mean it as the courting gesture it was. Did he?

"I'll try my best to make some time," he said, interrupting my mental spiral.

Tap walked me back to my room, bade me goodnight with a bow, and continued on toward the main hall. I glanced back the other direction, realizing that the seemingly normal hallway was like some of the walls off the living area and great hall—there was no visible end, just a vague fade into blackness and a sense of there being something solid just out of sight.

The workshop door was on the side of the hallway where Tap's room was, but there was another across from it on mine. Now that I knew what beautiful madness the workshops door contained, I tried not to wonder too hard about what might be behind the other.

CHAPTER 11
TAP

"YOU'RE MAKING EXCELLENT progress," I commented as I entered the library. One whole side of the table now had fully visible chairs.

Phin turned around, pleased by the compliment. "You think so? I can't wait until I can see this whole table. It's a lovely piece. Did you make it too?"

I shook my head. "No, this set is well beyond my abilities. The dining table and chairs in the kitchen is as far as I got. I learned pretty quickly that my strengths lie in much smaller pieces."

"Well, it's got a beautiful grain." She paused to wipe at her eyes, and my chest tightened.

"Are you well? Is the dust bothering you?"

She shook her head. "No, I'm fine. My eyes are just tired. I just didn't stop to rest or wash up like I normally do. I did six crates today. I think that's a personal best."

"Very likely, that's quite a lot to be sure. If the dust bothers you—"

"I'm alright, I promise." She pinned me with that violet stare and a lopsided grin. "But I appreciate the concern."

"As you say. It's getting late. Are you hungry?"

She slid out of the chair, pushing a pile of deals out of her way as she rose. "I got in such a good rhythm, I lost all track of time. Yes, I'm starving actually."

I gestured for her to go ahead of me, breathing in a nose full of her lavender-and-parchment scent as she passed me up in the doorway, close enough her arm brushed mine. Electricity sparked, and a wave of desire washed over me.

I was going to go mad soon.

Every nerve in my body was strung tight every second of the day because of the mate bond. Phin was never close enough, or when she was near, she was smiling too brightly, too innocently, for me to reconcile the fierce need to claim her as mine with who I'd always believed I was.

The bright light of her soul shone through more every day since she'd gotten away from that church and all the rules the priest had imposed under the guise of keeping her safe. Her voice, still rough and quiet, would crack and my anger would rise. She'd casually mention some other way she was made to suffer in the name of safety and my veins would boil, my demon aching to get out. To take revenge. On the priest, her parents, all the circumstances that led to her coming to live here.

But never with her.

None of this was her fault, and I would suffer this pain for eternity if it ensured she was safe and cared for.

The violent emotional swings were exhausting.

I found some peace in the rituals that kept me occupied for tiny bits of time—cooking, tidying, my rounds up and down the rows of doorways in the great hall. Bringing her teas and snacks to be sure she was soothed and never hungry. But it was never enough.

She sat in the chair she favored at the table, making enthusiastic noises over the plate I'd made for her. I couldn't help but preen at the compliment, and the burn behind my ribs eased a bit.

"This smells wonderful." Her stomach rumbled, and she blushed as she picked up her fork.

"I should have brought you something more substantial midday."

"You brought me plenty," she said over a mouthful of roasted potatoes. "I lost track of time is all, you're not responsible for that." She chewed and swallowed several times, following her hearty bites with a long drink of water. I nibbled and watched, anxious that she was so ravenous. When the food finally began to settle, she slowed down. "This is delicious as always. Thank you for always cooking. You don't have to, you know. I can always put together something for myself. Or for both of us. I wouldn't mind."

"It's my pleasure. But perhaps we'll work out a rotation." I wouldn't suggest one myself, but if she needed to take charge of a meal or two to feel useful, I'd accept her wishes. And I'd have to make sure to leave some kind of snacks for her in the library for days like this. Phin skipping meals altogether would not do.

"What's the green vegetable?" She'd eaten around that item, pushing it off to the side.

"Seir called it chard. He said it was one of Merry's favorites and a lot like spinach. Before I cooked it, some of the leaves were partly yellow, and some red as well as green. Very pretty."

"Mmm." Her gaze grew distant and she stopped eating, instead just moving her food around the plate, all enthusiasm gone.

"Is something wrong?"

Phin's eyes snapped up. She took an intentional bite, then another, leaving the greens as they were. Then she lied to me, though it was out of politeness, so I didn't hold it against her. "No, nothing's wrong." When she spoke again, her question took me completely by surprise. "Do all the doorways work all the time?"

"Yes and no. Why do you ask?"

One of her shoulders lifted in a shrug. "Just curious. There are so many. Seems like an impossible task to watch them all.."

"Not impossible. Not easy, either, though, I'll admit."

"What kinds of things are you looking for when you watch them? I'm not sure I understand quite why they need to be monitored so closely. Aren't portals fairly complicated to use?"

I considered the simplest way to respond. "They are. To use them, a person must know where one is, how to activate it, and be able to visualize where they're going or the person they're hoping to travel to at the very least. But there are realms and worlds beyond ours, where the knowledge is much more freely shared. Sometimes, doorway paths get crossed, or a creature gets lucky and ends up somewhere they don't belong. Malice isn't always at play, but it's best to be cautious, because sometimes, it absolutely is."

Phin's head tilted. "We used portals in and out of Heaven. There were three or four locations my father preferred, all linked to doorways around where we lived. I wonder if they still work." Her mouth flattened.

"None of the doorways to the celestial plane under my purview have been decommissioned recently. And by recently, I mean in the last say, ten or twenty earth years. Maybe more. I'm happy to check the files, if you can give me relatively close locations."

"Could I use one then? Would it be that easy?" Her voice went soft, the confidence and volume she'd earned since arriving here faded.

I clutched my fork so tight my knuckles whitened. "I don't see why not, if you know the entry point and how to activate one. But—"

"Obviously that's *not* something I want to do," she interrupted me. "Not unless I could be invisible or something. I'd be walking right into the very thing I've been hiding from, what my parents were keeping me safe from by leaving me at the church." Voice raspy, she sagged in her seat, sipping at her water. The bond flared irritably behind my ribs.

"Do you think your parents are there?"

Phin met my eye and started to shake her head, then switched to a nod. When she spoke again, her voice was quieter than before to reduce the irritation. "I honestly don't know. If they did, there's no reason they wouldn't have come back for me." She straightened, panic in her violet gaze. "If the portals work, and you manage some of the ones that go to Heaven, does that mean they could just come here? That's a direct path and they know what I look like."

I shook my head. "No. While they are active, they also cannot be used without permission, and even then, under a specific set of circumstances only. I could not go there directly either. There's a permanent agreement in place, one that cannot be broken or changed without the explicit and complicated sign-offs and the undoing of many layers of magical binding from those in charge of both places."

Phin relaxed, a gentle smirk lifting one side of her mouth. "Paperwork again."

"Always." I reached for her plate. "Are you finished?"

"Yes, thank you. But I can wash. You cooked."

I relented but tapped my finger against my bouncing leg in an effort to keep myself seated. "Not so thrilled about the greens, then?"

"Sorry, but not really. I ... overdid it with fresh greens once. I've never really recovered."

I detected a hint of misdirection in her words, but she was telling the truth. That was a story I desperately wanted to hear, but I resisted asking. She seemed to share things perfectly well if given time, and I could be patient. Most of the time.

Unable to sit any longer, I set to making us a pot of tea.

Phin dried the plates, then stacked them carefully in the cabinet. As I poured the boiling water into the teapot, I mused over whether I should ask if she'd prefer a different kind of stoneware, or perhaps some delicate china with a pretty pattern instead of my plain, somewhat inconsistently thrown, pottery to use.

"If I told you my father's name, do you think you'd recognize it?" She leaned against the countertop, drying her hands on the dish towel. Her eyebrows dipped. "Or perhaps there's a reason you've never asked?"

I dropped the kettle onto the stove a bit harder than I intended to, some of the water splashing back out. "I'm curious about most things where you're concerned, Phin."

"So is this like the files? It wouldn't change anything, so why ask?"

I choked on a laugh. "Perhaps. Though, it's more just me trying to respect your privacy than anything else. Would you prefer I were nosy?"

Phin made a sound, the start of a word that she abandoned. "Maybe. You're welcome to ask anything you like, Tap. If I don't want to tell you, I just ... won't."

"Fair enough." I got down two cups and poured our tea, adding a small spoonful of honey for hers, as she'd started making it that way for herself after Seir brought us a jar. They were keeping bees in the glade now, on top of everything else. It was downright domestic, and I wasn't sure I wasn't a little jealous about it. "Was your father of the old guard then? If you think I'd recognize his name?"

Phin's head bobbed as she took the cup from me, and I had no choice but to follow her out of the kitchen into the living area. She curled her legs under her as she settled into the corner seat of the sofa, and I took my place in the recliner.

"He was. Would that be strange? If you knew him?"

"Perhaps." It was an interesting prospect to be sure. "But having met him once or twice and knowing him are two very different things." I waited for her to continue, the changes in her facial expression telling me that this was not a simple topic for her. Nor should it have been—angelic and demonic names could be used for harm in the wrong mouths.

"My father's name is Radueriel."

"Ah." I curled my fingers around the steamy teacup, giving her my undivided attention. As far as names went, that was one I was sure everyone knew. "Then you come by your love of scribe work, libraries, and organization honestly."

Her eyes lit up. "Yes. I believe so too. You know him then?"

"Of him. I may have met him once or twice during my time in Heaven, but we were not well acquainted. I'm sorry."

"No need to apologize."

"He has a bit of a reputation. Are the rumors true?"

She smiled, and it was like someone had brought the sun into the room with us. "Which rumors would that be?"

"Top of mind is that he was quite high ranking."

"I suppose he was. I remember someone asking him once what it was like to be above even Metatron. My father said some things back to them that I worried would get us kicked out. Nobody ever asked that again."

"I'm guessing he didn't behave like someone with special permissions then?"

The tiniest snort came out of her nose. "No. Though I heard it repeated enough times to learn that my father was, in fact, a powerful man, he never behaved as such. He just wanted to be left alone to his books for the most part, though him sneaking me into the archives would probably have ended poorly had we ever been discovered." Her nose scrunched. "Aren't you also quite high ranking? Wasn't it only princes and dukes and the like that fell?"

"Jumped," I corrected her. "I suppose I am, though I don't participate in the systems of Hell that would award me any kind of tangible power. I hold my post here, monitor the doors, keep to myself. What would I even do with sixty-six legions?"

"That sounds like a lot." She smiled, her sweet nature more and more evident as she grew comfortable here.

"I suppose it is. My brothers mostly have twenty or so each. Though none of them really have use for them either." I rumbled a laugh, realizing that I was looking at the only reason any of us would have had for calling upon them in centuries. "Though if Heaven picks a fight ..." I shrugged and Phin shifted, understanding crossing her face as she nodded.

"Do you have a title?"

I shifted in my seat, uncomfortable. I'd never cared for the labels, meaningless as they were. "I do."

She watched me expectantly. "Well?"

I sighed. "I am a Mighty Prince as well as a Great President. But those are just words. They bring no value to my life, nor do they make me anything other than who I am."

"My father was a Great Prince, and he felt the same. Rank and power didn't appeal to him. Things like music and art did. Chasing butterflies in a meadow or trying to figure out the mathematical music of a stream moving over rocks."

"I recall talk about him being a poet. Those things certainly sound like something a poet would enjoy."

I hadn't thought it possible, but her face brightened even further, her pride in him evident. "He was. Every word was important to him. He absorbed knowledge in the archives like it was water and he was parched earth." I wondered if she noticed that she'd behaved very much like a poet herself just then. Her body had taken on a levity while speaking, her shoulders back and chest out, everything about her quietly confident. Radiant.

She was beautiful.

"Keep going," I said quietly, encouraging the burst of happiness to continue when she started to sag back into herself.

Phin sighed and set her tea on the side table. "I really can't think of anything he couldn't do, a kindness he didn't perform. He loves my mother with every bit of himself, and I was probably very spoiled by them both."

"You seem the opposite of spoiled, Phin."

She shrugged. "Well, that was a long time ago. Things are different now."

"What's your mother's name?"

"Terra."

"That's lovely. You obviously take after him. What does she look like?"

Her eyes closed and a slow smile spread across her face as she fell into her memories. "She's our opposite. Eyes so dark they're nearly black, The most incredible, warm smile. She always kept her hair braided because it was long. It had grown past her waist last I saw her. It looked wavy when she let it down. I often wished I'd gotten her dark-brown hair instead of Father's silver, her warm brown skin." Phin rubbed her arms and reached up to touch her very short curls. She cleared her throat and took another drink. "I had the best of both worlds growing up, in every sense. He always made sure we had everything we needed, that we spent as much time as we could in Heaven. But we also hated leaving my mother behind, so we went back and forth a lot."

"She couldn't go with you because she was human."

"No, she couldn't. But she never made us feel guilty about it, she knew it was important. Said that was what she signed up for when she fell in love with an angel."

"Were they fated?" I asked, the words quiet, my heartbeat pounding in my ears.

"Yes, they were mates." Her response was breathy, the way her eyes locked onto mine when she said the single affirmation sent a jolt of awareness through my whole body.

I had to swallow before speaking again, the tension suddenly thick between us. "How did they meet?"

"My father had come to Earth to find a certain book. The church, the vault there, it's always been somewhere those kinds of things happen to end up."

"There are still several priceless items there, and that was Armaros's excuse for visiting, so I can only imagine. My brother Vassago did actually locate one of his beloved tomes in that building once upon a time."

"Really?" Her eyes danced. She shifted around in the seat, her chin propped on her hand. It was distracting how engaged she was, how interesting she made my stories—*me*—feel. "Anyway, he was looking for a book and my mother was with her family, traveling through. Love at first sight and all that." She blushed. "Father always said there was simply no way he could have let her go after watching her single-handedly manage their caravan camp. Sold him immediately that she was not just beautiful, but capable and not afraid of hard work."

"Mate bonds do work in mysterious ways," I said, noncommittally, my own bond burning fiercely as I stared at her.

Melancholy returned to her tone. "I miss them so much." She stood. "But I feel better after talking about them. I've kept them as secret as I have myself the last number of years."

I reached out and took her fingers in my hand as she passed my chair. "Perhaps if you do that more I can help carry the burden of your grief. I try to be a good listener."

She blinked at me, a sheen in her eyes. Her throat worked as she swallowed. Phin opened her mouth but gave up and just nodded. Then she bent down and pressed a kiss to my cheek.

I sat there for several moments, thoughts scrambled as I processed what had happened. When I finally remembered to breathe again, my heart pounded to make up for the brief interruption.

A sniffle reached my ears as Phin retreated down the hall. My chest ached at her grief. I'd do anything in my power to ease it even a little bit, to take it from her, anything and everything I could to ensure her happiness.

There was simply no other choice.

CHAPTER 12
PHIN

I T HAD TAKEN quite a lot of convincing, but I'd finally gotten Tap to concede that if he was going to do all the cooking it was only fair I clean up sometimes. Yet again, he'd made us a lovely breakfast, so I rushed to take up the plates before he could.

"That's not—"

"I can help. Fair is fair, is it not? You cook, I can clean."

"But you're a guest," he frowned.

"I thought I lived here? At least for now," I countered, heart pounding as I hurried to scrub the plates with soap and hot water.

Tap was flustered, more color than usual in his cheeks. "Well, of course, but you deserve to be comfortable—"

"I'm perfectly comfortable, thank you. I've never slept so well, nor had as much leniency in my work schedule. I can certainly pull my own weight when it comes to chores. Perhaps we could work out a new schedule? One that divides things more fairly?" He opened and closed his mouth twice without uttering a word. "Good. We can work on that later?"

Finally, he rediscovered his voice. "Alright. As you wish."

"Good." I beamed, happy to have finally gotten my thoughts voiced where such things were concerned.

While it had been a lovely couple of weeks-worth of pampering, I wanted to feel useful, especially since I wasn't even sure the man slept. Once, I'd caught him dozing in his recliner when I got up to get a late-night snack, but that was the only proof I had he ever slept at all—he either never used his own bedroom or was a master of stealth coming and going from it.

My workload had changed so drastically, I was actually becoming a little bored, and I definitely had guilt over being waited on. With no scheduled time to get up, no need for applying a carefully crafted disguise, no waiting for doors to be unlocked or nagging church bells dictating every hour of my day, I was living a whole life of leisure. And that didn't even account for the demon bringing me snacks and tea throughout the day, or my own personal bath with endless hot water. Or the workshops. Some extra chores, given my current levels of comfort were *welcomed*.

After a moment's hesitation, Tap mumbled his thanks and left the room.

When I was finished and wandered out to the hall, I found the brothers already mid-conversation.

"—needs real sunlight. An afternoon in the glade would do you both a world of good. Nobody goes in or out unmonitored, and it's warded." Seir's volume increased as I passed through the living area and approached the hall proper.

"I can't keep leaving, Seir. I've taken several trips recently, not to mention the other hours I've been away."

"But you *can*, brother. And you should. It's not healthy to work like you do, never has been. When was the last time anything serious happened?"

"There's been something unusual happening with some of the dormant doorways lately. Surely that shouldn't be just brushed off? Especially considering there are angels out there hunting Nephilim?"

I heard two huffs of frustration, hilariously opposite, and the owner of each one easily identified.

"By all means, investigate. I'll help you even. But you need to work less and get out more. That remains true." Seir groaned. "We've had this particular conversation entirely too many times. I'm so *bored* of it."

"Imagine how I feel then," Tap countered.

I paused at the edge of the hall, finding Seir with his hands on his hips, scowling at his brother.

"Say yes."

"Who will be watching if you're with us? Assumedly Merry and Coltor will be there as well?"

"I've already asked Keplar if they can monitor for the afternoon. It's covered."

"And what will you owe to Hell for such favors, Seir? What will I?"

"You'll owe nothing. The details of arrangements I make are none of your concern. Besides, I'm still technically employed there. My unit leader doing me a favor and watching the gates is on him, not me, and certainly not *you*. Say. Yes."

"You are reckless, brother. Impulsive. Infuriating."

"You love all that about me."

Tap grunted. "I cannot make choices like this for anyone but myself. We'll need to discuss it with her."

"Discuss what?" I asked, causing both men to spin my direction. Seir's face broke into a wide smile and Tap regarded me calmly, pushing his glasses back up from where they'd slid down his nose while one hand idly turned his rings. I'd come to learn rather quickly that both habits were tells he was anxious. A demon who got nervous so easily was incredibly endearing.

Seir took a large step toward me, but Tap held him back by his shirt. If anything, this amused Seir, and he allowed his brother to effectively leash him as they approached.

"Seir has suggested that we travel earth-side."

I'd surmised as much, but the blunt way Tap said it still shocked me. I was too used to Father Morton dancing around things and was still working on my tendency to expect trickery. "What for?"

"Sunlight. Plants. Animals. Food that isn't prepared by *him*."

A smile cracked my face. "The food here isn't bad. For the most part, it's been an improvement over what I was eating before."

"Only for the most part?" Tap asked, looking crestfallen. "It was only the greens you didn't like, right?"

Seir groaned. "Oh no. That's awful! What terrible mistreatment did you get in Vincara that you could say such a thing?"

I laughed then, unable to keep the bright burst of mirth from tickling up my spine. Seir was a special kind of entertaining, but more than that, the exasperation on Tap's face had done me in. Both of them stared at me, which only made me laugh harder. Unfortunately that led to me coughing due to my irritated throat and I had to raise my hand in reassurance as Tap's expression clouded over.

Tap's hand grazed his chest, a soft rubbing motion just over his heart as Seir clapped him on the shoulder.

"So? What do you say?" Seir prompted, bouncing on his toes. "Would you like to get away from here? Breathe some fresh air? Meet some new people?"

My heart stuttered. Suddenly I did. I wanted a change of scenery more than anything despite the fact that I was very happy in my new residence. "That would be nice," I said, but my mood began to slip almost immediately as I remembered why I'd come here. "As long as it's safe." I looked at Tap. New people were a terrifying prospect, even if seeing a new place had its charms.

"It's one of the most secure places I can think of," he answered, reaching up to twist his earrings idly. "If you'd like to go, I wouldn't be concerned about your safety there."

His answer felt strange. "You'd be coming as well, I assume?"

He nodded stiffly. "Yes. I suppose I would."

"Are there a lot of people?"

"No, just a few, and everyone there is ... family." One of Tap's eyebrows raised as he completed his thought, as though saying it that way surprised even him.

"So that's a yes?" Seir asked, eyes bouncing between me and his brother.

"Yes. Please. I'd like to go."

Seir clapped his hands before placing them on my shoulders and steering me back toward my room. "Wonderful! It's not nearly as cold as in Vincara, but you'll still want a coat."

I stiffened, realizing I'd misjudged the offer slightly. "Wait, we're going right now?"

"When else? Do you have other plans today?"

"Seir," Tap chided gently, slowly following behind us with a shake of his head. "Easy."

"Sorry. If I'm being too forward just say so. I'll stop." He grinned again, the expression familiar, but I couldn't quite put my finger on why.

"It's okay. I don't really have plans, just more sorting."

"Exactly. And that will go on for ages no matter what, so why wait? Just imagine how wonderful the sun is going to feel on your face! I'd bet it's been months. Winter in Vincara is long and gloomy."

He wasn't wrong. "Alright," I agreed, my cheeks beginning to get sore from smiling as I went into my room and plucked the old, too-large coat out of the armoire.

When I came back, Tap was doing something that appeared to make most of the portals power down, both of them in their own coats.

"Ready?" Tap asked, and when I nodded he gently tucked my arm through his and led me toward one of the doorways. I looked at his breast pocket to find my feather threaded through the but-tonhole again. It seemed he moved it from piece to piece to be sure it was seen. I blushed, and he patted my arm, misunderstanding why. "It'll be fine."

Seir glanced back over his shoulder as he dove through first, smiling wide.

I wasn't sure if Tap's words were meant to reassure himself or me. In the end, it didn't matter, because the conversation ended the moment we stepped into the portal.

CHAPTER 13
PHIN

THE HEAVINESS OF the slightly humid air was the first thing to register as we exited the portal at our destination. While definitely colder than the evenly temperate crossroads, it was also far warmer than Vincara.

I marveled at the dense greenery in every direction as Seir led us down a narrow, worn footpath. As far as I could see were trees, grass, and even a few patches of colorful flowers despite the season. Animal life was also plentiful, birds noisy in the trees or flying overhead and squirrels and other woodland creatures scampering around in the underbrush as we walked.

It was lush, vibrant. *Alive.*

"Reminds me of the gardens," I muttered, attention unfocused as I took in everything around me.

"I can see the resemblance," Tap agreed. "This glade is also a rather special place." The corner of his mouth tilted as Seir proudly scampered ahead, narrating and pointing things out.

"The hot springs are over there, and the new beehives aren't far beyond that. Merry and Coltor live down that path, and the ruins are a bit past them. Our place is just up ahead, we'll start there."

We passed a series of hot springs and a little cabin that looked new as we walked toward a thriving stand of trees. Just at the edge was another cabin, this one clearly very lived in and cared for. Garden beds lined the house, all overflowing with vegetables despite the thin layer of frost. As we approached, two sets of wind chimes hanging from the edge of the front porch tinkled different tunes as a light breeze blew through.

A woman opened the door of the cabin as we approached and gestured with her arm. "Welcome! Come on inside."

Tap urged me to go first with a gentle press of his hand at the small of my back. I nodded politely at the pretty woman as I entered her small but comfortable home, pausing behind a plush sofa. There was a healthy fire going in the hearth, and the whole room smelled like cinnamon and apples. Nostalgia gripped my lungs and I swallowed over the lump in my throat. My mother nearly always had a simmer pot going with fruit and spices, and sitting in front of a warm fire was where we all shared how our day had gone after supper. I tried to shake off the sadness that inevitably crept in when I started to think about what might have become of them.

"You owe me a jar of pickles," Seir teased, pausing to kiss her on the mouth after pulling the door closed behind himself.

Tap seemed to notice the same moment I did that he'd never removed his hand. He stared at me with concern for the space of a heartbeat, clearly having picked up on my tension. I nodded to indicate I was fine, and the warmth of his touch fell away.

"So I do," Hailon laughed.

"The fresh air is quite nice." Tap gestured to his brother. "Maybe leave it open a little?"

"Good idea." He opened the door so just a sliver of light came through at the edge, enough for a bit of air to flow. I took a deep breath, some of the tension easing out of my shoulders and back. "For my pickles, I'd like green beans. No! The little baby beets." He licked his lips as though already tasting them. "Please."

"I'll see what I can do my next trip to d'Arcan. I'm not sure what's left in the cellar. Between you and Magnus, we'll have to triple our pickling schedule next year."

"Better quadruple, to be safe." Seir winked at her and continued into the kitchen.

"We'll need to put in more garden beds then."

"Merry will be thrilled!" He grinned at her, and as her head tilted, added, "Just tell me where to dig, Moonflower. You can have a hundred more if it means I have pickles whenever I want. Shall I pour the tea?"

She shook her head and turned her attention to Tap. "I'm so glad you came, but if I'm being honest, I wasn't sure he'd convince you. I know venturing out is a considerable undertaking."

Tap cracked a grin that set my thrumming nerves at ease. "If I were you, I'd have bet the pickles too." He leaned in and kissed her chastely on the cheek. "It's always good to see you, Hailon."

She leaned back and sighed. "One of these days I'll make it to the crossroads and save you the trouble of leaving. I really do want to see the great hall." She turned to me. "Hello. I'm Hailon. Seir's—"

"Wife," he confirmed with a smirk and strong nod. "My incredible wife." He kissed her cheek as he passed us by with the tea before setting them on the table.

"I don't recall being invited to a wedding," Tap said, but the tilt to his mouth let me know he was teasing.

"Unnecessary formality," Seir waved his hand.

I accepted the hand Hailon held out, which showcased a ring that argued Seir was correct. It was a simple band with a piece of obsidian in it. Unusual, perhaps, but pretty. As I met her eye, I was momentarily stunned. The coloring of them was beyond unique—the left a deep brown on one side and a light jade on the other, the right bright blue and opaque yellow. Despite her youth, Hailon's hair was nearly all white with just a few threads of pitch black which was intriguing as well. But it was the burst of warmth that passed between us when we touched that truly surprised me. "Phin. Pleased to meet you."

"Please, make yourselves at home."

Tap pulled out one of the dining table chairs for me. I sat, blushing as both Seir and Hailon watched us intently.

"You're helping set the deals library to rights?" Hailon asked, pushing a plate of finger foods my direction.

"Yes."

"I fear I didn't accurately describe the scope of the job before she agreed to it," Tap said, tone light but eyes still apologetic. He quickly added a healthy drop of honey to my cup before doing the same to his own.

"It's a big project, but I don't mind. It's nice to see the progress every single day." I curled my fingers around the steaming teacup and brought it toward my face. It smelled faintly of oranges and warmed my whole body when I took a sip.

"I bet. I feel the same way about pulling weeds or cleaning up. If I can see a difference, I feel like I've been very productive," Hailon agreed.

I nibbled on the tasty little jam covered toasts I'd taken as Tap spoke kindly about how much progress I was making already. I felt like he was exaggerating quite a bit but appreciated the praise.

Hailon turned back to me, patting my hand where it sat on the table in a friendly manner. Another jolt of awareness jumped between her hand and mine. Her head tilted to the side. "What's that about, I wonder?"

I blinked. "You feel it too?" My voice came out as a whisper.

She smiled. "I do."

"That means you're ... you have ..." I stumbled over my words, unsure how to formulate my thoughts coherently. I'd never met anyone with angelic blood outside of Heaven.

"I'm a null," Hailon offered. "I've a bit of everything in me. Perfectly balanced, or at least that's the claim. I beg to differ though, because I didn't even get wings." Her gentle smile helped me breathe evenly again. "I've never had that happen with anyone else."

"There aren't many of us."

"Hmm. I can relate to that too." She patted my hand again. "Nulls are very few and far between. I didn't even know what one was until I was informed, myself."

"Tap always was a bit contrary," Seir teased. "Can you imagine what the boss would say if he knew you'd hired an angel to sort out the contracts? That you're living together at the crossroads? Picturing his face will keep me entertained for days." He hooted with laughter.

Tap paused mid-bite and blushed, trying to swallow the bit of bread he'd eaten without choking. "Can't imagine he'd be all that surprised, honestly. He knows how I am." Seir found his response even more amusing, and Tap cracked that low, gentle smile again. Butterflies swarmed in my gut, and I drank some tea to disguise any outward signs that a simple smile had had an effect on me.

"Boss?" I asked.

"Lucifer," Tap said softly.

"Oh."

"It's easy enough to forget that at the end of the day, that's who Seir's actual employer is." Hailon sighed and shook her head. "Saints know I keep trying. It's very stressful sometimes."

"He's not that bad," Seir insisted. "It's not like I'll ever be summoned back again, I made sure I negotiated those terms. And you've met Lilith. Do you think she'd tolerate him if he was truly awful?"

Hailon laughed. "We had all of ten seconds worth of interaction, so I'm not sure that's enough to gauge an understanding of what she'd tolerate. Besides, she seemed incredibly angry with him, so ..." Her head tilted.

Tap huffed a breath. "So, same as always?"

Seir's smile went wide. "Naturally."

I blinked, trying to absorb the conversation as much as possible while reeling from how casually they were discussing *the* Lilith and Lucifer. The way the pair of them were being discussed as, well, a pair. I picked at my toast and watched them talk, nodding or giving short responses where appropriate, my thoughts too fast for me to sort through them or speak coherently.

"Care to take a walk outside?" Seir asked me after the snacks and tea had been depleted. "I did promise you sunshine."

That, at least, I could answer. "Yes, please."

He walked ahead again, gesturing this way and that as he pointed out where the best berries grew, the easiest place to find a bunny, should one want to, and even his favorite shrub. Hailon glanced behind her shoulder more than once, a look of amused apology on her face. Tap loped slowly beside me, looking around with one corner of his mouth tipped up.

"You get used to him," he told me again, barely louder than a whisper. The words tripped down my spine, the timbre of his voice strangely resonant in my chest.

I closed my eyes and tipped my face up, the sun bright and warm, as promised, and the air fresh and crisp. "He's just enthusiastic. It's actually really sweet that he's so proud of his home."

Tap nodded his agreement as we turned down the path that Seir had indicated would take us to where others lived. The dirt trail widened a little, clearly very well-traveled. Before long, a cabin with another building next to it came into view.

I was too busy staring at the incredible stained-glass window at the front of the structure as we got closer to notice the massive horse grazing in the yard. We were a few paces away, when it suddenly lifted its head and looked right at me.

I froze.

"Pleasure to see you again, Jacks," Tap said calmly, one of his hands coming to rest on my shoulder. "He's bound to Merry. He's a friend." As I stared, the horse bowed his head as though in greeting.

"Hello." My throat was tight, but I managed to speak after what felt like a very long moment.

Hello, little Nephilim.

I stared at the beast, and he stared back. I couldn't help speaking aloud as I worked through my confusion. "Wait. Did you ...?"

It's a neat little trick, he answered in my head, *but doesn't work on everyone. Have you never spoken with a creature this way before?*

"Only one. I thought ... I thought I'd imagined it," I confessed aloud.

Well, I'm flattered then. Welcome to our glade."

I cleared my throat. "Th-thank you. It's a lovely place."

You'll find you're well cared for here, Jacks assured me. He stared back as I glanced around, every single set of eyes fixed on me. I burned with embarrassment, though logically I knew I had nothing to be ashamed about. *These are good people. You can trust them. You have my word.*

"Alright, Phin?" Tap asked, but I couldn't respond to him. I was too caught up in the conversation happening inside my head.

"How did you ..." I cut the question off, but the horse was unbothered and knew exactly what I was asking.

Their nature is irrelevant to who they are as people, how they behave. Their goodness. Though I'd bet you already figured that out, yes? I nodded stiffly. *As for the other thing ... I see you, youngling. Do you see me?* As I watched, the ghosts of wings appeared at his sides. I gasped. *Ah, you do! Not even my mistress can see them. It's truly my honor then.*

"Phin?" Tap took a shoulder in each hand, holding me steady and sending my pulse racing. "Jacks? Would you mind including me in your conversation?"

The horse bobbed his head. *Apologies, I meant no harm. I was just welcoming her. Not every day an angel wanders through.* At that, he turned away and loped into another patch of grass, tail flicking behind him.

"He wasn't causing trouble again, was he?" a female voice asked. I looked over to find a woman with bright red hair approaching from the direction of the cabin. "He looks innocent enough, but he really does enjoy giving a good fright. I have to check around the corners of the house every morning before I walk around or else I get a surprise." The horse nickered and wandered even further away. She laughed. "See? He's not denying it, cheeky devil." She opened her arms and gave Tap a brief hug. "Lovely to see you out and about," she teased, reaching out a hand to me. "Hello. You must be Phin. I'm Merry."

"Nice to meet you."

"Sorry about Jacks. I think he gets bored sometimes. With only me to talk to most of the time, he's got to find other ways to entertain himself." Her head tilted. "Though I will say, Seir does okay, and Jacks and Coltor have come to an odd understanding, so they communicate fine, when they want to. But he's got a lot of free time and nowhere to channel his energy. Aside from scaring me, that is." Her volume increased for the last, and the horse made a noise that sounded a lot like laughter.

"It's okay. I've just never had that happen before." It was true enough.

"Oh, that first time can be a bit rough. I remember very well." She gestured toward the building next to her cabin. "Would you like to come have a look? It's finally finished inside, and the greenhouse is all glassed in." There was a general agreement that we would, and she turned, leading us down the trail.

"You grew the starberries?" I asked.

Merry turned around, beaming. "Yes! That was a wonderfully successful experiment. I wasn't sure the seeds would take given that they aren't earth native, but they have done so well, and in a very short amount of time. Remind me before you go, I'll send more with you. We can barely keep up with how much fruit we're getting. I'll likely have to make some jam. Not that I'm sad about it, they're delicious." Merry mounted the stairs and took us inside the secondary building, my breath catching as I took in the lovely space.

The office was arranged like a cozy living room, the size similar to that of the library she'd helped with though without the incredible height. Off the back was the greenhouse, and as a result the rest of the space was warm enough from the concentrated sunlight that I shrugged out of my coat. Tap reached over to take it, adding it on top of his own folded over his forearms. As I looked past him, I saw that Seir, who was last in, had propped the door open with a carved wooden cat for a doorstop.

"There are several things I'm starting off for Rylan. They haven't yet figured out where they want the new garden. It's difficult because it needs such special preparations but I wanted to get the seeds in soil before ..."

My ears began to ring as I recognized several of the plants. Memories came in bits and flashes, panic taking hold despite my intentional slow breaths and the reassuring mental chant I started out of reflex.

This was not then, here was not there. I was fine. Nothing like that would ever happen to me again.

But it made no difference. I was not stronger than the wave of numbness that crashed over me. I glanced at Tap as my fingertips went numb and I lost all control of my muscles.

His panicked face hovered over me as I fell to the floor.

CHAPTER 14
TAP

THE FUGUE STATE Phin had gone into at the church had been peaceful compared to whatever this was.

She'd paled, gone still, then collapsed like something had physically crashed into her. It was lucky I'd had our coats on my arm, they served to cushion her fall as I dove to reach for her.

"Phin?" I couldn't resist calling out to her, even though I knew she couldn't respond.

"What can I do?" Merry asked, urgency in her tone.

"I'm not sure," I admitted.

"Let's get her on the sofa," she suggested.

I scooped her up, unnerved by the complete absence of her as she continued to blink and breathe, but not respond.

"This is kind of how you were, Merry," Hailon said tensely.

"Yes, it does seem rather familiar, doesn't it? It's definitely no fun from that side of things, I can tell you that much. Does this happen often?"

"I've only seen her do this once before. It was triggered by the church bells. There are obviously none here, so I'm not sure what may have caused it. If it's the same, she can hear us, she's just ... stuck for a bit."

"Mmm. So very like how it was for me, then." Shadows passed by the front windows. "Sorry, looks like I have other company, I'll only be a moment. Hailon, could you maybe make her something to drink? I still have some of the elixir as well, it's the pink one in the cabinet next to the stove."

"I'll come with you." Seir followed Hailon out the door, leaving me and Phin in one part of the room while Merry opened her lovely stained-glass window and two huge birds came to perch on the sill. It seemed Archimedes, my brother's black owl, and Belmont, Greta's raven, were also making a visit.

I sat on the floor in front of the sofa and took one of Phin's hands in mine. I angled my grip so that my first two fingers could press into the vein in her wrist, the painful flare of the bond reassured by her heartbeat steady under my fingertips.

"One of my sisters-in-law is an alchemist. I'm betting there's a remedy of some kind she could brew up for you. She did the same for Merry when she was unwell." Phin's eyes blinked slowly. "We've got several healers in the family as well. I should have thought to ask if you wanted to be examined after having seen this happen at the church."

Merry smiled as she approached us again, leaving the window open, the familiars watching us with interest. "Well, there's no better place for this to have happened, I can assure you that, Phin. These folks all got a good trial run caring for me in such a state not all that long ago. I was new to this place, this life, and all the animals decided they wanted to start talking with me. Problem was, I wasn't really prepared for it and when they all tried to do it at once ... it kind of broke me for a little while." Her smile was gentle. "I'm no stranger to being trapped inside yourself. If you want to talk to anyone about it ..." She let the thought dangle and rose to help Hailon and Seir with the tea.

Phin's fingers twitching was the first sign she was coming back to herself, the second a low groan.

"How embarrassing," she whispered. "I'm sorry."

"None of that," Merry insisted. "This is an elixir Greta made for me when things were bad," she said, holding up the vial with shimmery pink liquid inside. "Do you want to try some?"

"I have a healing ability as well," Hailon offered. "If it's something I can mend, I'm happy to help."

Phin opened and closed her mouth twice, clearly awed by the attention. "No, thank you. I don't think any of that is necessary, but I appreciate the offer. Odd as it seems, this is pretty normal for me."

"Well." Merry handed over a cup of tea. "Should you change your mind."

"Thank you." Phin went quiet as she coddled the tea, but she had regained her coloring and otherwise seemed recovered. "The plants," she said cryptically.

"Sorry?" Merry frowned.

"Some of your new seedlings. I recognize some of them. They're all poisonous?"

"Yes, they're for d'Arcan's future poison garden."

Phin nodded tightly, the look in her eye positively haunted. I bristled, the bond flaring painfully.

Merry's cheeks pinked as she took in Phin's expression. "Oh. I see. I'm so sorry, I didn't mean—"

"I know you didn't. How could you? They're just plants. Please don't apologize, the issue is mine."

"Still, I feel terrible. Are you sure you're alright now?"

"Yes, I'll be fine." Phin straightened her shoulders. My chest eased. Whether she thought so or not, she was very strong. Her eyes landed on the birds still lingering on the windowsill. "Are they ...?"

"Introduce yourselves to the lady," Hailon prompted.

She gasped, eyes wide as they communicated with her in their own way. I was excluded again but didn't mind. I knew Archimedes very well, and Belmont was becoming just as much a fixture in the family as Rylan's owl.

There wasn't much space, but they each did their own version of a bow, spreading their wings and bobbing their heads.

"Nice to meet you," she whispered.

"What mischief are you two up to?" I asked.

New friend coming. Old friend. Archimedes sent, blinking his round gold orbs before turning his head back her direction. Phin frowned at his words.

"Those are different things, yes?"

Same.

I sighed, sure that there would be no progress had if I argued with him. "If you insist."

Belmont rarely spoke to me directly, but he made that loud knocking sound particular to corvids and blinked several times as he stared at me with his one good eye.

"Have you come to deliver a formal invitation to visit d'Arcan, then? Or just examine the new residents of the crossroads."

Yes. Archimedes put his wings out and fluffed his feathers, blinking at me as they settled again. Cheeky bird.

"Tell Rylan I'll consider it."

"Oh, you really should visit soon if you haven't," Hailon enthused. "The new dormitory is well on its way, and I think Magnus and Grace may be moving into their new house soon. I can't believe how much they've gotten done despite the cold weather. It must have killed Magnus to use the city's masons and other craftsman. They'd have moved in months ago had the stone kin been the ones in charge of building the structures."

"They really do work incredibly fast," Merry nodded. "Days is all it took for these cabins to be all but final finishes."

"When was the last time you went to d'Arcan, Tap? Was it the wedding?" Seir asked, smirk on his mouth. He was instigating again.

"You know it was."

"Then you're overdue. Surely going there is nearly as safe as coming here." My brother winked at me as he crossed to the window to pet the birds.

"What is d'Arcan?" Phin asked.

"A collegium in Revalia," I explained. "My brother Rylan's institution. They teach various skills to budding mages."

Belmont made the knocking noise again.

"Belmont's bonded, Greta, is the alchemist Tap mentioned. She lives there. She's mated to Vassago, another brother of ours," Seir explained.

Phin's brow crinkled the slightest bit at the word *mate*, but she nodded slowly. "I remember seeing Revalia on a map."

"Well, just let me know when you're ready to visit," Hailon said. "I'm there at least a couple times a week, I'm happy to accompany you."

Phin nodded, eyes gone a bit glazed. I squeezed her hand and she turned my direction, giving me a reassuring smile.

"You really do have the most gorgeous hair color," Hailon commented. "Mine's gone mostly white, but the silver tone to yours is just lovely, Phin."

"Thank you."

I was not overly wise in the ways of women, but I could see Phin warming to the casual conversation, though she still looked a bit dazed. It seemed as though it might benefit us all for Seir and I to go find something else to do, if only for a short time.

"Seir, would you walk with me to the ruins? I'd like to check on something."

He glanced between me and the women, who had all gathered around on the little sofa. "Sure. Is Coltor there?"

Merry nodded. "Last I saw him, he was taking care of something at his hut. You may pass him on your way."

"Perfect." I looked to Phin. "Alright?" She nodded.

The moment Seir and I were out the door, he groaned. "They were just getting to the good stuff. You're terrible at identifying when to leave a conversation, brother."

"It seemed like they could use a moment to get better acquainted," I said.

He huffed but cheered again as we started down the path. "What are we looking for?"

"Cracks. Gaps. Anything unusual."

"You mean exactly what Coltor looks for every single day?"

"More eyes, and all that."

He narrowed his gaze. "You don't really have anything to check on."

"Nothing specific. Though I do want to know if any of the dormant portals here have been behaving strangely or if I'm dealing with an anomaly."

My brother kicked at a clump of dirt and chuckled. "You owe me some good gossip for this."

"I suppose I have some of that. I keep forgetting, I need to pass a message to Coltor. And perhaps you or Hailon could take it to Magnus as well."

"A message?"

"Yes, from Tormund."

Seir stared at me, perplexed. "Have you met him, then?"

"Yes. He was guarding the church in Aymonroux."

His head tilted to the side. "He was?"

"Yes, he introduced himself when I went back without you. Seemed very amused I'd returned."

"I'm disappointed I missed that." He sulked for a brief moment, then brightened again. "I've earned a jar of pickles from Hailon and now gossip from you. I'm gathering owed debts all over the place. Must be my lucky day."

I wondered if my brother ever noticed that fortune was nearly always in his favor, but said nothing. I just enjoyed the fresh air and sunshine he'd been right to suggest we get.

Not that I'd ever tell him so.

IT WASN'T UNTIL we walked out of the boundary of the glade and into a more heavily forested and rocky area that we came across Merry's stone kin mate, Coltor.

He was standing in the ruins of Castle Emankor, to the untrained eye nothing more substantial than a few half-fallen pillars and floor stones covered in moss. What those of us who knew better could see was a hall not unlike the one at the crossroads, though smaller and with far fewer gateways to other places.

"Welcome back." Coltor ducked his head and reached out, his grip firm as he shook my hand.

"The wards are much stronger," I said, the sensation of the magic surrounding the glade, and especially the ruins, heavier than the last time I'd visited.

Coltor nodded, looking pleased. "Thanks to Ophelia, they've come a long way. I still can't believe she's visited more than once. But she's a very good teacher. Hopefully my efforts only get better thanks to her additions."

The ancient stone kin sorceress was known for her solitary living in her little hut inside the Dread Forest, which was named so mostly because of her terrifying presence and powerful wards. They were potent enough to make even powerful mages like my brother Rylan and the strongest of stone kin kind want to flee once they got too close to her home.

"Definitely something nobody could have predicted," Seir nodded, eyes wide.

"Your brother Tormund sends his greetings," I said, and Coltor's eyes went wide.

"Where on earth did you happen to encounter him?"

"Vincara. He's been posted there, I guess. He looked well."

Coltor nodded. "Unexpected news but appreciated. So, what brings you out here?"

I scanned the few doorways that were visible, finding the same calm, gentle energy that flowed through the crossroads. The old magic in the ruins was its own unique presence as well, like a sparkling wine bubbling against my skin.

"I've seen some oddities lately. I just wanted to see if you were experiencing the same."

"Oddities?"

"Inconsistent activity in some doorways that have long been dormant. Several of them I personally decommissioned."

A crease formed between Coltor's pitch-black eyebrows. "I've had a few momentary sparks the last little while, but I looked into them as soon as they happened. Nothing concerning. I figured it was just normal magical energy build up releasing."

I pushed my glasses up my nose. "Do you recall which ones you investigated?"

"It's all recorded. I can make you a copy of my logs."

"I'd appreciate it."

"Should I be concerned? Am I looking for something in particular?" Coltor crossed his arms, expression serious. He was nothing if not just as dedicated to his post as I was. I appreciated that about him more than he knew.

"I don't know yet. But I'll keep you informed if I learn anything."

He nodded solemnly. "I'm sure you didn't come all the way here to do the same job you do at the crossroads."

"The ladies are bonding," Seir chuckled.

"Ah." Coltor gestured to the stones, and we all took a position. "Be my guests then, there's certainly plenty to go around."

Together, the three of us performed a check of all the open portals. The routine was so much like what I spent my every hour doing that it brought a sense of comfort. Mostly, it was incredibly dull, our job, but occasionally, something wandered out of its realm, or magic went rogue and had to be contained. There was a sense of accomplishment that came with making sure everything was in its place.

"Well, that will make patrol a little simpler tonight," Coltor said, brushing his hands on his trousers. "Appreciated."

"My pleasure," I said, and I meant it. It was nice to see a different hall for a little while, and finding no disturbances always settled a very particular part of my soul.

"Oh. Hello there."

I turned, curious who Seir was greeting. At the edge of the ruins, just where the path back into the glade started, sat a sleek black dog. Its pointed ears were straight up, slender snout angled to scent the breeze.

"Where'd a *dog* come from?" Coltor asked, sounding offended that something had slipped through his defensive measures.

"That's no dog," Seir grinned. "Well, it is. But it's not."

"You're doing it again," Coltor sighed.

"Doing what?" Seir asked, only smiling harder.

"That thing where you talk nonsense."

"He does that quite a lot," I agreed, taking a step toward the creature, who was sitting quite regally, just watching us. Waiting. "But in this case, he's making sense."

Coltor grunted. "I've got two mad demons on my hands at once then. Lovely."

"Not at all." I reached out with my mind, offering a greeting to the animal. It responded with annoyance that it had taken me so long to acknowledge its presence. "This is no dog. It only looks like one. This is a hellhound."

Coltor straightened. "Looks like a dog to me." It was distant, but I heard the low growl of discontent at his comment. "My mistake." He held his hands up. "So, what, exactly, is a hellhound doing here?"

The hound stood and turned around, walking several paces back toward the cabins ahead of us.

"She snuck through a doorway when we weren't looking. Didn't you?" Seir was thrilled to have been the victim of the hound's stealth.

"Snuck. Through." Coltor looked ready to chew on some rocks in order to vent his frustration.

"They do that sometimes."

He turned his horrified expression on me. "How do we fix that?"

I shrugged. "We don't. There aren't many of them, and they're usually on very particular missions, so it's best to just be friendly if you see one. They'll complete their business and move along soon enough."

Are you coming? I'd like to see my mistress. The hound swung her head around, impatience clear in her bright amber stare.

"Mistress?" I asked.

Yes. It's been a very long time since I've seen her. I need to be sure she's alright. I know she's here; I can smell her. Her head swiveled around again. *Her scent is on you, too, demon.* Hound or not, her judgmental eyes scraped me from head to toe, and I had the irrational need to pass her inspection.

"What is your mistress's name?" Seir and Coltor were watching my one-sided conversation with rapt attention as we walked.

She's called Phin.

As my thoughts caught up to what she'd said, my heart stuttered. "Phin?"

Yes, that's what I said. Hurry up.

I glanced over my shoulder and found both Seir and Coltor as speechless as I was. Seir met my eye, many of the same questions I had reflected in his expression.

"Tap, wouldn't that mean ..."

"Yes," I confirmed.

If Phin was bonded to a hellhound, she was part demon.

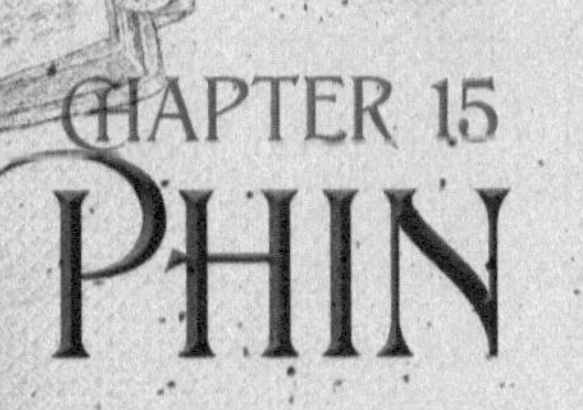

CHAPTER 15
PHIN

AFTER I'D REASSURED both Hailon and Merry that I was perfectly steady on my feet, they'd taken me back outside for some fresh air.

I'd only had a handful of episodes since my arrival at the crossroads, and they'd all been fairly easy to manage. A few minutes, frozen with deals in my hand in the library was far nicer than standing out in the frigid cold of the churchyard. Even my ability to think and speak clearly had improved. I supposed I'd been due a bigger one, but the situation couldn't have been more mortifying.

The odd pair of birds had followed, circling above us as we toured Merry's vegetable beds and flowers, her voice soothing as she listed the names and possible functions for everything she had planted. I appreciated that she had such enthusiasm for ensuring that not only was everyone well fed, but that there was beauty year-round. The climate of Ravenglen was not all that different to Vincara, and the plants in both Merry's and Hailon's gardening beds reminded me of the smaller one my mother kept outside our home in the forest. The ones at the church, sadly, suffered from my less than green thumbs, though the herbs usually did okay as they required very little attention.

I turned my face into the sun again, reveling in it while I could.

"Is it alright if I touch you, Phin?" Hailon asked quietly, her hand hovering above my shoulder. Her kind expression left me nodding. "There's a feather, just here, but I need to adjust your collar. This coat ..." She quirked her mouth and focused, tugging on something at the back of my neck with one hand and holding my shoulder with the other.

A burst of warmth rushed across my skin where her hand rested, even through the heavy fabric. She caught my eye and smiled, keeping contact while presenting me with yet another breakthrough feather.

"There we are. So pretty. Matches your hair."

I took it from her, copying Tap and threading it through the buttonhole on the outside breast pocket of my coat. "Thanks."

"Sure." Her brow furrowed. "I'm sorry if this is forward, but would you mind if I use my gift to see if there's any healing you need? You won't hurt my feelings if you say no," she said calmly. "It's just that I've never tried with anyone angelic before, I'm honestly really curious if it will work any differently, especially considering how we react to one another."

I glanced over to find Merry casually fussing over her plants, not paying attention to us but likely still hearing everything.

"I don't see what the harm could be."

"I'll be quick."

My shoulder warmed a little more under her touch as her eyes closed and her head tilted to the side. Her face went through several emotions, but she remained silent.

"Her gift has gotten very well trained in the last little while." Merry nodded, presenting me with a small bouquet of winter wildflowers she'd picked and tied together with a bit of string. "Some sunshine to take back with you."

"Thank you."

"Must be strange to live somewhere with no sunlight?"

"It isn't as difficult as I thought it would be. Tap has set up the windows so they get brighter and darker like they would if we were elsewhere."

"Really? That's clever."

"Did you ever notice the ceilings? Or that the walls sometimes don't look solid?"

Merry nodded. "I couldn't put my finger on it for the longest time because I was mostly in the one library and it has a ceiling. But coming and going from the hall with everything open does make the space seem really ... boundless. It definitely takes some getting used to."

I nodded, relieved that she understood what I meant. "Yes, that's it exactly."

Hailon made a small noise in her throat. "Sorry to interrupt. Phin, what does it feel like before you have an attack?"

I swallowed, unsure if my heart was suddenly pounding because I was nervous or because I was about to have another episode.

"It usually starts with my heart. Sometimes it beats so fast I can't breathe, other times it's like it's stuck in my throat instead of my chest." I lifted my hand, resting my palm against the beat. "Occasionally it's like it's stopped and has to restart. My fingertips go numb. I lose control of my muscles."

"That sounds terrifying." Hailon's tone was full of sympathy but missing the pity I expected.

"It is."

Merry came to stand at my side and wrapped both of her hands around the one of mine that held the bouquet.

"When I was stuck inside my own head, I couldn't even make my eyes open when I wanted them to most of the time. Everything was too heavy. Is it like that? Like you're underwater, and everything is impossible to lift or move?"

"Yes." Tears sprang to my eyes against my will, the genuine nature of these kind women taking me by such surprise I didn't know quite what to do with myself.

"Well," Hailon exhaled and patted my shoulder before dropping her hand. "You're quite healthy, Phin. But your heart does have a ... flaw? Maybe damage. I can't really tell which, organs are very complex. Not that it matters, but it's perhaps part of the reason for what happens. And your throat and vocal cords are very irritated. I could maybe help with those things, but I don't have to do anything today. And we can recommend other healers if you want another opinion."

"Does the dust bother you too?" Merry's face scrunched up. "I'm terribly allergic. It makes me sneeze, itch, and get terrible headaches. I suspect it's more to do with the paper in the old contracts than the crossroads itself, but it's definitely better when I work on the documents from here instead."

Several thoughts all sprang up, demanding attention at the same time. Because I couldn't sort them out, my words also got tangled when I tried to answer. I opened my mouth, but only some vague noises came out.

"Not allergic," I managed.

I shook my head, then nodded, trying to convey that while I didn't doubt Hailon's abilities, I wasn't sure I was ready to do anything drastic. Not to mention that I had a pretty good idea what had happened to cause the damage.

Hailon and Merry glanced at one another.

"Well. You think on that, okay?" Merry still held my hand between hers, and without a word they had steered me back toward the office. "For now, let's get back inside where it's warm. I've maybe got a book or two we could peek at for other suggestions."

"There's no rush on anything, Phin. Just know that I'm here if you'd like me to try."

I bobbed my head, the hot tears back again. I had no idea how

I'd been pulled from a life where I was invisible into one where I was freely given so much attention, but I was grateful.

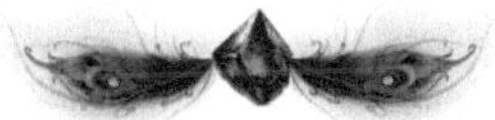

ONCE WE GOT settled back in the cozy little office, Merry and Hailon held a whole conversation by themselves while still making me feel as though I'd been included. My nods and hand gestures were somehow enough for them to clearly understand what I was trying to convey.

Merry took back my flower bundle and plunked it into a little cup of water on the small table that sat to one side of the sofa. Books were pulled from her shelves and flipped through, more tea made and drank, and copious notes written on a piece of parchment, all while I sat, stared, and marveled at how interested they were in trying to fix whatever was wrong with me.

"I'll take this to Greta." Hailon patted the pocket that contained her sheet of notes. "She's got the best resources for this kind of thing. Lovette may know something too, I'll see if I can get out to the conclave to chat with her. And Rylan is also a healer, so you're in good hands."

"The best." Merry nodded in agreement, her red curls bouncing. "What happened to me nearly broke my mind completely, and these people and their amazing gifts set me to rights."

I tried to mentally file all the new names they were saying, but it wouldn't really matter until I actually met the people they belonged to. Faces helped me retain names far better than descriptions.

As they were chatting and I was trying to focus on getting my tongue to work right again, I heard a sound that made me freeze.

"Did you hear that?" Merry jumped to her feet and opened the stained glass window. As though they'd been waiting, the birds ducked in. "A little space, if you please," she requested, elbowing her way through the middle of them, peering around, trying to find the source of the sound. "Lots of creatures live here in the glade, but dogs are few and far between. Actually, there aren't any at all that I've seen, not since the creatures all gathered before I took my place as Keeper." As if just realizing what she said, her brown pinched. "Cats either, actually. The only one I know is Calla's Morticia. That's odd, isn't it? Oh." She turned to face the door just as it was pulled all the way open by a massive man with long dark hair. Before he could step inside, a sleek black hound passed him up and came straight to me.

Throat tight, I found the only word I needed. "Ramsey?"

Mistress! You've grown so beautifully. A whine came from the hound's throat as she rested her chin on my knee, her tail wagging fiercely.

A laugh burst from me and I slid off the sofa cushions to the floor, wrapping my arms around her neck, and let her lick my cheek, not caring that we had an audience.

"I really do hear you," I whispered, still clinging to the animal I believed I'd never see again, the one I'd last said farewell to after I'd been handed off to Father Morton. She'd promised to return after looking into a lead on the people I was being hidden from, and I'd never seen her again.

After lamenting the loss of my parents and my companion to Father Morton, I'd been convinced that all of the conversations we'd had in my head since I was a child had been one giant figment of my imagination. How foolish I'd been to believe him. I couldn't help but wonder what else he'd made me believe that wasn't true.

I have missed you very much, mistress. Are you well?

I nodded, tears flowing freely despite my joy. "How?" I asked, hoping that was enough to convey what I was truly asking.

I have journeyed far, mistress. I'm sorry I had to leave you. She whined again and sat, soulful eyes looking into mine. *I loathe that I will have to do so again. But I will always come back.*

"Why?" The single word encapsulated several more questions. Lucky for me, Ramsey had always understood me just fine.

That is a very long story. She looked up at the people who were very politely giving us time to make our greetings. *How have you come to know so many demons and stone kin and witches?*

"Also a long story."

We have much to catch up on then. Ramsey chuffed and settled down, laying her body across my legs right where I sat on the floor.

"Isn't this wonderful!" Seir said, looking like he was ready to burst out of his skin with excitement. "Ramsey, is it? Welcome to the glade." He performed a flourish of his arm and a bow.

Ramsey glanced at me. *He's odd. I like him.*

"Me too." I realized then, looking between Seir and Ramsey why he'd always seemed so familiar. He had animated facial expressions—joyful, enthusiastic, frustrated—just like a hound. Thankfully my low laugh at the revelation was covered by the other goings-on of the moment.

Ramsey tilted her head in that way only dogs can, examining both Tap and Seir. *Princes?*

"Indeed." Tap bowed as well, adjusting his glasses when he straightened. "Pleased to meet you, Ramsey. I'm Tap, and that's Seir." She gave a little snort and dipped her nose in response. "I've met a few of your sisters through the years, though, I'll admit it's been quite a long time since the last."

I've heard of you, Watchman. You maintain the doorways and the familiar bonds. Rolo and Freyda have both spoken kindly of you.

"That's a very fancy title you have for me. I'm honored. Though, Merry handles the bonds now." He gestured to her.

Keeper. Ramsey thought loudly, watching Merry. The declaration was edged with surprise.

"Yes, hello. Pleased to meet you."

The birds both flapped and preened on the windowsill, clearly trying to get her attention.

New friend. Old friend. Archimedes repeated, which absolutely made sense now. The birds both moved to the edges of the sill, and Jacks poked his head through.

You have found many friends, mistress. Some more strange than others.

No need to be rude, hound. Jacks's voice came into my mind, and I heard Merry squeak as she looked nervously at Ramsey.

Not rude, demi-beast. True.

Even through the walls of the office, Jacks's stomp was clear. *Cheeky. Greetings to you, hound.*

He pulled his head back out of the window, letting loose the whinny that sounded like laughter as he moved away from the building.

After a brief, tense moment, Merry walked to the large man with long hair and threaded her arm through his. "Phin, Ramsey, this is Coltor."

He lifted his hand in a gentle wave. "Hello."

I nodded in greeting, running my hand over Ramsey's fur. "Stone kin?" I guessed, putting together what Ramsey had said with Tap's description from that afternoon at the church.

"Yes. Nephilim?"

I couldn't stop the stunned laugh that burst from my throat. "Yes."

"Pleased to meet you."

"And you." I was relieved that my ability to speak was returning even if it was only a couple of words at a time.

"Today has been entirely unexpected." Hailon breathed out heavily. "I'm not sure why I thought we'd have an uneventful afternoon, that's simply not how things tend to go in this family. I'm Hailon. Pleased to meet you."

Ramsey tilted her head again. *A null? Very rare indeed. I am relieved to find that you are so well protected, mistress.*

Relief washed over me. I trusted her assessment, especially as it echoed not only my own feelings but also what Jacks had told me. "I'm so happy to see you." I closed my eyes and pressed my cheek to the top of her head.

Ramsey seemed exhausted now that she was relaxed, licking at her paws before settling her chin between them across my lap. I wondered when the last time she'd really rested was.

"Well." Seir clapped his hands gently and turned toward the door, which was still propped open a bit by the cat doorstop. "Who's hungry?"

CHAPTER 16
TAP

WE ALL SHIFTED from the office to Merry's cabin, where the smell of something delicious cooking was heavy on the air.

"We'll be right back," Hailon said. "I've got some other dishes at ours, left them cooking while we took our walk."

She and Seir ducked out the door, my heart squeezing happily when my brother propped it open with one of Merry's many wooden carvings without any prompting.

"I'll get the other table set up," Coltor said, pausing to press a kiss to Merry's cheek before moving her little round table and chairs toward the back of the sofa.

"Good idea," Merry agreed, opening the oven and letting another burst of mouthwatering scent out. Even Ramsey licked her chops.

"I'm happy to help carry," I offered.

"No need." He gestured to the cabinets that faced the main room. "We've got this down to a science lately with all the visitors." He reached under and pulled up until a tabletop I'd assumed was just the cabinet backing was horizontal to the floor. He then pulled out legs that were hinged and hidden underneath, creating an instant table extension that more than doubled the seats Merry's little table would have provided.

"Incredible." I adjusted my spectacles and marveled at the ingenuity, squatting down to see how he'd attached everything.

"It's come in very handy lately." His words were slightly grumbled, as though visitors were a sore spot. I could understand that completely.

"Chairs?"

"Seir will bring his. And there are these." He walked down the short hallway and opened a closet, extracting a few wooden chairs that were folded completely flat.

Again, I marveled at the design, poking and examining how they moved. "Fantastic."

"I'm happy to share the plans," he said, giving me a genuine smile. "Though I can't take all the credit. Several of the craftsman who came from the conclave to work on the cabins are the ones who created the design."

"Well, they're brilliant. I'd love to have the plans, thank you." When I'd have time to make tables or chairs was a mystery, but it was a project that excited me, and that alone made it worth pursuing.

"I'll copy them when I do the logs you need," he said, chest puffed with pride.

"Can I help with anything?" Phin offered.

"I think we're all set, actually, but thank you. Make yourself comfortable. Ramsey, would you like something to drink?"

The hound walked into the kitchen, she and Merry having a private exchange. Merry filled a large bowl with water and set it on the floor, and the hound immediately started drinking.

Phin went to the sofa and sat in the end seat, Ramsey settling between her feet once she'd drunk her fill.

"You too, Tap. You're a guest, please relax." Merry motioned at the couch, and I went to join Phin at her command.

I was the recipient of a sweet, gentle smile as I sat, and my heart thudded happily.

"How long has Ramsey been with your family, Phin?"

Ramsey perked an ear at me. Her chin rested on Phin's thigh, and she cracked one eye open to stare at me. *Careful, demon. It's impolite to ask a lady's age.* There was a subtle change in the depth of how her voice registered that indicated she'd only responded so I could hear.

I mean no disrespect. It's just genuine curiosity, I promise. A habit leftover from all the time I spent managing familiars.

"As long as I can remember," Phin said.

Both of Ramsey's eyes opened and she pinned me with that potent amber stare. *I was with Terra before Phin was born.*

"How wonderful you could be reunited." I fidgeted with the tiny scraps of black lacquer that remained on my nails and spun my ring. "Am I right to assume you'll be going with us to the crossroads?"

The naked hope on Phin's face made the bond flare painfully. I rubbed my hand over my chest, trying to ease the ache.

For tonight, yes. But tomorrow, I must leave again.

"Tomorrow?" Phin's voice cracked and so did my heart. Even Ramsey whined.

I'm sorry, mistress. I have tasks that are not yet complete. But I will come back to you, as soon as I can. I promise. Ramsey's glare made me shift in my seat. *You and I must speak privately later, demon.*

I dipped my head, subtly acknowledging her statement.

The door to Merry's cabin opened fully, and Hailon came in, arms stacked with baking dishes and bowls. Behind her was Seir, somehow balancing multiple chairs on each arm as well as more food.

I jumped up to help, and before long, the table was set, the food was spread across every inch of Merry's countertops, and we were all seated with a full plate in front of us. Ramsey had been treated to her own plate as well. Merry had gone so far as to ask her whether she'd like some of each dish and how much.

"This is my favorite thing, I think." Seir held his cutlery in his fists like a toddler, moon-eyed over his food.

"What, the roast? Or the green beans?" Hailon asked, sampling one of the beans she spoke of.

"All of it. All the time." He breathed in, head back and eyes closed. "We did so well on stew while we traveled, Moonflower, but I have deeply enjoyed the many hearty meals we've had since."

She laughed and patted his forearm. "Me too."

"Please, everyone, eat up." Merry glanced in the kitchen and shook her head. "There's nowhere to put all the leftovers if you don't. I hope you know you'll be taking some home with you, Tap."

"I expected no less. The same thing happened at your ceremony, no matter that I made my esca—*exit*, early."

Coltor chuckled. "And my kin were cooking then as well. Every kitchen in the glade was overwhelmed."

"Yes, I had meals for a week. Everything was delicious, I was disappointed when it was all gone."

"It would be no trouble to send something now and then. We should have thought of that before now, to be honest," Hailon said. "Seir has mentioned more than once how concerned he is that you're not eating as much as you should."

I raised my eyebrow at my brother.

"What?" he said, unrepentant. "I've told you so directly many times. I bring you groceries."

"You do."

"Still, we can surely send a casserole or leftovers now and then." Merry nodded. "We always prepare as though we're trying to feed the whole of d'Arcan and not just ourselves. Best to share it rather than have it go to waste."

"You're giving away my leftovers?" Coltor asked, looking positively bereft.

"Oh, for saint's sake." Merry laughed. "We'll figure it out."

"It's really not necessary," I argued, "but I appreciate the concern."

"Speaking of d'Arcan, should we discuss a day for you to go?" Hailon asked. "I've got plans to be there day after tomorrow and again on Wednesday, which is ... five days from now."

"Phin?"

"Oh, I ..."

"We'll let you know. Though I promise it will be soon."

Phin had gone quiet again, but she seemed relieved, happily sampling the variety of foods on her plate. Thankfully, there were no greens to be found.

"How does it work, exactly, a Nephilim having a hellhound?" Coltor asked. Seir and I blinked at one another, and Merry kicked his ankle under the table. "Sorry. Is it rude to ask that?"

"Since when do you care about rude?" Seir teased. "Do you even remember how we met? You picked a fight with me and then made accusations at Hailon. I had to throw a knife at you."

"I'd like to think I've grown since then, demon." Seir only laughed harder.

Phin looked up from her plate. "Hellhound?" Ramsey came around the edge of the kitchen cabinets, eyes fixed on Coltor.

"Maybe I misunderstood—" Coltor very quickly turned an alarming shade of red.

"I thought ... Can't hellhounds only bond to demons?" Phin frowned, her violet eyes locked onto mine. Everyone lowered the amount of noise they were making to be sure they could hear her speaking.

"Yes, that's true," I said gently.

"But my father is an angel and my mother is human." She stared from one of us to the next, stopping again when she got to me. Her attention made the bond flare in my chest.

"Humans can have a mixed magical heritage, many times without even knowing."

"So, my mother ..."

Part demon, mistress. Finished with her food, Ramsey came to sit beside Phin, her chin in Phin's lap. *Mostly, in fact.*

"Which means I'm ..." Phin set her fork down and lowered her hand to her lap. She swallowed and inhaled a deep breath through her nose. Her hand trembled as it reached for mine, and I greedily accepted the invitation, lacing our fingers together. I traced my thumb along the edge of her finger, hoping the gesture brought her the same kind of comfort it did me.

"That changes nothing, Phin. You are still everything you knew yourself to be," I said softly.

"I'm sorry. Saints, I apologize, I didn't mean ... I just was being nosy," Coltor hastily babbled apologies.

"Mother told me you were blessed by a cherubim when I was born. That's why you never seemed to get older and were able to pass from her care to mine."

The sound of Ramsey's startled laughter rang through my mind. *A cherubim? That sounds like something she would say. I honestly thought you knew, all this time. I don't know why your parents kept it from you. Your mother has many talents similar to those of a wise woman or a hedgewitch, but she is indeed a demon.*

"Perhaps it wasn't just your angel nature responding to my touch then," Hailon said gently. "I know it doesn't help anything, but I didn't know my mother was a demon either, not until very recently. I won't insult you by saying that I know what you're feeling right now, but we seem to have quite a bit in common."

The silence was heavy for several heartbeats.

"I still went to Heaven. Frequently. How? And if I could go, why couldn't she?"

"I expect that it's nothing more complicated than the fact that you are still half angel, and she was not. That alone would be enough," I offered.

"Could you go?" Her head tilted. "As a fallen. Could you go back if you wanted to?"

I looked at Seir who shrugged. "Perhaps."

Phin closed her eyes, shoulders sagging. "Safe to assume you never asked?"

A surprised laugh bubbled out of me. "Yes, that's right. As I explained, there are rules. Lots of paperwork restricting the use of portals to and from Heaven from the crossroads. But I could ask, if you want me to. Seir—"

"I'll speak with Keplar," he responded immediately, knowing just what I was after. "Surely there's a codex somewhere with rules about inter-planar travel that include information beyond just Hell and Earth."

"Thank you."

Ramsey whined and Phin looked down at her, relaxing noticeably as she used her free hand to pet the hound's fur.

"Merry, do you happen to have any spirits?" Phin asked quietly.

"Spirits? Like ghosts or—"

"No. I ... I'm sorry to be so rude, but I could really use a drink."

"Oh! Absolutely."

Our hostess dashed into the kitchen and returned with a bottle, passing it and several small drink glasses around the table.

"Oh, I'm not sure that one's a good idea, that's stone kin home brew, it's—" Coltor tried to warn her, but it was too late.

Phin locked eyes with me again, just as she gulped down a solid two fingers' worth of the clear, potent grain alcohol Merry had provided her with. She grimaced, inhaled through the burn, and then coughed. I patted her back, but she indicated she was alright.

"Bottoms up." Merry took her own drink, though barely a sip in comparison, smiling encouragingly at Phin as she picked up her fork.

Dinner progressed as normally as any meal could after a revelation like that. Between Ramsey and I, we made sure that Phin ate most of the contents of her plate as well as the pie Hailon had made for dessert. Despite that, by the time she'd finished a third drink I was certain I'd be carrying her home and that she'd be in bed most of the next day.

None of which bothered me one bit. She was welcome to have whatever reaction she thought was appropriate to help her process what she'd learned.

I could only assume she felt the same way, because through the rest of dinner, the conversation, the goodbyes and promises to see one another soon, she never let go of my hand.

"DO YOU NEED to visit the bathroom? Or did you want to change into something else?" I flushed hot, unsure what I would do if she actually said yes.

"No, I'm 'kay." Phin sighed deeply, already half asleep as she snuggled into the bed fully dressed. I pulled her blankets up around her, torn between relief and worry that she might have to stumble in there later anyway.

"There's a pail just here"—I lifted her arm, making sure she touched the small bucket I'd put next to her bed with her fingers—"if you feel unwell."

"'Kay."

She was going to, I could almost guarantee it. She'd only made it a handful of treacherous steps across Merry's porch before I'd scooped her up and carried her back through the glade to the portal. The bond had been very pleased by the weight of her in my arms, the smell of her hair so close to my nose. She'd leaned in and kissed my cheek again, and I'd stopped breathing for several steps. Even my demon, lately agitated and restless because of the unfulfilled bond, seemed settled thanks to the close contact.

I very much liked being useful to her, a safe presence she'd been comfortable enough to lean on.

I craved more of it, in fact. Infinitely more.

"There's water on the bedside table, and a vial of medicine. If you wake in the night, you should take it. Drink as much water as you can."

"Mmm."

"Ramsey will be here with you. And I'll be either in my room or the great hall."

Phin patted the bed and the hellhound put her nose where she could feel it. A faint smile crossed her face and she relaxed fully, her breathing too slow to be anything but deeply asleep.

I looked away from my mate to the hound. "Do you want to speak in here?"

We should leave her to rest. I'll come back when we're finished.

I bobbed my head in agreement and we exited Phin's room, leaving the door open like she preferred.

Out of habit, I walked straight past the living area and into the great hall, beginning my routine checks as Ramsey kept pace right beside me.

Do you not rest, Watchman?

I paused, glancing around as I initiated the transfer of control overactive doorways back to the crossroads from Hell. The shift in energy as they came back to life around me settled my nerves. "Perhaps not as often as I should." She sat in the middle of the walkway, eyes fixed on mine. *Has Phin acknowledged your mate bond?*

The breath I'd taken stalled in my throat. "You are very straight-forward, Ramsey."

I don't often have time or energy to waste on frivolity, demon. Does she?

I shook my head. "We have not discussed it, but no. I don't believe she's even recognized it as a possibility yet."

But you do.

"Yes. From the moment I saw her, I knew."

Her head tilted. *This doesn't bother you? Is it not painful?*

"It is often bothersome, yes. But I have her near me. She is fed, comfortable, safe. I cannot and will not ask for more unless or until she's adequately prepared. Mate bonds are eternal. That shouldn't be entered into lightly."

The potential length of eternity between a demon and a Nephilim was genuinely endless. The idea that she could change her mind or regret our bond was beyond paralyzing. I had to eliminate as much possibility of that happening as I could.

Your stance is wise.

I waited, unsure if I should be requesting her blessing or expecting further questioning. The hellhound remained quiet.

Unable to stand it any longer, I asked, "Could I be so bold as to ask what it is you've been looking for in your travels?"

The people hunting my mistress have been doing so for far longer than she knows. While her trips to Heaven were indeed for her benefit, they were not just for her education, nor for her father to perform his duties. I have been hunting them, in return.

I straightened. "Have you found something? Is that why you were able to seek her out now, after such a long time?"

I believe I have. You and the other demon and the stone kin, you were discussing activity in dormant doors. That is almost certainly connected to the trio I've been following. Every time I catch up to them, they manage to slip away. Their skill with the portals rivals that of any hellhound.

I didn't care to hear that one bit. "Trio?"

Angels. Two men, one woman.

My mind flickered to Father Morton telling Phin about the people that had been in the village. "They were looking for her in Vincara not long before I brought her here."

Yes. I tracked them there as well. It was torturous to be so close to her and not be able to reveal myself, but it wasn't safe for either of us.

"I'm sorry. This kind of separation must have been very difficult for you both."

I am very anxious for a time when I can be at her side again.

"When you are able, you're welcome here, for however long she wants to stay."

Do you anticipate her wanting to leave?

"I am mindful of all possibilities. It is not guaranteed that she will either recognize or accept the bond, and once she is no longer in danger, she may choose to live a life elsewhere."

Ramsey tilted her head. *My mistress has stumbled into very unusual circumstances yet again, it seems.*

I bit my tongue, though I was dreadfully curious about what else the hound's *again* implied. That was twice she'd mentioned something from Phin's past that was almost certainly both very important to understanding who my mate was and so personal it was closely guarded.

"My brothers and I, as well as the stone kin, are already look-ing into several mysterious disappearances. All couples that the respective councils forbade to be together. All parents of unique, magically talented children. It is too much of a coincidence for none of the cases to be related. There may even be some resources in Hell willing to assist in checking on suspicious activity, old doorways, things like that."

That is very helpful. I will return as soon as I can. I promised her I would, and I meant it. I'm ready to be done wandering, being away this long was never the plan. Especially not after ... She sneezed, as though allergic to whatever had happened in the past. *I need to be with Phin. Too many times, she has been left alone.*

"She never will be again, if I can help it." It was a vow, and hung on the air between us, though not with the extra sparks that had come along with the one I made with Father Morton in the old language. "Are Phin's parents still alive, Ramsey?"

I believe so. I think I would know if my former mistress died, due to our connection. I am tied to Phin now, but some link to Terra will always remain. That knowledge and a faint draw to wherever she is has kept me hopeful that I might find her all these years. Her head swiveled the direction of the bedrooms. *I'm going to go rest. You should as well.*

"I will as soon as I'm done," I agreed, though there were no minutes or even hours I could assign to when that might be.

The hellhound disappeared from my sight, and I resumed my tour of the doorways, thoughts consumed by possibilities and an acceptance that visiting my brother's collegium was in my very near future.

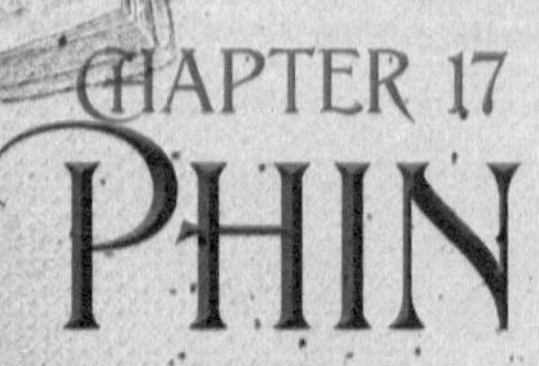

CHAPTER 17
PHIN

THE PAIN, PARTICULARLY the aching throb behind my eyes, was the first thing I became aware of as I woke.

"Oh, saints." Even whispering hurt.

I turned on my side to find the window lit brightly enough it was probably midmorning. Squinting, I groped for the glass of water Tap had so kindly left on my bedside table. Propping myself up on my elbow, I drank slowly, hopeful not to upset my stomach. Once I was sure the water wasn't coming back up, I reached for the vial of pain reliever and drank it as well, willing it to work swiftly.

"Ramsey?" I called, worried I'd missed getting to see her again before she left. "Are you still here?"

After a moment, her head appeared over the end of the bed. *I'm here, sleepyhead. How are you feeling?*

"Terrible. I just wanted to be sure you hadn't already gone." Every word stabbed at me, the headache more vicious than any I'd ever had excepting one.

I stayed to keep an eye on you. If you're not one to drink, stone kin homebrew is a bold way to start, mistress. She was making fun of me, and I deserved it.

"I just needed my mind to be quiet. I knew that would help."

Ramsey whined. *I understand, mistress. And I am equally confused and sorry your mother didn't tell you the truth. I don't know why that was kept from you. But as your demon said, it changes nothing.*

"He's not *my* demon," I scoffed, carefully moving my body the rest of the way upright, and letting the waves of nausea pass before trying to get all the way to my feet.

Ramsey cocked her head to the side. *If you say so.*

Her words itched at my brain, but I couldn't think well enough to worry about them at the moment. The memory of getting up to leave the little cabin and tripping over my own feet on the way out the door rose up. "Oh saints. I was so drunk he had to carry me home, wasn't I? I think I even laughed about it." I buried my face in my hands. The memory of his warm fingers threaded through mine made me groan into my palms. I'd even held his hand. And for how long? Hours? And then I kissed his cheek.

If it's any consolation, he seemed completely unbothered by that development.

"It's not." Mortification set in. I'd made a fool of myself in front of him *and* his family.

Do you need help? I can get the Watchman, and we can see if he feels any differently today.

"No!" The exclamation had me sucking in a breath through my gritted teeth. It was too abrupt, too loud, and hurt my throat as well as my head. "I can do this part myself, thank you very much. And then maybe some breakfast will help." I reached up and pressed my cool fingertips against my temple on one side, the throbbing behind it wildly painful.

You can just think our conversation at me, you don't have to speak. Maybe that will help too.

I tried what she suggested as I made my way to the sink. *Can you hear me?*

Perfectly.

How convenient. I wet a cloth in cold water and pressed it to my face and neck. My eyes were red and irritated, my throat dry and achy, like I'd spent the night breathing smoke. I resorted to splashing water directly onto my skin and drinking a bit from my cupped hands. Once slightly more revived, I made use of the toilet and very gently brushed some of the knots out of my hair, which had finally gotten long enough to tangle. Even my scalp was sore. *Will this work when you're far away?*

I don't know. We'll just have to try and see what happens.

Cheered by the possibility, I pulled on my most comfortable leggings and oversize tunic, surprised by a gentle rap at the door just as I turned to find some heavy socks. The toes of Tap's shoes and the long outline of his body were visible in the gap where the door was cracked.

"Phin?"

"Yes, you can come in," I said, pushing the door open.

"I thought you might be hungry." He held a tray in his hands, one with strange legs on it. "Though I expected to just leave this on the dresser, if I'm honest. I'm surprised you're up. Are you feeling alright?"

"Yes, I'm okay."

Go sit in the bed, mistress. Ramsey instructed, her laughter clear inside my thoughts.

I did what she asked, Tap visibly relaxing as I made myself comfortable with pillows at my back. "Oh." My gasp was audible as he settled the tray across my lap, the reason for the design now obvious. "I could have gone to the kitchen."

Tap ducked his head and spread the items out across the tray. "I wasn't sure what would sit best, or if you were feeling ill, so I brought a bit of everything." He moved the dishes apart, revealing that he'd made me toast with jam, a bowl of hot grain cereal with syrup and dried fruit, plus a bowl of halved starberries. There were also three cups on the tray, a small one of apple cider, a mug of tea and another tall glass of water. "The sweetness helps when my stomach's off sometimes." He gestured at the cider.

"This is so nice." My voice was thick, awe and confusion warring in my chest.

"One more thing." He reached into his back pocket and produced the little bouquet Merry had given me, safely tucked into in a lopsided vase I suspected he'd made on the pottery wheel in the workshop. As I stared, Tap set the vase on my bedside table, turning it so I'd get the best view of the pretty little wildflowers.

Oh my, mistress. Breakfast in bed? Flowers? You are indeed well cared for here.

Ramsey! I scolded, my face hot. She just laughed again and hopped up onto the foot of the bed so nimbly the mattress barely registered her weight at all.

I could have blamed the effects of having drunk the spirits or my episodes, but those things were not to blame for my racing pulse. Tap had performed all these tasks hovering over me, his face mere inches from mine. His arm brushed the sleeve of my tunic, the scent of him in my nose as I tried to slow my breathing.

"Thank you." Even my voice had stopped working properly.

"The pleasure is mine." If I hadn't been so close, I wouldn't have seen the blush that stained his cheeks and even spread to the tips of his ears as he met my eye. "I'll come back in a while and get the tray."

"No, you don't have to. I'll take it and wash the dishes when I'm finished. I need to get to the library anyway, I'm already—"

"Please don't say late." He shook his head. "Because you're not. You're having a very well-deserved lie in. You don't have to go in that room at all, not today or tomorrow or the next day unless you want to."

"But—"

"No. Phin, please. Rest. Take care of yourself. The library project is not meant to consume all your time, nor is it a race. Take the day. I'll come back later to check on you. Ramsey." He bent at the waist, not quite going into a bow as he addressed her. Then, not waiting for my response, he strode out the door, leaving it open a few inches like I preferred.

As I sampled the hot cereal, Ramsey's cackle was loud in my aching skull. *Well cared for indeed.*

I have no idea what's going on, I admitted.

Really? Because it looks to me as though you've stumbled into a lovely situation. Accept the kindness, mistress. You deserve this.

"What is *this*?" I asked quietly.

Comfort. Consideration. Kindness. All things you've lacked for some time.

I had no response to that because Tap had definitely offered those things from the very start.

Whatever the medicine had been, it had finally started to work, the pounding in my head lessening to a dull throb. "How long will you be gone this time?"

I don't know. She settled her chin between her paws, watching me. *Hopefully not long. I will return to you, Phin.*

"I know." I worked my way around the tray, a bite of this, then that, a sip of hot tea, then the apple cider. Finally, I broke off a bit of the toast and offered it to her. She accepted it happily, smacking her tongue long after the little taste was gone.

"Where did they go, Ramsey? Why didn't they come back for me? Why did they leave me there?" My voice cracked. I stared at my beloved hound and she stared back, her chin coming to rest on my foot.

They couldn't, mistress. Nothing else is possible. They wouldn't have stayed away unless they were unable to get back to you. None of us would.

"I hope they're okay."

Ramsey didn't answer.

It was childish, I knew. There was no reason a woman of my age should be so hung up on their parents doing what they thought was best to keep me safe. But I missed them terribly, and had more questions for them than I knew what to do with. Having gotten just a taste of life outside the church, meeting Tap's family and friends, seeing Ramsey again after so long ... it all reminded me just how little I'd actually lived for the last decade.

It was difficult not to compare my new life to how I'd lived at the church, especially now. I'd shrunk myself further and further under the guise of safety, not realizing that the bits of me getting chipped away shouldn't have been a required sacrifice.

Perhaps it had been true, that distancing myself from others was necessary, but it had not all been in my best interest. Even with my parents, there had been some of that, especially during my visits to Heaven. I was less, simply by virtue of the fact that my mother was not also an angel. I was not allowed to study the same things, go into all the buildings.

More than anything, it was shocking and a little disappointing to discover that the first people to truly accept me exactly as I was and to care about my wants, needs, and safety were demons.

Tears slipped down my cheeks, the mess of emotions swirling around inside my body getting the better of me. I realized then that I hadn't yet taken my tincture. Carefully, I moved the tray to the floor and got up to get it. Ramsey followed me, her ears perked and twisting as though she could hear several other conversations happening where I only found the gentle hum of the crossroads.

I'm afraid it's time for me to leave, mistress.

Already upset, I started sobbing in earnest. "Sorry," I apologized, knowing that the only thing crying was going to get me was another headache. "I don't know what's the matter with me lately."

You've been through much, even if it doesn't seem that way. Do as your demon says and rest today. Perhaps tomorrow as well.

"He's not *my demon*," I insisted weakly. "And I have far too much to do to just lay around. Though perhaps I'll go get a book or a quill."

That's the spirit.

I sat on the floor and threw my arms around the hound, her head heavy on my shoulder. "I'll miss you. Be careful."

Always, mistress. When she looked at me from near the door, her eyes glowed red instead of the amber they usually were. *Be well and stay safe.*

"I will do my best."

Do not be afraid of what you feel. You are not broken, Phin. And the Fates are never wrong.

"I ..." I stared at Ramsey, thoughts muddled. "I don't understand."

You will. Her eyes flashed ruby, and a faint puff of black smoke trailed her as she went out my bedroom door.

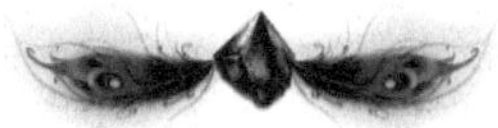

I EMERGED FROM my room after waking from a nap I hadn't intended to take.

After Ramsey left, I'd indulged in a long hot soak and then finished up all the leftovers on the tray of food. I'd lay back on the pillows to test how bad my headache might be, and the next thing I knew, I was groggily blinking back awake. The window was bright, so I hadn't slept the day away, but it still felt like I was forgetting something because of how off my routine I was.

Carrying the tray and all my dirty dishes to the kitchen was my first task, washing up was the second. Once that was finished, I decided to put together something for dinner, since Tap usually cooked and I had what seemed like unlimited time.

Just as I was putting the dish into the oven, Tap came through the doorway.

"You're up. Did you get some rest?"

"Yes, I fell back asleep."

"Good." He nodded enthusiastically, peeking around me at the mess I was cleaning up from my dinner preparations. "You didn't have to do that. I was just coming in to start."

"That's okay, I can take a turn now and then."

"How long have we got?"

"Perhaps an hour?"

"We should be quick then."

"Quick?"

Tap gestured for me to follow him, leading me down the hall to the workshops. He pressed the engraving for the library, and when he opened the door I gasped.

"When did you have time to do this?" I asked, rushing over to the beautiful new second writing desk and chair.

"Seir and I can get many things accomplished when we have a limited timeline, apparently. He responds very positively to being challenged. If it's not to your liking—"

"It's perfect," I gushed, running my finger over some of the intricately carved details in the edging. The wood was a wine color, and the grain pattern in the top had been set to resemble a starburst with alternating light and dark pieces.

Pleased, Tap gathered inkpots, quills, and sheets of parchment. "I rarely use my desk anymore. If there's something you need more of, please take it from there or the shelves. Nothing is off-limits."

"This is beyond generous, thank you."

He dipped his head at the praise. "Well, I'll leave you to it." He turned to leave.

"Wait. Could you please stay? You don't have to join me, but I'd like your company."

He turned back, movements hesitant. "Of course."

I settled into the plush chair, wiggling around and rearranging things until I had everything I needed just within reach. I dipped my quill and realized I had no idea what to put on the blank page under my hands.

"What's the matter?"

"I always copied words down. Now that I have blank pages and endless ink, I'm not sure what to write."

"It doesn't have to be words," Tap suggested as he pushed his glasses up. "Perhaps you could start with some pretty flourishes on the edges of the page?"

I experimented with the quills, going through three before I found one that was the right weight in my hand and left the best line. He pulled a sheet of the heavy paper toward himself and dipped a quill, grinning softly as he drew the same symbol over and over until the ink was faded and broken. It was an interesting blend of symmetrical crosses and loops, but it wasn't centered and had some other details that I couldn't quite figure out. Tap set the quill down and smeared the final one, which was mostly just ink splotches, with his finger.

"What's that?"

"My sigil."

"Oh." A demon's sigil was in a way their signature, their true name. If one had a sigil, they could in most cases, use it to summon that demon, or in some cases do them harm. And he'd just drawn it for me, several times, as though it were of no significance. "It's lovely."

His cheeks pinked and he moved to pick up the page. I simply held the corner down with one finger, indicating I wanted him to leave it. His silver eyes widened, but he ducked his head and let go.

After a long moment of intense eye contact, Tap wandered over to the bookshelves. He ran his finger over spines and ducked down to see what the bottom shelves held. Eventually he chose a few tomes and set them all on the low table between the sofas. I did my level best not to stare, but there was something incredibly attractive about his wide-shouldered stance as he evaluated the shelves and the way his jaw clenched as he adjusted his spectacles.

"Hailon will be going into the city tomorrow," he said. "Would you like to join her? Visit d'Arcan? Or would you like to wait a bit longer?"

I glanced up from studying the sigil he'd drawn. There were perhaps ten drops, which was only ten short days' worth left in my vial of tincture. As much as I wouldn't mind putting off another new experience for a bit, I needed to speak with the woman who might be able to help me very, very soon.

"Yes, I'd like to go."

"We'll plan for it then." Tap sank into the sofa cushion and began to flip through one of the books. He set it down and repeated the process with the others he'd selected. I smiled, watching as he returned to the shelves, gathered several more and began flipping.

"Are you actually reading those?"

"No, I'm ..." He paused, silver eyes meeting mine. A flare burst behind my ribs, a hot awareness that took me off guard and made me gasp. "Are you alright?"

I rubbed at the skin over where the ache was, perplexed at what might have caused it. "Fine. But I should probably avoid drinking for a while."

He chuckled. "That's probably not a bad idea. When was the last time you had something that strong?"

"Never." I sifted through my memories for an answer. "I only ever drank ale, rarely even a little bit of wine." I smiled, one memory rising to the surface. "My father had snuck a bottle of sparkling mead back with us from Heaven to serve with my cake my last birthday with them. I drank one glass and had a floaty head all night."

"Perhaps a glass of wine now and then, so you better understand how it affects you." He pointed at the books. "And I'm not reading, I'm trying to find a particular lettering style. It's one of my favorites, quite beautiful. I think you'll appreciate it. I just can't seem to recall where I last saw it."

The ache flared again, over and over as I drew curves and lines, swoops that led nowhere and angles that aligned with the page edge while Tap looked through books in search of that specific lettering. We simply existed together until the smell of our dinner floated in through the half-open door and he insisted we go eat before it burned.

I felt better afterward than I had all day, Ramsey's words echoing in my head.

CHAPTER 18
PHIN

"I**T'S ALRIGHT IF** you don't want to go with me today." I'd practiced those words at least a dozen times since getting dressed. I had summoned up all my courage to finally voice them as I scooped several halved starberries onto my spoon.

Merry not only had sent another basket of the little golden fruits with Seir but had also promised them weekly as long as they kept producing. I was enjoying every single one while they lasted.

Tap froze, his eyes wide as he looked up from his plate of eggs and toast. "Do ... do you not want me to accompany you?"

"No, no, that's not it at all. It's more that I worry I'm taking you away from something more important. I just need a tincture, and I'm not even sure they can help me."

In truth, I absolutely did want Tap with me to meet even more members of his family, but Hailon would be there too, so it wasn't like I was going into a room full of only strangers. Unless she didn't come, of course. Anxiety crept over my skin like a hot, unwelcome blanket and I did my best to push it down.

Tap set his fork down and slid his plate forward, lacing his long, graceful fingers together as he stared right through me. "You trust us all that well?"

My breakfast sat mostly uneaten thanks to the massive storm of butterflies swirling around in my stomach. "I suppose I do. Should I not?"

"We're plenty trustworthy, in my estimation. Naturally, I have a bit of a bias about it, though."

"Jacks told me I could trust you, so did Ramsey. And once I got past the first couple of weeks and you continued to behave the same way you had at the start, I couldn't help but believe you were as kind as you seemed."

Tap's face brightened. "I'm flattered, and very pleasantly surprised that you feel confident enough to go alone. It hasn't been that long since you came to stay here, after all. And you were right to have hesitations then." He shrugged and pulled his plate back in front of him, finishing off the last of his meal quickly. "It will be a lot like our visit to the glade in many ways, but with more people. Are you prepared for that?"

I swallowed. "As much as I can be, yes."

He nodded, wiping his mouth on a napkin. "Can I be honest with you, Phin?"

"Of course."

"I feel a bit foolish."

I set my spoon down roughly at his admission. "Why?"

He sighed, and one corner of his mouth tilted up. His expression changes were often minute, but even a tiny bit of joy changed his normally serious demeanor. "When I was making the argument that you'd be safer here, it honestly didn't occur to me that there were places just as protected. Not at the time, anyway."

"Like where Seir lives?"

"Yes, and like d'Arcan. Venturing out into the city of Revalia proper will have its risks, but Rylan is a mage. Between the various talented members of my family and attendees at the school, surely there's a token or trinket or spell that could help to disguise you." My nose wrinkled. Tap chuckled, the sound low and raspy. "No hair colorant or oversize secondhand clothing required."

I brightened but was hesitant to get my hopes too far up. "What exactly did you have in mind?" Tap got to his feet. I waved him off as he reached for my dishes.

"Seems only logical you'd need to do some shopping. Surely the wardrobe you brought with you could be improved upon? More items would mean you didn't have to wash every few days."

I barely contained my excitement at his words. Nearly everything I owned was worn to bare threads and chosen specifically to conceal my shape. The thought of some new shirts, a coat that fit properly and even a dress or skirts was almost too much for me. It had been many years since clothing was something I could choose based on my own desires and taste.

"Yes. So much," I managed, breathless at the prospect.

Tap's smile widened. "Good. It's a large city, I'm sure you can find anything you need. Bathroom goods, foods you like. I'm guessing any number of my sisters-in-law would take great joy in showing you the best parts of the markets. Once we get a method of concealing you arranged, of course." He stepped toward the doorway. "I'm going to make sure Seir is settled in. Just let me know when you're ready and we can leave."

I picked up my bowl of fruit with renewed appetite, more excited than I'd been in a very long time.

It wasn't until I was putting on the terrible coat I couldn't wait to be rid of that I realized it wouldn't matter where we went, or what I wanted to buy. I didn't have anything to trade, nor any coin.

Tap picked up on my mood change as I approached the hall.

"Everything alright?" he asked.

"Fine."

His brow wrinkled, and I glanced up to find Seir watching me, his head tilted to the side.

"I heard you may venture into Revalia with the ladies today?"

"Perhaps." I forced a tight smile, but Seir was not buying it, and narrowed his eyes.

"Nervous?"

"A little."

He crossed his arms. "No need to be. Hailon knows all the best places, and if there's something she can't find for you, Grace or Calla will know exactly where to go."

I nodded again, tears prickling. "That's okay, I don't need to go shopping."

Tap frowned at me, confusion evident. "I thought—"

"It's not necessary to do all that today. I just want to see if someone can help make my tincture. That's the most important thing."

"I have confidence that Greta will have a solution for you, but what we discussed earlier—"

"It's fine, really. I don't need anything."

"Phin? I'm confused. Earlier you seemed so excited."

Before I could open my mouth again, Seir interrupted us both. "Tap?"

"Just a minute—"

"No, brother, this is important." He stood in front of Tap, making sure his full attention was on him before speaking. "When was the last time your librarian received her wages?" He raised his eyebrows in emphasis, hands lightly gripping along Tap's upper arms.

Tap froze and stared straight ahead, looking through Seir and into the vague dark shape of the wall far behind him. After a long moment he released a tight breath and strode off in the direction of the bedrooms.

"Wages?" I asked.

Seir clucked his tongue. "Saints. You'll have to excuse him, sometimes his brain is going too many directions at once. All these doors, all these jobs … important details get missed." He narrowed his eyes. "Have the groceries I've been bringing gotten used or are they being thrown out?"

"I beg your pardon?"

"Has he been remembering to eat? Every day, maybe even more than once?" Seir's eyes rounded, the concern for Tap in them on full display.

"Oh. Yes, he hasn't missed a meal since I got here. In fact, he insists on doing nearly all the cooking. I've managed to get him to allow me to make a meal or clean up sometimes, but it took some work."

"And linens and things, they're changed regularly?"

"Yes, as far as I know."

"He's dressed and bathed daily?"

I nodded, confused by his questions. "What do those things have to do with anything?"

"Just one more, if you'll humor me. Is he sleeping?"

"I … don't really know. I never hear him go in or out of the room he said was his, but that doesn't mean anything. Once I found him in the recliner when I got up in the middle of the night for a drink of water."

He tutted, nodding enthusiastically. "As I expected. His focus is just elsewhere. Sorry Phin, that's not your fault. I'll talk to him."

"About what?"

I never got an answer, because just then Tap came back, carrying something in his hand. His cheeks were pink. "Forgive me." He held an envelope out to me, one that was as thick as my thumb. "*Foolish* seems to be the word of the day. I thought for sure we'd already spoken about this. Unfortunately, I must have only practiced the conversation in my head. I apologize in advance for next time, should there be one." He blushed a slightly darker shade, and it made him seem very young. "Your wages, starting from the day you arrived. I calculated weekly, so you're due more very soon. Unless of course you need the funds advanced to purchase something in Revalia, in which case I'm happy to do that. Or I could buy it for you myself, I'm not averse to that either. If it's for your room, that should be my responsibility. In fact—"

"Tap," Seir said gently, and Tap paused, inhaling deeply. It was fascinating, the way they balanced one another. Just the other day it had been Tap telling Seir to slow down.

"Anyhow. I'm sorry. I won't be offended if you remind me should I forget something so important in the future."

"Please take him to task when he needs it," Seir added helpfully, earning a chagrined scowl from his brother.

"It's okay. I wasn't even aware I'd be getting wages. I thought the agreement was just that you allowed me to live here and kept me hidden in exchange for my work in the library." I glanced inside and sucked in a breath. "Oh. This is too much." I nearly choked as I counted the paper notes.

Seir chuckled. "Merry said that once too. But she was wrong then, and you're wrong now. Say thank you and enjoy your hard-earned coin."

Tap agreed as he anxiously turned his earrings. "Your time is valuable, no matter what circumstances brought you here. You've done a lot of work since you arrived. More than I managed in several decades, in fact."

The lump in my throat expanded and the tears became very difficult to hold back. "I've barely started. This seems unbalanced."

"You made her cry, brother. Well done," Seir teased.

Panic crossed the kind demon's face. "I'm so sorry, I didn't mean to—"

I waved my hand. "No, no, I'm okay. I promise. I just went from excited, to sad, to happy. I'm a mess lately, my emotions are all over the place." I blotted at my face with the tails of my shirt and tucked the envelope into one of the pockets over my chest on the inside of my coat. "But I'm okay. Thank you. Is it safe to walk around with such a large amount? I've never had money like this before."

"I'm sure someone will have a spare pouch or belt you can borrow until you can purchase the one you like. I'm happy to hold some if you like." Tap frowned. "You've never had pocket money?"

"Sure, but not like *this*. I was rarely allowed to go into town on my own on Earth, and there's a very different order to things in Heaven. Both places, my father usually took care of everything." They both bobbed their heads in understanding. "Then when I went to stay at the church, I relied on Father Morton. I wasn't allowed to hold a job outside the church, and he didn't have spare coin to give me."

"Well," Seir clapped his hands, something I noticed he did when he'd decided a topic was settled. "No time like the present for you to experience the Revalia markets! I look forward to seeing what you bring back with you. Have a wonderful time!" He gently pushed his brother and me toward a doorway. This one had a telescope symbol on it, whereas the one we'd taken to visit Seir's glade showed the outline of a tree.

"I promise to figure out a better way to remind myself of the important things, Phin. It seems as though ..." He scowled, staring off into the distance again.

I understood him fine. "Right as you get a handle on one thing another slips away?"

His lips parted and he blinked at me. "Yes. Quite." The soft lift of his lips made my chest ache. "May I?" he asked, arm lifted so I could tuck mine underneath.

The corner of his mouth twitched up as we stepped forward together, his silver eyes locked to mine as the portal swallowed us up.

CHAPTER 19
TAP

"O H," PHIN GASPED, looking up at the massive stone building in front of us. Her breath made a plume of steam, her lips rounded as her eyes traveled up to the observatory.

"Yes, it's quite something, isn't it?" I patted her arm and stepped forward, bringing her with me.

"Do you visit often?" She blushed. "Sorry. That's a silly question."

"That's alright. No, I don't. I was here just over a year ago for Rylan and Calla's wedding. I don't leave the crossroads much."

"You've been out several times recently." Her smile was arresting. She seemed proud. My heart thumped hot and heavy behind my ribs.

"I have. And if Seir asked me, I'd blame him, but realistically, I think I've got you to thank."

Her mouth dropped open and her cheeks turned the most delightful shade of pink. Suddenly shy, she stopped meeting my eye, though to my great pleasure, she didn't let go of my arm.

As we approached the double doors of the magical collegium's main building, my sister-in-law Calla opened them for us.

"Welcome! Come in, please, it's freezing out there. Hailon just arrived too."

Once we were all inside where it was warmer, I accepted her hug and kissed her on the cheek. "You look well."

"I have no complaints." Calla, my brother Rylan's mate, and a powerful earth witch in her own right, smiled at us. She was on the taller side for a woman and her stride was long as she stepped over to hug Phin. "So nice to meet you! Welcome to d'Arcan. I'm Calla. You're Phin?"

"Yes, hello."

"I've heard so many wonderful things." She paused, head tilted as she took Phin in. "Aren't you beautiful." Calla glanced between the two of us, her happy smile impossible not to reciprocate. "Come on through." She started down the wide stone hall at a brisk clip, taking us past several rooms. "Students are in, but we won't be bothered in Vassago's classroom."

"Is he not teaching then?" I asked, slightly disappointed I'd be missing seeing him do so.

"Not today." She caught my eye and got a devious look. "Specialty instructors are only twice a week." She held the last of her commentary until she'd opened the doors of said classroom wide and walked us inside. "So your brothers often have free time."

The brothers in question looked up from where they sat across from one another on plush furniture, one with a book in his hand and the other a ledger, an assortment of snacks and half-drunk teacups on the low table between them.

For such a large room, it felt cozy. The fire was lit and burning heartily, the furniture was soft and plush. Across the room, two columnar windows made from thick slabs of rainbow glass threw gentle colors over the floor. My brother's worktables were a system of organized chaos specific to him, and I was oddly cheered by the familiar items sitting upon them.

"She's being mean to me again," Vassago said with a grin as he closed his book and got to his feet. Rylan was only a step behind him. "Have a word with her, would you?"

"I will not. She's perfect as she is. And she's not wrong," Rylan replied, a cagey smirk on his mouth.

Calla crossed behind Vassago, giving him a swift thump on the back of the head with her hand as she passed.

He chuckled. "See? Mean." Despite his words, his light tone conveyed that this was normal teasing between them, as did the little squeeze he gave her hand when it came to rest on the back of the sofa near him.

"Get your hand *off* my wife," Rylan said. Vassago held his hands up as though surrendering, chuckling a hearty laugh.

"You wouldn't know *mean* if it bit you," Greta, his mate, laughed from across the room. She was busily pouring something into tiny vials on her worktop, a cauldron steaming next to her. "Nice to see you, Tap."

"And you, Greta."

Hailon stood near her workstation, putting the vials into a wooden device with many little slots so they could be carried all at once. "Nice to see you both again so soon," she gave a little wave.

"You know how I feel about you threatening me with a good time, Dragonfly." Vassago smirked, the sharp points of his fangs denting his bottom lip. He was as fair as Phin, blond hair so light it was nearly white. Dressed in cream and silver, he was in every way opposite to both myself and Rylan. "Good to see you, brother." He pulled me into an embrace, thumping me on the back. As he released me, he held out a hand. "Pleased to meet you, Phin."

"Yes, welcome. I'm Rylan. I'm the headmaster here." He, too, shook her hand.

"Hello." Her eyes were wide as she looked from one of us to the next.

Calla was quick to reassure her. "Harmless, the lot of us, I promise. Well, mostly." She winked at Phin, and I could see Phin's shoulders relax just a little. "Please, make yourself at home."

"Magnus will be here shortly. He's speaking with the council," Rylan said. "He mentioned you've been working on a project for him?"

"Yes, I've got several things to discuss with him, actually, so that's good timing." I was growing more certain that the disturbances in the long dormant doors were related to the disappearances Magnus had asked me to look into, and what Ramsey had told me corroborated that. Unfortunately, my daily responsibilities hadn't allowed time for me to fully look into each one personally yet. I was hoping that the stone kin would be able to send some of their people through to assist with that part.

Calla had intercepted Phin and was plying her with tea and honey cakes on the sofa. Greta and Hailon both hustled over, and between them they were doing their best to make her comfortable. An odd flash of thought had my heart stalling in my chest. It was natural, the way they looked talking with one another. Like she fit right into this odd little family of mine.

"Tap? Alright?"

"Mm? Yes, fine." I snapped back to the current moment and found both of my brothers staring at me, identical smug grins on their faces.

"Ah. Well. I should have thought to ask you to bring your mirror. I've got a new enchantment that may allow it to work better," Vassago said, walking toward one of the tables.

The women were all well into their own conversation, Phin giving me a slight nod of reassurance that she was fine as I followed my brothers.

"I'm not sure a scrying mirror will ever work reliably from the crossroads. Most methods of communication like that have a difficult time getting through the energy fields between the planes."

"Only one way to find out," he said as he sorted out some supplies. "I'll make you another with the new method, and if it works, we can update your old one as well."

He had me pick from several different sizes and shapes and began the task of enchanting it.

I looked at Rylan. "Could I impose upon you for a favor?"

"Of course."

"I'd like for Phin to be able to go into the city. But she needs to be disguised somehow, if she's going to be anywhere that's unwarded or unprotected." Despite my quiet request, I'd gotten the attention of the women and the room went quiet.

"I'm sure we can manage something." Rylan rubbed his chin. "Were you thinking a trinket? I could also perhaps use a misdirection cantrip like I often do for myself when I go into the city."

I shook my head. "I don't think a cantrip will work." I didn't elaborate, but he must have seen enough explanation in my eyes. "I didn't have anything specific in mind, it just needs to keep her hidden."

"What about the invisibility thing you can do?" Vassago asked.

I shook my head. "Not only am I horribly out of practice, I have to be touching someone for it to work. That'll be fine for other situations once I revive my skill with it, but not for enabling her to go without me. She should also have some freedom to move from place to place if she likes."

"Hmm. Something spelled and worn would likely do the trick. Are we obscuring or disappearing altogether? How potent does it need to be and how soon were you thinking?" He moved toward one of the cabinets near the back of the room.

"Today if possible, so she can visit the glade and go shopping in the city, whenever she likes."

Rylan nodded thoughtfully. "What are we avoiding?"

"Angels." Phin's voice was quiet but clear. Her cheeks pinked as silence swallowed the room.

My brothers both blinked a few times as they looked between us. Relief washed over me when they finally reacted.

"Well, of course." Vassago nodded, hands still moving over the mirror.

"Naturally. We can't have a Nephilim just running around unprotected in Revalia. That's an invitation for Heaven to pick a fight, and the humans here don't need to be stuck in the middle of any of their frivolous battles." Rylan pulled several things out of the cabinet and brought them over to the table next to where Vassago was working. "It was bad enough when we had lower level demon hordes popping up." He sighed. "I'm so glad that's done with. Phin, would you mind coming over here for a moment? I need to know which object you prefer I use."

She did as he requested, selecting a delicate bracelet with a small amethyst stone. It matched the necklace she wore. I had some suspicions about her necklace, and Rylan got a decent look while she was at the table. She'd mentioned before in passing that it was her mother's, but it looked far too similar to the ones the other women in our family had come to be in possession of one way or another not to be intrigued. His eyebrow was raised as he stole a look my direction while fastening the bespelled item around her wrist.

Then everything stopped again as Phin burst into tears while laughing at the same time. Just as she did, Magnus came striding through the open classroom doors, Grace at his side. They stopped, seeing that they'd walked into a tense moment.

"I'm so sorry," Phin apologized through tears and laughter together, wiping at her face as she returned to the sofa. "I'm *such* a mess lately. I'm just ... confused. Overwhelmed, maybe. Everything I thought I knew about demons is wrong. And I thought I had already come to terms with that, but I guess I haven't, actually, because sometimes it feels like I've gone completely mad. You're all so sincere!"

"Should we not be?" Vassago asked, head tilted to the side as he handed me the completed mirror. "Though we are an interesting group, I'll give you that."

"No, no, I just ..." Phin threw her hands up and wiped at her face again. "You knew what I was when I came in?"

"Yes," Rylan said. "I'm afraid it's not common for any other kind of being to have your particular features, Phin."

"Not to mention Seir has a big mouth," I muttered. "And there are two nosy birds living here who happened to be visiting the glade the same time we were."

"Yes, there's that." Vassago smirked. "But you are rather obviously angelic. Violet eyes and silver hair are a dead giveaway."

"But you have—"

"My eyes are *gold*." Vassago's smile was gentle, but his tone was insistent. "Occasionally red. Not violet. At least, not anymore. Though that color did suit me very well." The cad actually batted his eyelashes at her.

"Fine, but what about my mother?"

"What about her?" he countered.

"According to Ramsey, my *hellhound*, she was mostly demon. Whatever that means. Doesn't that, I don't know, cancel out the angel in some way?"

His eyebrows raised. "It's been an age since I've seen a hellhound, how wonderful. I hope we'll get to meet her soon. But to answer your question, no, not at all. Your father was a full-blooded angel?"

"Yes."

"You simply take after him."

Phin blinked, disarmed by his exaggerated gestures and charm. She looked around again, some of her energy clearly flagging.

"And you're all fine with me being here? You just gave me jewelry that will keep me safe. Jewelry that's probably worth more than everything I own at the moment, except maybe my mother's necklace. And you even made it match?" She frowned, gripping the pendant in her fist. She cleared her throat several times before continuing, the rasp fairly severe because of how much she was speaking. "Simply because angels are dangerous, and I'm hiding from them, even though I also am one."

"Correct," Rylan said. "That's a very succinct explanation, well done. And I wouldn't mind getting a closer look at that necklace sometime. If you don't mind."

She frowned, eyebrows pinched together. "Are you not at all suspicious? Do you not see me as the enemy at all? I'm one of *them*. At least, enough of one they're hunting me."

"Perhaps you are, but you came here with him." Rylan gestured at me. "You've made no threats, nor have you asked us for anything at all. To be clear, we all know very well the danger involved with being the focus of an angel's attention. Doesn't even matter why. We know how eager they are to jump to violence. If we can prevent that from happening or protect you from ending up in their sights at all, we will."

"That's it? You just ... believe that I'm not like the rest of them?" Her volume had risen, louder than I'd ever heard her speak, her throat clearly irritated. I began to spin my ring, nervousness over her agitation overriding my calm.

I stepped toward her, bond raging in my chest. "Phin, we can—"

"Yes." The answer came from everyone in the room at the same time, silencing us both.

"Should we not?" Vassago asked, tilting his head to the side and watching her in a way that was almost certainly how he stared at students when he felt they were close to coming to the correct conclusion and he wanted to encourage them along. "You did just argue that you're part demon. Would you accept that as a reason?"

Phin stopped to process that for a moment. My heart swelled. This was the embodiment of everything I adored about my family. I was firmly reminded that I needed to spend more time with them, that I had likely missed quite a lot while cloistered away at the crossroads, buried under my responsibilities. That I'd pushed them away for the same, erroneous rationale—that I didn't have time, when really, that time would have mattered more had I spent it differently. But it was not the moment to catalog my regrets.

"I ... yes?" Phin finally answered.

Vassago looked pleased. He spread his hands in front of him, palm up. "Then that's the reason, if it must be."

She was silent for several beats as she considered this. "Please don't misunderstand, I am grateful." Phin took a deep breath and rolled the new bracelet around her wrist. "But I'm also struggling to understand. Things would absolutely *not* be the same the other way around."

"We know," Vassago chuckled.

"Oh, how we know." This from Magnus, who stepped forward with a gentle smile on his mouth. "Hello to you, little Nephilim. My name is Magnus. I believe you met Coltor not long ago? He is my son." His gaze drifted to me, and he inclined his head a bit in acknowledgment.

"Yes, I did. Pleased to meet you." She stared up at the man who was mountainous even in his human form, her hand invisible as he shook it within his larger one.

Grace stepped up next to him. "I'm Grace. I do my best to keep this whole lot in order, school included. If you need anything while you're here, you let me know."

"Okay." Her lips parted again as though she was going to ask something further but she abandoned the thought, instead reaching out for her cup of tea and scowling into it as she sipped. Her body relaxed, the act of greeting the pair of them a necessary and welcome distraction.

"Shall we adjourn to the observatory to talk?" Rylan asked. "I have some charts I need to show you, Tap."

"And I have news from the council," Magnus added. "No need to bore everyone else with the details."

"Good idea," Calla confirmed. "That way we can chat and get to know one another a little better before we head into the city. If you're comfortable with that, Phin?"

A bit dazed but with confidence, Phin nodded.

Rylan turned back to his wife. "Be safe."

"Always."

Rylan and Vassago kissed their wives on the way out, and I met Phin's eye again to be sure she was okay with me leaving her alone with my sisters-in-law. She nodded again, still looking as though she had a million thoughts happening at once.

"We'll take good care of her," Grace assured me, patting my shoulder.

Once we were out of the room and headed up the stairway to the observatory, Vassago clapped me on the shoulder and flicked the feather in my pocket, a devilish grin on his mouth.

"So, brother, how is it that you never leave the crossroads, but you've somehow ended up finding your mate?"

CHAPTER 20

PHIN

"THERE, MAYBE NOW you can take it all in. Breathe a bit." Grace scuttled around the table, organizing and cleaning the mess and somehow rearranging things so that it looked like a whole new plate of snacks had appeared. "If it's still too much, just say so, we can give you some space to yourself."

"We're a lot." Greta nodded.

"You're all so kind." My throat was very sore from my outburst, and I sagged back against the cushions. So much for a good first impression.

"All the good intentions in the world don't always negate the fact that there are quite a few of us—and most big personalities as well. I'm sorry if we've overwhelmed you," Calla said.

"I'm fine, really. Tap told me I'd get used to Seir, and I have. I suppose that's true for more than just him. Seems I'm included in that, actually." I put my face in my hands. "I can't believe I spoke to you all like that. I haven't been myself at *all* lately. First I drank too much when we visited the glade, and now this. I'm so sorry."

"Don't worry yourself one little bit. We can all take a bit of warming up to. Frankly, you seem a delight. I love a woman who isn't afraid to ask questions straight out like you did." Grace laughed and took a seat in the chair next to Calla. Greta was on the sofa next to me, though she'd left a generous distance between us on the cushions.

Hailon came over and pulled me into a brief hug, my body lighting up everywhere she touched me. "Please don't think twice about your visit the other day. You didn't do anything the rest of us haven't and you deserved a stiff drink. Besides, I had a similar outburst in this very room not all that long ago. It's hard to understand why they are the way they are and do the things they do. But trust me, this is all real. Your problems are now their problems. It's just who they are. And being upset or noisy or even a little combative won't put them off. Promise. Some of them thrive on it." One more quick squeeze and she released me, moving off to pour herself a tea.

"Hailon mentioned you needed a tincture?" Greta asked, her eyes flashing with excitement. "She gave me some notes about the other thing, but let's start with that." She gestured vaguely to her worktable.

"Yes. Are you the ... apothecary?" The word felt wrong, but my thoughts were too heavy to sift through efficiently for the right one.

"Alchemist," she replied proudly. "What kind of tincture did you need?"

I glanced between the women, realizing that I did honestly feel quite safe with them, newly met or not. I wasn't sure what to think about that, having been suspicious of just about everyone the majority of my life. I was sure that's what had pushed me to the outburst, I simply didn't know what to do with the dissonance I was experiencing. "A suppressant."

"Okay." Greta got up and crossed the room, pulling down a couple of oversize books from the shelf behind her workstation.

"What are we hoping to keep away? Some kind of rogue power? Magic?"

My ears got hot. "My cycle."

"Oh," she said thoughtfully. To my surprise, there was absolutely no judgment in her tone. "Probably this one instead then." She pulled down a different book and replaced the ones she'd taken before.

"Are you looking to stall fertility?"

"Yes, but it's more complicated than that," I said, voice cracking.

Calla rose and took Greta's place on the sofa, her hand over mine. "You can trust us. I swear it. If you'd like to be alone with Greta, or have us recommend an apothecary in the city instead, that's fine too."

"No, no. It's just ..." I swallowed, throat dry as I sorted my words carefully before explaining. "It's different." I blushed hot, shame over something that I had absolutely no control over coursing through me. "It's like ... going into heat."

"That's fascinating." Greta watched me with rapt attention, the books forgotten right in front of her. "Horrible, to be certain, but fascinating. Do all Nephilim go through this? I've never heard of that before."

"My mother said that my generation is the first to be this way, and not all of us are. There's a sickness of some kind, and the population of Heaven is shrinking. She thinks this change is to encourage more angelic pairings. More babies. For some it's monthly, for others only once a season, but it's incapacitating."

"How long does that last?" Calla inquired. "It's a rather precarious place to be, sounds like. I'm assuming that's the ovulation period?"

"Yes, the height of fertility. Three days, sometimes four or five." I could feel the tension and frustration in them on my behalf and needed some space from it. I stood and crossed to where Greta was waiting patiently behind her table and took out the precious little vial. She accepted it with great care, examining the contents with her eyes before sniffing at it.

"Who made this for you last?"

"The apothecary in Aymonroux. They said they couldn't make it anymore."

She nodded. "Okay. Do you know the recipe? Or even parts of it?"

I shook my head. "No, we never made it ourselves."

"I see. Does it do anything else for you? Are there side effects?"

"Nothing terrible, but when I take it, I can't use my wings. I've been getting some breakthrough feathers, but that's all."

Her eyes snapped to mine. "I'll definitely find a way to change the formula so you can access them if I can." Her head bobbed as she flipped pages. "And your voice? Is that related?"

The question threw me off. I'd been raspy for a very long time but wasn't sure how it was connected, and said so.

"No worries. Can you tell me about the other thing? I know Hailon offered to help already, but perhaps I can too. It might be related even."

I turned and looked behind me, finding Calla and Grace respectfully listening, concern etched into their faces. "I have episodes. My heart races, I go numb. I can hear and see what's going on around me, but I can't react. They never last very long."

"We have experience with that too." Grace gave an encouraging smile.

"The tincture I have used to help with the episodes a little more than it does now. I don't have nearly as many since I moved to the crossroads though. The church bells used to set them off."

"Church bells?" Calla frowned.

"Father said something about the metal being forged with blood." There was a general grumble over that fact.

"You were having one every hour?" Hailon asked, horrified.

"Never that frequent, no. Getting caught outside was the worst. If I was inside, it was better, and if I was downstairs even more so." I left out the part about the vault doors, realizing now how not normal that was, no matter if it helped.

"How long will this last you?" Greta asked, holding the bottle to the light. There was a terrifyingly small amount left again.

"Eight or nine days. I take a drop every day."

"I hate to ask, but may I take a sample?" She must have seen the panic on my face because she insisted, "I only need a single drop. With that, I can hopefully work out what's in it, and what all it's meant to do." My fear screamed at me to tell her no, that even one drop was a whole day's worth of treatment I was risking, but I agreed. "Well," Greta said, a glint in her eye. "Seems I've got a new, urgent project!" She handed the vial back to me after carefully measuring her one requested drop into an empty dish.

"Thank you."

"My pleasure. Do you happen to know why they couldn't make it anymore?"

"No, sorry."

"That's okay! I can make a good start I think. And I can visit the apothecary, get the recipe maybe." She came back around the table and we rejoined the other ladies in the sitting area. "Vassago would probably love an excuse to visit Vincara again, he spent an age at the monastery once upon a time." Her head tilted to the side. "Actually, I should try to get out to speak with Ophelia." Everyone seemed to agree that was a good idea.

"Sorry, who's that?"

"Oh! She's also family, easiest to say she's a many times great-aunt of mine. Or something like that. She's a stone kin sorceress and has a wonderful library and an incredible amount of knowledge." Greta patted my knee. "In any case, we'll find out for you, one way or another."

I nodded, in shock at how easily I'd just been welcomed into their group.

"I can pay—"

"Family doesn't pay." Greta waved her hand, laughing.

"I'm not—"

"Oh, no mistake. You are." Grace nodded, smiling widely.

"It's true," Calla confirmed. "I'm afraid once you've been invited here, there's no going back." She laughed. "That sounds ominous, doesn't it? I promise I don't mean it that way."

Hailon laughed. "I apologize for repeating this, but you get used to it."

My heart thudded behind my ribs, joy flooding in where there should have been hesitation. There were demons and witches and stone kin welcoming me like I was one of them, no questions, no qualifiers. I trusted it because I trusted Tap and Ramsey and Jacks.

I trusted it because I *wanted* it.

I craved what they were offering me as an only child who had never been angel enough for schooling beyond the basics, nor for the elders or the council to recognize my talents or interests. The same elders who only wanted me now for my functioning anatomy.

But these people? They had shown no ulterior motives or disingenuousness. I couldn't help but desperately want to be a part of something like it seemed they had. To be like they were.

As I mused over how changed my life had become in the last few short weeks, the conversation moved smoothly to what Grace was preparing for dinner.

"You really must stay," Calla insisted. "There's nothing like Grace's shepherd's pie."

"They say that about everything," Grace said humbly, waving a hand.

"Because it's true. We're going to have to build even more apartments and get you a larger kitchen if people keep moving in because of your meals," Greta laughed. "We already had to get a bigger family table." Grace waved her hand, but I could see the affection in the teasing. These women adored one another. There was no fakery or cattiness. This was love. Family.

My heart throbbed with a desire to have that.

Calla persisted, "It will give us more time to get to know you. Besides, we never see Tap. I really would love to have everyone here for a big family dinner. Wouldn't that be so lovely?"

Grace nodded. "I'd hoped for something over Yule, but we had too many other exciting things going on. At least we were all together. Mostly." She frowned for a brief moment but caught me looking at her and turned it into a smile instead.

"I wish it were warmer, I'd walk you around the grounds," Calla lamented. "Maybe next time."

"Yes, next time," I promised, and the smiles I got in return made my heart do a funny flip behind my ribs. They carried the conversation on, making sure to include me as we prepared to go as a group into the city to shop.

Tears prickled again, unexpected and from a mix of happy emotions I was unused to feeling.

THE CARRIAGE RIDE into Revalia proper was fairly short, but between the women I was with, I got a full education on everything I could see out the little windows as we passed. The library and cathedral were hard to miss, even from a distance, and there were people moving about in droves as though the cold was no bother at all. I'd never seen so much life in such a compact space.

The city was impressive as well.

"What are you looking for?" Grace asked, enthusiastic at the prospect of showing someone new around the markets.

"Clothing, I guess?"

"What kind?"

The words were out of my mouth before I even processed having made a decision. "A dress, maybe two. Warm leggings. A coat that fits me, maybe some new tunics?"

Grace beamed. "Cloak and Dagger to start then, perhaps the tailor by the bridge. We'll get you squared away in no time."

I pulled out my envelope of money. The currency in Vincara was different, and it wasn't like I was able to shop regularly there. I had no understanding of what things cost here, only that the envelope seemed to contain quite a lot of paper money. "Will this be enough?"

Calla gently took it, and her eyes widened as she flipped through. "Oh, yes. More than. But even if it weren't, we'd make it work. There's no shortage of coin between us."

Satisfied, I stowed it away in the inside pocket over my chest and tried to keep track of where we were in relation to the collegium.

The carriage slowed as foot traffic grew heavy, then pulled to the side and stopped altogether.

"Come on. We'll go on foot from here." Grace led the way, Calla and Greta both giving me reassuring smiles as I climbed out after her. With the sun at its peak and the buildings blocking most of the wind, the temperature seemed to have warmed quite a bit.

"Thank you, Clem. Do you mind waiting a while?" Calla asked.

"Not at all, ma'am. You ladies take your time. I'll be right here. Send for me if you need something carried." He sagged in the seat, tipping his hat over his eyes. How he was going to sleep out in the cold was a mystery to me.

Calla stopped to rub the horses' noses, and then I was tucked between them all and swept toward a shop. I'd never been shopping with anyone besides my mother, and having four other women there to advise on how something fit or how a color suited me was a novel and thrilling experience. Once the ladies working the shop found out what I was looking for, I was sent to a little room with a curtain for a door and brought an assortment of things to try on. Every time I was in something new, I had to walk out to see how it looked in their incredible person-sized mirror, as well as get approval from the council of women accompanying me.

"Definitely the lavender, though the pale green suits as well," Calla said with finality as she stacked two new tunics onto the counter. She'd confiscated my envelope for safekeeping, tucking it into her little bag once I'd taken my coat off.

"Merry will be sad to have missed this," Hailon lamented, holding two equally beautiful hooded cloaks against me, gauging fit. "She loves to shop." Her head tilted to the side. "Well, she's getting used to it, is probably more accurate. She likes to browse, and will help me choose things, but I still have to convince her to spend on anything for herself most of the time." She pursed her lips and consulted the others. "The gray? Or the brown?"

"Gray," Calla and Greta said in unison.

Grace smiled, taking it from Hailon and adding it to the stack on the counter.

The cloak, several tunics, three dresses, a weeks' worth of undergarments, and four pairs of leggings later, the shopkeeper was only too happy to wrap up my parcels and deliver them to the carriage for us as we continued on to the area of the markets with home wares.

"Do you all live in the city?" I asked as they led me down a street lined with tents and tables, each one a separate vendor.

"At d'Arcan itself, actually," Calla said, stopping to buy some delicate-looking candies from a man who clearly knew her well.

"Vassago and I keep one of the staff apartments upstairs too," Greta agreed, waving at a woman selling scarves.

"There's still one available for you and Seir, should you need it," Calla teased, winking at Hailon. "You too, Phin. We have a couple that are freed up at the moment. You and Tap are always welcome to stay if you like."

"Thank you."

"I have a small suite at d'Arcan, and Magnus technically lives at the stone kin conclave, though he mostly stays with me or at a way house close by. We'll be moving into a house soon," Grace said. "Still on the grounds at d'Arcan, though."

"Do you all teach?"

"Greta and I do, but only every great now and then." Calla shifted her parcels around. "Rylan and Vassago have regular classes, and Grace manages all the inner workings of the school."

"I have help! Thank goodness." Grace chuckled, pride making her cheeks glow. "My girls came to us shortly after Calla did. They get their education and help me with the chores." Grace chuckled. "Though Stella will likely be off soon, seeking her own way." Her smile faded a bit at the edges.

Hailon smiled at me, seeing that I was hesitating over asking another question. "Ask whatever you like, Phin. We're mostly open books." Greta nodded enthusiastically in agreement.

"How did you all end up there?"

Calla smiled. "That's several lengthy stories, actually. The short version is that the Fates put us there."

"The Fates?"

"Indeed." Grace's smile was slow, her response interrupted as she stopped to haggle over a basket of assorted cheese. "Come on. Let's get warm, shall we? The shop with hot chocolate is just over there." She swept us into a café, and we all settled into a table at the back once we'd gotten a steamy cup of chocolate and a pastry.

"How are you doing?" Hailon asked, leaning close.

"I'm okay."

She squeezed my shoulder. "This hot chocolate is to die for. Might put you off sweets for a week, but it's worth it."

I took a tentative sip and agreed. It was like someone had just melted down several bricks of chocolate and poured them into a cup. Just a few sips in, I was warm enough I took off my coat.

"What do you know about fated mate bonds, Phin?" Calla asked, her cheek resting on her fist.

"Not a lot," I admitted. "I suspect my parents were fated, but they didn't really talk about it. It's supposed to be pretty rare." They all wore a similar lopsided grin as they stared at me. Realization dawned, and I sat forward in my seat. "Oh. *All* of you?"

"And Merry, with Coltor," Hailon added.

"And Lovette." Grace omitted the mate's name, but I recognized Lovette as one I'd heard while speaking with Merry and Hailon in the glade.

"But how?"

Calla sipped from her cup of rich chocolate before speaking. "Multiple complicated stories, as I said. But that's what I meant by the Fates bringing us together. They had a significant hand in assembling this family." She reached into the collar of her shirt and pulled out a necklace. Greta did the same, and Hailon. Their necklaces all looked exactly like mine, just with different stones.

I floundered, opening and closing my mouth several times but never finding the words I needed to express my questions.

"Family heirlooms," Hailon said, "from our mothers."

I glanced down at the bracelet Rylan had made me, remembering his interest in my own necklace, and my thoughts spun, pondering what all of it meant.

"We're all here, Phin. For whatever you need. Just ask." There was nothing but sincerity in Calla's tone, and everyone at the table agreed with her.

My heart swelled. I believed them.

Seeing I was a bit flustered, nobody pushed. They simply left me to parse out what I needed from what they'd shared.

We finished our chocolate and continued to loop around the market streets, and I was encouraged to choose things that brought me joy. None of them were shy about picking items up either, and before long, we were headed back to the carriage with full arms and lightened purses. Not one of them had minded when I went quiet, all of them somehow able to keep me in the conversation even when I couldn't participate.

It was as perfect a day as I could have dreamed up for myself.

At least until we were within sight of the carriage and my heart decided to start racing, my fingertips went numb, and they had to catch me before I sagged to the cobbled street.

CHAPTER 21
TAP

THE WALK UP the stairs to the observatory stretched out as I mentally prepared and then discarded several responses to my brother. I ended up giving the simplest one.

"I suppose it's Seir's fault. He's the one who dragged me to Vincara." I had meant it as a joke but saying it like that felt wrong. It was nobody's *fault* I'd met Phin. It was truly the happiest accident that could have ever occurred. "Just blind luck, honestly. I'd never have gone there if not for him hunting down some seeds and things for Hailon."

"Tormund sent word after he first saw you there," Magnus chuckled. "He sends his thanks, actually. Now that she's no longer being cloistered in the church, he can be reassigned."

"He did tell me I could pass along a message. He said he'd see you soon." Magnus laughed. "How long was he there?"

"Twelve years."

"He's very good at his job, then. She only suspected a little bit." Magnus grinned proudly.

"It's a development none of us could have predicted," Rylan

added. "We only wanted to see you less overworked, perhaps to get out more. You finding your mate is well beyond anyone's imagining. She seems like a good match for you, though." He glanced over his shoulder at me as we continued to ascend, a smirk on his mouth. "The Fates sure are having a laugh on our account lately. Falling like stones, the lot of us."

I made a noncommittal noise in my throat.

"Are you not pleased by the development, brother?" Vassago queried.

"I am. But it is very complicated. Was it simple for either of you?"

They scoffed at the same time, and Magnus boomed with laughter, the sound of it echoing around them in the stairwell.

"That one"—he pointed to Rylan—"was in such self-loathing denial he had to do a spell before he believed it was real, and this one"—he shifted his finger Vassago's direction—"was convinced he'd accidentally do Greta harm. Terrified and foolish, the pair of them."

"Let us not forget how your face looked when Grace began aggressively returning your flirty advances, stone man," Vassago teased.

"Exactly. You nearly fainted right there on the dining room floor over a shirt color," Rylan chuckled.

"It was even odds she'd kill me for trying to woo her," Magnus insisted, but he didn't seem all that put off by the idea.

"Yes, one little human woman could definitely have taken you down," Vassago teased, eyebrow raised.

"I'd go happily," Magnus said. "Same as you."

"Fair enough."

"How does Phin feel about things?" Rylan asked.

"She ... doesn't."

Everyone came to an abrupt stop.

"Surely that's not right." Vassago pinned me with a look.

I shook my head. "She's not aware yet. At least not that I know of."

"And you?" Rylan asked.

"From first sight."

They muttered sympathetically, and we resumed the climb.

"Is the bond not agitated?" Vassago rubbed at his own chest with the question. "My ribs burned terribly."

"It's quite angry most of the time, but there's nothing to be done about that."

"I tried just about every remedy," Rylan commiserated. "Nothing worked. I'm afraid you're right."

"It's not that bad." The words even tasted like a lie, so I knew they didn't believe me, but they allowed me to pretend.

"Well, the best to the both of you. Hopefully things work out." Magnus clapped me on the shoulder.

"Thank you."

After what seemed like an endless number of stairs, we finally arrived at the observatory tower. The roof was closed due to the cold weather, but the round marble dome was still a wonder. A huge telescope was the focus of the room, but Rylan had added piles of cushions and several tables for keeping his massive star charts on. He walked straight to one as we followed.

"We're due an eclipse," he said without preamble, sorting through his stack and setting out several charts, one next to the other. "Just a few short weeks from now."

"Those happen rather frequently, do they not?" Magnus asked, poking at the massive charts.

"They do, but there's a pattern to this one."

"I'm not sure I understand." Magnus crossed his arms and scanned the charts, clearly confused as to why that might be significant.

"Celestial alignments can act as doorways," I supplied. "Or amplify existing ones."

"Yes," Rylan nodded, pointing to a section that matched up on every chart he'd set out. "There is an eclipse right around the birth of each of our mates. And"—he flipped pages, revealing another set of charts with the same eclipse denotation—"around the disappearance of every missing person we're searching for." He glanced at me. "Shall I assume Phin's parents should be included in this?"

I nodded. "Likely. They never returned after leaving her at the church in Vincara for her safety. I can ask Phin for specificity so it can be added to your charting. As well as for her birth." I touched the parchment, fascinated as always by my brother's talent. "But there are no portals linked specifically to eclipses," I said. "None that I know of would just spontaneously awaken because of an event like that. They'd likely have to be manually opened back up."

"But?" Vassago prompted as I looked closer at the charts, hearing the hesitation in my voice.

"But there've been some odd things happening lately that I need to investigate further. Decommissioned gates with activity. Coltor mentioned some odd surges in the ruins as well. We're monitoring as well as we can, but there's not much there to look into. Magnus, can you spare some soldiers? There are many to be evaluated, possibly watched from the other side for a while."

His brow furrowed. "I'll pull as many as I can. Might take a little time to organize, though."

I nodded. "They can go through Coltor, the doors in the glade. That may keep it a bit more covert if they're somehow watching the main gates specifically."

Magnus nodded. "I'll talk to him once I know how many and when." He scratched the stubble on his chin, the rasp loud in the highly acoustic space. "Brookes was the one responsible for arranging several of the disappearances, we know that for certain. He admitted as much. We suspect he had at least one unknown collaborator, someone who helped him to perform such an impossible task. Hugo and Auggie have already been dealt with.

We've interrogated and searched what we can, but he was clever and covered his tracks very well. They all created and exploited weaknesses within the council itself."

Magnus's sister Rowan, Greta's mother, was one of the missing. Calla's parents, who were a powerful witch and a stone kin, were counted among them. Hailon's too, a demoness and a warlock. Phin's likely as well. We knew for certain that Calla's parents had been strictly forbidden from marrying by the witch and stone kin councils. One could assume that Rowan had been similarly dissuaded from falling in love with Ris, who was now King of the Everwood in the fae realm. Hailon's parents had left her with her mother's best friend and gone on the run, much like Phin had been left at the church. A love affair between a high-ranking angel and an earth-bound demon seemed likely to have caused some trouble. The pattern was too strong to ignore.

"Ramsey has been following a trio of angels for years. They appeared in Vincara around when Seir and I visited, looking for Phin. She warned me that they are as skilled at using portals as hellhounds."

"If that's all true, we might be in for a bigger fight than we thought." Rylan sighed. "And here I was just going to ask if it would be possible to find a suitable place for a poison garden in one of your unused gates. I didn't think I'd have to be considering battle plans for angelic adversaries."

"We can do both," I suggested.

"Both it is." Rylan grinned, his dark hair swaying forward as he moved to restack his charts.

"I'll speak with Imogen," Magnus said. "She's been working on refining the Dark blades. If we're dealing with angels, we'll need more."

Vassago and Rylan nodded their agreement, and I knew if Seir were there with us, he'd be first in line to take up his blades. I inhaled, finding I was at ease, even with such a threat looming.

I was reminded again of the simple truth I had a tendency to forget once I returned to the busy isolation of the crossroads. There was magic in sharing a burden, and these men, my brothers, never made sharing worry or a duty one of us carried seem like a burden at all.

"—AT ALL. IN fact, I'm glad. Since we were able to examine you in the moment, I can adjust the formula to be tailored to your needs." Greta's voice echoed down the hall as we returned to the main level from the observatory.

"To the dining room, if you please," Grace said, catching us at the bottom of the stairs.

We'd had many things to discuss, and I was feeling slightly overwhelmed by all the new information dancing around in my head. My stomach, on the other hand, seemed to have been awakened by the very mention of the room where food was served.

D'Arcan's dining hall was one of my favorite places in the school. The woodwork was all very intentionally and beautifully done, from the broad rafters to the animals carved onto the pillars. I hadn't visited often, but this room had always felt like a place I wanted to be.

Phin seemed to think the same as she turned around, eyes wide as she took it all in. She moved from the pillar with an owl to the one with a bear and then to the wolf.

"Get everything you needed?" I asked softly.

She nodded. "So much. More than I intended." Her eyes widened as she breathed the words, but her smile remained.

"Wonderful."

The family table near the kitchen was much larger than I remembered it being. My brothers and their wives all settled into what seemed like their preferred seats. Magnus followed Grace to the kitchen, his hand resting on her back as she gestured enthusiastically, a smile on her face.

"Wherever you're comfortable," Calla encouraged Phin, and I waited for her to decide on a chair before taking the seat next to her.

"Anyway, Phin, as I was saying, just give me a few days. Hopefully I can come up with something." Greta nodded.

"I appreciate it."

Phin was clutching at her necklace as the other ladies discussed the trip into the city with my brothers. I reached over and squeezed her fingers. "Everything alright?"

"I froze. In town." My grip tightened, understanding what she was saying even with the brevity of her words. "I'm okay. It was short, and we were already on our way back to the carriage."

"The cathedral bells?"

She shook her head. "No. Just overwhelmed I think." At my expression, she added, "We drank hot chocolate." Her smile spread. "It was delicious, but it did make my heart beat faster."

"Ah. The sugar, perhaps."

Grace and Magnus returned, arms full of plates. They doled them out, then took their own seats. Glasses of water and cups of tea were poured, dinner a familiar organized chaos.

I took a tentative bite of the steaming hot food and found the flavor of the simple, comforting dish spectacular. And I wasn't the only one. Phin looked up at me as though she'd been shocked by what she'd tasted. I tried not to take any offense, as she'd never come close to that kind of expression with my food. But the indisputable truth was Grace was an incredibly talented cook.

"Delicious as usual, Grace," Calla said, all of us agreeing.

"If you find you don't like something we got you today, we can always take it to be tailored," Grace said to Phin, diverting from the compliment.

"Everything looked really nice though," Greta told her.

"I'm glad you found what you were looking for," I said. "Though the washing tub will probably miss seeing you so often."

"I won't miss scrubbing every few days. I had fun." She smiled, and the bond burned in response.

"Can we take a trip to Vincara?" Greta asked Vassago.

"Any particular reason, Dragonfly?"

"I want to visit an apothecary."

"Oh?"

"Yes. They have a recipe I need."

"You know the village," I offered.

"Do I?"

"There's a memorial to the priest you retrieved Lilith's book from in the church where Phin was living. The village is called Aymonroux now, after him as well."

"Truly? How incredible. They did have a significant vault there for such a small congregation." He squinted. "I'm afraid my memory isn't as detailed as I'd like, I don't recall what the village was called then. How did you find the selection at the apothecary, Tap?"

I shrugged "The proprietor seemed to have just about anything you could want, if I'm honest, and mentioned special orders as well. Seir and I both bought several things in addition to the plants and herbs he went there to find. Ink, needles, tea, candy. There were bouquets of flowers, wrapped and ready to gift even, despite the season."

"Are there farms there that operate year-round?" Calla asked, eyes turned to Phin.

She shook her head. "Not that I know of. But I didn't get out much."

"That's likely from the greenhouses," Vassago said. "The monastery has grown their own food that way for ages. Perhaps they've expanded." He turned to his wife. "I'll take you there any time you want to go."

"This week sometime? It sounds like they may have some of the rare botanicals we need to restock."

He thought for a moment. "After my morning class on Thursday we can. It's too cold to fly, perhaps we should portal." Vassago looked at me.

"Seir could escort you, or I could. Though you're always welcome to come and go through the great hall as a transition point if you like."

"Oh! Yes, let's do that." Greta placed a kiss on his cheek. "Good. I'm so excited to get to work on this."

Phin blushed and ducked her head.

"Seir's going to be very upset I got shepherd's pie and he didn't." Hailon looked far from contrite.

"He'll riot if you don't take him some," Rylan chuckled.

Grace laughed. "I'll make him a plate but tell him he's officially rationed on pickles. We won't have enough to last even until the soil thaws at this rate." Magnus chuffed. "I don't know why you're laughing, you are too."

He sagged. "I remember."

"We'll be planting more, I promise, Merry already has plans drawn up," Hailon said.

"Seeds have already been ordered for spring planting as well," Rylan confirmed.

Magnus finished his first plate and rose to refill it, gesturing for Grace to remain seated when she started to shift. "I'll get it. Hailon, if you wouldn't mind asking Merry if she could consult with a few of the aunts about expanding the beds at the conclave, we can contribute as well. Everyone loves pickles."

She laughed. "Of course."

"Better add more jars to the order, headmaster." Grace smiled.

"Already done."

Mostly, Phin and I watched the others and their easy conversation through the rest of the meal, the laughter around us vibrant and warm. Grace supplied a decadent cake for dessert, and I ate until I almost couldn't move.

But eventually, my restlessness was too loud to ignore.

"We should be getting back."

"I'm so glad you came," Calla gushed, getting to her feet and embracing me, then Phin. The gestures were repeated as everyone abandoned the table and walked us slowly down the hall toward the doors. "You'll want your coat."

"I'm plenty warm, and it'll only be a moment," Phin refused, her old coat folded over her arms. "Thank you, though, for everything."

"You're very welcome."

"We'll be through in a few days," Vassago said.

My arms laden with Phin's packages while Hailon carried leftovers for Seir and Phin possessed a selection of elixirs Greta had pulled from a cabinet, we finally walked out into the cold evening and through the portal, the familiar embrace of the crossroads calm and quiet.

I could only hope it wouldn't take long for the agitation in my body to disperse again.

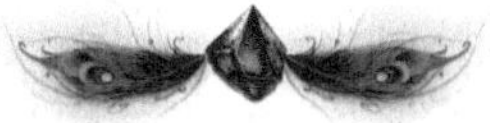

HAILON PRESENTED SEIR with his plate of shepherd's pie and took him straight home to the glade once he gave me a quick briefing, leaving Phin and I alone.

"Should I take these to your room?"

"If you don't mind."

I waited for her to go ahead of me and deposited them all on her bed. "You found everything you wanted?"

"More than. I felt a bit like a dress-up doll." Phin started unwrapping and sorting out the items, the stack shockingly large for as few bags as I'd had to carry.

"Oh?"

"Mostly I stood in the little curtained cubicle and tried things on. They handled which items, the colors, all that." A dreamy smile lit up her face. "I've never done anything like that before." She laughed, the sound bright.

I'd never once had the desire to shop in such a way, but I found myself wrestling with jealousy that I hadn't been there.

She held up the items as she took them to her armoire to be hung or reverently folded them before stacking them in her dresser drawers. A blush raced across her cheeks, and she stopped when she got to what I could only assume were undergarments at the bottom of the pile.

"Those are nice," I said, gesturing to the new decorative items as a distraction.

"They had so many things at the markets. I don't think we even saw half of the stalls."

"You'll have to go back, then."

She smiled again. "I'd like that." Her gaze went distant. "They told me something that sounds impossible."

"And what is that?"

"That they are all fated. They've all found their mates." Her palm scrubbed over her heart, but I wasn't even sure she realized she was doing it.

My breath stalled in my chest. "Yes."

"How?" The word was almost gasped as it left her lips. "The odds on that must be unfathomable."

"Indeed. It definitely defies all logic. And yet, it's true."

She looked away, frowning in concentration. Her hand strayed to the necklace dangling over her breastbone. At dinner, I'd noticed all my sisters-in-law had been wearing theirs as well. I could only assume she'd seen them too, at the very least.

"They told me I'm family."

"Then it must be true." My stomach swooped, acid rising in my throat.

"I never thought I would have any of this."

"You deserve everything."

Hundreds of thoughts crowded my mind as she stared at me, thousands of words backing up in my throat. I didn't dare give voice to any of them or I would want to say all of them. Confessions. Pleading. Explanation. It was likely none of it would endear me to her, and I didn't want to take the risk. I wasn't brave enough.

"Would you mind terribly making us some tea?" I asked, throat tight and chest painfully aflame. I was no longer sure what, if anything would bring some kind of relief.

"That's a good idea. Sure."

"Thank you, Phin." She smiled at me as I left her room. I stumbled across the hallway, hand clutching at my chest once I was safely out of her sight inside my own bedroom.

There was only one way I could ground myself again when things got like this. I quickly changed into different clothes, then crossed the hall and went into the room next to hers.

Chapter 22
PHIN

THE MYSTERY ROOM'S door was open.

I hesitated, but I'd checked everywhere else, and Tap was nowhere to be found. I called out but got no response. Curiosity overwhelming sense, I pushed the door all the way open and stepped inside, finding a space that was much like my bedroom but smaller.

As I processed what I was seeing on the floor in front of me, I froze. I breathed slowly through my nose as I took in the sight, each bit I looked at more stunning than the last. He was made beautifully, to be certain, but he was also an artist's canvas.

Tap was seated on one of the many cushions thrown around the space, his hair mussed like he'd run his hands through it over and over again. His muscular back was bare, save the tattoos in the old language that stretched across his upper back and disappeared over his shoulders. He wore loose linen pajama pants, but one side was pulled up as high as it could possibly go. That long leg was stretched out in front of his body and the other one was folded with the foot under the opposite knee. His lean stomach muscles bunched as he leaned over, using some kind of writing tool on his thigh.

Nearly all of the exposed leg was covered in ink, from thigh to toes, The arm on that side was the same, from shoulder to wrist; his long sleeves and cuffs had hidden it. Black whorls and dots decorated his skin, a complex network of curves, lines and shadows. The varying patterns all fit nicely together but it was clear innumerable little sections, most no bigger than a large silver coin, had been done separately over a broad span of time. The lettering from his back was a continuous mantle running across his chest, right under his collarbone and down his breastbone.

"Is this what you bought the ink for?" I kept my voice low and quiet so I wouldn't surprise him, unable to contain the inquiry any longer. "Did I use too much drawing on the parchment?"

Tap's head came up slowly, his silver eyes focusing as he took me in. It was like I was seeing him for the first time, and it took me a moment to figure out why he looked so different. It dawned on me as I noticed his thick eyelashes that he wasn't wearing his spectacles. "No, I still have plenty."

"Can you see clearly?" I blurted as I stepped forward, encouraged when he didn't flinch at the movement or order me to leave. It was odd seeing his bare face—the round wire spectacles were a part of what made him ... him.

"I do fine with this kind of close-up work," he said quietly. "I actually find it easier to do it without them. They tend to slip down my nose too much to be of much use otherwise."

"You could have them adjusted," I suggested. "Perhaps put them on a chain."

He shrugged one shoulder lightly. "Hardly seems worth the effort when I could just leave them off. Is everything alright?" He moved as though he might set the tool down, which provoked an odd twinge of sadness in my chest.

"Yes, everything is fine." His hand relaxed. "Oh! The tea is ready." The words felt almost silly once I said them aloud given what was in front of me. "I called for you but you never answered. So I came looking ..." I flushed hot, realizing that I'd hunted him down in a room I'd never been invited into while he was doing something private. "I'm sorry. I shouldn't have come in—"

"It's alright." He seemed far calmer than usual. His motions and speech which were normally quiet and easy were even more gentled, and slow. "If I were adamant about avoiding interruptions, I wouldn't have asked for tea. And I would have closed the door all the way."

Those words settled over me as I leaned a little closer. "This door is always closed."

"Exactly. You have an aversion to going into rooms with doors that are completely shut. You've never once asked about this one, nor tried to come in. You never, ever close yourself in a room if you can avoid it."

I blinked at him for several heartbeats, too stunned to even address how he'd pinned down and accommodated my subconscious habit.

"One day, perhaps you'll tell me why that is. Until then ..." He shrugged. "I've no complaint about leaving doors cracked. There's nothing here that needs to be hidden from you. Similarly, I can only assume that locked doors would be an absolute no for you. So, there are none here."

My pulse beat loudly in my ears as I absorbed what he'd said. Finally, I found my voice again. "You even made sure the doors were propped open when we visited the glade."

"Yes." Tap's brow creased.

"The classroom doors at d'Arcan were left open as well."

"I can't claim credit for that, but I was very happy to see it. Were you anxious at d'Arcan? Or in the city?"

"A little in the carriage, only because it was so full. I don't ... It's not on purpose, the doors. I don't even realize I'm doing it. But you noticed."

He blinked slowly, hair falling across his eyes as he nodded. "Yes."

Tears burned in my eyes. I'd spent most of my life hiding, but Tap *saw* me. From the first moment, he'd been able to see past all of the layers faster and more clearly than anyone else in my life ever had.

I pulled a cushion next to his, trying to get my throat to work properly again as I blinked away the tears. I rubbed a hand over my chest as my heart squeezed and blood roared in my head. I breathed slowly, counting in sets of four and eight to try to settle myself. "How does it work?"

He fidgeted, rolling what looked like a modified quill between his fingers.

"It's not much different than writing, though it requires more pressure. Plus a bit of enchantment, in truth. Vassago's talent is dreadfully convenient for such things." Tap resumed drawing the S shape he was working on when I interrupted, then made dots in the middle of the loops and drew a couple of complementary lines to tie it in with the art around it. After setting down the quill, he ran a damp, soapy cloth across the skin, removing the excess ink and tiny droplets of blood that had welled up.

"They're beautiful." I stopped myself just short of touching the fresh line.

His silver eyes blinked twice in rapid succession, and the corner of his mouth turned upward. "You are truly something else, little feather." I smiled wide, finding the compliment in his words and glowing at the nickname. "Would you mind bringing the tea in here?" he asked, picking the quill up again. My heart galloped behind my ribs as I stood. "I'd like to do a bit more."

"Of course."

I dashed back to the kitchen and scrambled to collect the pot and cups. When I got back, I tucked myself into the cushion next to his, awed as he elaborated on the simple lines. It looked so effortless, but I was sure I couldn't begin to fathom the number of hours he'd spent practicing this artform. It had taken months of careful practice and a heartbreaking amount of scrapped parchment before I produced something worth Father Morton keeping.

I sat silently to watch, Tap's movements careful and controlled. The muscles in his forearm flexed and rolled as he worked, his strong, capable hands performing a measured dance with the quill and cloth.

The pot of tea slowly disappeared between the two of us, sips taken from mismatched cups during brief pauses in his concentration.

"Why do you use this room to tattoo?" I asked. "Why not another workshop?"

He shrugged. "There's so little equipment required, it didn't seem efficient to create a whole workshop honestly." He glanced up, surveying the darker-toned wood walls. "This room originally started as a meditation room, but it turns out I'm terrible at clearing my mind. Unless, of course"—he lifted the magical quill"—I'm drawing on my own skin. Or putting holes in it."

"Holes?" At my shocked tone, he chuckled and ran a finger along the hoops in his ears. "Oh. Are those the only ones?"

Tap's lips parted, but he said nothing. I blushed hot when he only responded by very gently shaking his head. I wasn't sure my imagination could be trusted, so I diverted my eyes back to his leg.

"It used to be, I had to sharpen a piece of wood down into a fine point and score my skin over and over again, then rub ground charcoal and ash into the wound left behind."

"That sounds painful."

"Mmm." Tap's thoughtful noise was nothing more than a rumble in his throat. My skin warmed at the sound. "Indeed. Tedious, as well. The methods have improved, but the idea is unchanged."

Tap ran his fingers through his hair, frowning at his leg as though waiting for inspiration before applying the sharp end of the tool to his skin once again. "It took ages for me to do even a simple design when I first started. I've used just about every kind of pigment and ink available over the years. I prefer to use only black now, but these here"—he gestured to a set of whorls and dots that looked a bit like flowers if I imagined the rounded parts as petals—"these were red once. The stems done in green. I even had some yellow over here, and purple." His eyes drifted to me, like he was coming out of a daydream. "The purple in particular faded very quickly though, from a deep plum to violet, like your eyes." I braced, his gaze intense as he studied me without blinking. "Very disappointing. The ink, I mean, not ..."

"My eyes?" My throat was tight, the simple words strangled to barely more than a whisper on their way out. The fierce heat under my breastbone had returned, and I nearly gasped as it flared when he raised a hand, fingertips brushing along my jaw.

"Yes. They're the most beautiful thing I've ever seen. They have haunted me mightily since my first glimpse of them through that apothecary's shop window." His admission came as a low rumble, his eyes boring straight to my soul after twice dropping to my mouth. My heart swooped and then squeezed painfully in my chest.

"I'm sorry."

His palm settled warmly over my jaw, the pad of his thumb absently rubbing along my cheek. "Please don't apologize. It's been one of the sweetest tortures of my life. A gift." His fingers lifted and threaded through a curl over my temple. My pulse thudded in my ears, breath splintered and painful as I stared at him in shock. He'd never behaved like this before, and I wasn't sure how to respond. "Silver hair. Violet eyes. But I'd have known you anywhere even without those traits." Tap paused, and I could see the seemingly disconnected thoughts coming together behind his eyes. "Charcoal and ash. Fair for use in tattoos as well as hair colorant." He frowned. "What they had you doing to your hair was a paltry disguise at best. Your eyelashes looked all wrong. It was truly an awful ruse. Did anyone actually believe it?"

I choked out a harsh laugh. His thoughts seemed disordered sometimes, but there was a logic to them that I understood. "Between Father Morton's insistence that I was a young man, the clothes, the hair, my name ..." I shrugged. "Nobody said otherwise, even if they did suspect something was off. Though, to be fair, nobody said much of anything at all. It was better that way." I parroted the words I'd been told a thousand times, words I accepted even when I wanted to rail against them.

His eyes raked over me again and I shivered. "You were there a significant amount of time."

"Yes." More than eleven years, if my tracking of the seasons was correct. Long enough for me to understand that the way humans grew and matured was different than how I did. Faster. My relatively privileged existence prior to that had done little to prepare me for the reality of living as an angel in hiding among humans.

"You must have been terribly lonely. Stuck in a life you weren't allowed to actually live, a place you were forced to the edges of under a guise that hid your true self." Melancholy weighed down his tone, and his gaze shuttered as he looked away from me and back to his leg.

"Yes." I reached out and briefly squeezed his hand, seeing the same reflection of myself in him that I believed he saw in me. I might have been lonely everywhere I went, but he'd been buried here, suffocating alone. Fracturing under the weight of his responsibilities.

"It wouldn't matter to me if you were a different version of yourself," he added, head tilting one direction then the other as he plotted his next design. "I would have done the same, feel the same. I would still have recognized you. It is not your vessel that intrigues me, but rather the soul within it. Don't misunderstand," he added quickly, a flush to his cheeks. "This vessel is perfect. But there is far more to you than just that, Phin."

I felt as though I'd been struck by lightning. The pressure in my chest shortened my breaths nearly to pants as my mind spun wildly with questions I wasn't sure I was prepared for the answers to. He seemed far more confident in whatever he thought this was than I did. I held it gently, whereas he seemed sure it wasn't that fragile.

"How ... what ..." I inhaled through my nose, forcing the words all meshing together in my mouth to settle before I tried to speak again. "What does that mean, exactly? How do you feel about me?"

His mouth tilted up on one side. "I can see your pulse pounding in your throat." His eyes, had gone bright red and were fixated on that spot, his fingertips gliding over it so softly my skin tingled in the wake of his touch. His canines and the teeth next to them had sharpened, his tongue forked at the tip as he ran it over his bottom lip. "I can smell how you feel right now, see it in your face when your thoughts tangle around one another like mine do. Does your heart feel like it's being crushed? Like it's been set on fire right there in your chest? If so ... I think you know."

CHAPTER 23
PHIN

I GASPED A SHALLOW breath at Tap's brazen words, feeling the shape of every single one as they scratched and scraped their way through me. The unexpected appearance of his demonic features should have put me off, but I didn't feel any fear or offense. He wasn't wrong, and I wasn't scared of him. Where fear should have been pulsed a heavy desire. A need I'd only felt once before, but this time it was untainted. *Real.*

I was drawn to him like he was a flame I needed to burn myself on before I'd truly accept it was dangerous.

He studied me as I hesitated, his thumb tracing over my throat as I swallowed, his fingers wrapped lightly around the side of my neck. His eyes tracked the movement, then landed back on my mouth. I was focused only on breathing, the crushing sensation in my chest bordering on pain. My hand lashed around his wrist, holding it in place.

"I'm not going anywhere, Phin. I've been waiting right here for centuries. A little while longer doesn't trouble me." He inhaled and shuddered as I copied some of his movements with my free hand, my fingertips dragging along the sharp line of his jaw, my thumb catching his bottom lip and pulling it down.

Heart pounding, blood rushed loudly in my ears as Tap's eyes slid shut and his head tilted back. His neck was fully exposed to me, a sign of trust. Surrender.

My thoughts narrowed to the ache in my chest, the hollow throb between my thighs.

"Tap?"

His eyes opened dazedly, his lip soft under the pad of my thumb. "Yes, Feather?"

"Will it mess up the new ink if something rubs against it?"

A crease formed between his eyes, and he shook his head, gaze returning to my mouth. "No. Why?"

"Will it hurt?"

"Far less than doing it in the first place. Why, what—" His eyes widened as I shifted my weight, throwing one leg over the both of his so I was straddling his lap. The apple in his throat bobbed as he swallowed and his eyes flashed red as his hands came to rest on my hips.

"Phin. You …" Tap's voice trailed off into a breathy whisper, his eyes slipping closed again as my hands threaded through his hair.

I followed the impulses that had overtaken all my senses, reveling in the little sounds he made, the twitch in his fingers as I scraped my nails along his scalp. One of his arms rose and he tugged one of my hands away from his hair, pressing soft kisses into my palm. He groaned as I rested my lower half more firmly against him, shifting gently side to side as I settled in more comfortably.

"Saints." Ruby greeted me when he opened his eyes instead of silver, the soft gaze of pure adoration nearly undoing me.

Warnings flared faintly in the back of my mind, but I ignored them, instead remembering Ramsey's words to trust myself, my emotions. This felt *right*. I would not fear something that everything in my body was telling me it wanted.

Tap was good. He was safe. He would never push, never ask for more than I was willing to give. If anything, I was the one crossing boundaries.

My heart raced as I leaned in, pressing my lips to Tap's. We were both cautious at first, but fire caught between us almost instantly, the embers we'd been harboring easily fanned into flames. I held his face gently between my palms, doing my best to keep up as he began to devour me whole, his tongue tentatively tasting before tangling with mine as his soft lips turned needy and pulled everything from mine they could.

One of Tap's hands swept up to the middle of my back under my tunic, a warm, gentle pressure between my shoulder blades as he pulled me closer. The other arm went solidly around my lower back, dragging me in and down against him. I could feel his desire for me through our clothing, and I instinctively rocked myself against him, reveling in the rush of sensation the pressure gave me. My motions elicited another rumble from his throat, and he released my mouth to nibble a path down the side of my neck.

Soon nothing existed except the warmth of his touch, the gentle rasp of his skin against mine. His mouth was on mine, or mine on his; I wasn't sure it even mattered. The warm, cozy room with low lighting and no ceiling became a place where time was suspended and nothing mattered but us.

Tap's red eyes were glassy as they tracked my tunic being shrugged off and discarded on the floor. I lifted his arms by the wrist, placing his warm palms over my breasts and holding them there.

His breath left him in a rush, and he leaned us forward, trapping me underneath him on the cushions.

"Phin." It was only my name, but it came out of him so reverently I felt the prickle of tears in my eyes.

"Yes," I whispered in response, hoping he understood how many ways I meant the simple word.

Tap growled, and his forked tongue appeared as he lowered his face to my neck. Dueling points lashed against the skin a second before I felt the sharp edge of teeth, but he moved down my throat to my collarbone so quickly there was barely time for me to feel it. As he slid one hand down to the cushion underneath me for balance, the other slid down my breast until it was fingertips against my pebbled nipple instead of palm. He gently pinched the aching tip between his fingers before switching hands. I moaned out when fingers were replaced by his hot, wet mouth. He alternated until I had to tug him away from the sensitive flesh, my breath coming in short gasps.

I pulled him back up my body and lifted my head so I could kiss him again. He lay his whole weight against me as he slowly mapped my mouth with his tongue. His arousal pressed against my aching core, and I wrapped my legs around his waist, breaking the kiss to nip at the tender flesh just under his ear, the little hollow behind his jaw. I sucked hard for a moment, Tap making a noise that reminded me there were somehow still too many clothes between us.

My hands slipped from his bare shoulders to my leggings, and I wiggled and shifted until I could slide them down. He groaned against my mouth, one of his hands in my hair and the other helping me get the fabric down my legs, then removing his own before coming to rest between us.

I sucked in a breath, intense sensation rioting through my body. The pad of his thumb circled my overly sensitive clit and then pressed gently against my opening. Tap's breath was hot on my neck as he continued to drive me closer and closer to the peak only to back away again, his thumb going farther and farther inside me each time. My hips drove upward, and I tugged on his hair.

"Yes," I said again, nodding for good measure as I saw hesitance in his eyes. "Please."

He removed his hand, and the next time I lifted up, I could feel the heat of him there instead. We locked eyes, the thumb he'd been teasing me with in his mouth. His eyes slid closed as he removed the digit, and he seemed almost pained as slowly, his body entered mine. Something felt cooler than skin temperature as he worked his way in, and several times I felt an extra bit of pressure at the edges of me, but I couldn't think past the sensation of fullness.

Once he was fully seated, he stroked along my cheek with the backs of his fingers, sweat dotting his brow. I started to lift my hips again, doing my best to get the friction I needed. He grunted, his eyes closing as his muscles bunched and flexed, each movement careful, intentional.

"Phin. My lovely Little Feather." He bent down, mouth pressed to mine as his hips began to roll with more speed. I locked my feet around his waist and tilted my pelvis so his strokes hit a spot inside me that brought stars to my vision.

Tap's arms wrapped all the way around me as he scooped me into his chest. My body trembled under him, and I became aware that I was making sounds that started from somewhere deep in my chest that didn't even sound like my voice. As he drove into me, a growl rumbled in his throat. Pleasure washed over me in a hot wave, my muscles spasming as an orgasm swept through me.

Tap breathed my name again, the same prayer as before, just as he surged forward one final time. His whole body shuddered as his black, bat-like wings snapped out wide, his release barely a breath behind my own. He sagged, lips resting against my shoulder.

As I came back to myself, I realized that the discomfort in my chest had eased to something bearable. It had become something I could almost ignore but was still inescapably aware of.

Tap's eyes had settled back to silver when he finally opened them, and he ducked forward to plant soft kisses against my forehead, my cheeks, my eyelids. I mourned the loss of his wings when they tucked themselves away as quickly as they'd emerged. He gave similar treatment to the corners of my mouth, then gave me one final kiss before leaving me alone. A hot flush crept over my face as I fully realized what we'd done. Just as I started to spiral into anxious worry about where he'd gone, he returned with a warm washcloth.

"I can—"

"Please." He waited for my nod to lower the cloth between my legs, gently cleaning away the evidence of our mutual release.

He disappeared again, but when he returned, he lay next to me on the cushions. Even as the sweat from our exertions dried, my body was overheated, and I was glad for the lack of blankets or clothing.

I rolled onto my side and rested my ear against his chest. I quickly started to doze with his fingertips stroking softly down my arm and his heartbeat steady under my ear.

As I fell asleep, I turned the word *mate* over and over in my thoughts, wondering whether I could trust myself and my responses to him. But wanting to. Desperately wanting to.

I'd never considered finding a mate, but if the Fates were offering, I wanted it to be him.

CHAPTER 24
TAP

THE HIGH-PITCHED HUM of a gate activating drove me instantly from peacefully asleep to fully awake.

It took a moment for me to get my bearings, the room a different brightness and orientation than what I was used to. I looked over and found Phin asleep on the cushions next to me, and the memories of the previous evening crashed over me like a wave.

I focused on the bond, finding that my chest was sore, but the burning ache had gone.

"What have I done?" My voice was a ragged whisper as the reality of my impulsive actions settled in.

I tugged on my pants before rushing into the hall to find the source of the noise. Stalking up and down the rows, I followed the light hum until I located the right doorway. It was an old one, though not one of the decommissioned set I'd marked for investigation like I'd expected. A long-haired piglike creature ambled in and out of the portal several times, looking forlorn and lost. The third time it poked its head back into the hall, I was able to corral it fully away from the doorway.

"How did you manage to get in there?" I asked it. They had mind speech, but faint and very broken. It took several minutes, but I was able to discover where they belonged and send them back through the correct portal.

As the rush of the urgent lost creature situation wore off, reality weighed me down. Cursing myself, I returned to the room where Phin still lay curled in a ball sleeping, hesitating in the doorway. Guilt gnawed at me as I traced the lines and curves of her form with my eyes, remembering exactly how they felt under my lips and hands.

"Foolish demon." I scooped her into my arms and carried her back to her room, surprised at the warmth of her skin despite the fact that she'd been uncovered since we fell asleep. She shifted and relaxed under the weight of her blanket, and I left her there, shame sinking further into my skin.

After tidying the room, I sat on one of the cushions with my head in my hands. I'd allowed myself to disappear into the silence that Phin's presence gave me. Tattooing or piercing my flesh always provided a level of grounding and clarity, but this had been different. My mind had emptied completely with her warmth against me. I'd sunk to a place where I was allowed to just exist, just feel. The bond had been soothed, and my mind had been stilled. There had been nothing but her, and she was more important, more vital than the air I breathed. The peace of her touch was a shocking and blissful respite from the usual onslaught of tangled, overwhelming thoughts that never truly stopped.

I'd done something irreversible, drunk on the quiet she provided. The bond was almost certainly sealed, and she had no idea we were even mates. I'd done the very thing I'd never wanted to do. I'd stolen her choice. The ramifications would last literally forever, and she'd be well within her rights to hate me for it.

After going through my bathing and dressing routine I returned to the hall, all the thoughts and plans and sounds I'd been so relieved to unburden myself of, if only for a short time, piling back on.

There were six doors that needed to be inspected for unusual energy patterns—not including the one that the pig creature had come out of—nine that were closer every day to being decommissioned due to lack of use and three that needed secondary alternates created nearby because of how much use they were getting. Meals needed to be planned and prepared, and I was hopeful that Seir had remembered my request for more laundry washing powder.

My list of need-to-dos and things to watch grew longer as I paced. Top of the list was finding a way to turn back the clock so I could undo this mistake. I needed a way to unseal the bond I wanted more than anything I'd ever had in this life.

Just as the portal for the glade activated down the next row, I realized I perhaps it wasn't impossible after all—I just needed a powerful mage. And I knew exactly where to find one of those.

"Good morning!" Seir sang, headed for the living area.

"Over here," I called, and he spun on his heel. "Did you remember my soap?"

"I didn't forget it, but I also don't have it today. Hailon wanted to mix up a trial batch before I brought you some."

"Hailon's making it? What's wrong with what you were getting at the market?" He followed me as I made my way back toward the living area.

"Grace is always showing her interesting new things. Soap and candles are the latest. Sometimes the new hobby lasts, sometimes it doesn't." He shrugged. "I'm not going to complain. One of them gets me pickles, another candied fruit. Candles and soap seem like nice additions."

"Can you mind the hall for a bit today? I need to talk to Rylan."

"Sure. But didn't Vago just make you a mirror?"

"I need to talk to him in person."

"Okay." The way he was scrutinizing me made my face burn.

Faint light started creeping up the false windows. Soon, Phin would be up, and the least I could do was have something ready for her to eat. "Am I feeding you too?"

Seir frowned. "No. I ate before I came, like always. What's wrong with you? Are you ill?"

He reached over to feel my forehead and I dodged. "I'm fine."

"If you say so. I'm going to go get started. Maybe some extra-strong tea is in order? Do you have coffee? That might be better. I'm guessing you didn't sleep? Again?"

"I slept."

"Mmm. Sure you did." Seir narrowed his eyes at me and stared, even as he took several steps back into the hall.

I fled to the kitchen and prepared a quick breakfast of eggs, toast, and fruit. I left Phin's plate and a pot of tea on the table for her after I ate as quickly as I could, straight out of the pan over the sink, one eye on the doorway.

Seir and I worked in silence for a while, his occasional humming or chatter to himself unusually grating. I was so tense I was getting a headache, and I hated that he'd noticed my mood immediately.

"Good morning! Thank you for breakfast!" Phin called, and when I answered only with a tight, *you're welcome*, Seir stomped over from several rows away and stared directly into my face.

"I'm officially concerned. What's the matter with you?"

"Nothing is the matter with me, I'm fine."

Seir gasped and turned my head to the side with a finger on my jaw. "What's this?" he poked at a spot right behind my jaw. "You have a bruise. What an odd place to get injured, brother. How did you manage such a thing?" His eyebrow went up and his smile spread, the mirth in his eyes prodding at my raw emotions.

"None of your business, Seir."

Seir inhaled. "Tap. Did you and Phin seal the bo—" I smashed my hand over his mouth and hustled him to one of the farthest rows, looking over my shoulder like Phin might be standing nearby to overhear. I knew better, she was in the library, but the fear of that happening still had my blood pounding.

"Would you be quiet?"

My brother's features went serious at my stern tone. "Why are you so grumpy? Shouldn't you be celebrating?"

I shook my head. "She still doesn't know."

His eyes went wide. "What?"

I sagged. I wasn't angry with him, I was angry with *me*. "I've ruined everything, Seir." My voice caught and the anger turned inward, my eyes burning with tears.

"Hey. Hey, come on. It can't be that bad."

"I don't see how it's not. I acted selfishly. Now the bond is sealed, and she doesn't know. I have to find a way to break it."

He inhaled slowly through his nose. "Okay, let's go one step at a time, okay? Where's your mirror?"

I gestured vaguely toward the living quarters. "The familiars library. Why?"

"I need some support for this conversation, and we can't just leave. But Phin is right next door, so that doesn't feel like a very good option."

I remembered the one Vassago had just made me. "I have the new one. But we haven't tested it yet."

"Yes, good." Seir charged toward the living area, and I loped behind. "Where can we have some privacy?" I picked it up from the side table next to my recliner, considering the most secure place to go. "We can go to one of the workshops."

He brightened. "I've never seen those rooms before. It'll be an adventure!"

Resigned to proceeding with whatever he had planned, I quickly ducked into the first library and pulled the face-sized mirror down from where it hung on the wall just in case. Through the crack in the double doors leading to the deals library, I could see Phin pacing back and forth as she sorted. My heart clenched, a guilty flash of acid churning through my gut.

"Come on then," I said to Seir, leading him past the kitchen and down the hall. I put my palm over the paintbrush on the workshop door frame, regretting having chosen that one the moment Seir noticed the portrait of us all still lingering on the easel.

"Are you making any progress, brother?"

"Not in a while." I sighed. "But I'll finish it."

"I know you will," he said, voice full of pride. "I've never doubted. And look, I'm already here and quite handsome!"

The corner of my mouth twitched despite my foul mood, and I settled the mirrors on an easel in front of the small sofa to the side of the work area. Regretful, I went to the door and turned the lock. I hated doing another thing I'd told her I wouldn't. While there was almost zero chance Phin would come looking for us, I didn't want her to stumble into this conversation.

Seir was already seated so I took the spot next to him before speaking the words to activate the glass. A confused Vassago appeared in the new mirror, but the older one remained blank.

"Is this the new mirror or the old one?"

"New."

"Well, that's one question answered. Good morning to you both. To what do I owe the pleasure?"

"Is Rylan there?" Seir asked, before I could even open my mouth.

"Yes. He and Magnus are working on something to do with the eclipse situation."

"Can you bring them both in please?"

"Of course. Everything alright?"

"Tap is having a bad day."

Vassago frowned in confusion as I stayed silent and spun my ring irritably. "Give me a moment."

Soon enough, both of my brothers and the massive stone kin man were all visible in the mirror.

"Are you alone?" I asked, feeling foolish over how uncomfortable I was with the idea that my sisters-in-law might overhear whatever this conversation was going to be.

"They're at the markets," Rylan confirmed. "Are you ill?"

"No, I'm fine."

"You look awful," Vassago agreed.

"And good morning to you both." Neither looked apologetic in the least.

"What can we do for you, Tap?" Vassago asked.

"He's in a bit of a situation," Seir tried to break it to them gently, but my nerves were too frayed to continue the idle chatter.

"I need to know if there's a way to break a bond once it's sealed."

The harsh chorus of "*What?*" made my ears ring.

"Is this a hypothetical?" Rylan shifted forward.

"No."

"You were just here. We spoke about you having found your mate. What's happened?" Vassago asked.

I dropped my aching head into my hands. "This was a terrible idea."

"No it wasn't," Seir patted my shoulder. "Is there a way to break a sealed bond, Rylan?"

He shook his head. "I've never heard of one that's more than theory, though there are always stories, usually involving a complicated ritual and someone either going mad or dying. Denying a bond is different, of course. We know what happens there." His golden eyes flicked between me and Seir. "Would you care to explain why you're asking? I can't answer very well without knowing a bit more."

I braced myself. "I'm only saying this once." It was almost comical the way they all leaned forward to be sure they heard me properly, Seir included. "Last night we ... I allowed myself to turn off my mind for a few hours, to just *feel*, just *be* ... and the bond was sealed. Phin still hasn't acknowledged that she even feels like such a thing exists for her. So, I need to unseal it. She needs to be given her choice back."

"You stopped thinking?" Seir asked, quiet awe on his face.

"This, precisely. Since when are you capable of that?" Vassago asked.

Magnus smirked, his gaze empathetic. "Since her, I'm betting."

"This was the first time." I realized after the words left my mouth that they held a very heavy double meaning.

Seir blinked at me, clearly hearing what I'd left unsaid. "Tap. You really haven't lived outside of this place."

"I've lacked nothing."

"That's a blatant lie," Vassago chuffed. "Of course you have. You are too responsible, always have been. You and Orobas have that in common, and neither of your posts should ever have encompassed all the duties they have. You should have never accepted. Lucifer was cruel to pile on like he did. We don't even get to speak with Bas because of where he's cloistered. I'm still awed he showed himself at Rylan's wedding. But I'm getting off track." He inhaled to calm himself. "I wish you would have told someone you were struggling well before you were absolutely drowning. We would have helped."

"Perhaps you're right." I accepted his judgment.

"You've been very unlike your normal self in recent days, Tap." Rylan's serious expression broke with a smile. "Not that I'm complaining. It suits you, actually living a little. You should absolutely continue."

"I think you all forget how lovesick you were in his same position," Magnus interjected. "As I recall, your brain power was something equivalent to mashed potatoes. I think that one's still stuck there, sometimes," he teased, pointing at Seir. Seir just grinned back.

"You are not exempt, stone man," Vassago reminded him. "I recall you drooling into your shirt, stupefied, on several occasions."

"I suppose that's true enough. But everyone's allowed weak moments."

"Not like this," I muttered.

Vassago shook his head. "You made a *mistake*. Perhaps your first. Everyone's allowed."

"A mistake is sending a creature through the wrong portal," I argued, thinking of what had woken me in the wee hours, venom in my tone. "Not sealing an eternal mate bond with someone whose whole life has already been largely dictated by others. Did you or did you not all give your mates a choice?"

"Alright," Seir interrupted, gesturing widely with his arms. "Anyone have a suggestion? A useful one?"

"Tell her," Rylan said plainly. "The longer you wait, the worse it will be." He might have been right, but I froze inside at the very thought.

"I can speak with Greta to see if she has any ideas, but she'll have questions," Vassago sighed.

"You could perhaps go visit Ophelia," Magnus suggested. "At your own peril, of course. She may have knowledge about bonds even this haughty archmage does not." He reached over and clapped Rylan on the shoulder. Their interesting friendship had changed much for us all. "Though breaking mate bonds is one magic I'm not sure actually exists. Not without fatal consequences."

"Greta mentioned asking her about the tincture formula for Phin but she hasn't had a chance to get out there yet. Perhaps you both go? Get some answers all the way around. Seeing her was very informative when Greta and I visited."

"And for us, as well," Rylan confirmed.

I glanced at Seir. "Don't look at me." He shrugged. "You know how much Ophelia did for Hailon while I was in Hell, not to mention how she's looked after Merry and helped with the wards in the glade. I'd never say a word against her, and not just because she's terrifying. I make mistakes constantly, so honestly, I'm just glad it's someone else this time." Unable to help myself, I huffed a rough laugh.

"This has been incredibly demoralizing and largely unhelpful. Thank you all," I said, words heavy with sarcasm.

"Anytime," Rylan chuckled.

"Glad to know the mirror works. Use it as often as you need," Vassago nodded.

"Best of luck to you," Magnus grinned. "If you're visiting Ophelia, take some salted licorice."

"I likely won't have a chance to get any but noted."

We said our goodbyes, and the mirror went dark. I stared at it for several moments after they were gone, feeling both a heavy sense of foreboding but also a lot lighter.

"There," Seir said, getting to his feet. He picked up one mirror, and I took the other. "Now you have a plan. I'll ask Hailon to let Ophelia know you'll be coming, they get on well. One step at a time." We headed toward the door, relief washing over me when I unlocked it. Out in the hall, Seir spun on me. "Can I see some of the other ones?" He had on that begging pup expression again, the one I could never resist.

"I suppose."

He beamed, and I was gifted another small window of not thinking about everything all at once while my brother pushed all the symbols on the door frame, gushing over each and every workshop he looked at. Faced with what I was, I appreciated the distraction more than he knew.

It seemed it wasn't a mage I needed, but rather a sorceress. One with ancient knowledge and insight into things much of the world had already forgotten.

Thankfully, I also knew where to find one of those.

CHAPTER 25
PHIN

I THOUGHT AT FIRST that I was imagining things, but after he spent the whole of dinner unable to meet my eye, I had to admit to myself that Tap was in fact, avoiding me.

My stomach was knotted as I dried the last dish. He was standing right next to me at the stove but might as well have been at the far end of the great hall.

"Tap?"

"Yes?"

"I was thinking about spending some time practicing with my quill. Would you like to join me? Maybe keep looking for that lettering style you wanted to show me?" I cringed at the desperation in my tone.

His response was painfully slow, but my shoulders relaxed a bit when he finally answered, a quiet, "Okay."

"Would you mind bringing the tea?"

"Of course."

He followed me down the hall, and I pressed my palm to the little book to access the library. The silence was heavy as I got settled at my beautiful new desk. Tap sat stiffly on the edge of a sofa cushion, still avoiding my eye.

My heart squeezed. I didn't understand what I'd done wrong. He was not exactly being cold to me, but he was unbearably tense and resisting even the most basic conversation. I'd gotten one-word answers and diverted eye contact all day.

The only logical conclusion was that he regretted what we'd done. Nothing else made sense. And the very idea of that made my chest feel like it was going to collapse.

Quill in hand, I practiced my favorite scroll design with ex-aggerated loops and swirls in the rich blue ink. Over and over, I drew them, lining all four edges of the page before I swapped for the gold ink and did a thin outline of them all to change them from flat to more realistically dimensioned. Tap was flipping through books, but I wasn't convinced he was seeing anything on the pages.

I called out for Ramsey in my mind, wondering if perhaps she could lend me some of her wisdom on the situation, but unfortunately there was no response. Not that I expected one, there hadn't been anything but silence since she left the crossroads, but I was already upset and that just dug the blade into my sore emotions a little bit deeper.

I did another row of symbols, then another round of outlining. When I finally reached for my cup, the tea was cold.

That was my limit, apparently, because tears began to flow as I fought the urge to spit the tepid mouthful of brew back out. I put my face in my hands and sobbed silently, shoulders shaking and heart sore. At the same time, I felt completely out of control. Crying over such things, over *anything*, really, was unlike me.

It was my sniffle that finally made him look at me, and I could see the change in his demeanor immediately.

"Phin?"

"Tea's cold," I managed over a shuddering breath.

"Here." He rushed over with the pot and swapped out my cup for a new one before he poured. "Sorry, I didn't bring the honey. I think it helps your throat."

"I don't need it." His thoughtfulness about how I drank my tea made the tears come faster. "Are you angry with me?" I stuttered, and he nearly dropped the cup on my freshly drawn pages.

"No, of course not."

"Then why won't you look at me? Do you regret what happened?"

Horror crawled across his face. "No, no. Of course not. I'm sorry. I didn't mean to make you feel that way, especially after ..." He trailed off. "I'm sorry." I could hear the sorrow in his voice. Perhaps it made me a fool, but I believed him. He never moved to comfort me physically though, which was still very strange. He'd never withheld even simple touches when he had the opportunity. "Phin, I ..." His eyes dropped to the paper I'd been drawing on. Whatever he'd been about to say, he decided to keep to himself. "Tomorrow, I'm planning to visit Ophelia."

The name was familiar, but I couldn't quite place it. "Ophelia is the ..."

"Stone kin sorceress."

"Oh yes. Greta mentioned going to visit her, to ask about my tincture."

"Vassago told me that she hasn't had a chance to see her yet. So I thought perhaps we could go."

I brightened. "Yes, I'd be happy to if it will speed up that process." The faster we could work out the recipe, the sooner I could stop worrying about running out of the only thing keeping my cycle and perhaps more of the freezing episodes at bay.

"Good." Tap remained serious as he returned to the sofa. "I ... I'm sorry. Truly," he repeated, but didn't elaborate.

Something was still wrong, the tension sitting heavy between us, the total opposite of what I'd felt only the night before. But like him, I wouldn't push. Not yet.

Hopefully getting out in the world again helped. I wasn't sure I could stomach the tension if not.

"THE WARDS AROUND her hut will likely feel heavy. They're designed to keep people out, to make them want to avoid her part of the Dread Forest altogether. If you feel like you want to run away, don't panic. It will pass once we're inside." Tap's warning as we traveled out of the city gates in the carriage from d'Arcan didn't ease my stomachache one bit.

His odd behavior had continued, though he'd offered his arm before we stepped through the portal. He was wound as tight as could be, and I hated every second of the awkwardness between us. It hadn't even been like this when we first met. I hated it.

The forest became denser on the sides of the road the farther we went, and then it was like we were swallowed up by the greenery altogether when the carriage turned onto a narrow lane. Before long, I understood all too well what Tap had meant with his warning about the wards.

Pure panic roiled through me, the urge to scream and go back the way we'd come overriding all other senses.

"Just breathe through it, we'll be there in a moment," Tap said gently, his own teeth clenched.

The carriage came to a stop in front of a little round hut. There were flowers blooming in the window boxes and what looked like the remains of a garden off to one side.

"Here." Tap reached for my hand as he exited the carriage, and I gladly took it, seeking anything that would temper the wild need to leave this place. "Thank you, Clem. We'll make our own way back."

The groom dipped his head. "Sir." He immediately steered the clearly spooked horses back the other direction, disappearing down the dirt lane at a fast trot.

He approached the door and knocked three times. After several long heartbeats where I struggled to keep my feet planted where they were, the wooden door opened, revealing a squatty old woman with pure white hair.

"Hello, Tap. Hailon sent word that you'd be coming."

"Greetings to you, Ophelia. I apologize. I come bearing no gifts today. But I'm happy to make a special order, if you have any requests?"

She scanned Tap up and down. "I'll forgive you this time, I suppose. But I'd like a portal of my own one of these days."

Tap blinked. "Truly?"

"Yes, yes. My days of sitting in denial that company won't keep showing up regardless of my opinion on the matter are over. Having one here, one I can control that's safe under my wards, will simplify the process for everyone. And I won't have to go all the way into Revalia when I want to visit the glade or the conclave."

Tap blinked as he took in this information. "I'd be happy to create one for you, it's no trouble at all. I can likely do it today, as long as you have the components I need."

"Good." Then those rheumy blue eyes turned on me. "Always something new with you demons. Come in then." She led us into the cozy little dwelling, and once I was over the threshold, the urge to leave with haste disappeared. The smell of freshly baked bread and the warmth from the oven also helped put me at ease. "Bread needs a few more minutes, but the tea should be steeped."

The space was small but filled with bits and bobs that illustrated immediately who Ophelia was. I took in the stacks of books and papers on every available flat surface and abundance of precariously positioned houseplants and clusters of rocks and crystals and knew she was my kind of person.

We passed through the kitchen to a small living room and into a

U shaped seating area arranged in front of a fireplace. Tap waited to be invited to sit, which seemed to amuse the elder stone kin.

"Go on, demon. Sit yourself down. And you"—she turned to me, her smile genuine but missing several teeth—"sit next to me? If you please." She patted the cushion to her right.

Tea was doled out in dainty little cups, the scent of alcohol heavy as I lifted mine to my mouth. I took a tentative sip, the burn of whiskey hot in my nose as I swallowed.

"Ophelia, this is—" Tap started, but a curt wave of a hand stopped him.

"She can speak for herself, I'm sure. I'm Ophelia, but you already knew that. Go ahead. When you're ready, young lady."

"Hello. I'm Phin," I said, unsure whether or not I was trampling some unspoken rule of etiquette.

"Pleasure to meet you, Phin. What brings you all the way out here?"

"A tincture?" I was entirely unsure of my footing around this woman. She was clearly ancient, and she exuded a strength the likes of which I'd never encountered before outside of some angels even my father seemed hesitant to be around. "Greta is helping me. We're unsure of the exact formula."

"Ah. Well, if anyone can work it out, she can." Her tone rang with pride. "But I'm happy to see if I can help. May I take a look at you? I don't meet many Nephilim."

"Sure." I sat stiffly as she held my hand in hers, one soft fingertip tracing the lines in my palm. She nodded and made some thoughtful noises in her throat as she continued up my arm, following the blue veins from elbow to wrist, then went back again, leaning her face close to my palm.

"Why is it, that you and your brothers keep showing up here with your fascinating mates? It's like clockwork. Is there something about my quaint little home that draws you all in?" My breath caught in my throat. Ophelia's gaze turned to Tap and mine did as well, his expression apologetic as she continued, "A Nephilim bonded to a hellhound?" She laughed. "How wonderful. Which one?"

"Ramsey." I could barely breathe her name over the word *mate* rattling around my head very loudly.

"Oh, yes! She's been through here a time or two. Rolo too." Her enthusiastic nod was oddly comforting. "But I thought she belonged to ... oh. Are you Terra's girl, then?"

I choked up immediately. "You know my mother?"

"Yes, yes. Not well, mind, but she and I have met several times. Gifted with hedge skills, she is. An earth witch at heart, if a demon in body." My emotions swelled at this, that my mother might have sat where I was. It was silly, but any connection after such a long separation was more than welcome. "She's quite lovely." Ophelia patted my hand. "As are you, my dear. Where is Ramsey, then? Will she be joining us?"

"Not today."

"No? Unfortunate. Why not?"

"That's a long story," Tap offered.

"Well, we've got time. Perhaps once the bread is done and that tea starts to warm your soul you'll be ready to discuss that. But truly, if you lot keep trying to outdo one another with interesting mates, we're all going to be in serious trouble. There are three more of you princelings, after all, aren't there? If this keeps escalating, one of you will be mated to a deity!" She started to laugh, finding the thought so funny she slapped her own knee and swept away a tear. "Though perhaps that's exactly what they're all afraid of. Wouldn't that be something?" She hooted through another round of laughter and shook her head as we just stared at one another.

"It's true?" Elation filled my chest, confirmation that I hadn't misunderstood what I was feeling between us. Just as quickly, my heart plummeted again when Tap spoke.

"I'm sorry." Two simple words, ones he'd repeated over and over lately, but they still stabbed straight through me.

"What's this now? What are you apologizing for?" Ophelia asked, continuing her inspection of me despite the fact I wasn't sure I was even breathing correctly. Her fingers gently gripped my chin as she turned my head, then traced along my ear.

"I didn't mean for the bond to become sealed. It wasn't intentional. We were just ... and you ..." He shook his head. "Don't misunderstand, I don't blame you, Phin, I would never. It's my fault. I wasn't thinking of the consequences, only that I was ... that we ... it was peaceful." He closed his eyes tightly, chin falling to his chest. "I'm explaining this very badly. I want to make it right. I thought Ophelia might know of way to break the bond. So we can fix it."

I sank into my seat, head spinning. For all I knew he'd spoken eloquently and my thoughts were the thing that was stuttering, but I didn't think so. We'd gone from Ophelia declaring we were mates to him stating he wanted to sever our bond at stunning speed, and I was struggling to keep up. I rubbed a hand over my heart, trying to soothe the faint throb of pain. "You want to break it?"

Ophelia's hand dropped away from me and she tsked. "Am I to believe that *you* of all creatures neglected to think something through?" He sagged further. "Truly?" When he turned his head, a furious blush stained his cheeks, and she began to laugh in earnest. "Oh my. Today is a banner day indeed! They do say there is a first time for everything, and now, I may have seen it all."

"I already got a version of this speech from my brothers," he complained.

"Good." She huffed a breath. "You'll live through one lapse in judgment, I promise." A bell went off in the other room. "Tap, would you please go take the bread out of the oven? Come with me, Phin."

Tap rose and went the short distance into the other room, and Ophelia leaned in close to my ear while patting the top of my hand. "Don't you worry." Then she pulled me to my feet and steered me to a little nook that was both behind her favored chair and the kitchen. A table sat under a stained glass window, an assortment of crystals, herbs, sand, salt, and other items scattered across it. "Flip it out of the pan and onto that cooling rack," she called. "And butter the top, while you're at it." As she rearranged the items on the table, she spoke in a low voice. "I'm betting that's not really what he wants. Am I correct to assume you weren't aware?"

"Not exactly. There were lots of hints, though. Admittedly I was the one who instigated the ... bond sealing." I flushed furiously hot, wondering what magic it was that had me speaking so freely with this woman I'd just met over such a serious matter. Perhaps I'd been wrong to assume it was just whiskey in my tea, as I'd barely had more than a sip.

"Guilt, then. For such smart men, they certainly have their moments. There is a way." Her gaze went distant for a moment. "If that's truly what you both want." She looked at me, blue eyes piercing. "But you need to be absolutely certain. Undoing such powerful magic is not without consequence." Her words settled heavily in my gut. I'd gone from being certain to being unsure what I wanted, so I just nodded. "You come back here, and we'll perform the ritual. Don't go to anyone else and don't attempt anything yourselves. But honesty first, yes? Make him explain before anything is decided. You seem plenty compatible to me, and if you are not in objection, then he's just stuck in his head, like always."

"Alright." Her urgency clawed at me, panic rising again as the mysterious negative possible outcomes battered at my emotions.

"Anything else I can do for you while I'm in here, Ophelia?" Tap called back.

"It has to cool before it's cut. You're free to come sit again, I suppose."

She stepped away to gather a few more items, and I was happy to see a knot of amethyst crystals join the other stones.

"Hold this." She placed a small bundle of wood shavings tied together with twine in one of my hands. "Finger?" I held my empty hand out, and she pricked my index finger with a needle I hadn't even seen, squeezing a drop of my blood into a tiny cauldron near the edge of the table. She tossed a glance at Tap as I sucked the sting away and tsked again. "I'm almost disappointed. You really are the most even-tempered of the bunch, even all wound up, aren't you?" He just frowned at her and crossed his arms. Ophelia chuffed, a smile on her mouth as she lit the tiny, low candle under the cauldron. She sprinkled some salt, some paper shavings and a bit of the wood from my bundle into it, then handed me a bell.

"Ring that." I shook the little instrument, but it just clanked hollowly. "Losing my touch," she muttered, moving things around the table with haste as acrid gray smoke started to rise. "Try again?"

"Sorry," I apologized when the same thing happened a second time.

"No, no. It's not you. Something's wrong." She grew pensive. "Are you wearing any stones?"

I nodded, pulling my necklace out from under my shirt and flashing her the bracelet Rylan had made for me. "Just these."

She shook her head and opened the stained glass window a little to let the smelly smoke out. "No, that's not it, though I'd like a better look at that necklace. Anything else?"

I dug my vial of tincture out of my pocket. "Just this."

Ophelia took the bottle from me and pulled up the cork, giving the contents a thorough sniff. Pensive, she ran her finger around the edge of the top where the cork sat and tasted it. Her face screwed up into a grimace. I could relate, the potent, bitter flavor had never been enjoyable, and it always burned as it went down. I stood there stunned as she upended the vial into the cauldron. The scant remaining drops of my daily treatment were gone, just like that.

"No!" I gasped.

After a moment's consideration, she added the glass bottle too. Despite the fact that the tiny cauldron was only heated by a single candle, the vial shattered and crumbled, the vessel belching plumes of acrid gray smoke as the contents burned.

"Trust me, it's for the best. Ring the bell?"

I couldn't respond to her request over my panic. Ophelia reached over and shook my arm, and the bell rang clearly, the sound piercing. My heart immediately started to gallop, and my fingertips went numb. Horrified it was happening at such a time, I struggled to stay upright as the smoke in the cauldron shifted to a strange pale yellow shade and started to take a defined shape.

Tap was suddenly there, a steady presence behind me, his arm around my body for support as I sagged. My blinks were heavy as I fought my body's attempts to shut down. This was too important to miss because of a silly freezing episode.

There, in the smoke, were the smiling faces of my parents.

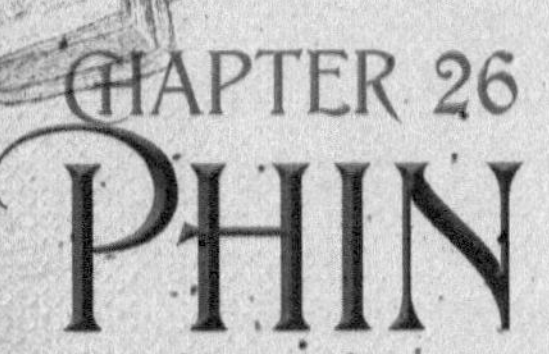

CHAPTER 26
PHIN

I COULDN'T SPEAK, AND my ears felt clogged, the tone of the bell resounding in my head even though it had been taken from me and placed back on the table.

The yellow smoke had formed a portrait of them, and they looked so detailed, so real it brought tears to my eyes. It had to be some kind of illusion, but they appeared to be actively looking at me, smiling at me. My mother even raised a hand and blew me a kiss, the same way she'd done since I was a child. If ever we locked eyes from across the room, or out the window of our house while I was playing in the yard, that's what she did. I hiccupped a sob, and my father's expression changed, sadness tugging at his eyes. His head tilted to the side, his cheek resting against my mother's curls.

My strength returned enough that I was able to reach a hand toward the smoke just before it dissipated.

"Does that mean they're alive? That they're okay?" The tears had made my voice even rougher than it usually was.

"I can't know for certain, but I'd like to think so." Ophelia took the bundle from me. "Your father. May I ask his name?"

"Radueriel."

"The poet?" she laughed. "Terra always did have a soft heart."

The words felt like a compliment, and when she saw my smile, she patted my shoulder.

Tap's grip loosened when it was clear my body my own once again. He hesitated but dropped his arms completely after a moment.

Ophelia looked over my head at Tap, her eyebrow raised. "Tell me again why you want to break your bond?"

He sighed. "It's complicated, Ophelia."

"It doesn't have to be, demon. You're just stuck in your head, like usual." He sighed, and she tossed her hands up, leaving us standing there as she stalked into the kitchen. She returned in short order with a sliced loaf of bread and fresh pot of tea. She settled into her seat with a steaming cup and waited for us to serve ourselves. "Tell me, then. Your long stories. Let's see if I can help you uncomplicate them."

"Where would you like us to start?" Tap asked, picking at his bread.

"Wherever suits you. I need to know it all, do I not?" When neither of us were forthcoming, she sighed and leaned to one side. "Perhaps at the beginning, then? How did you two happen upon one another in the first place? It's not like droves of Nephilim are just wandering about the continent."

He glanced at me and I nodded, indicating he could continue. "I discovered Phin when I visited Aymonroux with Seir. She was living in the church."

"And why were you in Aymonroux, Phin?"

"My parents left me there, with the priest. For safekeeping."

"Nephilim are rare but not generally threatened nor considered a threat. Not on their own. So, what is it you were being kept safe from?"

"Heaven."

"What for?" Ophelia seemed moderately impatient with our short answers.

"There's an illness. Me and other Nephilim are being sought out so we can help them repopulate."

Tap growled, and Ophelia grimaced, clearly disgusted by the notion. "Indeed? Well. That explains a few things." She frowned. "She's staying with you at the crossroads now?"

"Yes."

Her head bobbed, and she reached out with a grunt, splashing more whiskey directly into the teapot before pouring herself another cup. "It's definitely a difficult place to find unless you already know how to get there. Seems a good place to hide, to me. Your hound didn't stay?"

"Ramsey is hunting the angels who are trying to locate Phin."

"Ah, well, good for her. May she be successful in her search." She lifted her cup as though offering a toast, then threw the whole thing back in one gulp.

"She met us in the glade not long ago. Hopefully her quarry doesn't evade her much longer," Tap said.

Ophelia nodded solemnly. "And you're keeping yourself occupied at the crossroads, Phin?"

"Yes, I'm organizing the deals library."

Ophelia brightened. "That suits, yes, yes." Her gaze narrowed. "Tell me then, what happened when the bell rang?"

"I have freezing episodes." I explained it to her as I had to Greta, how my heart races and I lose control of my muscles. She grew more thoughtful the longer I spoke.

"In Aymonroux, the church bell was forged with both demon and angel blood," Tap explained. "It seemed to trigger them, her own blood responding to the remnants in the bell. But they happen randomly also. Is there something similar in yours?"

Ophelia shook her head. "No, mine is just plain iron, I've had it since I was young. Watched it being forged myself. But there may be something about the tone that triggers them. The mind is a complicated place." She reached out a hand. "May I see your necklace?" I slipped the chain over my head and placed the pendant in her palm. "Terra was wearing this each time I saw her." She turned it over, then held it up to the light. "And her mother before her I'd imagine, though I never met her. When did she pass it along to you?"

"After I got sick once, when I was younger." That was true, if intentionally vague about what had happened to make me unwell.

"Wise. Amethyst offers protection and healing. It's also said to be helpful in boosting mental clarity." She handed it back.

I blinked, understanding more clearly why my mother had given it to me when she had. "I didn't know that."

"Did anything improve once Rylan gave you the bracelet? Did the addition of more amethyst help at all?"

At Ophelia's look, I held out my wrist so she could look at it as well. "Maybe. I'm not sure."

"This one is spelled. Partial invisibility?"

"Yes, so she could go into the city without drawing any unwanted attention."

The sorceress's head bobbed. "I have to admit, the archmage does nice work. This is good protection, Phin. Keep it on whenever you leave the crossroads."

"I will."

Ophelia took another slice of bread and smeared it liberally with honey. She ate the entire thing before speaking again. "Now then, to the reason you came." I tensed, already trying to organize my thoughts. "That awful tincture, who made it?"

"The apothecary in Aymonroux."

"And how often were you taking it?"

"Daily."

"For how long?"

"Since I was taken there. Ten or eleven years."

She grumbled several colorful words under her breath. "It was not properly made."

"I don't understand." The painful prickle of worry settled under my skin.

There was a heavy knock on the door, and a woman's voice called out for Ophelia.

"That'll be Imogen. Tap, would you mind?"

"Of course." He rose to answer the door, leaving us alone again.

Ophelia shook her head. "It was bad magic, Phin. You're better off without it."

Panic started to take hold. "I'm not though. Without it ..." Mortified, I gave the simplest version. "I'll basically go into heat. For days."

"I'm truly sorry for that but continuing to take that tincture was not a viable option." She gripped my hand, urgency in her tone. "I tasted quieting cane. Hemlock. Foxglove. Effective at suppressing a number of things no doubt, but dangerous, lazy work. *Poison*, Phin. Greta took a sample?"

My blood went cold. Hemlock and foxglove were well known toxins. "Yes, she did. I've never heard of quieting cane, what is that?"

She just shook her head. "It burned going down, yes?" I nodded. "Because it was actually *burning* you, child. It's no doubt to blame, at least in part, for why your voice is the way that it is." She shook her head. "I'd bet she's figured it out herself by now, but tell Greta I tasted those things. She'll understand."

More confused than ever, I looked up as Tap led a tall, broad-shouldered woman into the room. She had long dark hair and a gentle smile, though she was built like a warrior.

"Greetings, my girl," Ophelia said. "Imogen, this is Phin, Tap's Nephilim mate."

"Ophelia." Tap sighed her name and pinched the bridge of his nose. It might have been funny if the whole situation hadn't left me feeling so off balance and nauseated.

"It's true." Ophelia threw her hands up, unapologetic.

"Hello." Imogen raised a hand. "Pleasure to meet you. Sorry to interrupt, I didn't know she had company today."

"You're all welcome here." Ophelia waved her hand dismissively, and I was curious as to why that response made Tap's eyebrows go up and Imogen smile, but that question would have to wait.

"Imo, come have a seat. Get yourself some tea and a snack. I've got to look for something these two need, and he's going to make me a portal. Tap, come with me." She waved him over to a set of bookshelves at the back of the room. While nothing was truly that far away, it was enough that their hushed conversation was too quiet to hear.

Imogen did as Ophelia asked, methodically spreading honey over the soft bread but sniffing at the tea after pouring only a tiny bit and setting it right back down.

"Are you the one my brother Tormund was keeping an eye on? In Aymonroux?"

I startled at the question, then vindication settled in. I'd been right, the statue on the church roof *had* been moving. "I suppose I was. Though I never got to meet him, of course."

She nodded. "He just arrived back at the conclave this morning, so perhaps one day soon you will. He was posted there for quite a while."

"Could you thank him for me? Sounds like he may have been responsible for misdirecting at least a few of the people I was trying to stay hidden from."

"I will." She smiled, clearly pleased by the idea.

I wasn't sure what to say after that, and our brief conversation hit an awkward lull. After she'd finished her bread, she gestured at Tap and Ophelia, who were huddled together over an old tome she'd put on a reading stand. Tap's shoulders were hunched and tense, and Ophelia was clearly telling him something it didn't appear he wanted to hear. He then stalked over to the table with all the crystals on it and started assembling something in another little cauldron. Ophelia followed behind, watching over his shoulder.

"You chose a good day. Usually she's not so accommodating," Imogen said, but her smile made me wonder if she wasn't quite telling me the truth. Her eyes dipped to my necklace. "That's pretty. Family heirloom?"

"Thanks. And yes."

She nodded. "So interesting they all look so much alike."

Somehow, I'd put it out of my mind that the other women had similar jewelry. I fought the urge to reach for the pendant, opting instead to sip at my tea that was mostly whiskey and regretting my choice.

"I'm the forge mistress at the stone kin conclave. I'm working on some Dark blades now, to better defend against the angels, should things go sideways. But for you ... perhaps something more specific." Her head tilted to the side as she scrutinized me. It should have made me feel uncomfortable, but there was nothing threatening about it.

"That's very kind, but I'm pretty miserable with weaponry."

She laughed, and the sound reminded me immediately of her father. "Well, still. Everyone needs a good knife. Maybe we can find you something you feel comfortable with? I'm sure there's lessons to be had as well, if you care to learn. Myself, or my sister could show you, though Calla is also very skilled." She tapped her finger to her chin. "Honestly I'd bet anyone at d'Arcan would be happy to catch you up."

"I'll keep that in mind. What's a conclave?"

"That's what we call our settlement outside of Revalia."

"There are a lot of you, then? Stone kin?"

Imogen reached for her cup, then seemed to remember she didn't want it. "Yes. We have grown steadily in numbers over the years we've been there."

"And a ... Dark blade? What's that?" I felt like I'd stumbled into a whole other world and it was exposing just how sheltered my upbringing had been.

"Oh. It's a sword or dagger, is all. Just forged in a way that enhances its effectiveness against angels. Some fae too." She shrugged. "Greta is largely responsible for our understanding of them, actually. Light blades are forged with angelic essence—blood or a feather usually—and are more dangerous against demons. Dark blades are forged with demon essence and are more effective against angels and fae." She frowned, seeing me tense. "Sorry, did I say something wrong?"

"No, no. It's just, I'm both, so it sounds like I'd be in danger from either one."

"Plain steel is always an option, though of course still deadly." She nodded empathetically. "In any case, it seemed like a good idea to get started on some additional weapons for the armory, given the circumstances."

It was me. *I* was the circumstances. My presence required an entirely new batch of weapons to be made. My stomach twisted. No wonder Tap was uncertain about having sealed the bond.

Tap stepped away from Ophelia as she started laughing and they joined us back in the small living area.

"Thank you, Ophelia," Tap said, even giving her a little bow.

"Think about all I've said," was her response. "Both of you. I appreciate the portal. Set it up on your way out?"

"Of course. Nice to see you again, Imogen."

"Tap."

I stood as it became clear we were leaving. I turned to the sorceress, confused, and a bit relieved that we were going. "Thank you."

"Come back to see me if you need to, Phin. My door is always open to you."

Flattered, I responded that I would, said my goodbyes to Imogen, and followed Tap outside.

He remained silent as he led me to one side of the yard, the weight of the wards pressing down the second we were out of the cozy hut.

"Here," he said softly, reaching out for my hand. My heart leapt and I took it, stunned as I watched him pour what looked like black sludge out of the little iron cauldron onto the trunk of a massive tree. The thick liquid dripped and expanded into an arched door shape. "Ready?"

I nodded, and he pulled me along with him through the new portal.

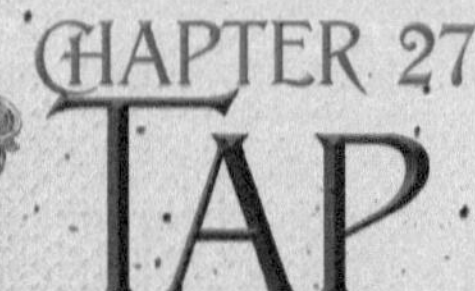

CHAPTER 27
TAP

SEIR GREETED US the moment we stepped back into the hall, his normally jovial expression serious. He forced a smile. "I'm glad you're back. A new doorway directly to the Dread Forest? She *does* like you. Did you have a good visit?"

Phin glanced between us and excused herself. "I'm going to go freshen up and get to work."

"You don't have to—"

She waved her hand, already walking toward the living area. "It's alright, it will be good for me."

Seir looked at me. "It went well?"

I shook my head, unsure what the appropriate answer to his question was. "What is it? Why do you have that look on your face?" I asked.

"Three angels were spotted outside the glade," he replied, expression grave. I glanced over my shoulder, glad Phin hadn't lingered. That was probably the very last thing she needed to hear right now. "They were on the same road that Hailon and I took when we fell into the ruins. Coltor said they looked as though they were searching for a break in the wards, like they could sense they were there."

"When?"

"This morning. Coltor was late coming back from patrol. Hailon filled me in just a little while ago."

"They've moved on though?"

"Yes. They continued north on the road, never stopped, and didn't turn back. He followed them to be sure. Coltor said they seemed confused about how they'd wandered into a village in the Emankor Valley, but the magical boundary did its job."

"So did he," I confirmed. "Do you think it's possible they showed up there by accident?"

"I don't know, but them showing up anywhere she's been feels like more than coincidence."

My gut churned. I agreed. "Was there any sign of Ramsey?"

"No, but Coltor was watching them, not what might be coming up behind them."

"Phin didn't have her bracelet yet when we visited," I mused as I turned the ring on my index finger, thoughts spinning like they were trapped in a whirlwind. "Did you warn Rylan and Magnus to be watchful?"

"I'm headed there next."

"Good." As he turned toward the doorway to d'Arcan, I heard the high-pitched whine of the gate activating and put my arm out in front of him. "Wait."

Vassago and Greta stepped through, both dressed in heavy coats but looking perfectly thrilled to be going on a little excursion.

"Welcome," I greeted them.

"What's the matter?" Vassago asked, immediately noticing our expressions.

"Angels were spotted outside the glade," I said. "Seir just finished telling me about it."

Vassago swore.

Greta lifted her hand cautiously. "Sorry, but which way to Phin? I need to speak with her before we continue on to Vincara."

"I'll show you." Seir hustled away with Greta on his heels, leaving Vassago and I staring at one another in the hall. "Would you like to sit?" I gestured toward the living area, and he followed. Seir joined us shortly after we'd gotten settled.

"Is it possible they're tracking her?" Seir asked.

"I don't see how."

"Where is your new mirror?" Vassago asked.

"Here." I gestured to the low side table beside my recliner.

"Good. Keep it close. I'll test it from the village. If it works from there as well, I'll try to fix your original on our way back."

"I'll go ahead to d'Arcan and fill Rylan in," Seir offered, not hesitating to make for the portals. "Bring me back some flowers, would you, Vago? As many white ones as possible."

"For you? Or for Hailon?"

Seir's grin finally appeared. "Hailon, naturally."

"Of course. For *her.*"

Seir scoffed and was gone.

Vassago glanced around. "What a strange place this is, brother."

I couldn't help but laugh at the way he cringed into himself, as though the space around him was offensive in some way.

"I'm wounded. You spent decades in a sarcophagus below a monastery and now live in a magic school, but *my* home is strange?"

He sputtered a laugh just as Greta reappeared. "Fair enough. Did you get what you needed?" Vassago asked her.

"Yes, I'm ready now." She pinned me with a stare that told me she wasn't overly happy with me. I wondered what all she and Phin had shared in the short time she was gone. "The libraries are fantastic, Tap. I can understand why Phin is so happy here."

"That's very kind of you to say." The compliment struck as deep as her glare, and I barely stopped myself before asking her if Phin had actually said that, especially after our morning. Her happiness mattered as much as ever.

Vassago got up, and I walked them both to the doorway they needed to access the little village.

"Should we bring back a bouquet or two for Phin as well? Since you may not get out for a bit?"

"Alright." I was disappointed in myself that I hadn't thought of it first now that he'd mentioned it. Something like that would probably make my impending apologies go a little further.

"What flowers does she like best?" Greta asked.

"I don't know," I admitted, stomach rolling unhappily. "Though she seemed quite happy with the wildflowers that Merry gave her in the glade."

"We'll choose a few. Maybe she'll tell you once she has some in front of her to select from."

Greta spun on my brother, mouth open. "You sneak. Is that how you did it with me?"

He chuckled. "Perhaps it is, Dragonfly."

"And here I thought Belmont somehow clued you in."

"I should let you continue to blame the bird," he joked. "But I also have a habit of following you around the markets. So really, figuring out your preferences—especially before Grace can—is an ongoing challenge I happily accept." He drew her close and kissed her temple, her frustration melting away. Their dynamic was so warm and natural, it was easy to feel a bit envious of their bond.

"Is there anything else you need?" Greta asked me.

"Not that I can think of, thank you."

"Of course." Greta waved just before they stepped through.

I did a quick check of the portals, the unique hum each of them made registering in my mind as I walked past. Activity as a whole was low, which should have been a relief, but instead felt suspicious. Seir still hadn't returned and I was restless, so once

I'd completed my rounds, I made a tray of tea and finger foods for Phin and carried them into the library.

Nearly the whole table had been cleared, and I could see that she'd arranged a system on the long, bare tabletop for more efficient sorting. Her brow was furrowed with focus as she paced back and forth along the far side of the table, tossing contracts in their corresponding crates. Normally, I'd just leave the tray and go, but something drew me to stay.

"Shall I pour it, or leave it in the pot?" I asked. She was frowning, muttering to herself. I wasn't sure she'd even noticed I was in the room with her. "Phin?"

Her head snapped up. "Sorry, what?"

"Tea?" I gestured to the tray.

"Oh, yes, thank you." Her head dropped, and she scooped up another armful of paperwork, pacing and whispering to herself.

I prepared two cups, and pulled out one of the chairs for myself, watching as she continued without pausing for two more stacks.

"Phin," I said her name gently, worry beginning to claw at me. I'd watched her work before, but this was unlike anything I'd ever seen her do. After what she'd learned this morning, I couldn't help but feel responsible for her distress.

She collected and distributed another stack. Then another. At the third, I stood and walked over to her, realizing as I got close that her face was dotted with sweat. As she hesitated, reaching for another pile of contracts, I rested my hands on her shoulders. "Phin. Stop." Her breathing was erratic, and she shifted as though she might try to pull away. All at once, her body sagged, and I stepped back and braced as she fell into me, wrapping my arms around her to balance us both. I stilled, the shake of her shoulders indicating that she was crying.

"It's my fault," she gasped. "They're in danger because of me."

I gripped her harder. "What? Nonsense, everyone is fine."

"The angels nearly found the glade! Greta was here, and Seir said—"

"Coltor noticed them straightaway and made sure they kept their distance. He's been guarding the ruins of Emankor Castle, which is right next to the glade, for ages. He's very good at it. There are powerful wards around the whole area. Seir and Hailon are there, and Merry—"

"They could all be hurt because I went there. The angels were looking for *me*. Imogen said they're making swords specifically to fight angels. That's *my* fault." She hiccupped and my heart slammed against my ribs. "Maybe Father Morton's approach to all this was just fine." She sniffled and looked up at me, eyes rounding. "I'm sorry." I held fast as she tried to pull away.

"No." The word came out as a growl, and she stiffened. I gentled my tone. "His approach was suffocating. A punishment when you did nothing wrong." I took a deep breath and tried to clear the red from my vision and the fire from my lungs before continuing. My mate was distressed, and I was fully prepared to take on whatever opponent I needed to in order to soothe her, to convince her that this wasn't her fault. Even if that was me. "Nothing and no one would get through without someone noticing, is my point. Merry alone would have every creature in the glade alerting her. Jacks is there as well, and he's not exactly a regular animal. Do you trust me, Phin? Despite what happened this morning, what you learned. Can you trust me a little while longer?"

Those bright violet orbs shimmered as she blinked. "Yes."

I gazed down at her, willing my sincerity to break through whatever panic she'd worked herself into. I ran the backs of my fingers down the side of her face, the little sigh she made feeding my needy soul. "Please believe me when I say that no harm will come to you, nor to them. This is not your fault. And Father Morton may have been well intentioned, but he went about many things in a way that actually did you harm, and I will not forgive him for that." Phin only stared at me. My heart was racing, her lavender-and-parchment scent in my nose and her warmth pressed up against me. "I will never forgive myself for the same reason." She rested her face against my chest, and I bent to kiss her forehead before I could stop myself. Her skin was fevered, a match to the burn in my chest.

"I don't understand, Tap."

"I know, Feather. But I promise to explain." After a long moment I straightened, indulging in a chance to lean my cheek against the top of her head. "Come. Rest yourself." I pulled out a chair and slid her into it, then poured her a hot cup of tea. Her hands trembled as she lifted it to her mouth, and my gut rolled again as I reached out to help her. "Are you truly that scared?"

Her lips thinned, and I could see the moment she decided not to deny it. "Yes." Her eyes flickered to mine, then dropped back to the table. "I know what they want me for. I know they will hurt others to get it. I'm sorry."

I hated that she was apologizing for this, for anything. "They won't get near you." A growl edged my words again, and I saw her blink in surprise. "Please don't apologize. I knew the risks when I suggested you come to stay here. I do not regret anything about that. Nothing. Understand?" I did not look away until she nodded in agreement, but I could see the question plainly on her face. I knew the conversation was coming, whether I was prepared for it or not. "Good."

"But—"

"I don't regret what happened last night, Phin. I swear it."

She rubbed at her forehead. "But you said you wanted to break the bond."

"Not because I don't want to be mated to you, Phin."

"Then why?" The tears in her eyes made me feel like the lowest wretch to ever crawl out of the pits.

"Because I was panicking. I wanted to undo a mistake—"

"So you think what we did was a mistake?" Her voice rose sharply, the pain in it cutting straight through to my bones.

"*No*." I shook my head firmly. "No."

"Then *what*? I trusted you. I trusted myself. And now I don't have the slightest clue what's real and what's not. Everything feels ... too big." She gestured vaguely, and then curled in on herself as though trying to contain it.

I took her hand between both of mine. "This is real. Everything I said last night, everything you feel. All of it." I inhaled, organizing my thoughts so as not to cause her any more stress. "My mistake was that I took the same thing from you everyone else has, Feather. Your choice."

She frowned. "No, you didn't. I participated freely in what happened, Tap. I was the one who kissed you, remember? Nothing happened that I didn't want."

I stared into her violet eyes, willing the right words to come, hoping that I hadn't already ruined everything. "Would you have done the same if you'd known it would tie you to me forever?" My chest ached when she didn't respond immediately, but I tried to be patient.

Her brow furrowed, and her jaw muscles flexed. "I wouldn't ... There's no way I would have pushed that far if part of me hadn't known," she whispered, stealing my breath. "I chose, Tap. Just because we didn't discuss it, though we probably should have, doesn't change that I had already thought it through." She glanced around the table, and I watched her wrestle with whether or not she should go right back to the frenetic sorting to push away the uncomfortable emotions.

"Alright. We can discuss it more later if you like. But for now, I think you need some rest. You don't look well." I pushed the plate of fruit and cheese toward her.

"I'm not hungry. But ... I think I'm going to take a hot bath.

Maybe I'll try to nap." She got to her feet and took a few steps toward the library door.

"I'll check on you in a while?"

She hesitated in the doorway, her hand on the wood. Eventually, she nodded.

I sat there for several minutes, willing the burn in my chest to settle before collecting the tray and returning it to the kitchen. As I rinsed out the cups, a shrieking teakettle noise went off, which was odd, because the stove wasn't lit. After listening for a moment, I rushed out to the living area to find it was coming from the new scrying mirror Vassago had given me.

"Are you already finished?" I could see Greta over Vassago's shoulder, the both of them bunded up and collecting fluffy snowflakes on their clothes.

"Yes, we have everything we came for. I'll have to come back to visit the monastery another time, it's just too bloody cold today." Greta stuck out her tongue to catch some flakes behind him. "Was just checking the range on your new device, see you in a moment."

The glass went dark, and they were walking through the portal from the little village before I fully made it into the hall.

"Good trip?"

"It's a cute place," Greta said, handing over three wrapped bundles. "The apothecary had a ton of things I didn't expect."

"I felt the same way when I visited. Was the old man there today?" I led them toward the first library, where the main mirror had been returned to the wall. Vassago's mist crept over his skin, pale gray and wispy as he worked on making the adjustments.

"Yes, the proprietor was there. Unfortunately, he'll be taking an extended leave. His daughter will be running the shop in his absence." His eyes connected with mine and flashed red.

I frowned. "That's unfortunate." Not to mention slightly suspicious.

"Indeed. But it's in his best interest."

I frowned. "Explain."

Vassago smirked. "I left the priest for you to deal with. The apothecary was rather apologetic. He claimed it was a crisis of conscience that led him to tell Phin he could no longer make the tincture."

"So there isn't an actual issue preventing it?"

"No, there is," Greta's tone was sharp. "There's an herb that's become very difficult to find. But instead of seeking out an alternative, he'd just been using less and less of the more expensive herbs."

"So, it was actually getting less effective?"

"Yes. And there were other modifications approved by Father Morton." I could tell by the disgust shared between them that I wasn't going to like whatever came next. "Among other things, the apothecary added in hemlock, foxglove, and quieting cane as they were readily available and had similar effect as what he couldn't source. I don't know what the Heavenly alternatives might have been for the original formula."

My blood flashed icy, then rage took over. "Aren't those all—"

"Poison." Greta nodded. "Damaging to mind, heart, and voice, respectively. All three are known poisons separately, but together? Even just her normal dose of a drop a day?" She clenched her jaw and her fists. "I'm sure that's why Ophelia destroyed the rest of it. That alone explains her irritated throat and likely her episodes as well." She shook her head and stepped toward the double doors that led to the deals library. "Is Phin still in there?"

"No, she went to her room to rest. She wasn't feeling well."

Greta frowned. "Tell her I'm working as fast as I can. The blue elixir I sent with her should help with healing and the light green with silver shimmer may do a decent job with some of the other symptoms until I can get the new tincture made."

"I'll tell her. Thank you both."

"Our pleasure. Did Seir ever come back?" Vassago asked.

"No."

He grunted. "I'll be trying again from d'Arcan. I'll let you know if he's still there. Perhaps he went straight home."

"That's what I assumed."

They made their way back to the hall, Greta more and more pensive.

"Everything okay?"

"Yes, it's fine. If she needs anything, just send for me," she said ominously.

"I will." I caught Vassago looking around again, face pinched as though he smelled something rotten. "Come visit any time."

"Perhaps I will. Go wait by your mirror."

"You are not in charge here, Vago. But thank you for bringing the flowers."

He grinned and pulled me in for a quick embrace, and once he let go I kissed Greta's cheek and bade them farewell once again. I'd barely gotten into the library when the mirror howled a terrifyingly human sound, and his pleased face showed through the glass.

"That's awful. Can you change it to the teakettle sound like the other?"

"Will you hear it if I do?"

"Yes. Who in the world *couldn't* hear that?"

He chuffed, highly amused. "Rylan. He never seems to hear it unless it's the most terrible noise possible. Too many stairs and distance between rooms, or at least that's what he claims."

"Well, we're not dealing with the same kind of space here, so the whistle is much preferred to the howl."

"I'll change it." It was nice to see Vassago in such good humor.

We spoke through the device long enough for him to tell me that Seir was in fact still at the collegium, and that he, Rylan, Magnus, Coltor, and several other stone kin soldiers were working out a guard rotation for both the glade and Revalia, and Magnus would be sending several units through to the doors that Coltor had noted with unusual activity.

The angel sighting had put everyone on high alert, and they were wasting no time setting up some defenses just in case.

While using the mirror was a bit strange, it was nice to be able to speak to them easily if I needed to. There was no telling what trouble might find us in the coming days, and I told them so. Without hesitation, they informed me that the whole of the stone kin outpost, plus our family, would respond in kind should something happen.

When I finally signed off and headed toward the kitchen to assemble something substantial for us to eat, grateful if exhausted. That peace didn't last, though.

I'd just begun peeling a potato when I heard something heavy fall, and Phin's muffled cry.

CHAPTER 28
TAP

I BURST THROUGH PHIN'S bathroom door and found her hunched over on the floor next to the tub, water splashed all over the room.

She looked up at me, fear and pain in her eyes. She didn't speak, but I could see the plea for help plainly written on her face. Her arms moved to cover her exposed flesh, and I surged forward.

"Saints." I grabbed one of the plush towels she'd left on the counter by the sink and wrapped it around her body. "Are you hurt?"

Phin cried out again in her quiet rasp as her wings partially erupted from her back and then retracted again. "I don't know what's happening," she gasped.

Phin groaned, and the appendages violently burst through again and fully extended, the silver feathers looking wilted and worn, like they were ready to molt.

"Can you control it at all?"

"No. I'm trying, but it's like they're separate from me. Like they can't ... hear me." Phin's body curled in on itself even further and she stuttered a pained cry as they retracted again. "I haven't used them in a very, very long time." She sobbed, and the bond roared. I despised how helpless I felt.

"Shall I pick you up?" I asked.

Phin nodded aggressively, and I wasted no time scooping her into my arms. I hated myself for feeling relief because I was holding her considering her discomfort. She was burning up. I tucked the towel around her more securely when one of the ends flipped open and held it closed with my arm. I carried her out of the bathroom, intending to lay her in her bed only to find that it was stripped to the bare mattress. After a brief hesitation, I took her across the hall into my room.

My private chambers were set up the same as Phin's, though done in a darker color palette. Where hers was cream and pastels, mine was navy and charcoal. I preferred my mattress on the floor rather than up on a frame, and I had amassed a pile of assorted pillows, blankets and cushions over the years in an effort to make the bed the more appealing place to sleep. None of them had worked on me so far, but the collection of them all piled off to one side made the space look inviting enough that Phin reached for the bed as we got near it.

I laid her down on her side and went to my armoire, pulling out one of my oldest, softest shirts. It had been made with custom openings in the back for my wings to slide through. I hadn't worn it in eons.

"Here." I helped her shrug into it, mentally cataloging the sprinkling of freckles across her shoulders, the grouping of moles in the shape of a star with one very short leg on the right side of her ribs, the faint silvery scar across her lower back on the left. I inhaled firmly through my nose as my chest burned and my cock twitched, the sight of her in my clothing affecting me far more intensely than I'd dared consider.

She groaned and pulled her knees into her chest as her wings appeared again, flaring wide. I reached out and stroked along them, several feathers falling out. I collected them, impulsively stuffing them into the little pocket on my shirt right over my heart.

"Can you feel me touching them? Or are they fully disconnected from you?"

Phin made a very different kind of noise, one that made my brain stop for several heartbeats. I began to sweat, and struggled to stop the inappropriate visions from flashing across my thoughts, the ache between my legs rapidly becoming as profound as the one in my chest.

"Yes."

I removed my hands like they'd been burned, forcing several slow breaths so I could calm down. This was not the time to fall prey to my own base desires. "I'm sorry."

"It's okay." She sobbed quietly as they retracted again, curling into herself on the bed. "What do I do?"

"I don't know. But you're welcome to stay here as long as you like. I'm sure this is more comfortable than a cold bathroom floor." I moved some blankets and pillows closer, and she reached for the ones she wanted, curling herself around a pillow, burying her legs under a blanket.

I did my best to soothe Phin as her body racked itself again and again, minutes stretching into hours as we lay there together. Sweat dotted her forehead as she quietly screamed her throat raw, her wings so aggressively punching out several times that I'd worried about her breaking the fragile bones and had collected a whole pile of damaged feathers. I didn't know where to put my hands, but I was unable to keep them to myself with my mate writhing in pain before me. At one point I gathered her into my arms and pulled her across my body, her face buried in my chest as I gently rocked us both. I stroked her hair and apologized for my inability to stop what was happening to her. I reassured her she was going to be alright and that we'd figure out a way to stop whatever had gone wrong even though I had no idea where to begin with such a thing. I would have promised her anything if it would have soothed her even for a few minutes.

Eventually, the time between episodes finally started to stretch, and then they were finally gone altogether. I forced myself to rouse as I started to fall asleep.

Phin was dozing on my chest, and her eyes fluttered open as I brushed some damp curls off her forehead. "I'm going to go get a few things. You'll be alright?"

She managed a weak nod and slid off me into a stack of pillows. I climbed to my feet, loath to leave her in such a state but eager to at the very least find her something to eat. She had to be exhausted after all that, and I'd been interrupted while preparing dinner.

Every step I took toward the door increased the pressure in my chest, but I forced myself to ignore it. I left her there, on my bed, in my clothes.

I'd never been more hesitant to leave nor more eager to return to that room.

I USED TOWELS to clean the water off the floor in her bathroom, then I threw them and her discarded clothing in the washing tub. I went back into her room and pocketed her jewelry, hopeful getting it on her skin would help. After checking for the right colors, I also took the elixirs Greta had mentioned. The new mirror Vassago had made me joined the other items after I did a speed-walk through the great hall, checking as well as redirecting and disabling as many gates as I could. When I finally made it back to the kitchen, I prepared a tray of food and drinks, driven to tend to her needs even if I wasn't sure what they might be. The bouquets of flowers Vassago had brought me from Vincara all got hastily dropped into one large vessel, and I carried that in the crook of my elbow, pleased that there was a lovely fragrance to the bundle.

When I got back, Phin had woken and was finishing up her own project. I nearly dropped the tray as I took her in. My shirt was puddled around her thighs as she sat on her heels, arranging pillows and blankets along every edge of my mattress. She was sniffing them before she put them down, frowning with pensive focus as she moved everything to her liking. Some of her feathers were tucked into the folds of the fabrics, an intentional mixing of her scent and mine.

She glanced up, finding me lingering in the doorway. "It felt wrong." Her hands went between her knees, like she was trying to keep them from reaching out again.

"It looks very comfortable now." I gestured with the tray. "May I?"

Phin's eyes shone with pleasure that I'd asked her permission, but her expression changed in a flash. "It's your bed," she whispered. "I should have asked *you*, not the other way around. I'm sorry—"

"No, this is nice. I like your arrangement much more than what I had. Do whatever you need to do to make it comfortable."

Her smile was timid, but the glow in her eyes thrilled me. "I thought you might want something to eat."

"In your bed?"

I shrugged, setting down the tray in the middle of the nest-like configuration she'd created. I lifted the vase from between my arm and body and handed it to her.

"Thank you." After burying her face in the bouquet, she set it on the low bedside table. As she turned back, Phin reached over her shoulder, rubbing at the muscle where her wing ways were hidden.

"Does it hurt?"

"Not really, just sore." She shivered. "I hope whatever that was is over."

"Me too." I tested the temperature of her forehead with the back of my hand, relieved to find her cooler than before I'd left. "Feeling better?"

She nodded. "Yes." Her mouth opened like she was going to say something else, but instead, she picked up a piece of cheese and turned, taking a proper look around my room. "I actually was starting to believe you didn't have a bed or anything, that maybe the room was just empty."

I chuffed a laugh as I poured us both some tea. "Why would you think that?"

"I never hear you come or go from this room. I'm not even sure you sleep."

"I do. Just rarely in here. The recliner has been where I've sought rest for a long time."

"I find it impossible to believe you find that chair more comfortable than this mattress," she grumbled, shaking her head as she reached for another snack.

I sighed. "It's not about comfort so much as convenience. If I'm in the recliner, I can hear the doors."

"Hear them?"

"Yes. Each of them has a unique sound when activated. Even while sleeping, I can hear activity from there and respond if needed."

"Mmm. I noticed they all look different; I guess it makes sense they sound different as well." Her brows pinched together as she chewed. "Can't you make it so they don't work while you sleep? You did something like that when we went to the glade."

"Yes. I did it just now, in fact."

"So why not every night?"

I shook my head and reached for an apple slice, my body responding to her calm, muscles relaxing and heartbeat slowing. "It limits use of the doorways too much."

"So why aren't there more locations they can be watched from? Like in the glade?"

"That would put the full burden of watching them on someone else. It's *my* job."

She frowned. "That's too much for one person though. You'll get sick. Nobody can function on no sleep. Have you ever asked for help? Told someone it's simply too much?"

"I have help now. Seir and Coltor can assist. Occasionally, Seir calls in a favor, and the majority are monitored from Hell. Merry has taken over the familiar bonds, and you're here for the deals. It's infinitely better than it was. But I've done it this way always. For centuries." I bit back the lie that almost slipped out, the one where I told her I was fine. I knew I wasn't. I was better, but I had been slowly breaking for a very long time, and it would take a while for me to be fully back to myself.

"But it's still too much. And it sounds like you're doing things the old way just because. Maybe there are more efficient methods you could employ. You know, if you asked some questions?"

"You sound like my brothers." I couldn't stop the smile that tugged at the corners of my mouth.

"I can't help it if they're right." She huffed. As she reached for a teacup, her eyes widened in alarm, and her body stiffened.

"Phin?"

"Wings." She panted the word just before they slowly slid out, flexed, then retracted. "That one was better." Her upper body trembled. "Didn't hurt as much."

"That's good," I said, remembering the items in my pocket. "Here." I dropped her jewelry into her hand and set the mirror and elixir vials on the tray next to the cups. "I thought maybe these would help."

"Thank you." She looped the necklace over her head and fastened the bracelet around her wrist. She picked up the little vials and inspected them both, the shimmer catching the light.

"Greta said the blue for healing, the light green for the other things, and if you needed anything, to reach out. I'm sorry, I wish I would have remembered earlier. Would it help to speak with her? I know you did earlier, but perhaps whatever this is changes things?"

"Yes. I think I should."

I activated the mirror, and Vassago's face popped up.

"Miss me so soon, Tap?" he teased.

"Hardly. I've seen your face more in the last few weeks than in the last several decades, brother."

Vago snorted. "And what a treat that must be for you, you're welcome. What can I do for you, brother?"

"Phin would like to speak with Greta, if she has a moment?"

Vago's playful expression dropped into concern. "Of course. I hope everything is alright."

I looked at Phin, who was taking in the device with wide eyes. "Not really. Phin is experiencing some odd symptoms."

"Odd how?" Greta's face joined Vassago's in the glass. She pulled a pair of protective spectacles up off her eyes, resting them on the top of her head as she looked between us.

I hesitated again, but Phin nodded that I should continue. "She's been feverish. Her wings broke through and retracted many times over the last couple of hours. They are unresponsive to her control."

"Mm. Phin?"

"Yes?" Phin, who had been allowing me to guide the conversation thus far, clutched a pillow to her chest.

"I don't know how long it will take me to make a new batch. Not long, once we can find some of the difficult-to-locate ingredients, but that has to happen first."

Phin clenched. "Ophelia destroyed what I had left."

"So you said, I'm sorry. But she was right, it was for the best. Are you taking the light-green elixir?"

"I will."

"Every day, or at least as many as possible." She raised an eyebrow and Phin nodded that she understood. "You've mentioned not feeling like yourself several times, what does that mean exactly? I want to be sure I get this right."

Phin shifted next to me, picking at a thread on the shirt. "Before I moved to the crossroads, my freezing episodes were more frequent. Now they aren't as often but they're unpredictable. I was pretty numb when I lived at the church, if I'm honest. I thought at first when I got here that maybe I was just remembering how to feel again." My heart squeezed for her, for all the years she'd been forced to exist as a shell of herself. "Now, everything is extremes. My emotions, my hunger, even my ... temperature." Phin's eyes widened and Greta nodded gently.

"I'm moving as quickly as I can, I promise. But I think you need to prepare for the possibility that it's already too late. You will likely start to heal from the side effects of the harmful parts of the old formula as well, which may cause new symptoms."

My stomach rolled. "Too late? For what exactly? And what are we healing?"

Phin's mouth tightened, but she didn't address my questions.

"The apothecary had only guessed what herbs would work based on the sample from your original version of the tincture. I was thinking maybe we'd try shepherd's plight? It's difficult to find, perhaps more so even than bride's bane, but wouldn't come with some of the negative side effects. Given what Ophelia tasted ..." Her mouth tightened with frustration. "I want to find you the right recipe, Phin. We're basically starting fresh."

"The trio of angels visited not long before they could no longer produce it for you, didn't they?" I asked, remembering Father Morton mentioning that during our first visit. Phin nodded. I made eye contact with Vassago, and he quirked an eyebrow. Perhaps the apothecary had been encouraged by the visit to stop making the thing that kept Phin safe. That was a mixed blessing, given that they were poisoning her to keep her hidden. I spun my ring, wondering if I could work in a little bit of time with my tattooing quill. It seemed the beginning and end of my stress came back to setting ink lately. "There are several places that might be suitable for Rylan's poison garden I haven't had a chance to explore yet. Either of those herbs might grow wild in those places. We can check? If it will help." Anything to help. And I wasn't even positive I knew what we were talking about, though if bride's bane was involved, I could make a reasonable guess.

"Yes. Please," Phin answered quickly.

"Of course. I'll ask Seir if he can mind the hall so we can explore a few starting tomorrow morning."

Greta nodded, expression grave. "Good luck. I'll see if there's anything else I can find in the meantime, and I've already asked Rylan to check with his sources to see if they have any leads. Starting the mix without either bride's bane or a suitable replacement and an incomplete formula won't do much good. There are other elixirs in my books, I've just not found one that meets all the requirements yet. But I'll keep searching for you."

"Thank you, Greta."

"Best to you both. We'll be in touch soon." I severed the connection, which left Phin and I to stare at one another.

"I won't pressure you for details you don't want to share, Phin, but could you reassure me that you're alright at least?" My pulse was loud in my ears, my hands unsteady from the way my blood was surging. It wouldn't have surprised me if my demonic features had started to show as out of control as I felt.

"I'm okay. I mean, I'm not sick. It's a … fertility thing."

I inhaled slowly through my nose. "I do most of my tattooing when I'm agitated, and I could use a little bit of focus right now." I realized as I said the words she might think I was implying something more since that's what had happened before. "Just tattooing, not—"

She cracked a smile and silenced me with a finger to my lips. "I know. But could you do it in here instead? I wouldn't mind watching, but I also don't want to leave." Even she seemed confused by that, but I was proud of her for asserting her desire.

"Of course. I'll go get my things."

I left her there, looking adrift in her sea of blankets and pillows, every part of my routine upside down.

She looked like every dream I'd never allowed myself to have. I hoped I'd get to keep her.

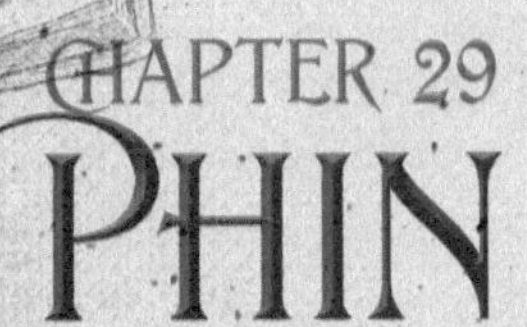

CHAPTER 29
PHIN

WHILE TAP WAS gone, I made use of his bathroom. He was always so tidy it seemed like I'd stumbled on a secret when I discovered his bathroom counter was rather cluttered with products. His shaving cup and brush needed a thorough cleaning and a new bar of soap. His razor blade was starting to rust. Several glass bottles in assorted shapes, sizes, and colors sat in an order only he understood, awaiting use. I pulled the cork from one and sniffed, discovering what had to be his aftershave. Clean towels hung in half-folded disarray on the bar while the used ones lay in a sad pile on the floor, and several items of clothing were also mixed in the mess.

It was nice to get a glimpse at his chaos beyond a dirty teacup left on the table next to his chair or a shirt forgotten in the laundry room—the flaws made him seem more real.

I climbed back onto the firm, oversize mattress. After arranging a spot for Tap to sit, I snuggled in with several pillows at my back and three cuddly blankets.

Shortly after I'd gotten comfortable, Tap returned with his quill, inkpots, and somehow, more snacks and a freshly brewed pot of tea.

"I didn't know if you'd be tired yet, or ..." He trailed off, stacking the new items on the tray alongside the old ones.

It was quiet between us as he got set up, the only light from a lamp he lit and set on the table next to him. He removed his spectacles and put them next to the light.

The dark color of the walls and floor, the coziness of the décor ... all of it had me sinking into the mattress. I couldn't understand in the least why he couldn't sleep here.

I silently watched him start another small section of tiny designs on his leg before finding my voice again, the rhythm of the quill point against his skin hypnotic.

"That's my scroll," I whispered.

He paused, peering closer at the marks he was leaving. "Is it? That was not intentional." He glanced over at me. "May I use your design, Phin?"

For some reason, the idea made me want to cry again. "Yes. Of course you can."

"Thank you." His mouth twitched into a gentle smile, and he continued.

My eyes strayed from him to the huge vase on the table. It was packed full, flowers and greenery spilling over the edges of the pottery.

"The bouquet is beautiful. Where did you get all those flowers?"

"Vassago and Greta picked them up in Aymonroux."

"Oh." I smiled as a happy memory bubbled up. "The shop would sometimes gift the ones nearing the end of their bloom that hadn't sold to the church. Father would have me put them in little vases at the ends of the row of pews." The uneven lip and off-kilter handle hinted that the pottery was likely his. "Do you have them in a pitcher?"

The tips of Tap's ears went pink. "Yes. I was in a hurry."

"Well, it works perfectly."

"As a vase perhaps, but as a pitcher it falls a little short. I forgot to put on a spout or even narrow the lip so that it would pour well. I went through a phase of making functional vessels—pitchers, pots, cups. Thankfully my skill improved as I went along."

"Maybe I need to visit that workshop. I always wanted to see if I could make a bowl or plate," I said, which earned me a smile. "They smell nice. The flowers."

"Do you have a favorite?"

"Irises and tulips," I said without hesitation. "They always bloom early and aren't afraid of a little frost or snow. Once those flowers start to break the soil, I know I can hope for warmer weather soon. And the color, of course; both come in lovely shades of purple."

"Very logical. I'm afraid there aren't any of either in this bouquet."

"That's alright. My only complaint about them is they don't have much of a fragrance. And these are nice, something in there smells lovely. I'm not a fan of most greenery."

His mouth twitched, and he looked up from his work. "I gathered."

"But the bits of ice leaf and fern they use in the bouquets don't bother me." He dipped his quill in the pot of ink and looked away, focusing on his work. I appreciated that he was trying to put me at ease, take the pressure off me. It allowed me to find my words much easier. "There was ... an incident, in the gardens." Tap's silver gaze flitted to mine, the quill in his hand tilted away from his skin. "I had just turned sixty. Because I went back and forth so often between Earth and Heaven, the way I aged wasn't as predictable as being in either place all the time. On top of that, any angel born around the time I was is ... different."

"Different?"

I nodded and sat up, needing something in my hands as a distraction. I poured myself a tea and picked up one of the little finger sandwiches he'd brought. "My mother guessed it was a response to the angels not being made."

Tap's head tilted. "Is it an illness? Are adult angels becoming unwell? Dying?"

I shook my head. "From what I understand, established angels don't seem to be as affected as newer generations. But the bestowing of wings on new arrivals isn't working. New angels are not being made."

"That sounds rather desperate indeed. For how long?"

"I'm not sure, but as long as I can remember."

"You said your generation is different?"

I swallowed, focusing on the smear of tea leaves in the bottom of my cup that resembled a crescent moon. "Yes. We're ... equipped ... for more earthly types of reproduction."

"While not all were, that's been true of quite a few of the angelic line for a very long time. Nephilim wouldn't exist otherwise."

"Not like this." I fidgeted. "Many of us now have a very pronounced fertility cycle. Like some animals have." I could see the questions flit across Tap's intently focused face, but he remained silent. "Some have one every month, others just a few times a year." I explained to him as I had to Greta, that when you succumb to it, you are completely indisposed for at least a few days.

"That's ... I don't even know what to say about that." He bowed his head again, the quill scratching along his skin with intensity. "And that's what the tincture was for? To stop that from happening?"

"Yes. I've taken it since my first cycle."

Tap settled back against the cushions, arranging himself in a way that he could work a bit easier and still look at me. "Something happened in the gardens, you said?"

I drank the rest of my tea and returned the cup to the tray, even the memory causing my heart to beat faster. "I was with some other Nephilim, and we were sneaking around where we weren't allowed to be. I wanted to see some of the creatures." I swallowed. "Instead, we found a walled garden." Tap's head raised for a moment, but he seemed to understand that his work with the quill was keeping us both focused. "We just thought it was something restricted, something we weren't allowed to enjoy because we were Nephilim and not full angels. Admittedly, we all had chips on our shoulders about being treated differently, so it felt like we'd won something by getting to just walk right in. We should have been more cautious." A tickle in my irritated throat sent me into a coughing fit. Tap stopped his design and I reached for more tea before he could, sipping until I had eased the sensation and continued in barely more than a whisper. "The stone walls were three times as tall as me, with vines growing all over them. The flowers were blooming, everything looked so healthy, so beautiful. I was enjoying looking around when I suddenly got very hot and felt a little out of sorts. I sat down to rest, not realizing that nobody else was as far into the garden as I was. There were four men and two other women with me. I could see the two other women being carried out, so I can only assume it was because they were feeling the same way I was. But they'd all been closer to the door. They'd heard the patrol coming." I exhaled, remnants of the fear from the moment I realized they had all gone increasing my pulse.

"They *all* left you there? *Alone*?" he spat, clearly furious.

"I don't think it was intentional. And the door had been wide open when we went in, so there was no way for them to know that it would lock behind them as they ran out, or that there was no latch or even a handle on the inside. They were just scared of getting in trouble. Probably worried about the other women, since they'd collapsed the same as me."

Tap stopped working and stared at me, his mouth halfway open in horror. "You are far too generous, Feather."

"Maybe."

He swallowed, nostrils flared as he breathed. "How long?"

"Four days." The quill clattered to the floor. My throat tightened, remembering only flashes of what even then was like one long fever dream. "The whole of my first estrus cycle. My father found me after. I don't remember that part though. Or much of the next couple of weeks."

Tap scrunched his eyes closed. "Saints."

I could see the intricately designed beds and walkways lined with plants clearly in my mind, the deceptively beautiful blossoms, the common-looking greenery. "I ate what I thought looked familiar. But there were no truly safe plants in there."

Tap rumbled a noise low in his chest. "A poison garden."

"Yes. Between hallucinations, my heart beating either too fast or too slow, and bouts of getting sick, I had to contend with cramping and a … a *need* I didn't understand and couldn't soothe. At that point, nobody knew. Nobody could have explained what to expect when such a thing happened. And I kept choosing what I thought were edible greens or berries only to end up more unwell. I left a different person than I entered."

"Phin." Sympathy infused his tone, and he reached for my hand. I let him take it, appreciating the warmth of his skin and the way he pressed my palm to his cheek.

"I'm doing much better now, but many of my memories from before and shortly after that are fragmented or missing. I don't know how much to trust the ones I do have, but when they feel right, I do my best." He flinched, my pointed wording landing as I hoped.

"That had to be … indescribable."

"It was." I took a deep breath and reached for my tea, my throat raw and raspy from having spoken so much. "If not for Ramsey, I'm not sure I would have recovered."

"Were you not taken to the healers?"

I shrugged. "I was. I've never seen my father so angry and scared, I do remember that much. But there was only so much they could do."

"Bullshit." He spat the word with such force I startled. "I'm sorry." He squeezed my hand and then let go of it, pushing his fingers through his hair as his eyes flickered between red and silver. "They had the whole of the angelic council at their disposal. Divine healers. They could have undone any injury a plant toxin had given you. Physically, mentally, it wouldn't have mattered. They could have helped. Especially soon after it happened."

His words left me feeling vindicated. After I'd recovered and had a chance to reflect, I'd thought the same thing. So had my parents—the lack of expedient help for me was one of the last straws as far as his affinity for the council and Heaven in general for my father.

"My mother did her best, and my father was still able to get me some medicines and things from Heaven. My original tincture, too. Mostly, I'm fine."

"And the others? The Nephilim that left you behind?"

I shrugged. "I never saw any of them again. I was recovering, and then when I went back to Heaven, it was always to go straight to the archives with my father." Tap's mouth hung open, his rage palpable.

"I think my freezing episodes are probably related to what happened somehow, though that doesn't explain why the bells triggered them so much, or why they didn't start until I was living at the church." I'd thought about Hailon's offer to try to repair my heart quite a lot since our visit in the glade. I had hesitated out of fear that nothing would change, even if she could heal some of the damage. For the same reason, I'd never tried any of Greta's elixirs. I was finally mostly functional, even with those brief moments of being frozen inside my own body. But knowing now that the tincture was contributing, I was seriously reconsidering.

"Even I reacted to the blood in the metal. You were reacting both as an angel and as a demon, so it was twice as bad," Tap said, sympathy heavy on his quiet voice.

"Perhaps you're right. But the tincture isn't—wasn't—really working anymore."

"Phin, your tincture was being made weaker."

"What?"

"Greta and Vassago, they spoke with the apothecary. It was being diluted. Some of the herbs replaced with poison."

I flinched. Ophelia had told me what she'd tasted. I'd believed her, of course, but hearing it again, especially from him was jarring.

"That ..."

"It's a partial explanation, at least. If it was damaging your heart, every time the bells rang your blood responding would make you feel weak." Tap was somber, though I could feel the undercurrent of anger there as well. "Your wings are part of the cycle then, your fevers?"

I nodded slowly. "I can only assume so, yes. I haven't used my wings since before that day in the garden."

He rumbled a disapproving noise deep in his chest. "We need to find those herbs."

"It may already be too late." Even I could hear the defeat in my voice. "And Greta doesn't even have a recipe."

Tap leaned down to cup my face with his hands. "We'll go tomorrow. We'll find what you need, Phin."

"And if we don't?"

"We will," he said again, more forcefully.

"You can't know that. What if none of those places has the herbs, or—"

"We will find one of them, or an alternative. Covenants be damned, I'll go to Heaven myself and speak to the healers. My mate won't be made to suffer any longer, I will not stand for it!" The growl in his voice had returned. His eyes flashed red and his chest heaved as he caught his breath. Tap pulled his hands away from my face, fisting them as he curled into himself, putting his body as far from me as he could without actually moving. His eyes were wide as they settled back to silver.

I stared back at him, the charged word hanging there on the air between us.

PHIN

"SO, YOU REALLY are my demon," I whispered, repeating the words Ramsey had said to me, the truth of them landing in my gut like a punch. My chest ached, and I realized I'd been in varying stages of hope and denial for days, maybe weeks.

"Does that make you my angel then, Feather? Can you forgive me for what I did? What I might still do to Father Morton and perhaps that apothecary?" He seemed incredibly young and oddly insecure as he waited for my reaction.

"I told you before, I knew what I was doing that night. There's nothing to forgive you for—I was the one who climbed onto your lap for saint's sake. As for them ... I don't know. Do you truly want to break the bond?"

"No." He shook his head.

"How long have you known?"

His eyes shifted away. "Always. From the very first day."

I sucked in a breath. "What?" That truth smacked me across the face, more proof that if I'd been smarter, if he'd said something ... the whole tense mess between us could have been avoided.

"I'll accept if you're angry with me, but there was no other way. I wanted you to have time and space to yourself before laying something so heavy on you. It had to be your discovery, your choice. It will always be, even now. You should have gotten a say about whether we sealed the bond or not. Instead, you get to choose whether we keep it. It isn't quite the same choice, but it's yours." He swallowed, gathering up the inkpot and quill and setting them aside. "And ... I was afraid."

"Afraid?"

"Forever is a very long time, Phin, particularly for us. I don't ever want you to regret your decision. Once the bond is sealed, there's no going back. At least not without severe consequence. Much easier to avoid it than undo it."

"Why would I regret anything?"

He put his glasses back on. "I can think of several reasons."

"Such as?" I could see how uncomfortable he was, but I wanted to know why he was so timid about this.

"I'm a mess. Literally and figuratively. You've seen the workshops, the library. I forget half the things I'm supposed to be doing at any given time. I selfishly seek familiarity. I don't like to go outside my routine and doing so usually results in me becoming more agitated and less organized. I live in a place with no sunlight or fresh air—and I very rarely leave. I have operated here alone for literal centuries." He shrugged. "I know of the world, the way of things, but only because I have experienced small glimpses through the doorways. Seir is responsible for much of my knowledge, honestly, and my other brothers to a lesser extent."

I swallowed, my heart thudding warmly behind my ribs. He was scared. And for once, I was not.

"Well, lucky for us I'm good at organizing. And you've created a very comfortable place to live, the workshops for one, are incredible. You're forgetting the very reason you wanted me to come in the first place—it's safe here. There's instant access to anywhere someone could ever want to go if they start to get bored or need to shop or visit somewhere outside of this place. I know just as little about the world, perhaps less."

"Yes, I suppose that's all true. But what if it's not enough?" I heard what he hadn't said. What if *he* wasn't enough. My chest squeezed empathetically. I'd been less than enough my whole life.

Despite how hard I'd been ignoring the signs, now that the truth had been spoken I felt nothing but a sense of relief. It made sense to me. We were cut from similar cloth, with just enough variation in the pattern to complement the other.

"When you suggested I come here ..."

He shook his head, expression pained. "Not entirely unselfish, but absolutely for your safety. Nothing I said to you or Father Morton that day is untrue. Armaros is not to be trusted."

I studied him, from his chipped nail lacquer and the ring he spun when he was nervous to the earnest silver eyes behind round wire spectacles.

"I believe you." He straightened. "Coming here has changed everything about my life. In a good way."

A smile softened his pensive expression. "I'm very glad to hear that."

"You would have just dealt with the pain from the unfulfilled bond forever? That's what it was, right? The burning? The ache."

"You felt it too?"

"Yes."

He lifted one shoulder. "It was not my preferred outcome, but yes."

"But can't you go mad if you ignore it?"

"Eventually. It would take a very long time, though, and we're well beyond that point anyhow." He lifted his eyes and reached for my hand. "Do not make a decision out of guilt, Phin. Those things are irrelevant. If this is not what you want, the alternatives aren't important."

"What are these severe consequences? Ophelia wasn't specific."

"It doesn't matter. I would bear the entirety of them. She agreed to that."

I shook my head, and Tap looked startled when I started to laugh. "So both foolish *and* stubborn."

"Sorry?"

"Not just you, but if it applies, do with those labels what you will. They all knew, straightaway. Jacks, and Ramsey both made a point to reassure me that my instinct about you and your family was correct. Everyone essentially gave me their blessing, nudged me in the right direction. I'm the last to figure it out. To admit it." Overwhelmed, I pulled blankets and pillows around me as my thoughts crashed into one another, memories and new exclamations of hope colliding. Having my hands busy helped, so once I was done with the bedding, I rearranged everything so it wouldn't fall and set the tray of snacks on the floor next to the mattress. I took a deep breath, summoning my bravery. "Can I have a scroll too?"

"You want me to tattoo you?" His eyes were wide.

"Yes, please." I held out my arm. "Right here." I pointed at the inside of my wrist.

"It will hurt."

I shrugged. "I don't mind." He hesitated, then stood. "What's the matter?"

"I want the other ink. The blue." Tap strode with purpose from the room and returned a few minutes later much the same way. He took his glasses off again and set them on the low bedside table next to his lamp. Gently, he cradled my wrist in one hand and took up the quill with the other. "Ready?"

"Yes."

He bent over my wrist, more intently focused on the small design for me than I'd seen him at any point for himself. The pain of the quill piercing into my skin was sharp and hot but bearable, and it was fascinating to watch the curves take shape under his hand. He traced the lines twice, then wiped away the droplets of blood and ink with the cloth. It was perfect. As he released me, I pulled my wrist close so I could admire it. When I glanced up, I gasped.

He was putting the same thing on his wrist.

"Tap."

"Feather?"

"I don't know what to say. But that feels ..."

"Like a promise. It's a good start, I think."

"But you only like black. And you don't have anything else on that side yet. It will stand out."

"Good. I want it to."

I flushed hot. I couldn't prove it, but in that moment, I was sure we were going to be okay.

When he was finished with his new mark, he moved away all the supplies and held his arm up next to mine.

"I love it."

His sincere silver eyes bore into mine. "Thank you, Phin."

I could only nod for a moment, my throat thick as the tears threatened again. I was an emotional disaster, and it was likely to get worse before it got better. He kissed my forehead, and I replied with one on his cheek.

"Would you lie here with me for a while?"

"Yes, of course." He put out the lamp before lying down stiffly on his back, claiming only a single pillow. I huffed and maneuvered him onto his side, then settled into the pile I'd collected, lying in front of him.

"I feel better when you're close," I confessed.

"Me too, Feather." His warm breath tickled as it blew across the back of my neck.

"I don't want to break the bond, Tap. But you should be warned—I also don't know how to be anyone's mate."

He rumbled a low chuckle. "Me neither. But I've been giving it my best effort. I promise to continue. Though you'll have to tell me which meals I've fallen short with so I can improve. No greens is easy enough to remember, but I need to know the rest."

I laughed outright, and for the first time in a very long while, I heard a faint resonance in it like I'd had before the incident. I wanted to be happy about that, but it also scared me. "Your cooking is fine. More than. You've been so wonderful. Truly. I promise to continue my efforts at balancing out those responsibilities. I've never been so spoiled."

"And I insist that you are anything but." His fingers brushed along my hip, tracing circles that made my skin tingle. "We'll figure it out together. There's no rush to do anything differently. Nothing has to change."

"Okay." I could feel him relax behind me, and my body responded in kind. "But what if I want it to? Like this. This is nice." He made a noise of agreement. "Perhaps we just agree to do things slowly? Like starting over, kind of."

"Then slow it shall be. You honor me, Phin. Thank you." His hand splayed across my hipbone, and I covered it with mine. Several beats passed, then Tap said, "Oh. I keep forgetting to tell you. There was actually a stone kin watching the church."

"I knew it," I whispered harshly, excitement flooding my veins. "But also, Imogen told me so today. Her brother?"

Tap chuckled and settled more comfortably behind me, his arm over my waist as he pulled my back against his front and rearranged the blanket over us. "Yes, Tormund. He's a lot like Coltor."

"You met him?"

"Yes, that day at the church. We had a brief talk."

"I have so many questions. Will we get to see him at some point, do you think?"

"I imagine so."

The quiet settled heavily through the room, my eyes harder to open each time I blinked. "Will you stay with me tonight?"

"As you wish. Get some rest."

With his steady breaths and strong heartbeat as music, I fell into the deepest sleep I'd had in a long time.

Chapter 31
Tap

I WOKE WITH BLANKETS tangled around my legs and Phin curled up in a little ball beside me, her forehead pressed against my chest. My body was loose and relaxed, the bond quiet. Even my normally tangled thoughts were clear, orderly. The windows were still dark, but I felt more thoroughly rested than I had in years. I hardly knew what to do with myself.

I indulged in a few more quiet moments before straightening the blankets and pulling them back over her sleeping form. Carefully, I slipped away from her and made quick use of my bathroom before heading to the kitchen with the tray and remnants of the previous night's snacks. I dropped the mess off and continued to the hall, tension returning almost immediately as I opened up all the doorways. After a quick check, I cleaned the dishes and started the kettle for tea. As I sorted out the pot, I made a mental list of where I wanted to take Phin.

There were three doors I believed had the best potential for the rare herbs, all in far-flung realms. One in particular seemed promising both for her herbs as well as for Rylan's poison garden, as it was uninhabited and had a very temperate climate. It was one of the doorways I'd decommissioned ages before as well. We'd start there.

I was just returning to the hall with my tea and a quick breakfast of bread and cheese when Seir came through from the glade.

"You're early today," I said, offering him a cup.

"There's a lot going on." He was not his usual chipper self for the second day in a row. I could all but feel the tension radiating off him.

"Anything new I should know about?"

He shook his head. "Coltor is taking the first wave of stone kin through his doorways with odd magical activity today."

"Good." I frowned. "Does he need you there to help?"

"No, Magnus stayed to supervise. They are only checking a few at a time so that the groups going in can be larger. Anything new here? Everything okay?"

I felt like a youngling the way my skin prickled at the thought of my mate. "All is well."

Seir brightened instantly. "Really?" He clasped his hands together in front of his chest, smile wide. "That's wonderful news. I'm so happy for you both. See? One step at a time."

"Yes, I suppose you were right. Are you available to monitor today? We're going to be doing a similar journey as the stone kin, though likely only one location."

"Of course. Which one? Just in case."

"Florissar. It's in the decommissioned area, light-green frame, dark-green serrated leaf at the top right and bottom left."

"Got it. I have a request in with Keplar as well. I suspect you may need to redistribute gate-monitoring duties again soon, and Hell has the ability and manpower to cover."

My temper flared. I knew it was irrational, that he was only trying to help and this was a logical step, but it felt like a swipe at my capabilities. "That's not necessary." My tone was biting, but Seir was unaffected. He even rolled his eyes at my outburst.

"I disagree. It's something we should have looked into for you ages ago instead of believing your claims that you were fine. Because you weren't fine."

"I have managed perfectly well," I argued.

"Of course you have, because you had to. But you don't even *sleep* most days, brother. That's not fine." He crossed his arms and sighed. "Things are changing, Tap. Even my position has become largely obsolete. They can help. It would still be just as secure. You'd get to personally approve anyone considered for the job, if it gets to that point. I promise." He narrowed his eyes. "Don't make me bring Phin into this."

"You wouldn't dare."

"I would." His grin was devious. "Because I can only imagine that she'll want a mate who has time to do things with her, opportunities to be somewhere other than the great hall."

"Seir." I pinched the bridge of my nose between my thumb and forefinger, a headache starting behind my eyes.

"Tell me I'm wrong, Tap."

I sighed. "You're not. I know you're not." My anger fled, leaving me feeling deflated. I knew he wasn't wrong, about any of it. The number of doorways had grown too large for even two locations to monitor. And Phin deserved more than scant scraps of my time.

"I'm so glad we agree." He leveled a gaze at me. "It's not admitting failure to ask for help, remember? Didn't it bring relief when Merry took over the creatures? Doesn't it make you feel lighter to know that Phin is sorting out the deals?"

My chin dipped toward my chest. "Yes."

"Then spreading out the shifts for watching the doors should allow you to actually *live*."

I froze, his words striking a chord deep in my chest. I'd said a similar thing to Phin, about her existence at the church. It seemed the Fates had wonderful senses of humor and loved to present their offerings in a way that left one taking a long look in the mirror.

"I hear you, Seir."

"Good! I'll keep you informed. Last I heard, Keplar was putting together a roster of potential candidates and possible locations for centralizing. I suggested that instead of splitting up the doorways themselves, we manage shifts based on location time so that someone always has a chance to rest. Might even allow Coltor to trade off doing nightshift sometimes, if he wants."

I shoved my pride down and nodded at my brother. "That's a reasonable idea."

He smiled and clapped me on the shoulder. "She's good for you."

"In the grand scheme of things, she just got here. Maybe I'm evolving."

Seir scoffed and snatched the remains of my breakfast directly out of my hand, finishing it in one messy bite. "I stand by what I said," he muttered over his mouth full of bread and walked away, leaving me staring after him.

Nothing new there, at least.

SWEAT PRICKLED AT my temples the moment we crossed through the doorway. Thankfully, we'd left our cloaks behind.

Phin pushed up the sleeves on her tunic as she took in the overgrown plant life that spread in every direction. "Wow."

"You okay?"

She nodded slowly. "I'll be fine."

I appreciated her bravery, but I remembered all too well her reaction to seeing the plants in Merry's greenhouse. "This way." My hand stretched for hers, and she flushed pink as she laced her fingers with mine.

We stepped high, carefully planting our feet through the crowding of vines, clusters of flowers and tufts of grasses that covered the ground. There were very few areas of just soil visible. Here, the plants ruled.

Not far from the portal was a small lake with a rock outcropping to one side. Beyond that the land began to slope upward rather quickly, and the foliage thinned out. Our chances of finding the two herbs Greta had mentioned were better at the increased elevation.

"It's nice here," Phin said. "Very quiet, though. Where are all the birds?"

"There are none. The only wildlife here are some rodent-like creatures, lizards, and some bugs."

Her eyebrows drew together. "Odd."

I swung our linked hands up and pressed my lips to her knuckles. "There are many strange places through the doorways. They all serve their own purpose, even if that purpose is a bit mysterious."

She smiled softly at me, and we were quiet as we passed the lake, which had become about half covered in a creeping water plant.

"Will you be able to identify what we're looking for? I'm afraid botanicals are Rylan's specialty, not mine."

"Yes. The bride's bane has small purple flowers and thin fingers on the leaves. The shepherd's plight looks like bolted mustard plant, but with tiny white flowers instead of yellow. The leaves look like the serrated ones dandelions have." Phin suddenly stopped walking. "Did you bring gloves? We shouldn't touch them with bare hands."

I patted the small satchel slung over my shoulder. "I have everything we need."

Both of us began to sweat in earnest, the sun hot on our exposed flesh as the incline increased. As the plants began to thin, Phin's intensity grew as she scanned for the herbs she was seeking.

"You should drink some water," I encouraged, letting go of her hand. Condensation formed quickly on the outside of the glass bottle the moment I pulled it from my bag and offered it to her.

"Thanks." She took a deep drink and handed it back. "I'm going to look over there. That fallen tree looks promising."

"Alright."

Her steps were high as she pushed aside vines and other plants. I took a moment to just admire her as she moved with intent. She bent in half, getting a closer look at something right up next to the rotting wood.

Her hand shot out. "Here!"

I moved as quickly as I dared over the uneven ground, already digging around for the bags and leather gloves I'd brought.

Just as she'd described, the bride's bane had starlike purple flowers clustered all around and down the stalk. They were open and deceptively pretty, all the way down to the flexible little leaves. Phin accepted the gloves and retrieved as much of the herb as she could, filling up the small canvas bag.

"Excellent eye," I said. "Do you want to see if we can find the other?"

"Yes. Both would be better, I think."

I just bobbed my head and followed her, looking for tiny white flowers but not overly confident I had a clue what I was doing. Phin started a course a little bit higher up and then walked horizontally, kicking over stones and moving tangled nests of vines with the toe of her boot. Just about the time I was ready to suggest we move on, that we could try another door, she yelped again and repeated her harvesting ritual with the other plant.

"This place was perfect," she enthused, carefully removing her gloves and placing them in the satchel.

"It was the most likely candidate. I think Rylan's garden would do well here, also. And there's nobody it could harm here." She looked pleased at that.

We made our way down the hill, stopping to catch our breath near the lake.

It was cool in the shade next to the water, the brackish smell a fair trade for a reprieve from the brutal sun and heat. I took the bag off and offered her the bottle of water. She sipped, expression peaceful as she blotted away the moisture from her face.

I'd looked away, gazing into the distance when Phin's harsh grunt had me spinning around. She was doubled over, fresh dots of sweat lining her brow.

"Phin?" Fear clawed coldly through my veins as she slowly sank to her knees, body curled in half.

She groaned, hands pressing against her abdomen. "No, no. It's so soon!" she cried out and her eyes filled with tears. Everything in me screamed to help her.

"Just tell me what you need, Feather, I'll do it."

She grimaced and trembled, unable to speak. Her breath shuddered, and she moaned out, the sound of her agony cutting into my thoughts like a blade. She looked terrified. After several long minutes, she sobbed and breathed shallowly, the worst of the pain seeming to have passed for the moment. "I ... need ... you."

I battled with myself as I sat on the damp undergrowth and pulled her across my lap. I cupped her face with my hand. "Not like this, Feather. This is not how we confirm our bond after what I just put you through."

"Why are you arguing with me again?" she asked through gritted teeth, though I could see the flash of humor as her mouth twitched at the corner. "I thought we settled this. If you don't want me, just say so." She laughed, but it was cut off by another surge of pain.

My demon roared, and I could feel my teeth lengthening despite her levity. "*Never* doubt that I want you, Phin. I told you before, I was haunted by you from the very first moment I saw your eyes through that window. I endured all that time knowing you are my mate and allowing the bond to burn me from the inside out. But this is not how I want to revisit intimacy between us. Didn't we agree on slow? This is the opposite of that."

"Doing nothing means pain." She panted as another terrible spasm gripped her. "I don't know that I'll be okay if I have to go through that again." Her words landed like daggers, and I clutched her to my body. "I am myself enough to decide, Tap. I know what I want. I choose you. I would always have chosen you."

I clenched my jaw, the words a knife straight to my heart. "Then we set our own terms. We're going to get you home, to a place where you can be safe and comfortable. Alright?" I cupped her face, blood on fire at the prospect of everything I had never dared to dream of being held between my hands. "Once you're past this part of the cycle, you have a rest period, right?"

She nodded. "Yes. At least a few weeks." She sobbed again. I hated every bit of this.

"Good. We'll send these to Greta so she can start working on what you need to keep this from happening again. Then we do what it takes to get you through this, the way you want to. Okay?"

"Yes."

"Can you walk?" She started to nod and got halfway up but couldn't completely unfold without pain. I put the satchel back over my shoulder and scooped her into my arms, all but jogging back to the doorway and leaping through the portal that would take us to the crossroads.

CHAPTER 32
TAP

I SETTLED PHIN IN a cool bath, opting to use hers so she had her own items for comfort as soon as we got back.

Seir's eyes were wide as I went back to the hall. All he'd seen was me bursting through a portal and carrying her at a jog toward our living quarters.

"What's happening?"

"I need a few days. Nobody in or out of this place. All doorways will be inactivated."

"Okaaay." He raised an eyebrow, watching as I began preparing to divert several portals. "I can do that. Is she alright?"

"She'll be fine."

He nodded but didn't press. "This could be a good test for Keplar's candidates, I guess."

"You have my approval for whatever you think is best, as long as the doors are monitored. I'll send word when it's okay for you to come back." I hustled my brother toward the portal back to the glade.

"You're acting *very* strangely," Seir said, trying to glance at me over his shoulder. "And that's saying something, brother."

"Leave, Seir."

He threw his hands up. "Fine, I'm going. But what about food? Do you need any supplies?"

"If I do, I'll use the scrying mirror."

"And if there's an emergency?"

"Mirror."

"And what about—"

"*Mirror.*" I shoved him toward the doorway, urgency drawing my demon to the surface. My wings snapped out wide, and my tail snaked out along the floor by my feet, tapping anxiously. My brother had the audacity to just grin.

"Ooh, it's serious then. Put your fangs away, I'm leaving. See you in a few days, I guess. Good luck?" He leaped for the portal as I moved to push him again, gone before I could make contact.

I hurried down the hall, disabling or diverting every last doorway, which I'd never once done before. It was eerily quiet when I was finished, the ambient hums all silenced, the chorus of noises the portals made that gave the impression the hall breathed unusually quiet.

My next stop was the kitchen. I collected what seemed like enough food and drink for a couple of days and delivered that to my room. Phin's bed was still missing sheets, but I could fix that if she preferred it over mine.

When I got back to her, she was calm but had turned so that her face was settled on an arm that was draped over the side of the tub, discomfort etched into her face.

"Do you want some of Greta's elixir? I have some of the regular pain remedy I gave you after the visit to the glade as well."

"Can I have both?"

I collected them and brought them to her, feeding her the liquids right there in the tub. I scolded myself for the response my body had to her lifting her slender neck and opening her mouth. I was nearly undone when she flattened her tongue to accept the elixirs.

"Do you want to stay in there?"

"Just a few more minutes." She sounded drowsy, but it seemed more likely she was just overwhelmed.

"Whatever you need. Shall I wash your hair?" Her gentle nod gave way to her body curling into itself, her face pressed to her knees until the wave passed. "I'm sorry," I apologized, wishing I could take on the pain for her. After rolling up my sleeves, I cupped my hands and used them to pour water over her short curls as she did her best to lounge in the tub. One at a time, I scrubbed in the shampoo, rinsed, then layered in some fancy floral-scented conditioning cream that she'd picked up when she went shopping with my sisters-in-law. Once she was rinsed again and had soaped herself clean, I helped her out of the water and wrapped her in a towel.

"Mine or yours?" I asked.

"Yours."

I scooped her up against me and carried her to my room, setting her down, towel and all, right in the middle of the large mattress.

"Clothes?"

"Do you have another shirt I could wear?" she asked, her expression bordering on embarrassed.

"You're welcome to anything of mine you like, Feather." I dug around in my wardrobe again, unearthing another old, soft shirt for her. She pulled it on and began arranging the pillows and blankets.

"Phin?" She looked up at me, sweat dotting her brow despite how cool her bath had been.

"Yes?"

"I'm here to help you, but I need to know what you need. I've never done anything like this before." The confession that had scratched along the edges of my mind for days lingered at the back of my tongue. "The night in the tattoo room, that was … You are the only lover I've ever had." My voice dropped to a whisper. "The only one I'll ever have."

"I've never done this part either." She shuffled around. "That night, it wasn't my first time, but it's the only one that matters."

I shoved down a flare of jealousy. It didn't matter who owned that part of her past as long as I was her future. "Then we'll learn together."

"Okay." Her face scrunched, and despite her efforts at disguising it, she groaned and curled up.

I felt helpless, standing there discussing steps and expectations when her body was causing her pain.

"I need you closer." She patted the mattress next to her, the wall of pillows and blankets she'd constructed around the mattress having made a little nest.

"Of course."

"Can I …?" She indicated coming closer, and I opened my arms wide. She snuggled her face against my chest, her ear above my heart. I could feel the heat of her forehead through the fabric of my shirt, the fever back and perhaps even worse than before.

"Is the medicine working?"

"I think so. The pain is a little better."

"Good."

I dragged my fingers up and down her spine, the floral scent of her soap heady in my nose. Her knees were tucked into my thigh, and the muscles in my stomach tensed as she inched her fingers under the hem of my shirt.

"Can I take this off? It's rough against my face." Her eyes were round, pleading. I could see the question embarrassed her from the blush on her cheeks.

"I already gave you one shirt today," I teased. "But I did say you could have whatever you wanted." Her pink cheeks deepened to red as I unbuttoned and shrugged out of my shirt. "Just a joke, Feather."

She smiled and took my discarded shirt, stretching it out along one edge of the mattress against the pillows. "Thank you."

"Of course."

Phin hummed as she traced the tattoos that ran along my chest under my collarbone, looped over my shoulders and continued across my back. "This tells your rank and titles. Your legions."

"Yes." My lips tilted up. "Not that anyone sees them but it's nice to have someone around who reads the old language. Less explanation needed."

"Mmm." She tensed and her fingernails dug into my side.

I didn't mind it nearly as much as I thought I would.

As she relaxed again, her hands ran up and down my ribs, my skin and muscles twitching in response. My head fell back, and I could only sigh when I felt the weight of her as she straddled my lap again, her lips resting against my throat as she settled her face there.

"Tell me what you want me to do, Feather."

She sat back, her face pinched, and her hips rolled. "Touch me back."

I inhaled slowly through my nose as she removed my spectacles, setting them aside on the little table so they wouldn't be lost in the tangle of sheets and blankets or damaged. Then I repeated what she'd done, flattening my palms against her ribs as I smoothed my hands up and down her sides.

Phin had begun sweating in earnest, and her body seemed to be moving of its own accord, hips undulating and her hands restless along my shoulders and chest. I suspected I knew what it was seeking, that release was the only way to calm the need wreaking havoc inside her. I leaned in close and sucked on her collarbone, and she arched into me on a moan.

"Everything is ... it feels like I'm on fire."

"I'll help you, the whole time. I'm not going anywhere, understand?" She nodded weakly. "Good. Is there anything you don't want me to do? Anywhere you don't want me to touch?"

She shook her head, hesitated, then shook it again. "I don't think so."

"Well, if you get uncomfortable, say ... library. I'll stop immediately. How about that?"

"Yes."

"Say the word. I want to be sure you are really with me, Phin."

"Library."

"Good."

She shifted, expression pained, and moaned in her throat. "Tap."

"I've got you. Shall we lie you down, Little Feather?"

I narrated my movements, ensuring she was aware of every step as I lay her back on the cushions and began to inch her shirt up and off, kissing my way from her navel to her breasts, pausing to suck each of the rosy tips into my mouth. Her hips jerked at the sensation and her violet eyes opened long enough to stare into mine for a beat before slipping closed again.

"Up." I drew the fabric over her head and off her arms, leaving it where she could reach. She tucked it blindly into the pillows next to where she'd stuffed mine.

Hands trembling as my blood surged through my body, I kissed her long and slow, nipping at her swollen bottom lip before moving on. Down the column of her throat, down the valley between her breasts, until I was slipping my fingertips under the waistband of her leggings.

"Off," she puffed eagerly, lifting herself up to help me. "Itchy. Hot."

I chuckled and peeled them down her legs, tossing them behind me. "You can add those to your design later." She didn't seem to care, her chest and even the tops of her thighs flushed with color. Her fingers threaded through my hair as I bent to kiss her stomach, then continued lower still, the scent of her forcing my demon to the surface.

"Phin," I breathed, making sure she met my eye. "I am myself, but not in full control of my dark nature either. I am completely undone by you, little mate." I shuddered a sigh, desire surging through my veins, my pants painfully tight as my cock swelled with need for her.

"Can I see the rest?"

I sucked in a harsh breath and released my wings as gently as I could, the weight of them still making the snap of the leathery flesh loud in the cozy room. Her fingers grazed the sensitive undersides as my tail wound around her leg, coiling from her ankle to her knee with the arrow-like tip tapping on her skin.

"I accept you just the way you are," she replied, shaking her head as though unsure why I was even concerned about it. "I *like* you this way. Always have."

A growl rumbled through my chest, and I licked out, my forked tongue laving a wet mark on her thigh.

Her hips rocked, and she moaned, breaths coming in shorter pants. "*Please.*"

"I don't want you to hurt, Feather. What is it you need?" I retracted my wings so they wouldn't be in the way, a surge of pride flaring when she pouted that they were gone.

Her hands fluttered over her womb, then she cupped herself. "I feel ... empty." She breathed, eyes widening with horror as the word came out.

Those words affected me very, very differently than they did her. My cock throbbed behind the laces of my trousers.

"Do you trust me, Phin?"

"Yes."

"You remember what to say if you get uncomfortable at any point?"

"Library. Tap, *please*." She moaned again, hips lifting, her body searching for any bit of friction it could get.

"I have waited lifetimes for this." I sighed and lifted one of her legs over my shoulder, calmly running my fingers down the length of her calf, then her thigh as I kissed her delicate ankle. Her skin jumped as I traced my path, and she made little noises that only made me harder. "I'll give you what you need, beloved. But I'm going to take what I want while I do it." She moaned out at my words, and I could see the rush of her arousal glistening against her skin in the low light.

I lowered my head and licked all along the seam of her, the noises she made feeding the sound of blood throbbing in my ears. Her sweet flavor burst on my tongue, and I groaned, gathering one hip in each hand, bringing my feast closer to my mouth. I watched her face contort and one of her hands pinch the tip of her breast as my forked tongue surrounded her clit from both sides. When I took her between my lips and sucked, she cried out, her body trying to buck away from my hands. I held her steady, only encouraged by that response.

"Please," she begged again, violet eyes misty as she watched me.

I swept along her opening with my tongue again before returning to my focused ministrations. As her thighs began to shake, I sank a finger inside her heat and reveled as her cries tingled down my spine.

"I ... can't ... I don't ..." She moaned and writhed, slick with sweat as her inner muscles fluttered. I let up on the suction I'd created with my mouth, laving her sensitive clit with the flat part of my tongue as I gently worked another finger inside her.

"You'll be just fine, Feather. You're doing so well for me." She panted as I combined the suction with quick flicks, and for a moment she stopped breathing. On a long moan, I felt everything inside her tighten, and then release in fluttering waves, her pleasure mine as she reached her peak with my face buried between her thighs. I shuddered, the pressure too much for me to contain. My spend soaked the seam of my trousers as I rumbled a groan against her flesh.

I gentled my pressure and withdrew my fingers, her eyes following me as I sucked on them before kissing along her trembling leg.

"Better?" She nodded languidly. "Stay where you are. I'll get us cleaned up."

I stripped my soiled pants off and wet a rag with warm water, willing my demonic features to retreat. I stared at myself in the mirror until the last of the red in my eyes faded, flattered that Phin hadn't cared one way or the other. When I got back to the bed, she had rolled to her side and was propped up on one elbow, drinking water.

"Thank you," she breathed, flopping back to the mattress once she'd had her fill. "But you—"

I shook my head. "That was my honor, Feather. And I got at least as much out of that as you did." She raised an eyebrow at my words but didn't contest them as I gently cleaned her up. "Though I'm also glad it helped." I lay down beside her when I was finished, and she immediately curled up across my chest. I pulled a blanket across us and she snuggled close.

I stroked down her spine until her breathing changed, then indulged in rest myself, unsure how long we might have until the next spike but longing for this kind of closeness for the rest of my existence.

CHAPTER 33
PHIN

I WOKE UP FEELING like every inch of my skin was too hot. Too tight. It was like I was on fire from the inside out.

Tap was dozing under me, my face pressed to his bare chest, one of his legs slung over mine. He was holding me like I was precious. My heart thudded and squeezed, but the sweet moment was lost to the sudden pain in my abdomen.

"What do you need?" he asked, voice dark and rough from sleep.

A groan was all that came out. I strangled the sheet, my grip white-knuckled as the pain rolled through me. My body throbbed as I curled into a tight ball. My throat was dry, and words simply wouldn't come.

"I'm right here," he muttered, kissing the top of my head. "Take what you need, Feather, if you can't use your voice. I am yours, and I will say our word if you do something I don't care for."

I leveraged myself over him, sweat already running in rivulets down my spine. The way he looked up at me, silver eyes full of longing and desire spurred my motions. As I rocked over him, my arousal slick against us both, he moaned and slid his hands up to hold my hips. I leaned forward to kiss him, and he met me eagerly, sliding one knee out and lifting just a bit so that as I rocked, the tip of his cock teased my entrance. But there was something else there too, something harder and slightly cool. I sat up on my knees and looked down at him, finding several bits of metal pierced through his rigid length.

My head snapped up, and his mouth curled into a vicious grin. His eyes shifted to red, and that devilish split tongue ran along his bottom lip.

"More needlework, beloved. My ears are not the only place I care to pierce when I get overwhelmed by it all. Though, I have removed many from other places on my body over time." He ran his tongue against his teeth, and I flushed even hotter somehow. Unable to meet his eye any longer, I looked back down and counted. There was a wide ring vertically through the tip, and six straight pins with round ends horizontally up the length of him. Seeing the question in my face, he said, "Yes, they hurt, but only temporarily. You'll have to let me know if you enjoy them or not. I'm happy to take them out, or add to my collection, whatever your preference."

I remembered feeling them that night in the tattoo room, but I hadn't really considered what it was beyond the passion of that moment. Now, having seen them, I registered every bit of what they'd felt like as they moved inside me.

One of his hands slid up my spine and curled against the back of my head, pulling me in as I settled down against him, both of us moaning as he slid inside fully. He seated so deeply in this position it stole my breath.

With my hands against his chest, I lifted and sank down again, my body following the same current as the desire swelling within me. Tap never took his eyes off mine, the same full complete surrender of control as he'd shown our first night together communicating absolute trust and devotion as I took and took and took from him to feed the flames inside myself.

He slid one hand along my thigh, settling it close enough his thumb could reach my sensitive clit as I rocked, and when he started to make gentle circles I nearly sobbed. The tip of his tail traveled from the wet space where we were joined to my rear entrance and I gasped.

"Okay, Feather? You remember your word if you don't like something?"

I nodded, the sensation new and intense but not bad. He used his hands and tail in tandem, supplying just the right pressure. My body responded by releasing more arousal, easing the way for it all to go faster, deeper. The pleasant pressure of him filling me so fully brought tears to my eyes and I moaned. I had a fleeting thought that in any other moment I would be horrified by how wanton I'd become, but in this one, I could not be bothered to care. I was nothing more than a body made of need and exposed nerves, and everything felt so *good*.

It only took a few full thrusts for a powerful orgasm to start building. When Tap felt the first flutters his control broke and he started to thrust up as I came down, intensifying every stroke as his tail followed the same rhythm.

My voice cracked as I cried out, my body convulsing around him as my climax washed over me in a hot wave. My wings emerged in one rough snap, but there was no pain this time, only a flurry of immature feathers and a warm white light.

Tap's smile was adoring as he looked up at me. "You're glowing, Feather." He reached up and drew his hands down the edges of my wings, causing me to shiver. He never stopped thrusting into me, chasing his own release. I leaned forward to swallow his moan as his face betrayed his climax, rocking gently to prolong the intensity as he shuddered beneath me.

"How do you feel?" he asked, hands firm on my thighs.

"Beautiful." I breathed the word, the truth of it ringing through my body. I flexed and relaxed the appendages that were finally responsive to my control, though they felt a little foreign and heavy against my back. I requested that they go wide, then stowed them away.

"As you should, beloved. You're the most gorgeous thing I've ever seen."

Panting, he drew me down and devoured my mouth with his, then pulled me against his chest. I trembled and he held me together, the flames soothed for the moment and my heart full to bursting with affection for the mate the universe had so lovingly gifted me.

TAP LET ME doze but only for a little while.

"We need to get you cleaned up and fed before your fever returns, Feather." I managed a nod and sat up, eyes heavy. "Which first?"

"Bath," I whispered.

"I'll go start the water." He planted a kiss on my forehead before setting a cup of water in my hands. "Drink."

I did as he said, the cool water soothing against my hot, dry throat. I'd nearly finished it when he returned, scooped me up, and carried me into his bathroom.

"I can walk," I argued.

"This is faster." He smirked, setting me down carefully in the hot water. "Temperature okay?"

I nodded, and he gathered some supplies, setting them on a stool he'd dragged next to the tub's edge. Then he climbed in behind me.

Pampered didn't feel like a strong enough word as he massaged my scalp with the shampoo again, working the suds along my shoulders and releasing any remaining tension there as well. He soaped a thick cloth and washed my arms and chest, my neck. He had me poke one leg at a time out of the water so they could receive similar treatment. I reached for the cloth, but he shook his head.

"Stand up, Feather." I did, and he wrapped one arm around my legs to hold me steady as he reverently ran the cloth between my legs. "Are you sore?"

"A little."

He nodded and helped me sit again, leaving me to soak as he took care of washing himself. I'd reached for him first but had been denied.

"If you start touching me, Phin, there will be no rest. And you *need* to rest. This is only the first day."

I'd pouted, but he was right.

Once he was done, I'd been bundled back into a plush towel. "I brought everything from your bathroom in case there was something you needed." He gestured to the unused side of his countertop. "I'm going to find us a clean sheet."

I nodded and took the opportunity to take a dose of the light-green elixir Greta had sent, brush my teeth, and apply some of the rich moisturizer for my face that I'd found in Revalia.

Tap fetched me once again, this time pulling me by the hand instead of carrying me. Once we were comfortable on the mattress he brought over the full tray and started feeding me.

"I'm not incapable of caring for myself," I said, after being offered the third bite of bread and cheese with some kind of preserved sausage.

"I know."

"So why—"

"Because I can." His eyebrow went up, and I swallowed, a flash of heat distracting me from the protest I'd half-formed. "Because I want to."

I didn't try to argue any further.

Once Tap was certain my stomach was full and I'd drunk enough water, he pulled me down with him and covered us with a sheet.

Sleep chased me the moment I was horizontal, and I fell into a peaceful place of semi-consciousness with his heartbeat under my ear and his fingers tangled in my hair.

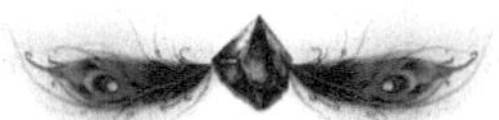

I WOKE HOT but with the need to relieve myself much more pressing than the dull ache in my womb.

"Phin?" Tap called as I slid off him and went into the bathroom.

"I'm okay," I replied, hurrying into his water closet. And I was, until I was washing my hands. The need attacked with a viciousness, my knees nearly going out from under me as I rinsed off the soap.

Within a breath of me crying out, Tap was in the doorway, urgency in his gaze.

"Help," I panted. He approached with clear intent to pick me up, to carry me back to the mattress but there was no time. "No. Right now."

"Here?"

"Yes." I nodded, the throb overwhelming, sweat making me feel damp everywhere.

His gaze turned ruby as he stood behind me, eyes fixed on us in the mirror. "You want to see yourself, Phin? How lovely you look as we cement this bond between us again?" I could only moan, and my eyes closed as his hand slid around my throat. "As you wish, little mate. I am yours to command."

I buckled further, pressing my bare ass up against his body, finding him hard and ready. "Now," I repeated, shifting back and forth impatiently. "I need you."

"Greedy little angel," he growled, making me repeat the word we'd agreed on if I felt uncomfortable before plunging into me from behind.

Sore or not, the moment he filled me up I sagged against the counter, his hand around my throat the only thing keeping my chin from falling to my chest.

Tears filled my eyes as he started to move, slowly at first and then with intent, my hips saved from banging against the counter's sharp edge by the hand towel he left folded there for the sink.

His eyes held mine, flickering between silver and red as I panted and moaned, his jaw flexing with every thrust. The ink on his arm was a stark contrast to my bare skin, and when he tensed the grip he had on the sides of my throat, my body responded by clamping down, making him groan.

"You'll surely bring me the most glorious of deaths, Phin. But more than that, the most beautiful life." He paused in his movements, making me cry out in complaint. "Can you use your voice, beloved?"

"Yes," I panted.

"Good. You're truly not afraid of my demon?"

"Still you," I argued. "I want all of you."

He moaned and bent, biting along the top of my shoulder as he pushed as far into me as he could go, his cock throbbing inside my walls. His forked tongue licked up my neck.

"What promises should we make to one another, Phin? It may not be the best time, but I want to remember this moment always." The fingers of his free hand dipped, and he began toying with my clit as he held eye contact with me in the mirror. His tail wrapped around my leg and pulled, making my stance wider. "I promise there will never be any other for me. Only. You. Forever." He punctuated with thrusts, stealing my breath and my thoughts. He drew out of me infuriatingly slowly, making me feel every piercing both as he pulled out and as he pressed back in. My thighs trembled, a climax hovering just out of reach.

"Yes," was all I could manage. It was breathy, desperate, but I meant it.

"I will give you anything you crave," he promised, dipping to suck at my neck. "And the freedom to live as you please."

I shook, the words unlocking something deep inside me. "*Tap.*"

"I will love you, Phin. In this lifetime and the next. I." *Thrust.* "Am." *Thrust.* "Yours." *Thrust.* "Understand?"

"Yes." I nodded as much as I could against the tension of how he was holding me, the back of my head against the top of his shoulder. "Please," I begged, tears nearly overflowing my eyes as the need to come overwhelmed me. I ground out the words slowly, having to search for the shapes of them before they could be vocalized. "I want nothing else but this. You. My mate. Forever."

His head fell back and his rhythm increased. The wave of pleasure in my blood finally crested, washing over me as I cried out, unable to control my body any further. Tap held me steady as he found his own release, his moan hot against the back of my neck. He turned my head with his hand, kissing me with a ferocity I'd not yet seen in him, which seemed significant given what we'd already been through together.

"Let's clean you up, beloved."

Boneless, I allowed him to pamper me all over again with a quick bath, water, food. Soft kisses and gentle hands cradled me, fed me, made sure I had what I needed.

I'd been terrified of what having a cycle meant for so long, I'd never considered that under the right circumstances it could lead to me feeling so utterly loved.

THE NEXT COUPLE of days passed in a blur, a similar pattern repeating.

Tap was always there, constantly aware of my needs and unerringly ready. He napped in short bursts and snuck out for more supplies while I rested. He made sure that I at least took the green elixir once a day, but also the blue when he remembered and the pain reliever when I needed it. I saw every side of him and adored him more for it all.

We feasted on well-aged wines he unearthed from somewhere in his endless eclectic stores, cheese, fruit, bread—anything that could easily be eaten with one hand. He brought us cakes and other sweet treats in the sleepless hours of the night, then we fortified ourselves with tea and hot grain cereal in the morning when he began to fret that I was going to suffer from lack of real food. He brewed tea that grew cold before it ever got poured a few times and brought me endless pitchers—ones from his later batches with spouts—full of water. I started to wonder how we even had any groceries left for his creative finger foods at all.

Mostly, we explored one another in the quiet moments between heat flares and sleep, hands and mouths mapping skin until there wasn't a single inch left untouched, untasted.

I requested to see Tap's full demon form several times, and each time he grew less timid about it. He spread his black, bat-like wings for me and showed off his whiplike tail. The red eyes were still thoughtful behind his round spectacles, still wholly him, and we both knew that his forked tongue was good at plenty of interesting things. His horns were perfect crescent shapes and shockingly sharp at the tips, which pointed behind him. There was nothing scary or unattractive about that version of him, and I told him so, as well as several new and creative ideas I'd had about his tail. We'd ended up tangled in the bedding with half a plate's worth of fruit or crackers smashed between us and the mattress more than once.

At one point, Tap asked if he could see my wings. It took some focus, but I was able to bring them out. I flexed and even flapped them, a gust of wind washing over us both. The feathers seemed to be regenerating and healthy, which was hopeful. When I pulled them back in, he gently kissed along the place on my shoulder blades where my wing ways were and traced down my spine.

"What is this scar from?" he asked, touching a spot along my lower back.

"I wish it were something far more interesting than what the truth is," I chuckled, chewing on an apple slice.

"No battle with rogue wolves then? Or a tragic swordsmanship lesson gone wrong?" he teased. "You did say you didn't do very well in your weaponry classes."

"Nothing so valiant, I'm afraid, though I have plenty of little marks from the short time I took lessons." I smiled, the old, mostly painful memories of failing my courses in Heaven suddenly no longer nearly as hurtful. "I was hiking in the woods near our house and lost my footing going along an embankment for a creek. There were rocks and broken tree limbs the whole way down. I caught a particularly sharp stone as I slid is all. Didn't bleed much, but it was the most hideous bruise for weeks. Took forever to fully heal."

"Mmm." He ran the tip of his tongue along the silvery line and then kissed it, making me shiver. When I glanced over my shoulder, he was grinning at me with obvious intent and that was enough to spike my temperature and need all over again.

Tap was dreadfully good at inciting the same desires he was masterful at satisfying.

"How are you so good at this?" I asked him while still panting, the white glow that had started to come from my skin when I was at the height of pleasure slowly fading.

He chuckled darkly. "I appreciate the compliment, Feather. Bringing you pleasure is truly one of my greatest accomplishments. It's also very nice to have a tangible guide letting me know when I'm doing something right." He ran the backs of his fingers down my cheek.

"Not going to tell me then?" I teased, reaching for a drink.

"I might never have taken a lover, but that doesn't mean I didn't have ages to do … independent research."

"Ah." I helped myself to several pieces of cheese and some grapes while my mind sifted through how to respond. "Wait. Those books, the ones you removed from the library"—he raised his eyebrow playfully—"before I started organizing. Was there something in them you didn't want me seeing?"

He choked on his tea. "Very astute, as always."

"There were a *lot* of them." I'd recognized what looked like medical texts, as well as some plain ledgers and even illustrated fiction.

"Nothing quite like a well-rounded education, Feather. Wouldn't you say?" His eyebrow went up again, and I honestly was beginning to question how much of what was spiking my temperature was the hormones and how much was just him.

"Where did you put them?"

"Why? Do you have specific questions?"

I shrugged. "Just curious where you learned some things is all."

"They're in the tattoo room. Bottom shelves, big cabinet."

"I didn't notice them in there."

He smirked. "There are doors on the cabinet disguising the shelves." I shoved ineffectively at his shoulder, and he laughed, catching me and squeezing me against his chest. "We can go back through them together if you'd like."

I would have argued further but he kissed me again, and I was useless against such a tactic.

Through it all, *library* remained unsaid as a hard stop while we were in the heat of things, but the consideration and safety of his insistence of having it at all embedded firmly into my soul.

Nothing could change my mind or my heart that the Fates had chosen exactly right pairing me with Tap.

Late on the third day, my body sore and spent, the fever finally started to wane.

"I think it'll be over soon," I sighed, drowsily lounging against him.

"We'll see," he replied, unbothered as ever, the pair of us tangled in yet another clean sheet.

"You're not tired?" I asked, unable to hold back the light chuckle.

"Maybe, but these have been some of the best days of my life, Feather. I wouldn't trade it. I'm honored I could be here for you in your time of need."

I laughed. "Your sacrifice is deeply appreciated, sir."

His smile stretched, and he kissed my forehead, arms tightening around me. "Get some rest. Real life doesn't have to exist just yet. Not until you want it to."

So I did. And no other indulgence had ever felt as decadent.

CHAPTER 34
PHIN

GETTING BACK TO our normal routine after the hazy days of my heat was more difficult than I expected. I was still tired despite having slept nearly all of the previous day and night.

Once my fever had broken for good, Tap replaced the bedding we'd been using for a final time while I bathed, then made sure I drank plenty of water and ate my fill before tucking me back in again. He'd spent the whole day carefully removing the rest of the linens to wash one pillow and blanket at a time, ensuring the arrangement I'd made wasn't too disturbed while I dozed on and off. I was proud of him for not returning to the hall, though I'm sure it was difficult for him not to.

I finally rolled my pleasantly achy body out of the bed a few hours after Tap brought me breakfast, kissed my forehead, and warned me that Seir was on his way.

"The elixirs Greta gave you are both gone, should I see if she can send more?"

"No, that's alright. I don't want to bother her with anything else; she's already working on my tincture. Besides, I haven't had an episode at all since ..." I thought back, heartened when I couldn't remember exactly when the last one was. "Before all this, anyhow. And I'll just take some of the pain reliever if I need some."

"Alright. I'll be in the hall if you need anything." I pulled him down for a thorough kiss, loving the way he melted into me. "Though if you keep that up ..." He squeezed his eyes closed and shook his head. "No, I have to go. Eat your food."

He gave a longing look back at me from the doorway, but sighed and left me there, making sure as always to leave the door open a couple of inches.

I knew it would be best if I got back to work as well, though the temptation to be lazy was awfully strong. Sinking back into the pillows, I allowed myself another few minutes before getting up and go into my own room for clean clothes.

As usual, there were plenty more snacks and tea waiting for me in the kitchen. I could hear Tap and Seir having a conversation as I crossed to the library, but I was too embarrassed to say hello myself. By now everyone probably knew what had caused Tap to completely shut down the crossroads, and while there was nothing shameful about it, I still wasn't sure how I was going to look anyone in the eye right away.

The library was calming in its familiarity, the stacks of deals right where I'd left them. I scooped up an armload, muttering to myself as I separated them out. I was settling into the quiet headspace I loved, the place where my body and mind just did what they were supposed to without me having to think through every step. It was the same place I'd always gone to when copying pages for Father Morton, and sometimes when I drew. Extreme focus where nothing else mattered and my mind was still.

"Silver in the crate, gold over here. Red over there. Silver, silver, gold." I paused, something flashing at the edge of my vision. "Silver ..." I turned my head quickly, trying to catch whatever it was that I was seeing. I gasped, finding a glow from within the piles. "Gold?" The glow changed, from white to yellow. Shaky, I focused on the deals in my arms. "Red." The single open deal in my hands emitted a faint red light. "Saints." I squeezed my eyes closed, quickly sorted what I had, then went to the farthest corner of the room and gathered up an armload of envelopes. With my eyes closed, I tried again. "Silver." When I opened them, several of the deals I held were lit with a white light.

Needing validation that what I was seeing was real, I finished with that set and left the library.

"Tap?" I called, my voice missing its usual rasp, and at least twice as loud as it had been in years.

Both he and Seir came around the edge of the hall at the same time.

"What's wrong?" Tap's question was strained, his pace hurried.

"Sorry, I wasn't trying to scare you. I'm fine."

"Phin, you yelled! How exciting!" Seir enthused. He gestured to his brother. "I think it scared both of us, but for different reasons."

I couldn't resist his offbeat humor and chuckled, but also I was sure he was telling the truth. "Can you both come look at something?" They glanced at one another but followed me into the library. "Gold," I said with intent. "Do you see anything?"

"Oh." Tap grunted, moving toward a shelf where yellow light glowed from multiple different envelopes.

"That's fantastic!" Seir leafed through several envelopes, exposing more of the light. "How'd you do that?"

"I have no idea. Silver." The light shifted again and both men reacted appropriately, small gasps and mumbles of appreciation. "Red."

"This is fascinating, Phin. Has this ever happened before?"

I shook my head, realizing I had no idea how to make it stop. "No, never. I'm honestly really relieved you see it too." I pulled out a handful of the red ones, wandering around the room to gather them. It really was very handy to be able to identify them so easily. "Green?" I said, wondering if that would throw off illumination. All the light disappeared.

"Fantastic," Seir clapped again. "I'll take this and bring you more empty ones," he said, picking up a full crate.

"Thanks."

He left the room, and Tap dipped his head, pressing a kiss to my hair. "That's a very helpful ability, Feather. What do you think it is, exactly?"

I shrugged. "I know about angelic Voice, of course, but I've never had a talent before."

"That you know of."

I couldn't help but agree. "That I know of."

"What about your father?"

I shook my head. "I never saw him use one that I can remember. We were in the archives a lot but there were no lights. He never spoke much there at all, actually." I frowned, wondering if his silence meant he was hiding his talent.

"Mmm. Well, I'm glad your throat is healing in any case. Do you need more tea? Water?"

I couldn't help but smile. Still catering to my every need, all the time. "No, I'm fine."

"Alright." He ambled out as well, and I happily dove back in, calling up the silver deals and wondering if I could beat my record of six crates before the day was done.

I'D ONLY MANAGED five crates, all told, but it had been a productive day.

After dinner, Tap and I adjourned to the living area. He was studying some kind of astral calendar while I repainted his fingernails.

"You should do yours too," he encouraged. "Or I can?" He seemed intrigued by the suggestion even though he'd been the one to make it.

"I would love that, actually, but I don't want black."

"We should ask Seir tomorrow, I'll bet he's got some blue or even purple lying about. He bought a few new bottles not long ago." He flipped a page. "If not, I'd bet he knows where to get you some in a hurry."

"Careful. They'll smear."

"I know." He glanced at me, eyes soft behind his spectacles. "What's your birthdate, Phin? I was meant to ask you for Rylan a while back, but I kept forgetting with everything else that's been going on. But also, that feels like something I should know. Something important."

"I was born on Litha, so early summer. Seventy-five years ago."

"Mmm." His eyebrows drew together as he shuffled the book-size pages. "There was an eclipse then."

"Really?"

"Yes. Do you know when your parents disappeared?"

I thought back. "They left me at the church in the spring, eleven years ago. I don't know the exact date."

He shuffled again. "He's never wrong about these things. How annoying," he muttered. "We're due another soon."

"Eclipse?"

"Yes, within the week if Rylan's charting is right, and it always is."

"What will that mean?"

"Hopefully nothing, but Magnus will be sending some reinforcements to help Coltor watch on his end, and Seir will be coming here. There's just been a pattern of something significant happening during those events, we don't want to be careless."

"Makes sense." I put the little brush back in the bottle and tightened the top. "All done."

"Thank you." He held his hands out in front of him and admired the shiny black lacquer.

"What's your birthday?" I asked, excited to learn something new about him.

"I don't have one." At my confusion, he tilted his head, amusement in his eyes. "I wasn't born, remember?"

I blushed. "Oh. Of course." I settled into the sofa, disinterested in the book I'd chosen but too lazy to go to the workshops for another. "You should choose one."

"Just a random day? Point at a calendar with my eyes closed?"

"Sure, why not? You should still have a day to celebrate."

He smiled softly. "I'll consider it. I'd be open to suggestions, of course."

The heat in my cheeks flared again. "I'll think about it. Do you have a surname?"

Tap glanced up, amusement all over his face. "No, I don't. Never seemed a need for one, honestly, as I'm here all the time. Rylan uses his old name, Stolas. Vassago chose one for himself many years ago, and Seir uses that one as well now, actually. Do you?"

"We used Engel, which looking back is a lot like them naming me Seraphina—hiding us in plain sight. But no, not really. Not unless my father was doing business that required paperwork here on Earth. There's no need for that in Heaven, first names are enough." For some reason, having no birthday or surname struck me as funny. "We're strange, aren't we?"

"Perhaps, but I like us that way." He stared at me for several heartbeats. "While you consider what date I should use, you should also pick the surname you'd like to have. That way, it's already sorted out when I officially make you my wife."

I gaped at him, lost for words as my cheeks burned and he just smirked, smug to have rendered me so speechless. Marriage hadn't come up yet, though now that the word had been said I found myself intrigued by the possibility.

We sat there a bit longer while he scowled at the calendar pages, but he finally set them down on his side table and stood, reaching out for me.

"Come on, Feather. Let's get you to bed." He took me by the hand and led me down the hallway. "Yours or mine?"

I fidgeted. "Would you be upset if I said mine?"

He frowned. "Of course not. Why would I be?"

"Because we've been using yours."

"Well, you have been doing wonders for the amount of rest I get in my bed versus that chair, but you should sleep wherever you're more comfortable."

"You can join me, if you like," I suggested, standing on my toes so I could kiss him.

"Maybe in a bit I'll take you up on that. I need to do a few things first."

"Alright."

He waited until I was out of sight in the bathroom to turn and head back down the hall. I bathed quickly and was just slipping into a thin old tunic when I heard the door creak back open.

"Are you finished already?"

The tips of his ears were pink as he shook his head. "No, but this is more important. I can go back out there once I'm done."

"Done with what?" I asked, flipping the quilts back and sliding into the sheets.

"Holding you until you fall asleep," he said, voice low and soft.

I melted; arms open to him as he joined me. He lay on top of the blankets instead of under them with me, but I was still able to curl into his side and rest my head on his chest. Like we'd done in his room, he stroked his fingers through my hair and up and down my spine, stealing away every bit of tension from my body.

"Sweet dreams, Feather." His whisper came from somewhere far away as I drifted, and I wasn't even upset when I felt him slip away. I knew he wouldn't be far, and that he'd almost certainly come back to me before I woke.

CHAPTER 35
TAP

AS I WAS preparing breakfast a couple of mornings later, a familiar bark echoed through the great hall.

I rushed out of the kitchen, torn over which should come first—finding Ramsey or waking Phin. As another bark echoed through the hall, Phin rushed out, short curls wild and eyes wide.

"Do you see her?" she asked, passing me up as she headed for the living area. "She answered me just now, in my head, but she just said *close*."

"I haven't gone to look, but I heard her bark."

"Ramsey!" Phin yelled, jogging down one row as the bark came again. "Where are you?"

A foreboding washed over me and I ran after her. Two gates activated at the same time, and I reached Phin's side just as Ramsey emerged from one door, paws touching the floor for just a beat before she disappeared again through the one across from it.

"Phin, get behind me," I warned, pushing her gently with my outstretched arm. "Actually, go get the mirror from the table next to my chair, please."

She frowned at me but took several steps down the hall. "Can you hear something I can't?"

I shook my head. "No, but something is wrong. Go, please. Quickly."

Phin's disappointment was palpable, but there must have been something in my expression that spurred her to obey my request with expedience. She returned quickly and handed over the mirror.

"What's going on?"

"I'm not sure, but I want to warn the others, just in case."

The hall remained quiet, and Phin grew fidgety. "I'm going to run and get dressed. Do you need anything else?"

"No, thank you, Feather."

I spoke the words to activate the mirror, and Seir appeared in the glass, his face swaying with his movements. "I'm on my way through to you," he grinned. "Need me to bring something?"

"Is there anything odd happening there? Or in the ruins?"

His face fell, hearing my serious tone. "Not that I know of, but I can check. Just a moment." I heard the heavy sound of his wings deploying, the ground racing through the glass as he flew directly there. Coltor and what looked like dozens of stone kin were all milling about near the doorways in the ruins.

"Ramsey just jumped gates here," I said plainly. "Do you have anything similar happening there?"

Coltor's expression was intense. He looked tired. "Multiple portals lit up briefly. I'm about to send some teams in to investigate." His eyes turned skyward. "The sky is an odd color, and everyone is extra nervy today. I'm thinking Rylan's prediction was correct." He held up a shiny new blade. "Imogen has delivered a whole batch of Dark blades, so we're well equipped. D'Arcan got theirs as well."

"I'll bring yours," Seir said, accepting sheathed blades from one of the soldiers.

"Good. Can you leave the mirror with Coltor, Seir? Show him how to use it? I have two here, so we'll both still have one."

"Yes, good idea."

"Hurry."

He nodded and disappeared from the glass in my hand, my blood surging anxiously the longer the portals were quiet. When nothing happened, I returned to the kitchen just as Phin came out of her room, fully dressed and very anxious.

"Did she come back?"

"Not yet. You should eat." I couldn't shake the sense that something big was coming, and that everything would be disrupted. Normally, eclipses brought some odd energy shifts, but nothing I couldn't manage. Perhaps I just knew more going into it this time, but this felt very different.

The whine of the portal to the glade sounded, and I called out once I heard Seir's footsteps. "We're in the kitchen. There's breakfast."

Seir strode through a few moments later, Phin hastily dispatching her toast and eggs. I'd brewed the tea so long ago it was barely warm enough to drink, but I still poured us all a cup.

"How exciting, I never get invited into the kitchen." His normal enthusiasm was missing. "Everything feels ... strange. Do you think that's just the eclipse?"

"You feel it too?" Phin asked and we both nodded. She sagged. "I'm so glad. I thought it was just me."

"No, something's coming." Seir nodded, his three sets of canines already elongated. "I feel like my skin is too tight or something. I'm itchy, full of energy with nowhere to put it." He shrugged, trying to rid himself of the sensation. "Anyway, here. Coltor said Imogen sends her apologies, she normally likes to deliver these herself, but she's patrolling at the conclave today. Things are odd there too. Rylan's even got the observatory open at d'Arcan despite the cold, and he and Vassago are taking turns watching the portal." Seir handed Phin the smallest of the sheaths.

"What's this?"

"Imogen told Coltor that this one is yours, specifically." He watched, clearly interested as Phin opened the toggle and pulled out a dagger. There was a polished ball of amethyst embedded in the rounded pommel at the end of the handle. The blade itself looked almost marbled, dark and light metals blended to make a blade yet not fully merged.

"It's beautiful. I'll have to thank her for it. I'm afraid it's wasted on me though, my weapons skills are very weak."

"We can practice," I assured her, already developing a training workshop in my mind where we could safely spar. Lots of cushions and mats, wooden training swords. Her handling me roughly and with determination on her face ... I quickly shut down the lascivious ideas my mind readily supplied.

"He was very insistent I tell you to be very careful not to cut yourself with it." He grew serious. "I've seen what one of these blades will do to a fae." He swallowed as he stared at her hand. "Please be mindful."

"I will, I promise." She slid it back into the protective leather covering. "The belt is very short, where is it supposed to go?"

"That looks like a thigh holster, Feather."

"Oh." She experimented with how to fasten it over the top of her leggings while I examined the stout Dark blade Seir handed me. "That makes sense."

"Angels, then?"

"That's the suspicion," he confirmed.

A gate activated with a painfully high-pitched whine just as Phin got the sheath comfortable on her thigh. Without a word, I left the kitchen, Phin and Seir following behind me.

I got to the hall just in time to see two men and one woman, all with violet eyes, step out of a decommissioned doorway. The portal they were using led to a green place much like Florissar, a place nobody lived or ever visited, where even animal life was scarce. Somewhere nobody, them included, should be.

It was almost as though saying the word *angel* had summoned them.

I unsheathed my new sword, holding it out in front of me as a warning as I approached them at a fast walk.

Hold, Watchman! Ramsey dashed out the doorway a few beats after them, stopping me from charging forward with violent intent. *I brought them here. They are not your enemy.*

Phin pushed past me as I lowered the blade, kneeling to accept an enthusiastic greeting from the hellhound as the three Nephilim huddled together watching us.

"I'm so happy to see you." Phin squeezed Ramsey again, then got to her feet, eyes widening as she took in the three people who looked quite a lot like her. She backed up to my side, the hound maintaining a post between us.

"Hello." The woman raised a hand in a timid wave. Her voice was low and resonant, like it encapsulated the tone of bells when they rang. She had the same silvery blonde hair Phin had, but long enough to be tied back in a loose braid that ended between her shoulder blades. "We're Nephilim, if that helps. Not full angels. We're not armed, either."

I felt Seir approaching from behind me, and his presence was confirmed when all three took a small step backward.

The three of them, upon closer inspection, seemed weak and hungry. They would be no match against two demon princes armed with Dark blades. I sheathed the new sword and turned my focus to the hound.

"Is there anything else coming out of that doorway?"

Not that I'm aware of, Watchman.

I approached the portal and deactivated it manually, just in case. "Ramsey, it would be helpful if you could explain," I prompted, eyes never leaving the three half-angels.

"Is that her name? Ramsey?" the woman asked.

Phin nodded. "Yes."

"She's lovely." The woman's eyes dropped to the hound. "It's been a bit difficult communicating, since none of us have the gift of mind speech. But she's gotten her point across well enough."

The corner of my mouth ticked upward when the dark-haired man shifted and ran his palm over his forearm. I was betting there were some teeth marks under his sleeve.

I wasn't overly upset about that, and I worried what that said about me.

I was wrong, all this time. Please extend them some grace, they deserve it. But they have some things to atone for as well. Do not mistake my kindness for total forgiveness.

"You're sure?" I asked the hound. Phin met my eye, clearly hearing the same thing I was.

Yes. I was chasing them, and naturally, they were running from me. They are incredible at maneuvering portals and staying hidden, but not because they are hunting Phin, though they were seeking her out.

"Is that not the same thing?" Phin asked.

No, it's not. They are trying to stay hidden, to survive. Just like you. Give them a chance to explain.

Phin took half a step forward, focus etched in her face as she looked between them as though trying to solve a puzzle. "Oh. You're some of the others from that day. From the garden."

Immediately my blood went hot.

I didn't even realize I was growling, wings wide and full demon features on display until I felt Seir's strong grip on my shoulder holding me back and heard Phin's voice calling my name.

"Stop! Tap! No, it's okay!"

I glanced from the now terrified Nephilim to my sweet mate and inhaled slowly as her palms came to the sides of my face. Her touch chased the rage back. It was not gone, but I could easily manage it.

Phin shook her head. "They are not at fault."

"You were hurt," I said, knowing I sounded petulant. "They left you behind."

"I was, but I'm okay now. I haven't even had an episode despite them being here, thinking and talking about it. That's a good sign, right?"

I blinked and realized she was right. There hadn't been any freezing episodes since she stopped taking that cursed tincture.

"I'll follow your lead, Feather," I said quietly. "But I will not hesitate if I feel you're in danger."

"I know." She patted my hand and kissed my cheek. When I looked up, the Nephilim seemed a bit confused by our interaction but not bothered. In fact, all three of them were holding hands, the woman clutching at both of the men who stood firm at either side of her, blocking as much of her body from me as they could.

Phin turned to them, moving to stand where Ramsey was sitting, but thankfully no closer. I was still on edge, regardless of how weak they might look. Things are not always as they seem, as Phin herself had proven.

"I'm Phin, obviously. That's Tap, and he's Seir." Seir raised a hand and waved but I remained still. "You're ..." Phin squinted. "Brinda?"

"Yes." Her hand fluttered to her chest, and she inhaled roughly her emotions naked on her face. "I'm so sorry, Phin. Apologizing could never be enough." She shook her bowed head. "I swear, we didn't mean to leave you there. It just happened, and the patrol was coming, and ..." Tears fell to the floor.

"That's how I remember it too; you were all just closer to the door than I was when it started. It wasn't your fault that your cycle hit like that. Mine did the same. I know you didn't leave me there or lock me in intentionally."

Brinda looked up, eyes wide. "Really? Thank you."

Phin dipped her head and moved on, pointing at the blond. "Harmon?"

"Yes, that's right."

Her head tilted as she looked at the brunet man. "I'm sorry. I think your name starts with a G? But I can't quite recall it."

He cracked the smallest of shy smiles. "That's alright, we didn't know one another very well. And you're close—I'm James." He rubbed his palms along the hips of his worn pants. "We're all incredibly sorry for what happened that day." He shook his head, eyes shifting to the ground. "Truly. We've been looking for you for a long time, both to apologize and to make sure you were okay. That they hadn't caught you too."

"Too? Who else?" I asked.

Brinda raised her hand. "Me. I was caught."

"But we got her out," James said, puffing out his chest. His cheekbones were too prominent, the shine in his eyes dulled. Their condition seemed worse the longer I looked at them.

"That feels like a rather important story," Seir commented, meeting my eye. I could see the gentle plea to take pity on these people in his gaze. He raised an eyebrow, communicating clearly that he wouldn't leave my side and if things went sideways, between us we could manage, regardless of what I decided.

I sighed, and he smiled. He really was a pain in my ass sometimes.

"Ramsey, can we trust them?" I asked, amused as she shifted and huffed while they straightened and stressed.

Yes, Watchman. I will vouch for them. And if I'm wrong, I'll be the first to help correct my error in judgment.

"I'll accept that," I told the hound.

Phin squeezed my hand, her big heart immediately offering aid. "It looks as though it's been a while since you've seen a decent meal?"

They tensed, something like hope flitting across their faces. In the end, Brinda was the brave one. "I suppose that's true. We haven't had access to a proper kitchen in a very long time."

"Right," I said, melting under Phin's imploring, pitiful gaze. "Seir, would you get them comfortable on the sofa? I'm sure we can find our guests something to eat."

He held out an arm and gestured for them to follow him. They did, at a safe distance, and likely only because Ramsey went with them. The mutual caution was reassuring.

"I'll help you," Phin said, linking her arm with mine. We were quiet until we were in the kitchen, Seir taking care of getting them settled.

"Are you alright, Feather?"

She nodded tightly as we assembled some sandwiches, gathered fruit and put the kettle on to make tea. "Strangely, yes. I don't feel any dishonesty from them, though ..." She frowned. "I'm not always the best judge of character. And it's really very interesting to see them again after so much time and what happened. It's not often I get to talk to people who look so much like me."

My heart squeezed, and I vowed to myself that I would do my best to get all the information I could from them while maintaining my mate's happiness. I didn't want to be the one to add to her pain over that part of her past if I could prevent it.

"What will you do with them?" she asked, unusually timid.

"That depends on what all they have to tell us, I suppose. It doesn't seem wise to host them here, but there are other options that could be explored." She brightened. "Again, depending on what we learn, and whether or not it's the truth."

"Of course."

Once we had the plates assembled, we took them out, Phin carrying a separate serving for Ramsey as well.

"Please, help yourselves," I gestured.

"Where's mine?" Seir frowned.

"If you're really that hungry, I can make you one too," Phin sighed.

"No." He jumped up, grinning. "I'm just giving him a hard time," he said, gesturing at me. "I don't really need anything."

Phin shook her head at him, but he just smiled back, the three of us doing our best not to stand too menacingly over the Nephilim while they descended on their meals. They ate so ravenously I felt a pang of sympathy. Ramsey finished quickly and curled up on the floor, alert, but relaxed.

It's been a very long journey, but I am glad to be here again. Congratulations, by the way, mistress. You've figured it out. I told you he was your demon.

Phin barked a laugh before petting her for a moment. "Yes, well spotted, I suppose." Her voice was barely above a whisper and there was a flush in her cheeks as she settled on the very edge of my recliner seat.

She watched them eat with a sympathetic frown, fidgeting until she couldn't stand it any longer. She left briefly and returned with more food, and they all looked at her with wordless thanks as that too was devoured.

The dynamic between the three Nephilim was clear—the men cared for her and she for them, though there was affection between the men too. The men pulled out the better-looking fruit and offered it to her, and she passed along the bits of meat she knew they'd like best. Their synchronicity, their bond, was beautiful to watch.

I froze as certainty passed through me. This needed to be protected. *They* needed to be protected.

I remembered what Phin had told me when we first met, that there might be other Nephilim out there, but they were no relation of hers. Seeing these three, I begged to differ. They were as good as family, perhaps cousins, if other labels failed. They required help, and I would do what I could for them despite the events of the past.

I pulled Seir off to the side. "Do you have any thoughts on where they could go if everything they tell us checks out? They can't keep running, and they can't be left at risk of being caught and returned to Heaven."

"There's an empty cabin in the glade. Perhaps d'Arcan? Rylan always manages to scrounge up rooms for strays at the school." His eyes narrowed, and he rubbed his chin. "Actually, we may be able to call in a favor with Ris."

"In the Everwood?" His suggestion to send them to the fae realm was interesting but perhaps inspired. Ris was Greta's father, and king of his realm. He would almost certainly have the means to care for them. That locale would be somewhat difficult to find and heartily defended as well.

Seir shrugged. "Just an idea."

"A good one." I patted his shoulder with a thump, and he smirked, appreciating the compliment.

"I do have those now and then, brother."

I didn't reply, which only made him laugh.

When they finished eating, Seir cleared plates while Phin and I settled in. She fidgeted, clearly ready to get the whole story from this odd trio of angels, who I was more and more sure we'd accidentally crossed paths with several times with already.

CHAPTER 36
TAP

"WHAT HAPPENED THAT day? After you left the garden?" Phin asked.

The Nephilim looked completely exhausted now that they had full stomachs.

"We made it back to my dorm," Harmon said quietly. "They came and took her while we were sleeping that first night." His jaw and fist clenched at the same time. She squeezed her fingers around his, but it was clearly a sore point for them all. "We fought, but they were stronger. We thought at first it was just because we had her with us overnight, which was against the rules. But it was so much worse."

"Who?" I asked.

"Councilman Armaros and those loyal to him." Harmon shook his head and ran his hand irritably through his stringy hair.

"We were promised special privileges," James continued. "Nice apartments. Access to everything the full angels have. We were told we were special. They swore they'd care for us since we had nobody else. So stupid to believe it," he sneered, pounding his fist into his thigh. "It was all lies. They took her to a breeding room and us to a cell."

Phin put her hand to her mouth, eyes shimmering with tears. "You have no family at all? None of you?"

James shook his head. "None worth speaking of. Our fathers were all soldiers, and our human mothers were elderly by the time we were allowed to get our schooling. We were housed in the dorms out of what little pity Heaven held for us. None of our families remained when we searched for them after escaping."

"I'm so sorry," Phin said. She frowned, as though just doing the math on her age versus that of her own mother. "They destroyed our home too. We were able to get away, but I haven't seen my parents since shortly after that."

There was a heavy silence.

After several long moments, I asked, "Apologies, but did you say *breeding room?*"

"Yes. They had a whole hallway of awful little cells in the basement of one of the fancy apartment buildings for higher ranking angels," Brinda said, voice low. "Bed, sink, toilet. Nothing else. Two meager meals a day. Not enough for me to keep my strength, just the bare minimum to keep me alive and healthy enough for their purposes. I wasn't ever let out to so much as take a walk; I just paced around my little cell. It was ten steps from the door to the wall, five from the bed to the sink. I made a game of it, to keep my sanity." She scrubbed her hands up and down her upper arms. "It was so quiet, so lonely. I couldn't hear anybody else down there with me, but that doesn't mean they weren't there." She swallowed. "I was visited by the full angels I was matched to breed with, as often as possible. Sometimes more than once a day, sometimes I'd get a day or two between."

My blood was roiling under my skin. "I would appreciate names, if you have them."

Brinda's face fell. "I'm sorry, but I don't have any. I never saw any faces. The angels I was matched with came only when it was dark and wore coverings. It was not ... intimate. I was made to face away from them, both so I couldn't run and for their anonymity." James and Harmon made angry noises and she sniffled, blinking away her tears before they could fall. "Councilman Armaros came by once a week to make sure I was still well enough to do what they wanted. Once, he brought a healer after ..." She shook her head but didn't elaborate. She didn't need to; we could all guess why just fine. "There was nobody else."

I glanced at Seir, who indicated with a slight head nod that he'd heard that as clearly as I had. The rage I felt down to my bones was reflected in his face, his red eyes and elongated teeth. They would pay, one way or another.

I turned to the men. "And your prison, it was elsewhere?"

James played with the frayed threads on his pant leg, clearly agitated. "Only female Nephilim are truly useful to them. Our potential breeding contributions are considered insignificant—they just want rid of us. The female angels that reproduce the same way we do are already matched with full angels, and anyone with an angelic parent that isn't completely evil would never stand for their offspring being treated in such a way, male or female." He looked away. "We were only a nuisance. So we were left to rot in a dungeon."

"At least we were together," Harmon said, strong affection in his eyes. "And that allowed us to plot our escape. So we could get back to Brin. Get her out."

"How did you escape?"

"Our guard got careless. We were intentionally compliant. Docile." His jaw rolled. "He liked to chat, though we rarely responded because that wasn't the point. He loved to hear his own voice. Though he did enjoy the challenge of getting a reaction out of us."

"He did, at first, too. Until we got smarter," James added.

"Yes. We learned. Watched. He had a bad habit of leaving his keys in doors after he opened them. One day, we got lucky. He went to use the toilet after leaving us near the tubs for our weekly bath. The keys were still in the lock, and he was across the room in a water closet, proving his diet was not to be envied." Harmon relayed the information in a detached tone that indicated he'd ventured back to that place in his mind.

James took up the tale, seeing Harmon's gaze go distant. "We were still dressed even, the fool. We glanced at one another, turned on the taps to make it seem like we were still there preparing to wash, grabbed the keys, and locked every door we could on our way out to slow him down. Then we ran like the devil himself was chasing us." He looked up, eyes wide. "No offense."

I couldn't help but smile and Seir was openly chuckling. "None taken."

"How did you know where she was?" Phin asked.

"The idiot had gleefully taunted us about how close and yet how far from us she was." Harmon snarled. "Told us more than once exactly where they were keeping her, what she was being put through."

"Were you able to find any other women?"

"Only her." James's somber tone weighed down the air. "We opened five other rooms before the guards came. They were all empty. But there were perhaps another twenty we didn't get to check." He swallowed and reached into his pocket. "I still have these." A ring with dozens of keys dangled from his fingers.

"And where you were kept, were there any other men?" Seir asked, perplexed.

They shook their heads. "Not many. Not anymore," James said sadly.

"There were four other cells. Nine other men. Only three still alive and one of those ... barely," Harmon breathed. Brinda whimpered and Phin closed her eyes, tears running freely down her cheeks. "We opened their cell doors on our way out. They all went their own way, and we've never come across them again. I didn't recognize any of them either." He sagged. "I hope every day that they are recovered and safe somewhere."

"Armaros was behind all this?" I bit off his name like a curse, eyes lifting to Seir who was as disgusted as I was.

"Yes. It's his *initiative*," James affirmed. "That's what he called it when he came every so often to see if we were dead or dying yet."

I recalled with rage how I had viscerally responded to the man that day in the church. "I came across him in Vincara, shortly after you had passed through. It's a wonder he didn't try to snatch Phin right from the church on the slightest suspicion she was Nephilim." I hated to be thankful for the tincture that had quite literally been poisoning her, but it had done a good job keeping her hidden from him, even at close range.

"You *were* there," Brinda gasped. "We were so close."

"He's too careful for that." Harmon shook his head. "We've been trying to find you, Phin, since we first escaped. Our first stop was to check the garden, but you were obviously already gone. The door was wide open again though, a clear trap. We've wanted to be sure you were okay, and to warn you. To apologize. This whole time. We went to Vincara because we'd heard a rumor that there was someone with eyes like ours in that village, a dark haired boy." I raised an eyebrow, and the corner of Phin's mouth twitched. "That was you, right? Not someone else?"

"Yes," Phin confirmed.

"I hate that us going there drew his attention to you. It seems we've put you in further danger, and I'm sorry for that too, none of this was how we intended."

They bled sincerity, and I found myself letting down my guard. They'd done what they could to survive and saved others in the process.

"I understand," Phin assured them. "So ... you escaped Heaven and have been running since then?" Phin asked. "How long were you held captive?"

"Two cycles," Brinda said. "The end of that first one and into the next."

"So four months or so?" Seir exhaled when she confirmed. "I'm sorry."

She nodded gently, accepting his empathy. "It could have been far worse."

"It should never have happened at all," James snapped. "To you or anyone else."

"You came for me." She patted him comfortingly. "You got me out. And those men. That's what matters."

Do you see the difference now, Watchman? They were running from that terrible councilman but also seeking you out, Phin. I misunderstood, I thought they were after you, mistress. I chased, they ran. I never realized someone was after them aside from me. Terrible mistakes, all the way around. The real enemy is that hideous angel, not them.

"Agreed," I sighed.

"Thank you for your kindness, but we really shouldn't linger here," Harmon sighed, shifting like he was about to stand. He glanced around as though just realizing where they actually were, and his face blanched. "We probably shouldn't have come here in the first place, but thank you, Ramsey, for your insistence that we follow you."

"Inter-planar transit rules are sometimes flexible, in times of emergency," Seir said, thoughtful. "This certainly qualifies for an exception. Besides, you were accompanied by a hellhound, and that by itself gives a certain leniency."

Ramsey lifted her head and panted lightly with a very pleased canine smile.

Your deference is appreciated, princeling.

Seir grinned, so she'd sent her message strongly enough for him to hear, as well.

"Surely you could stay long enough to rest?" Phin suggested, glancing at me to be sure I was in agreement. "Some decent sleep and a hot bath could do you a world of good. Another meal, as well, maybe? If you need to leave, it seems the least we can do is help you replenish your strength first."

"You've been so hospitable, we're very grateful. But we really shouldn't. Trouble has a way of following us." Brinda's sad tone made my heart ache.

"I insist," I said. "We have the resources to protect ourselves. A few hours should make no difference." I wasn't sure that was entirely true with an eclipse underway, but time would tell, and we could certainly manage protecting a few extra people should it come to that.

They all sagged visibly, tears forming in Brinda's eyes. "Thank you."

"Come on. I'm sure there are some clothes we can find for you as well."

Phin led them down the hall toward her room, Ramsey taking the opportunity to sleep, right there on the sofa. Seir and I followed behind the Nephilim, keeping a sharp eye on everything. Tension pulled at my shoulders, the invasion of my personal space unfamiliar and uncomfortable, but for a good cause. Before Phin came, not even Seir had ventured into the rooms beyond the living area.

Once Phin had them all tucked into her bathroom with soap and towels, she went straight across to my bedroom and began digging through the wardrobe.

I locked eyes with my brother, and he nodded, stationing himself right outside Phin's bedroom door. It wasn't that we didn't trust them, but it would not do to be careless.

"Is there something I can help you find?" I asked.

"You said I could have anything I wanted, yes?"

"I did."

"Well, I would like for Harmon and James to borrow some clothes. I have plenty to share with Brinda, but I don't think those two would fit in my leggings, no matter how many meals they've missed."

I smiled back and helped her find what she needed, equally amused and pleased that she'd taken my offer to heart. "As you wish." I kissed her temple, my front against her back and my arms bracketing her in as we sifted through my shirts and trousers. "Are you alright?" I asked softly. "This is quite a lot to take in all at once."

She paused, eyes going distant. A nod came, gentle at first, then more confident. "Yes. I think I am. I really don't blame them for what happened, I never ... *rarely* did. It was just terrible timing all the way around. And from the sound of things, I got the better end, all things considered. My father came for me, after all. I wasn't taken to a ..." She grimaced and my own stomach lurched. "Breeding chamber." She shivered, and I rubbed a hand along her back.

"What's happening will not stand, Feather. I promise you that." My teeth clenched, and I tried not to picture the destruction that such a deplorable effort must have caused over the course of years. "You will be safe, and so will they. As will any others they still have captive."

"It could start a war," she whispered, fear in her eyes.

"Then to war we shall go. I have sixty-six legions at my command, ready to be summoned should the need arise. My brothers have hundreds more between them. You have my blade, and theirs, and likely that of the stone kin as well. I don't particularly enjoy them, but I am not afraid of a fight. Especially not over someone as important as *you*."

My brave, strong mate turned and wrapped her arms around me, silently sobbing into my chest as she finally allowed the wave of emotion to crash over her. What she'd endured, what she'd escaped, and what others had been faced with hit her all at once.

"I wish I could talk to my dad. I have so many questions."

"I know, beloved."

I shushed her, held her, and vowed to fix it all, even go to war with Heaven itself, if it meant she'd be safe once and for all.

Aside from vowing my loyalty and love for her, I'd never meant anything more seriously in my life.

CHAPTER 37
PHIN

A QUICK PEEK SHOWED that the three Nephilim were out cold, all cuddled together in my bed. I'd been worried that it would be too small, but clearly that fear was unfounded. Harmon and James each hand an arm and a leg over Brinda, who was sandwiched between them.

Ramsey had curled up in front of my bedroom door to guard. She was sleeping, too, but I had no doubt she'd be up the moment she heard them stir.

Seir went into the first library almost immediately and closed the door behind himself, confusing me terribly. After a beat, he opened it a crack.

"Sorry, Phin!" he called, which almost made me laugh.

"What's he up to?" I asked as I followed behind Tap, who first went to the great hall and shuttered at least half the gates and then went into the kitchen and started stacking ingredients on the counter.

"He's using my larger scrying mirror I assume. A friend of his is the King of Everwood, in the fae realm. We may be able to send your cousins to him for temporary safekeeping."

What Tap had said was all real words, certainly, and most of them sensical. But it took me several tries to really grasp what he'd said. "Cousins? Fae king?"

"Yes. Ris is Greta's father, actually. And in a manner of speaking, they are cousin to you, are they not? All Nephilim?"

"Oh." I blinked, taking this additional information in. "I suppose that's correct enough, yes."

Tap's mouth twitched as he started chopping and sautéing what appeared to be a very large pot of hearty stew.

"Thank you," I said, emotions still riding me heavily. "For this."

He shook his head, bumping his glasses back up his nose with his wrist as they started to slip. "You owe me no thanks for this, Feather. This is simply the decent thing to do."

"And yet you're ignoring how rare it is to be so." I squeezed his arm and moved to chop or stir, whichever was more helpful. "Do you think it would be okay to eat in the first library? The table in there would be better to seat everyone."

"Yes, that should be fine. There's nothing so secretive in there they couldn't see it. And they wouldn't be able to do much with it anyhow."

Seir came in as I was stacking up bowls. "Ris is quite agreeable to our request," he said proudly. "His palace has plenty of open rooms, and there's always work for people to do. His soldiers are well trained and likely bored. They've been very efficient at clearing out all the disloyal since I was there last."

"That's good news, all of it." Tap sprinkled spices over the simmering pot of stew, the aroma already mouthwatering.

Seir came to peer over Tap's shoulder and added another couple dashes of spice, earning him a stunned glare from his brother. "I also checked in with the others. Rylan says things are odd, but aside from the sun beginning to disappear a little, there's been nothing else to worry over. Magnus and his teams explored the gates that signaled the energy surges, but they also found nothing unusual. Seems it's just the eclipse making things go a little ... off."

Tap nodded, but the pensive look on his face told me he didn't want to dismiss anything yet. "Won't be long then, if Rylan noted the sun is going dark."

They went off to check as many gates as they could while the soup cooked, and I took the opportunity to make some quick bread to have with it. That didn't occupy quite enough time, so I left all the doors between the living area and the deals library wide open and made myself sort for a while.

Ramsey finally alerted me that everyone was awake a few hours later, and I walked out the libraries to find her leading the three Nephilim back to the couch. They all sat, clearly still groggy and looking both as though they had slept well and like they needed to do the same thing for a week.

"I trust you slept well?" I asked.

"Very much so, thank you." Brinda smiled. "We haven't been in a bed like that in ages."

Years, I'd wager. Ramsey chuffed in my head. *They've endured much, mistress. Comfort is not something they've had much of.*

My heart squeezed, and I felt terrible for having ever complained about my circumstances at the church. It was not a competition, but I'd had it easy, compared to them. "I'm glad to hear that. Are you hungry?" They glanced between themselves, clearly embarrassed to say they were after having already eaten. "There's stew and bread. Get you full and warm before you go."

"You're being so kind," James said. "Thank you."

"It's nothing, really," Tap said from the other side of them, drawing everyone's attention. "Please also allow me to apologize for the impression I must have made when you got here."

"Your reaction was warranted. We understand and appreciate all you've done, very much," Harmon agreed.

"We'll bring everything, if you'd like to show them to the table, Feather."

"Of course. Come with me?"

They rose and, as a cluster, walked with me through the first door into the familiars library. They chose seats all in a row down one side of the table, Brinda still at the center between James and Harmon. They all looked around with awe, the tall shelves packed with scrolls and envelopes stunning no matter how many times I'd seen them.

Tap set down the huge pot while Seir dished out bowls and passed them around. Ramsey got hers delivered on the floor and sniffed at it.

"Not to your liking, hound?" Seir teased.

Just too hot to eat, demon. She sat back, doing the dog equivalent of an eye roll.

I laughed, startling Brinda. "Sorry, Ramsey and Seir are teasing one another."

"Oh." Her mouth twitched into a smile. "How fun. She's truly something else, isn't she?" Her awe of the hellhound made me hope there was a special creature in her future.

As directed, the three of them ate as though storing up what they could before they entered unknown territories again.

"Where did you plan to go after this?" Tap asked.

James shook his head, reaching for another slice of bread. He smeared butter over it before taking a bite. "There are a few places we know we can stay for a few days or longer before having to move on. Probably start with one of them."

"What if there was another option?" Seir asked, his grin playful.

"Like what?" Harmon asked. Brinda paused, spoon halfway to her mouth.

"Have you been to the fae realm at all in your travels?"

"No. We've only mastered the portals in this realm. It was hard enough finding places to go that were habitable and wouldn't immediately be deadly, we didn't dare risk going further, to somewhere inherently more dangerous."

"Fair enough. Would you go there, if it meant you no longer had to keep running?"

They all three stopped, looking from him to me. "They would not betray you like that, I promise. This is a serious offer."

"How would you convince the fae to take in three Nephilim who are being hunted by a dangerous member of the angelic council?" James chuffed, though he was not amused. "That's an awfully tall order."

"King Ris of the Everwood welcomes you," Seir said plainly before eating a bite of soup.

"And the catch?" Harmon asked. "What are we trading for such generosity?"

"Likely some light labor around the palace, depending on your skills, of course. Some gratitude to those who've provided aid. Information about those who wronged you and potentially some in-person testimony so they can be brought to the justice they deserve." Seir shrugged and the three had a conversation between themselves without ever speaking a word.

"That's it?" Brinda asked.

"Should there be more?" Tap asked.

I understood her confusion to my bones. I'd reacted much the same way when Tap brought me here. After leading such a life, the notion that someone would do a kindness for no reason other than it was right was definitely perplexing.

"You can go today," Seir said calmly. "I'll escort you myself, after you're finished eating. If that's what you want." He sat back in his chair. "Though if you want to continue on as you have, I respect that as well. Sometimes it's harder to let go of the familiar than to take a chance on the unknown."

"You're serious." James repeated.

"Quite." Tap nodded.

"I know you don't know us from Adam," Seir said, smirking hard, especially when James chuffed a laugh, "but the offer is genuine. Ris is a good man. His story is not mine to tell, but he was also imprisoned just for being who he is. He is beloved by his kingdom and does his best to treat everyone kindly. With fairness." He swiped his napkin across his mouth and leaned forward on his elbows. "Honest work. Ample food, warm bed, hot baths. What do you say?"

"Yes. Please." Brinda fought her tears, but they won in the end. She dropped her head into her hands and sobbed out her thanks, her two men comforting her and giving us their gratitude just as vocally.

For a day that had started off feeling wrong, I couldn't help feeling hopeful that we'd managed to turn everything around, at least for them.

AFTER THE MEAL, everyone gathered in the great hall near the portal to the fae realm. The one that led directly to Everwood was a deep, rich brown. There was a small pine tree in one corner and a red leaf in the other.

I briefly wondered if I would ever remember the symbols and sounds for all the places on the other side of the doorways like Tap did. As if confirming my question, when I looked at the one beside it, a doorway built from driftwood with a sprinkle of golden sand in one top corner and a shell in the other, I knew that it led to a place called Aevum Cay.

"Couldn't possibly be all of them," I muttered to myself. "Doors to the fae realm?" I asked quietly, and a row of four lit up gold, the ones for Everwood and Aevum Cay included. "Saints." I thought quickly as Seir educated our guests on what to expect in that realm. "Doors to cold places?" Several lit up, all up and down the hall, a faint white light hovering around them like it did the silver deals. "Doors to forested places?" Green illuminated these. I exhaled, wondering just how far my Voice talent extended and how many new surprises it would bring as I continued to heal.

It's wonderful that you're finding it again, Ramsey said in my head, startling me. She panted, smiling. *Your gift.*

"Again?" I asked. "How do you mean?"

Why do you think your father took you to the archives with him? Do you really not remember at all?

Saddened, I shook my head. "No, I don't. What all does it work on?"

One way to find out, mistress.

Cryptically helpful, as always.

Ramsey planned to accompany the three Nephilim to Everwood with Seir as another layer of familiarity. Despite not being able to communicate clearly, they'd built a level of trust.

"Thank you," Brinda said, drawing me close and giving me a brief hug. "We owe you so much more than we did when we arrived, but I'm grateful for such a debt."

"We'll see one another again, soon," I promised her, and I meant it. I wanted to talk with them, and any other Nephilim that might have escaped the councilman's grasp.

Tap activated the portal and just as Brinda moved to step through, every other doorway in the hall also came to life, flickered, then went dark again. Then they started to come on at random, but only for a moment before going out again.

"What in the ..." Seir glanced around. "Tap?"

"I think it's safe to assume we've arrived at eclipse totality," Tap said. "This has happened before, though not so widespread. We should wait until it settles."

Seir nodded and activated his small scrying mirror, trying to reach Rylan or Vassago at d'Arcan to confirm.

The pressure in the room changed. The temperature dropped. Portals hummed as they activated just to go dark again.

And somewhere amidst the chaos, Councilman Armaros stepped through the same portal the three Nephilim had arrived through.

The angel smirked as he looked around the great hall. I'd gotten very brief glimpses of him that day at the church, but now I was getting to see him straight on. He was tall, with the silver-blonde hair and violet eyes that gave him away as an angel. He was painfully beautiful, but his evil nature shone through, dulling any attractiveness. I shivered when his cold eyes landed on me, then my anger flared when he arrogantly winked at Brinda.

Seir tensed and stepped in front of the three Nephilim, clearly recognizing him as well as the threat he was. Ramsey had her teeth bared, a low rumble in her chest as she took up a defensive stance. Her eyes glowed red, and black smoke swirled aggressively over her whole body.

"How *dare* you step foot here," Tap growled. His wings snapped out wide, his demon features instantly at the surface. "You are breaking several Heavenly ordained rules by daring to come here." The angel just chuckled, looking at Tap like he was a child having a tantrum. It was odd to see, because Tap was taller than him by a few inches, especially in his demon form, so the angel's ego had him smirking while looking *up* at Tap.

"Armaros, this is *my* domain, and you are *not. Welcome. Here.*" Tap's deep, resonant voice boomed around the wide hall. I held my breath as he approached the angel, blade raised. "You are not now, nor have you ever been permitted to come to this place."

Seir stepped forward, handing the mirror to Brinda so he too could draw his blade. I saw a flash of Rylan's face in the glass, which was reassurance that they were at the very least hearing what was happening.

He just laughed, the sound like broken bells. "Oh, Tap. What a pleasure to see you again."

"I could not disagree more."

"You'll be made an example of for breaking the transit covenants," Seir warned, shaking his head in disgust. "You should leave."

Armaros shrugged. "Not if I've got the proper reasoning and leverage." The three Nephilim huddled together, backing as far away from him as they could get without falling through the portal. "You know, I was losing my faith in Father Morton there for a bit, but now, I think he deserves a reward for being so helpful." He turned to face me, wearing a grin that scraped along my spine. His words landed like punches, giving me further confirmation that Father Morton was not, and perhaps had never truly been, a friend to me or my parents. He was not even a good man of faith; so easily swayed by temptation as to reveal my location once I was no longer under his watch. Shameful.

"Absolutely not," Tap warned, the tip of his blade raised and aimed at Armaros's throat. "You don't even look at her. I will kill you where you stand."

"There's no need for ugliness. As we discussed in Vincara, that lovely little Nephilim has been chosen for our repopulation initiative. Demon mother or not, she'll make us some very useful angel offspring." Rage flowed through me, hot and thick. He didn't wait for a response before continuing, "We've waited years for you to reveal yourself, Seraphina. Your father did an excellent job of hiding you away. I was reasonable the last time we met, because I couldn't be sure it was you under that robe." His head tilted to one side. "I couldn't sense you properly at all then." He inhaled deeply, eyes sliding closed. "But I can now. And you're definitely ready to be matched. Even if you did dishonor yourself by spreading your legs for a demon." He sneered. "Apples not falling far from trees, and all that."

Tap unleashed a guttural sound of rage, and Armaros stepped back as Tap swung his blade.

"Come home, with me, Seraphina. Fulfill your highest purpose as a Nephilim."

My stomach turned at his words. "Heaven has never been my home," I replied softly, wishing I could summon the strength to be louder. I forced myself to stand taller, and push my shoulders back, pretending to be brave as though that would make it real.

"You mustn't judge based on how things used to be. You'll see, things are much improved for Nephilim since these three left."

"Left?" James huffed. "We *escaped.* Nothing that comes out of your mouth is the truth." The Nephilim's disdain for him was obvious, and when his eyes met mine, the plea for me to believe him was clear.

"Come now, James. I know your memories are probably a bit darker than I'd like, but privileges have been reevaluated. Everything is different now. And just think, if you're a carrier for a talent that's useful to us all, you'll be rewarded even more handsomely." He turned to face me again, and I had to force myself not to shrink away. "Come with me, Seraphina. Despite the nature you inherited from your mother, Heaven is where you *belong.*"

Behind him, Seir had quietly activated the gate to Everwood, and the other Nephilim edged right up against it.

I set my jaw, trying to be smart about whatever was about to happen. "No."

His pleasant expression disappeared, and Tap stepped even closer to him, rage pouring off him in waves.

"You request death by coming here. A slow, painful one for threatening her."

He was smug. "You wouldn't dare. To kill me would be to incite a war between Heaven and Hell."

Seir shook his head, a smile that was too sharp to be friendly on his mouth. "I very much doubt you're worth that much, Armaros. You're nothing more than someone who sits in a fancy chair somewhere and directs people to do his dirty work and useless errands. Nobody will miss you." I gasped, his words intentionally incendiary. I wasn't sure what he was playing at until Armaros began to tremble, a vein throbbing in his forehead and red streaks forming around his eyes.

"How dare you?" he boomed, and it was then I realized how unhinged he truly was. He raged, spit flying and the cords in his neck strained to snapping. "*I'm* the one who has figured out how to match angels and Nephilim for the best Voice outcomes in their offspring! All I do, I do for the good of Heaven. My initiative is the best possible scenario for you. A *gift!*" He swept his arm, vaguely indicating that he was including me and the Nephilim in his statements. "All of you are an abomination! None of you should have existed in the first place. Your parents stepped out of the light and fornicated with humans and witches and even *demons* to create you. At least this way, you can be useful. You can earn your place in the glory of the celestial plane. You should be *grateful!*"

"Grateful?" Tap boomed in response. "For what, exactly? Imprisonment? Rape? Forced impregnation? Death? You're insane."

"Such crude words!" He snapped. "I'm bringing *life* back to Heaven, there are several new babies thanks to me!"

Brinda gasped, and I did my best to hold my body stable, to not draw attention as I took tiny steps toward Ramsey.

"How many women would I be joining?" I asked quietly.

Armaros grimaced as though disgusted. "The previous vessels we managed to successfully breed were weak, but their progeny shall be strong. They're being raised by deserving parents, and they will want for nothing." He spun to me, a wild look in his eye. "Which is why we need her." He seemed to remember that Brinda was there too and turned her direction. "Them. We need them."

"You will never have either of them." Tap stepped forward, blade raised. "Or any other Nephilim."

Seir grabbed onto the sleeves of both James and Harmon, who in turn both held Brinda, and pushed them through the gate. He paused and followed only after making eye contact with Tap.

Ramsey quickly padded several doors down. *Come with me, mistress! I will keep her safe, demon.*

I hesitated, and that was a mistake. One heartbeat too long, and the plan was given away.

As I moved to follow my hellhound, the councilman pivoted and snatched at me, grabbing the fabric of my shirt. Tap rushed forward but the councilman was faster, spinning us toward the nearest active doorway.

Chaos reigned, a whole world of things happening in the space of a breath.

Ramsey barked, running and leaping at me as Tap's eyes went wide, his arm reaching for me as his blade swung down, the heavy sound it made cutting through the air forcing my eyes closed. Magnus's booming voice echoed through the great hall and then we were gone, my breath knocked from my lungs as we landed in a foreign place.

CHAPTER 38
PHIN

I GRUNTED, STRUGGLING AGAINST the councilor's grasp as I tried to get my lungs to expand. My heart sank when I realized I couldn't see the portal we'd come through, and that Ramsey hadn't made it in our jump. "Show me the door?" I whispered to the breeze, and the portal was visible as though it had always been right there. I breathed a little easier. According to this new facet of my gift, we were in a place called Prawlin. I didn't even know what realm that was in, but at least I had a name.

Armaros groaned as I forcefully threw back my elbow. "So aggressive, Seraphina."

I scrambled away from him as he reached up to touch a cut on his forehead, lurching to my feet. Remembering I was armed at the sight of his blood, I undid the latch on my little dagger and pulled it out, the weight of the blade heavy in my hand. I mentally chanted a reminder to keep the sharp parts far from my own skin. As I hid it as best I could by holding it behind my leg.

"Come along," he said once he stood, grabbing at my collar to pull me with him. In that moment I was half grateful I'd started leaving my jewelry on the bedside table unless we were leaving the crossroads. While the bracelet offering some invisibility might have been helpful, I would have deeply regretted breaking my necklace chain or losing either piece.

"Hey!" The tight grip he had on my shirt collar began to choke me and fear took over. He was bigger, stronger, and a full angel—I was no match for him. I tightened my grip on my new blade, waiting for a good moment to land a decent strike. "Do you really think he won't find me? He knows where every single portal leads."

"Not all of them," he chuckled darkly. "Have you found your Voice yet, Seraphina?"

"None of your business."

He *tsked* at me. "There's no need for such animosity. I know your father after all, and I'm a councilman. Shouldn't that earn me at least some respect?"

"Not after what I've learned about you, and much of that from your own mouth, no."

Fury burned in his eyes, and he jerked me by the collar, my teeth rattling as he shook me. "I am responsible for some of the boldest advancements in all angelic history!" I could only stare back, wide-eyed as he glared down at me. The angel collected himself, the change visible as he forced himself to be calm. It chilled me to the bone. He was truly insane. "Now. What is your innate talent? What is the gift you bear with your angelic Voice?"

"It doesn't matter, it's not useful here," I lied.

"No? Try me."

"I work in a library. My talent helps me organize the shelves."

He squinted, paused, then jerked me with him as he went left, through a stand of trees. Abruptly, he pulled me forward and we went through yet another portal, landing us in a place covered in ice. My landing was rough, my wrist bent awkwardly underneath my body, but my blade was still in my hand and by some miracle, I hadn't cut myself yet. I shivered immediately, my teeth chattering uncontrollably. It was colder than I'd ever remembered it being in Aymonroux; it even hurt to breathe. My eyelashes frosted over and I couldn't feel the tips of my ears within just a few steps. I turned to look and filed away that the doorway was marked Xylos.

"What talent does your father have?" Armaros demanded.

"I d-don't know, I never s-saw it."

He growled. "No point in lying to me, Seraphina."

"I'm n-not lying." I twisted the handle around in my hand, heart in my throat as I curled in on myself for warmth. I was doing my best to keep calm all while plotting to stab an angel in a place I didn't recognize with no way to get back.

"That's a shame. Perhaps I'll just have to ask him myself."

I stopped walking, and he continued on, my head bobbing as his momentum pulled me forward. "You know wh-where he is?"

"Of course I do."

The words *he's alive* pulsed through my mind over and over again.

"Ah. This way." He tugged at me again, and we landed in a hot, humid, green place that reminded me of Florissar.

"And my mother?" I thawed bit by bit, my wrist throbbing from how I'd landed on it.

He snorted. "What will you give me for that kind of information?"

"I'm not going back to Heaven with you."

Armaros spun on me, violet eyes blazing as he glared down at me. "Yes, you are. And you will do everything I say. It's too important for you not to."

I tried to decide what the right thing to do would be. I was not a fighter, and I wasn't even good at strategy. What would Tap do? Seir? One of the other strong, talented women in the family? I bit my tongue instead, which only frustrated him further.

"So arrogant. After all I've done. After all my research, I still have to prove myself." I followed behind, his grip becoming more lax. "Even Brookes, rest his soul, got proper recognition for what he did. All those couples, going against the express will of the councils! Pairing up and even having children." He shook his head. "Something had to be done to keep them from risking the safety of us all. Mating two strong powers together? Unpredictable and dangerous. Could throw the whole balance off. But my initiative will fix that! If the councils lost control over their factions, it would be disastrous ..." He muttered incoherently and shook his head. "And now, I'm the only one left! The only one who knows! That should be more valuable." He grumbled under his breath, something about titles and the council, but I couldn't make it out.

He was fully ranting, and I wasn't sure he even realized he was talking to me and not just himself. "What is it that you know?"

"Where the hiding place is, of course! Where they're all kept."

"Is that where my father is?"

He laughed. "Of course it is! Where else—" He stopped walking, mouth dropping open. My heart flew behind my ribs, my ears clogging with the sudden rush of excitement mixed with fear as he turned on me. "You little trickster!" I had only been going along with his mad rant, but I was sure he didn't see it that way.

"Take me there first, and I'll go with you," I said hastily.

"What?"

"Show me where they are, and I'll agree to go to Heaven with you. I just want to see them. They don't even have to see me back." He tilted his head and stared at me, clearly trying to detect any deception.

Armaros smiled, and it was full of teeth. How a man so beautiful could be so terrifying confused me. "Good. Good, good. I knew you'd see reason. Come along." I let him pull me through three more portals, the final one landing us in a bland, beige place, where everything felt ... empty. He'd taken a deep breath before the final jump, like he was preparing himself for the possibility that it wouldn't work.

"Where are we?" I asked. He had only walked a few paces from the portal before stopping.

"The hiding place," he said. But I could see plain as day that the portal was labeled Purgatory.

"Why did you seem afraid? Like you might be wrong?"

"Not *wrong!*" he roared. "It only opens during an eclipse," he huffed as though what I'd asked was ridiculous. "You're going to be a lot of work, Seraphina, I can tell. You're bright, inquisitive." He nodded and looked me up and down. "It'll be so much fun watching you break."

"Armaros?" I hated the way his name tasted. Sour, stale. Like moldy bread.

"What?" He stalked away from the portal, and I rushed to keep up.

"I lied."

He spun again, mouth open and shocked rage in his eyes. Holding the handle of my blade with both hands, I jammed the point down, aiming for his torso. At the last moment he stepped back, so the dagger actually sank deep into his thigh. The feel of the steel cutting through his flesh and stopping with an odd vibration as it hit bone made me gag, but I did what I'd been taught by my parents and twisted before pulling it back out. I almost lost my balance but managed to keep my footing. As he gaped at me, I backed away several steps, too stunned to run, even though my mind was screaming that I should do just that.

"You little bitch," he swore, gasping as the pain of what I'd done registered. He sat down hard in the dead grass and wasted no time ripping open the leg of his pants so he could see the damage.

The area around the wound was already black, tiny tendrils creeping away from the wound as well.

"What *is* this?" he asked. "How dare you! You'll pay for such insolence. You'll be punished! I'm a full angel, high ranking and of the old guard—" I cut him off with a wild swing of my blade, this one catching his forearm. He cried out, pulling the arm against his chest, mouth open and eyes shocked. "What have you done to me?"

"Far less than you deserve."

He blinked as though stunned I was still talking back to him in such a manner. I turned and sprinted for the portal, wondering how else my Voice might work. Scared to get too close at first, I screamed at it, giving our current location and every other place we'd stopped along the way. When I spotted Armaros back on his feet, hobbling my way, I closed my eyes, shoved my face into the strange nowhere space between the wood frame and screamed it all there as well. Then I pictured the crossroads and Tap, willing the portal to take me home directly. Unfortunately, it flickered and went dark just before I stepped in. I could only hope some part of my other efforts was successful.

"What have you *done*?" Armaros roared, the black spreading from the single stab wound now thick, following along every place that blood flowed through his thigh.

"Please show Tap the way here," I muttered, standing my ground, blade held in both hands out in front of me as the angel groaned and writhed.

There was a hum, and suddenly Ramsey and Tap both stepped out of the portal.

I hardly recognized my hound; she seemed larger than usual, her eyes red and teeth bared. Her black smoke poured from her all over, and she didn't speak to me at all. I'd never seen her so worked up.

"Thank all the saints," Tap breathed, sweeping me into his arms. "You called for me, Feather. It nearly knocked me off my feet in the hall it was so clear, so loud."

"It worked." I was equal parts thrilled and terrified by the potential power of my Voice.

"Yes, beloved, it did." He pulled me in, planting a fierce kiss on my mouth. "Are you alright?" Tap hastily checked me over, hands and eyes covering every inch until he was satisfied that I hadn't come to harm.

"I'm fine," I assured him. "What about the others?"

Everyone is fine, mistress. Your demon's family and the stone kin have everything well in hand. The crossroads is secure, and the other three Nephilim are safe in the fae realm.

Tap grimaced, appraising the angel's condition. As if taking that as permission, Ramsey latched onto Armaros's wrist over his shirt and tugged, making him cry out.

Weak, arrogant angel. Not even worth my effort to bite down.

"Don't bite him! The blade—"

I would not be harmed, mistress. Don't worry. But I can tell he would taste bad. She sneezed and sat right at his side, staring at him while he moaned and tried to shuffle away from her. *Coward.*

"It's moving so fast," I said, already seeing tendrils of black curling up from under Armaros's collar, creeping along his neck and over the top of his hands. I relayed what I could as fast as I could string my words together, the mentions of the council and the hiding place we'd stumbled into.

Tap's dark smile gave me an odd thrill as he approached the angel. "Speak." When Armaros didn't, Tap pressed into the bloody gash in Armaros's thigh with his thumb, eliciting pained shrieks from the angel. "I might be inclined to get you aid if you tell me what I want to know."

Armaros, more than a little panicked, began to repeat what he'd told me. There were a few other tidbits about the workings of Heaven, but he started to struggle to use his tongue fairly quickly. Before long, it was clear that there was no hope that he might survive the terrible poison that was my hybrid blade.

Armaros shuddered as the black spread through every vein. He babbled incoherently, hands fisting and relaxing uncontrollably.

I gasped, hand over my mouth as his chest was slower and slower to rise again. "Saints," I breathed. "What have I done?"

"What you had to. You saved yourself." Tap's tone was soft, placating.

"I k-killed him." The weight of my actions hit me all at once, and my knees buckled. Tap caught me, lowering me gently to a sitting position before kneeling beside me on the ground. He forced me to meet his eye with his hands on either side of my face. "Phin, beloved, listen to me. You just stabbed him. Understand? He took you, and you defended yourself." He took the blade from my hand, and with one sharp motion pierced Armaros's heart with it, the angel groaning out until the sound was only a wheeze. Then there was silence. "See? *I* killed him." He stared at me, those silver orbs insistent and unyielding until my breaths were no longer so loud in my ears and my heartbeat had settled to a more normal pace. "Okay?" I nodded, and he copied the gesture, relaxing his grip on me. "Good. Look away, Feather. You don't need to see this."

I did, eyes scrunched closed and hands covering my ears, but not until after the first meaty *thwack* of Tap's blade rending Armaros's head from his body had embedded itself in my brain.

CHAPTER 39
PHIN

"**P**ORTALS THAT BYPASS the crossroads *completely*. Only accessible during an eclipse." Tap shook his head irritably as we made our way across the grassy expanse, looking for any signs of life. "We underestimated the depth of their betrayal as well as their abilities." He frowned. "I've failed at keeping all the doorways secured. For years."

"You can't blame yourself for not guarding something you didn't know existed," I tried to reassure him.

"But it was still my job. My responsibility." His jaw clenched as he worked through the unhappiness this whole situation had wrought.

The landscape reminded me of the countryside. If there had been more trees and much colder, it would almost have felt like the region where my childhood home had been in Vincara.

"I wonder where we are, exactly," Tap mused as he reached for my hand. Once our fingers were laced together, he started walking.

"Purgatory," I said confidently.

"That can't be right." He paused, squinting as he looked around.

"That's what the door is marked."

His head tilted. "You can see that?"

I shrugged. "I can now."

"Mm. Then I trust you, Feather. It seems logical, actually. There's no color here, no brightness. There's existence, but not life. The air is still, like it can't even be bothered to make a breeze. It's as though time itself doesn't matter here, and that's intentional. Does it feel that way to you?"

I shivered. Now that he'd mentioned it, I couldn't avoid how strongly I felt the desire to leave such a place. "Yes. It feels wrong."

The landscape here was deceptive in every way. The beige dead grass was soft under our feet instead of crunchy, the flat earth somehow rising into invisible hills and valleys.

"That's it exactly. I don't see any sign of them, or anything yet."

"Ramsey, do you?"

No, mistress. My beautiful hound had not gone far from my side since they'd arrived. *But I feel my bond with your mother much more strongly in this place than I do elsewhere.*

That gave me such a surge of hope my eyes welled up. "I don't want to go too far from the portal," I said, irrationally afraid that we wouldn't be able to find our way back, particularly with my new talent.

"We won't."

I will go ahead, mistress. I'll use my connection to her as a guide. Follow me.

My skin crawled as I lost sight of her, the sense of urgency to leave reminding me of Ophelia's wards.

After another few minutes walking for what seemed like no gain in distance and no change on the horizon, I heard her bark.

"Ramsey?" I called, unsure what direction I'd heard her from.

Come, over this way. She walked ahead of us, still in a hurry.

Wary but trusting her, we followed the hound as she trotted at full speed a different direction than we'd been headed.

Tap stopped walking. "Look."

I followed his gaze and saw what had drawn his attention. Smoke.

The closer we got to the column of smoke, the harder my heart pounded. Crude rooflines appeared, then walls. Doors. Nothing was fancy, everything clearly made from whatever could be found nearby, but all completely serviceable little cabins.

Ramsey barked several times and dashed away, leaving me and Tap staring at one another and my heart in my throat.

As we crested a hill we hadn't seen and started down the other side, a whole settlement became visible. There were several homes, a well, lines for hanging laundry, and a rack over a big fire cooking some kind of meat.

Ramsey went from one little house to the next, barking and making as much noise as she possibly could.

Tap squeezed my hand, reminding me to breathe as one after another, people emerged from the little dwellings. I looked from one of them to the next, stunned at how many of them there were. Four women, and three men, arranged in couples aside from one of the women. The first couple was an auburn-haired woman and a large, sharp-featured man with long dark hair. The second, a petite woman with black hair, the man clutching her shoulders tall and willowy. The woman standing alone reminded me of Greta, if a bit older. They all looked cautious, confused.

All except one.

The tan woman with long dark hair exclaimed excitedly, gesturing for the others to greet the hellhound that was prancing around from one to the next, making enough noise to raise the dead. Next to her was a tall angel, one with long silver-blond hair and violet eyes, like mine.

"Saints, it's all of them," Tap breathed the words. "They're really all here."

I hiccupped a breath as the woman looked up, spotting us. And for the first time in years, I locked eyes with my parents.

I BREATHED IN the soft scent of my mother's hair, eyes closed as my tears dried. My father had his arms wrapped around us both, my body crushed between them.

It was everything I'd craved out of a hug for years.

My legs had moved of their own accord once the reality of my parents, standing within a short distance of me, had sunk in. Ramsey had joined our little reunion, the rest of the people around us smiling as they watched.

"I'm so happy to see you." I exhaled into her shoulder, and she kissed my cheek soundly before pulling away.

"Come. Say hello. Friends, this is our daughter, Phin." Everyone responded with a kind greeting, some a little wave. "And ..." she looked to Tap.

"I'm Tap," he said, dipping into a little bow. "I'm the demon of the crossroads. And I believe I know who you all are, but I'd love to meet you properly. I feel it's important you all know straightaway that your children are safe. All of them. They're grown, and thriving." A collective murmur of relief went through them, hands squeezed and emotions already bubbling over in the form of tears.

I glanced around at everyone, finding familiar features in most of them. As Tap slowly went to them one by one and shook their hands, I walked beside him and nodded in greeting. As they introduced themselves, my heart clenched tighter and tighter. All of these people were parents Armaros and his co-conspirators had stashed away here, people separated from their families by their unforgivable madness.

"I'm Rowan," She said. "Rowan Aurichal." The woman standing by herself said, eagerly putting out her arm.

"I thought so." Tap nodded. "I'd recognize those features any-where." Tap smiled at her. "Magnus has been desperate to find you." She hiccupped a light sob, tears filling her eyes. "Greta will be so happy to see that you're alright." She pumped Tap's arm another several times and then quickly wrapped her arms around me, squeezing me tight.

"Thank you both."

The woman with auburn hair took Tap's hand. "I'm Selene. This is Kaspar." She gestured to her large husband, whose features were similar to Rowan's. Stone kin lines were quite strong, it seemed.

"Pleased to meet you."

"We've been here the longest. I'm not even sure how many years now," she lamented.

"We left behind a baby, with Selene's parents." The man's eyes were kind, his voice deep and rough. "Sofie."

"I think she uses the name Calla, now," Tap said kindly. He turned to the other couple. "Unless you're Calla's parents?"

They shook their heads and the woman said, "No, our daughter's name is Hailon. I'm Wyn."

"I'm Oren. Pleased to meet you."

Tap shook both their hands and shifted back to my parents.

"Terra." My mother beamed as she enthusiastically patted Tap's hands between both of hers.

"Radueriel," said my father, saving Tap from her grasp by reaching to shake.

"How did you get here?" My mother asked.

"It's complicated," Tap said. "But Ramsey certainly gets some credit." The hound received several more pats in gratitude. "And Armaros, but his death is all I'm thankful for at this moment." His mouth flattened.

"Dead, you say?" my father inquired.

"Yes."

"What about that slimy stone kin councilman, Brookes? He's the one who brought us all here," Rowan asked.

"Him too. My brothers actually took care of him months ago. And several others thought to be involved before that."

My father's shoulders relaxed. "I'm disappointed to have missed such festivities, but good riddance." He rubbed his chin thoughtfully. "I'll need to get to Heaven with expedience, to report what's happened."

Tap nodded. "There are several doorways available to you. Someone can escort you back to Vincara, to one more familiar." My father inclined his head in thanks, glancing between Tap and I. He gave me a small, private smile that I immediately understood as approval. I never could keep anything from him for long.

"We can leave?" Hailon's mother asked, the hope in her face almost painful.

"Yes. And we should, quickly. The portal is only open temporarily."

There was a general rumbling and some hesitating, which I understood. Some of these people had been here for decades. This was their home.

"Will we ever be able to come back here after that?" Rowan asked. "I'm anxious to leave, of course, but there are things we've made here, things we've built. It wasn't always easy but it has been our life for a very long time. To just up and leave it all behind makes me feel ... odd." Her husband comforted her.

"I'm happy to see if I can change the pathways to the portal so that it is accessible more often once we return," Tap said. "But I can make no guarantees, I'm afraid. Purgatory is not usually under my purview."

"I understand," she said.

"Ramsey, would you mind going back through and alerting my brothers at d'Arcan that we will be arriving shortly with several guests? Collect everyone from the glade as well, if you please. And if you could also take the body? My brothers will have a place for it."

She panted, a smile on her face. *It would be my pleasure, Watchman. Shall I also take the head or would you like me to leave that for you?*

"Take it please. Though, how will you do both?"

I'll manage. I can change my size to accommodate most of him and fit the rest between my teeth.

I flinched at that visual, but said nothing. After a quick bump of her head for both my mother and I, Ramsey was gone.

"What's happened that we can leave now?" my mother asked.

"There's an eclipse," Tap explained. "And unfortunately, the portal only works during such an event."

"Alright then. There are many hands here." Hailon's dad took charge. "Load up the bedsheets with what you want to take right now. Between us we can surely carry the important things. The rest can wait until another day."

There was a hasty conversation about dousing fires, which items were most precious and whether or not to take the food as everyone dispersed to their own cabins. I stayed with my parents while Tap went to help Greta's mother, as she was the only one without a partner.

My parents both kept looking over their shoulders as they grabbed up the things most important to them.

"I can't believe you're really here," Mom sighed as she tucked away some interesting-looking yarn work.

"Me neither."

My father's smile turned into a smirk. "Tell me the truth, sweetheart, are you and that demon—" Mom lightly slapped his arm.

"Dueriel! You leave her alone! There's plenty of time for that conversation later."

"It's okay," I laughed, tears springing into my eyes again at the familiar banter. I could almost picture us standing in the kitchen of our little cabin in the woods outside of Aymonroux instead of this little hut in Purgatory. "He saved me from the church in Vincara."

Mom gasped. "Saved you?"

"Father Morton was working with Armaros. I don't know for how long, though. If not for my tincture, he might have captured me."

They both stared at me, horrified. "I don't even know what to say about that. I'm so sorry. We trusted him. *We* left you there!" My father was getting louder, and I put my hand on his arm to stop the tirade that I knew was inevitable at some point. But we didn't have time for that now.

"I don't think he was the whole time. It's complicated. But Tap took me to the crossroads to keep me hidden. Safe."

"The crossroads? That's actually quite genius." Dad looked impressed. "Explains why he knows so much about portals."

"We're mate bonded."

They both stopped cold and turned to look at me.

"Truly?" Mom gasped.

"Yes."

She sagged, clearly teary-eyed herself as she came over and crushed me to her chest. "Oh, Phin! That's such wonderful news! Unexpected, but fantastic. We only ever hoped for you to be safe, clearly, we should have dreamed bigger!"

"You were going to tell me you were part demon eventually, right?"

"I was, I swear it. We thought it was safer you didn't know. They've hunted all Nephilim for a very long time, my heart, Armaros isn't the first to have designs on using or eliminating angels with parentage they didn't care for. If they'd known about me ..." She shook her head. "How did you figure that out?"

"Ramsey. She said she didn't even realize I didn't know."

"I'm sorry, Phin. For all of it. Nothing went the way we expected."

That was an understatement. I wanted to tell her it was okay, but something held me back. Instead, I just nodded and helped her collect a few more things.

After we left their temporary little home for what I hoped was the last time, we split up to help the others. The cooking meat was packed up, and the fire doused with water from the well, and the houses were tidied and secured the best they could be until we made it back another time.

Once everyone had what they needed, we started walking toward the portal, Tap and I both carrying bundles as well. All told, there really wasn't as much as there could have been.

Everyone was quiet. The weight of the air itself didn't help, but there was deep reflection and anxiety in them all. Leaving this strange life that wasn't really one at all, and returning to one where you hadn't existed for years to lifetimes was kind of like that. Never mind the fact that they hadn't aged while stuck here. There was certainly going to be quite a lot to untangle down the line.

Tap took the lead as we approached the portal. "Everyone hold tight to one another. If we make a chain, it may simplify things." He glanced around. "I'll pull us through to Revalia. I want to say it will be eight different doors to get us there, so it will be uncomfortable for a bit. And it's winter, so the weather is very different there. I apologize, this will probably be uncomfortable for several reasons."

"I hate portals," Hailon's father complained, already pale. "But it'll be worth it."

"I'll make it as painless as I can. Everyone got a good grip? Good. Here we go." He smiled at me, going first, and I brought up the rear, a whole world between us.

AS I STEPPED out of the portal in d'Arcan, the cold was an unwelcome shock. There was a slim slice of black still over the sun, but it seemed we'd left Purgatory just in time—the eclipse was ending.

Ramsey scuttled out the doors the second they opened and ran between me and my mother. Calla's shocked face softened the moment she scanned the whole group in the courtyard before her.

"Saints," she breathed. "Please, come inside."

Everyone shuffled forward, Tap hanging back to wait for me.

"Ready for this part, Feather?"

"I'm nervous," I replied honestly, squeezing his hand as he laced his fingers through mine.

"Me too. But excited, as well. They've all been dearly missed."

Everything warmed considerably as the doors closed behind us and we followed everyone into the dining room.

At first, the silence was overwhelming. Then came the chaos. A plate breaking was the first noise, the next was sniffles. Chairs scraped the floor, then came full-on sobs. Exclamations and shouts took over, and then all the air disappeared again while everyone froze, afraid to move lest the moment break.

As the group moved toward the center of the room and stopped, I was able to see that Ramsey had indeed collected everyone. Hailon stood from where she'd been sitting at the dining table, Seir supporting her by the shoulders. Calla had gone to Rylan's side, and he had his hand around her waist. Greta's hand was over her mouth, Vassago a steady presence at her side. Merry and Grace were watching from near the kitchen door, clutching one another and both of them openly crying already. Magnus was the most terrifying one, standing silent with his mouth open as he stopped moving halfway between Grace and the table. In the end, he was the one who broke first.

"Rowan?"

"Magnus." Greta's mother breathed his name, then bent in half on a half-laugh, half-sob before standing straight again just in time for him to charge forward and slam into her with a hug so fierce it shook the room. "Oh, sweet saints. You're found. You're here." The mountainous man gave in to silent tears as he squeezed his sister.

That broke the tension, and the others shuffled forward cautiously. Tap squeezed my fingers again and leaned down to kiss my forehead.

"You're a marvel, Feather. You did this."

I shook my head. "No. I hesitated. I got caught."

He exhaled through his nose. "Perhaps, but you were brave enough, strong enough, to take on that angel all by yourself, knowing what could happen." His eyes turned to me, serious and bright red. "You will never risk yourself like that ever again, Phin. *Never.*"

"I have absolutely no plans to do so," I promised.

My parents joined us, giving the others some space. We sat at one of the long tables and Grace came over almost immediately to deliver a plate of snacks and a pot of tea. Then she was gone again, doing the same with some of the others who had broken away from the group to reunite with their loved ones.

Calla was timid with her parents, but Rylan was bridging the gap with his overtures to make them comfortable. Hailon and her parents were seated at one end of the long family table, with Seir standing protectively behind her chair. Greta was standing in front of her mother, who Magnus had finally released, their hands loosely clasped down by their waists for a moment before they embraced one another.

"Thank you," my father said earnestly, his eyes on Tap.

"No thanks are needed. Finding your daughter has been the biggest gift of my life."

Dad cracked a grin. "Obviously I have no ill feelings about

demons like many of my kin, but this is truly something else." He smiled, kissing my mother's fingers, gazing down at her adoringly like he always had. "Four princes of Hell in one room? Several stone kin from the original twelve families?" He shook his head, long white hair shifting along his back. "Nobody would believe it."

"Should I be worried that you're going to tell someone such sensitive information?" Tap asked in return. I could see the tiny lift at the corner of his mouth, but my father didn't.

"No! Of course not. We're friends, are we not?"

Tap chuckled. "Yes, I believe so." His expression grew serious. "What will you tell your council?"

My father grunted. "The truth. All of it. And if they ever want to see their numbers increase instead of the entire race crumbling to dust as they likely deserve, they'll take it to heart."

"What does that mean?" I asked.

"The reason the angel population is suffering is because I wasn't at my post."

Tap's head tilted. "Could you elaborate on that? I thought you were an archivist."

"I am." He glanced at my mother, and she smiled, giving him a gentle nod and a comforting pat on the hand. "I'm assuming, as friends, I can trust you with some sensitive information the same as you trust me?"

Tap smiled. "Fair is fair. Please, I welcome it."

My father, clearly nervous about whatever he was about to say, shifted in his seat and cleared his throat. When he spoke again, it was at a volume barely heard above the other chatter in the room. "My true Voice talent is quite literally speaking angels into existence. Much of my time in the archives was spent evaluating and filing the life records of all incoming souls. Once I used my Voice to approve them, they got their wings, work and housing assignments ... whatever they needed to officially become an angel. Without me, without my Voice, that process doesn't happen." I inhaled and openly stared at my father. I'd been with him, all that time, and never knew any of that was happening. "And, relatively soon, there will only be the oldest of our kind left. And I can only assume eventually, even they will fade and perish." He shook his head slowly. "*Nothing* is truly forever."

Tap stared, stunned at that revelation. "Nobody else knows your true talent?"

He smirked. "No. My lovely wife aside, of course. And *Him*, naturally, but He's been gone so long ..." He shook his head and turned to me. "I was trying to apprentice you, in a way, Phin. So that you'd be familiar with the archives in the event your talent worked like mine." His smile appeared, but it was sad. "But in truth, I'm glad that's not what happened. You'd only have been more valuable to them."

"In the end, Brookes and Armaros and their purist-mentality co-conspirators caused the very outcome they were trying to avoid?" Tap's smile broadened as he tapped his finger against the table. "That's almost poetic, actually."

"Truly." My father sighed and sipped at his tall mug of ale. The weight of his talent was clear in the way his gaze went distant.

"He was looking for a ledger, when we saw him in Vincara. The kind that might have record of all Voice talents ever gifted."

Radueriel shook his head with a smirk and patted his vest pocket suggestively. "Who would be foolish enough to lose track of a ledger with that much power?"

A loud caw and the beat of wings interrupted our conversation. Belmont had flown in and perched on one of the beams in the center of the dining room, his good eye turned to where Greta sat across from her mother. A man rushed in behind the bird, one with regal posture and a vicious scar across his face. He was moving so quickly his momentum was barely slowed when he grabbed onto the door frame and swung himself into the room.

Greta brightened and gave a little wave when she saw him, and I had the honor of watching her mother turn, her whole face crumpling as she took the man in. She sobbed into her hands for a moment. The man was not all that different from Magnus in his reaction.

"Rowan?" He called her name like he was trying to figure out if this was real or not. She popped up out of her chair and threw herself into his arms, and several of us instantly started to cry. It was impossible not to feel or respond to all the heavy emotions floating around the room.

"Look what your talent and heart have done, Phin. What good you bring to this world. I'm so proud of you." My dad pulled me in for a hug, and I disappeared into his warmth, suddenly just a little girl again, riding the absolute euphoria of having pleased her father.

For a moment, nothing else mattered.

CHAPTER 40
TAP

DINNER AT D'ARCAN was an unusually wild affair. Students were in, so Grace and her helpers were extra busy serving them at the long tables and hastily redirecting any nosy glances or gossip. The sheer amount of supernaturals gathered to eat should have been considered dangerous and disbanded, but it was just ... dinner.

The family table, which was being supplemented with the old round table on one end, was overloaded in the best way. Everyone sat elbow to elbow, and there was a feast spread down the tabletop. Joy and laughter abounded from every corner and there were at least four conversations happening at any given time. I kept checking on Phin to be sure she was holding up okay, but I needn't have worried—she was quite literally glowing with happiness.

Even Ramsey seemed to be having the time of her life. The hellhound, the birds, and Calla's stone kin cat were off in a far corner eating and teasing one another, chatting on about all their adventures and accomplishments.

The whole day felt very surreal, and I'd put Armaros completely out of my mind until Vassago patted my shoulder on his way to create a few scrying mirrors so that everyone could be in easy communication.

"We put him in the cellar, in case you're wondering. Between Calla's magic, Greta's elixirs, and some enchanted snow, he'll be held in his current state until we know whether or not his remains should be returned to Heaven." He made a face, as though he'd tasted something bad. "Those blades do nasty work. Effective, but very unpleasant."

Rylan had clearly overheard and muttered, "If they don't want him back, I'll happily burn him to ash. Lucky I didn't yet, honestly, I was tempted from the moment Ramsey dragged him through the portal." He grinned, "Might have put his body in a different box from his head, though, just for spite."

"Perhaps I should offer that to the three Nephilim who escaped from him?" I said casually.

Rylan laughed heartily. "You should. Ris! We have something for you to take with you when you go." My brother raised his cup and took a drink, smiling at his new in-laws like he hadn't just casually offered the head of an angel I'd beheaded, who was currently kept in his basement, to a fae king as a gift for some Nephilim.

I might be a touch grumpy and overstimulated sometimes, but I truly adored my family and all the beautiful madness they embodied.

Once the students had dispersed—which was rather quickly thanks to Grace hustling them along—everything settled down a bit. Logistics became the main topic of conversation as more tea and desserts were passed around. Those who had been retrieved from Purgatory suffered nothing more taxing than a wealth of options.

"There are plenty of huts at the conclave," Magnus offered. "You're all welcome, of course, for however long you need. Stone kin or not, you're all clan."

"We have apartments open here, of course," Calla added.

"There's only a single cabin open in the glade, but with some help from the stone kin, we could have more in short order, I'm sure." Seir nodded.

"My palace is perpetually available as well," Ris said. "We recently acquired three new residents, but there are endless rooms that could be put to good use, so long as you are amenable to being in the fae realm."

In the end, everyone chose somewhere different; for most, it was the place they could be closest to their children. Calla's parents took an apartment at d'Arcan and while Rowan chose to accompany Ris to Everwood, I suspected she'd be traveling both to d'Arcan and to the conclave frequently. Hailon's parents agreed to take the cabin in the glade.

It was Phin's parents who surprised me. We'd offered Phin's room to them, and their own once I could get one requisitioned and properly set up, but Radueriel was insistent that Father Morton and Heaven be dealt with immediately.

"We're going straight to Vincara once we leave here," Phin's father said sternly. "We'll consider resting in Aymonroux, but I want these matters dealt with. There's no time to waste."

"What about Mom?" Phin asked.

"I'm going with him," she said. Radueriel laced his fingers with his wife's and leaned in to kiss her forehead.

"But ... how will that work?" Phin asked, and my brothers and I all looked to one another, also curious.

"If they wish to prevent their own imminent collapse, they will allow my wife to accompany me inside the gates peacefully. If they refuse?" he shrugged and tossed back the last of his ale. "Then I will lose no sleep over it. I will deliver Armaros's corpse to their doorstep and go on to live my life here on Earth. I will make it my mission to punish anyone involved in his scheme and ensure there are never any Nephilim within their grasp ever again. Then I will avenge those who were captured, tortured, killed. Once that's done, I'll rest easy, never wasting another moment of my time thinking about that place or those who dwell there ever again."

Magnus's low rolling chuckle slowly gained speed and volume. "I like you," he said, raising his own tankard in toast.

"Yes," Vassago agreed with a smirk. "I believe you'll fit in here just fine. Welcome to you both." He raised his cup as well.

After a bit longer, goodbyes were begun, the energy of the whole group beginning to wane. Promises were made to align schedules so that they could all transition back to some kind of normal life as quickly as possible.

"D'Arcan is open to you," Rylan repeated, dipping to briefly embrace Hailon's mother. "We have ample resources, and there are many talents within these walls. Just ask for what you need, surely we can find a way."

Archimedes and Belmont flew low to the ceiling, their wings cutting the air with a heavy beat. The pair dove out the doors the moment they were opened, immediately taking to the sky. Calla's cat had wandered off to nap somewhere, and Ramsey had become glued to Phin's legs.

Hailon and Seir split off with her parents, headed for the portal back to the glade as Magnus squeezed his sister, then drew Ris in with a chuckle, his arms around them both.

"I'll see you soon," she said, the words a solemn vow.

"Yes, you will," Magnus laughed, releasing them both.

Ris and Rowan both hugged Greta for a long moment, then he tucked his wife under his arm. She looked up at him with the same moony expression he'd worn all through dinner. I could guarantee it would be a long while before any of these people took being able to see and touch their loved ones for granted.

"Please reach out if you need anything for the Nephilim," Phin's father offered.

Ris dipped his head and stretched out a hand for Radueriel to shake. "I will. Thank you. I'm happy to lend aid in whatever way you need should your discussions with Heaven go less smoothly than you hope." Then they too were gone. Vassago turned and took Greta to their own set of rooms.

Calla had escorted her parents up to their apartment already, and Rylan bade us good night to go to her, leaving us alone with Raduriel and Terra.

To facilitate their journey to Vincara, we first traveled to the crossroads. When we stepped through, I all but deflated as the tension left my limbs. I truly was an isolationist who loved being home at heart, and the quiet of the great hall brought immediate and tremendous comfort.

"Are you sure you don't want to rest?" I asked. "Heaven will be there after a good night's sleep."

"Your offer is appreciated, but I'm certain." Radueriel reached out to shake my hand, his grip firm. "I've been making preparations for a long while with no way to fulfill them."

"I'm more than happy to accompany you, if you'd like."

"That's not necessary, but I would not deprive you—either of you—your own vengeance on Father Morton, should you wish to take it."

I cannot wait to see the holy man again. Ramsey's black smoke plumed out around her, the tone of her voice in my head denoting a heavy level of sarcasm. *But I will return to your side imminently, mistress.* Phin patted Ramsey's head.

"You're the one he mistreated, Phin. If you want revenge, it's yours." Phin's mother's eyes were soft, but there was a rim of red around the dark brown, her ire clearly near the surface.

"I don't want anything to do with him or the bells at that church, ever again. If you want to do this, you're welcome to it. He made and broke promises to you, not to me."

"Promises with you at the heart, though. Your care." Radueriel frowned at his daughter, confusion in his kind violet eyes.

"He asked the apothecary to slowly *poison* you, Feather," I argued, realizing I'd been more thorough in devising as well as devoted to my own plot to repay him for his betrayal than I thought.

She shook her head. "His method was absolutely wrong, but he kept me hidden when it mattered. That tincture kept my cycle at bay and disguised me well enough Armaros didn't see me when he was sitting at a table five feet from me." I opened my mouth again, ready to list all the organs it had damaged while she was taking it, the freezing episodes, but I didn't get a word out before she put her fingers to my lips. "My father will take care of it, far better than I could, I'm sure."

"He'll be coming with me to Heaven. Justice will be served, one way or the other," Radueriel assured us.

"Good luck to you. And we will await a summons should you need any kind of assistance or testimony."

"We'll see you very soon, my heart." Phin's mom squeezed her tight and then they turned, vanishing through the same doorway that had carried me to the place I'd found my fate.

I DEACTIVATED ALL the active portals except the one that went to Aymonroux before taking Phin's hand and leading her to my bedroom. My nerves were frayed, but her trust in me as she followed without hesitation soothed my ragged edges.

I didn't speak as I ran my oversize tub full of hot water, stacked up clean towels, and made sure all of the necessary supplies were within reach. Phin accommodated my unspoken requests as I lifted her leg and removed her thigh sheath, setting it far back on the counter for safety. Her little grin and hazy gaze as I slowly peeled her tunic and leggings off nearly brought me to my knees. I shed my own clothes in silence, never moving further than a few inches from her. I couldn't stand more distance than that right now.

I willed my hands to speak for me, to communicate my adoration and concern as they traced every inch of her flesh, checking for the smallest cut or bruise, any injury or damage. I lifted her chin and turned her head, anger flaring at the faint marks left around her neck.

"My collar," she whispered. "He pulled it. Doesn't hurt."

I picked up one arm at a time and examined them like they were art pieces, memorizing a tally of small wounds as the rage built in my veins. To soothe the hot emotion, my mouth followed everywhere I touched, her skin warm and soft under my lips as I gently kissed her jaw, her shoulder, her hip, her stomach, her thigh.

By the time I finally wrapped my arms around her and kissed her properly, she looked as dizzy from the attention as I felt, and I held her tight to keep her from sliding bonelessly to the floor.

"Come on, Feather. Let's get you clean and into bed. It's been far too busy of a day for my liking," I muttered, voice rough.

She slid into the water first, and I climbed in behind her. We soaked for several minutes, her back to my front, my legs surrounding hers. My knees were sticking out of the water despite the oversize basin, though it was clear up to Phin's chin. She rested her head back against my shoulder and I dragged my fingertips along her limbs, loving the way she melted against me.

When the water started to cool, I washed her hair, then her body, then, against better judgment, I allowed her the comfort of doing the same for me. The simple acts were grounding. I was painfully alive under the scrape of her fingernails against my chest, holding on by mere threads when I gripped the edge of the tub while she straddled and faced me to scrub the shampoo into my hair, her perfect breasts right at eye level. I reveled in the defeat

I felt when my restraint snapped and I wrapped my arms around her waist, pulling her into me and making water splash out of the tub. I did not trust my tongue to make the right words, so the only sounds between us were squeaks and rumbles, groans and sighs. I worried that somehow, that might be worse.

When I could stand it no more, I scooped her up out of the water, drying us both quickly with the plush towels before marching her back into my room to the bed.

I lay on my side, head propped up on one hand as she arranged the pillows and blankets to her liking. When she finally lay down against me, my arms reflexively came around her, pulling her as close as I could get her. I listened to the steady rhythm of her breathing as she wound her limbs around me. The bond in my chest was quiet, but my heart throbbed happily.

Everything in me calmed. After years of restlessness, existing solely for the gates, she was my place to recharge.

The slow graze of my fingertips against her skin became more insistent, and she looked up to find me watching her, a thousand fantasies dancing behind my eyes. When she shifted up to kiss me, I exhaled like I'd been holding my breath for years. All the tension left me, all the stress. Nothing else mattered.

There in the dark, I showed her what her future held as mine. We rocked together, breaths heavy and senses heightened. I understood what it was to be cherished and cared for, gently loved and wholly satisfied. I could only hope she felt the same.

And as it turned out, we didn't need words to reconnect after what we'd been through. We only needed one another.

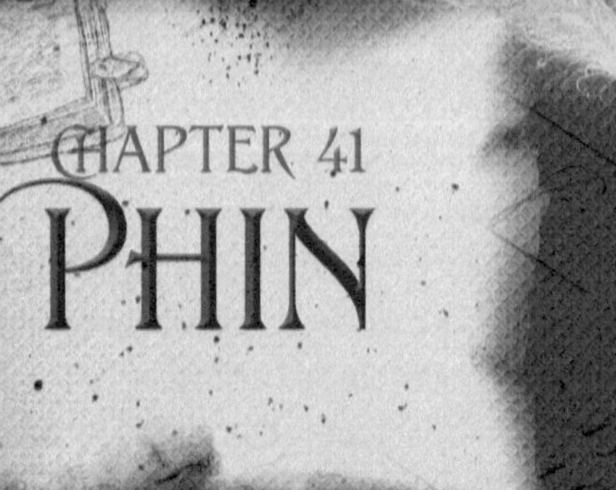

CHAPTER 41
PHIN

THE NEXT SEVERAL days passed in an odd mix of settling into our routine and wondering if something else was coming to disturb our peace.

The trial run of Hell sharing in the burden of watching the portals had been a resounding success, especially considering it was basically trial by fire with the eclipse. Seir, Coltor, and Tap spent time every day discussing logistics for converting that to a permanent situation while simultaneously trying to figure out how to find any other hidden doorways like the one that led to Purgatory, not to mention a way to re-route the path back to Purgatory itself.

Ramsey and my parents still hadn't returned, but they'd used one of Vassago's scrying mirrors to let me know they were safe and things were being dealt with. Based on my father's very pensive expression, things were not great on the celestial plane, but I had no doubt he would do everything he could to make them better.

Greta had stopped by with a new vial of tincture for me, one that only had to be taken at the first sign of my cycle starting. It wouldn't suppress my wings, or my Voice, but it wouldn't harm me like the last one. She'd tucked it safely into my hand and then squeezed me tight, apologizing that it had taken so long. I hugged her back and tried to assure her that I was just grateful to have it.

With the help of my newfound talent, I'd made it through all the deals on and around the table and was beginning to work through the first set of shelves so I could better clean up the rest of the floor. Unfortunately, that required me to shift some of those documents from their stacks and piles ... to the table. It was a work in progress, but I loved seeing the way everything was becoming more orderly day after day. I had lots of ideas for an improved method of maintaining new deals going forward, but that wasn't part of the project.

To my relief and joy, Tap had actually started to make a little bit of time for leisure activities since our return. He'd resumed work on the family portrait but asked me to keep that quiet, especially from Seir, but it apparently had become a running joke between all of his brothers that it was something he'd been attempting to complete for a very long time. He'd also started on some new woodwork, but I hadn't seen what it was yet as I'd been occupied with drawing.

"Feather, would you come with me somewhere?" he asked as I wandered a row of portals with him, a plate full of cookies I'd baked from a recipe Grace shared still in my hands.

"I don't see why not. Where?"

"Hell."

I stopped walking. "Am I ... allowed to go there?"

"Of course. You're part demon."

"It's the angel part I think might be a problem. Especially since I happen to look like one."

He shrugged, that ridiculously disarming grin on his mouth. "You were allowed into Heaven even as part demon, if you recall. Besides, you'll be with me. I tend to agree with your father on this—if my mate is not welcome anywhere I need to go, then that's their problem, not mine. And they'll have to deal with me personally about it." His smile widened as he saw how those words had affected me, and he dipped to give me a quick kiss before taking a cookie from the plate.

"He's absolutely correct!" Seir called from the next row. "And I'll be there, too, if that counts for anything." He jogged over. "Can I have one?"

I laughed, his pleading puppylike eyes never not amusing. "Of course."

He enthusiastically grabbed at the treat and crammed it in his mouth. "Delicious," he mumbled over the bite.

Tap just shook his head and sighed. "Are you ready?"

I froze, recalling how going to d'Arcan that first time had gone this same way. "Now?"

"Sorry, but yes. There's a meeting shortly. Even we didn't find out until just before I asked you."

Irrational panic rose. "Okay. Do I need to change?"

"No. You look beautiful, as always."

"Aw," Seir said from near a portal with red flames on a black frame marked The Pit. "You two are adorable. Shall we go?"

"Was that always here?" I asked. "I think I would remember it."

Tap offered me his arm, and after I hastily patted my hair down and straightened my clothes, I accepted. "It's a new addition," he said. "Ready?"

Seir stepped through before us, and as was my habit, I scrunched my eyes closed and held my breath until we were on the other side. When I opened them, I found myself in what was essentially a room like our libraries, just without all the shelves.

A shiny ebony table equipped to seat at least twenty sat in the middle of a room decorated with sculpted garnet wallpaper and gold fixtures. The fire was lit and burning at a cozy level. There were several small tables at the fringes of the room with armchairs on either side and low lamps on top. It should have come across as gaudy, but instead just seemed entirely fitting for the location.

Seir took another cookie off the plate and set it on the table.

"You brought them with you?" Tap chuckled.

"I certainly wasn't going to leave them behind," he chuffed. "I'm hungry and they're delicious."

The door we'd come through opened and a massive demon strode in, dropping a heavy folder on the table as he selected a chair.

"Thank you for coming on such short notice. I'm Keplar." He frowned in concentration as he arranged a crystal orb on the table in front of himself. "Shall we get started?" He seemed stressed, but once he glanced at Tap and I, he took a deep breath and relaxed. "Sorry. My workload is … not your issue. Like I said, I'm Keplar. I assume you're Tap?" He reached out a meaty hand and they shook.

"Yes, that's right."

"Nice to meet you. The crossroads is no easy assignment; you have my respect for how well you've held it all together."

"Appreciated." Tap blinked, his nod stiff with surprise. "This is Phin."

"Hello," I said, unable to keep myself from being shy in the presence of yet another massive demon.

Keplar's hand shifted to me. "Pleased to meet you, as well, Phin. It's not often—well, never, actually—that I get the honor of meeting a Nephilim." I only blushed harder and he cracked a grin. Then his eyes shifted to Seir, and he exhaled a long-suffering sigh. "Yes, and how are you, today, Seir?"

"Well, thank you, sir. Cookie?" Seir was positively bouncing in his seat as he shoved the plate Keplar's direction. The big demon took one between his finger and thumb, making short work of it in one bite. He nodded his approval, which gave me an odd surge of pride.

"Alright. Shall we get started? We'll get the other introductions out of the way all at once." Keplar adjusted a few things, and the orb threw three windows of light into the air above it, all of them slowly rotating around in a circle.

One of the windows showed an office with a squatty demon sitting behind a desk with a high counter in front of it and a cheery, red-skinned demoness standing next to them. The next was what I assumed was the forge at the stone kin conclave, because Imogen and Magnus were sitting side by side. The last window showed a room I recognized all too well—the archives in Heaven. I leaned forward in my seat, happy to see my parents.

"Good to know the orb and scrying mirrors work well together. That will aid communications immensely. Alright, we've got Seir, Tap, and Phin with me here representing the crossroads and the Emankor ruins. Rune and Meg are representing our assignments and records office. I've also invited stone kin forge mistress Imogen Aurichal and General Magnus Aurichal. Welcome everyone, thank you for coming. I've spoken with most of you separately, but I thought it would be beneficial to have everyone in one conversation." There was a general murmur of greeting and then Keplar launched right into what seemed essentially to be a business meeting. "If you wouldn't mind starting us off, Councilman?"

I flinched at the title, but it was my father who responded to it.

"Certainly. Negotiations here have stalled for the moment, but we're still compiling cases and locating those who were wronged under the current council. Overall, the current oversight structure is crumbling as supporters of Armaros are rooted out. I didn't plan to take a seat, but that's proven necessary to prevent further devastation to vital infrastructure. We'll be located here for the time being." I nodded as my parents looked at me, eyes pleading for understanding.

"Understood. General?"

"The stone kin and mage councils are also in disarray due to several of their members having been involved not only with Armaros, but in the broader scheme to forbid cross-species matches in order to limit the power of potential offspring. The rot has festered for too long and now that it's being excised there's quite a mess to clean up. Things are less stable than we'd like. Instability and desperation lead to violence, so we are braced and vigilant as we put things in order."

"Too true," Keplar nodded. "In that vein, forge mistress, we'd like to put forth a bid to commission your blades for at least some of our legions."

"I'm flattered," Imogen said, "but a bit confused. Am I wrong to assume that Hell has its own forges?"

"Not at all. They make our standard blades and will continue. But we'd like to contract you for the specialty pieces. Particularly, the Dark blades, though we'd like to have the combination Light and Dark available as well. One never knows what kind of enemy they might be facing, after all, and it seems we may be moving more toward fights that are delineated on stance rather than species."

She inhaled thoughtfully and glanced at Magnus. "I'm happy to look over any proposals, but as the only one currently tending our forge, my time and energy is limited, as are the resources needed for that kind of weapon."

"Fully understood. We'll gratefully accept whatever you can provide, and I'm happy to negotiate for materials in the contracts."

Imogen nodded. "Alright. I can agree to look over your proposition."

"Fantastic. Rune, I'll be sending an official requisition over shortly for approval."

"Make sure it's form 17-WR, not 14," she grumbled. "Fourteen is exclusive to punishment tools."

"I will."

The squatty demon just slowly blinked back, clearly not believing she'd be getting the right one. The red demon next to her, Meg, just smiled.

"I'm happy to report that the paperwork has been put through for amendments in the accord agreements between the planes." He looked up, making solid eye contact with everyone. "I personally am very grateful to be forming such a friendly alliance with you all, and I look forward to working with you. Rune? Any estimates as to when we can expect that to be approved?"

"My apprentice and I are working to clean up old documentation to be sure we have every loophole examined. We don't have an archivist currently, so we have to go through it by ourselves. It's a big project to tackle."

"Aren't they all," I sighed, not meaning to speak aloud. Meg nodded enthusiastically and my mother gave me a wink, noticing my discomfort at having drawn attention to myself.

"Where is our archivist?" Keplar asked, lowering the paperwork he'd picked up to examine.

"Retired. Meg is training but can't yet do it by herself. She came from the scheduling desk and I'm trying to make sure she doesn't quit on me."

"I wouldn't do that, Rune." Meg looked at the little demon with affection.

"Wait, so what's happening to all the stuff I'm bringing down?" Seir asked, sneaking a look at Tap and then me. "Merry worked through the familiars contracts, and now she's working on deals." He gestured to me.

"They're going to storage for now."

Tap's eye twitched, just a tiny tic, but I noticed. I inhaled through my nose, forcing myself to be brave.

"Maybe between us we can work out a better way so that it's not so cumbersome on either side?" I suggested. "There seems to be a lot of doubled or pointless paperwork."

The studious little demon looked at me over the top of her glasses. "Meg?"

"Yes please!" The relief in her face was palpable. "There's *so much* right now. And most of it just needless filing that will never be looked at ever again." Her words confirmed my suspicions and also made Tap twitch. I had a feeling that a conversation about simply asking a question was in my future.

Rune grunted and looked at my parents. "She's yours?"

"Indeed," my father said proudly.

"You're an archivist?"

"Yes ma'am, and she accompanied me as often as possible. I wanted her as my own apprentice, but that wasn't meant to be."

"Who was your mother?" she asked my mom.

"Toreen," Mom said with a fond smile.

"I thought so. She did a tour with my mentor the same time I was coming up." She gave a solemn nod and looked back to me. "You'd be welcome to the position, if you're interested. We can work out the fine points in a contract."

Seir leaned forward and looked at me with excitement, and Tap squeezed my fingers encouragingly.

"Okay."

Meg clapped her hands. "I'm so happy! Thank you, Phin, I'm excited to talk with you."

"Perfect. Next order of business ..." Keplar spoke about a few more things, most to do with the new distribution of management for the portals and other agreements between demons, angels, mages, and stone kin, but I couldn't hear a word. Blood rushed in my ears as I processed what had just happened.

"Thank you all for coming," Keplar said finally. "We'll set something up in a few weeks to check in." Goodbyes were said, and he tapped the orb, closing all the windows of light. "Good to meet you," he said, raising his hand to Tap and I. "Seir, come see me tomorrow, yes?"

"Yes sir."

"Good. I'm off to fill out Rune's forms." He sighed and wasted no time leaving and we were not far behind him.

"Come on, I'll take you to Rune," Seir said. "Meg's really nice, you'll like working with her."

"Am I accepting?" I said, heart pounding out of nervousness.

"Why wouldn't you?" Tap asked. "It sounds perfect for you."

"Don't I already have a job?"

He smiled and kissed my forehead. "No, beloved. You have a project. One that will wait until you streamline everything that's wrong with the rest of the system. Everything I should have questioned this entire time." He smiled. "A wise woman once suggested it might have been simpler if I had."

I just chuckled, pleased I didn't have to be the one to mention it.

"Storage, she said. I've brought down so. Many. Crates." Seir groaned. "They could have told me!"

As we turned the third corner in the labyrinthine halls, both Tap and Seir stopped, staring at another man who was walking toward us. Part of Seir's cookie even fell out of his mouth, landing on the floor in a pile of crumbs.

"I'll be double damned," Tap swore.

"Triple for me," Seir muttered.

The man was built larger than either Tap or Seir and wore leather armor that covered his shoulders and torso as well as wrist bracers. He carried two large swords, both slung across his back in a scabbard that had seen better days. The sides of his head were shaved almost to the skin up to the tops of his ears, but the rest of his dark-blond hair was long and wound up in a messy knot atop his head. There were at least as many rings in his ears as in Tap's, and small letter tattoos ran in a thin line down the side of his neck.

"What in Hell's pits are *you* doing here?" Seir chuckled as he threw his arms around the newcomer, their hands thumping along one another's shoulders heavily. "It's been an age, brother."

"Only since Rylan's wedding, but I agree, it's always too long between visits. Though I'm nearly done with my contract, finally, so perhaps that will change." He turned to Tap. "I didn't know you ever left the crossroads. You're as tied to that place as I'm beholden to the training grounds."

"Things change, Ipos." Tap smiled, and the pair embraced.

"And thank the Fates they do."

"Cookie?" Seir offered the nearly empty plate.

"Don't mind if I do," he said, eyes closing as he savored the first bite. "Hellfire. There's very little flavor in anything served at the grounds. These are fantastic." The two battled for the last cookies on the plate, but in the end Seir lost. Though it might have been fairer to say the cookies lost, as they were little more than a pile of dust by the end. Ipos didn't seem to mind, though, he just dumped the contents of the plate into his mouth. "My compliments."

"I can't take credit; Phin made them."

Ipos turned his eyes to me as Tap threaded his fingers through mine and squeezed. His dark eyebrows raised, golden gaze curious. "I assume that's you?"

"Yes, hello. I'm glad you like them."

"Beloved, this is our brother, Ipos. Ipos, this is my mate, Phin. "

"Pleasure to meet you, Phin." He stepped forward to shake my hand. I was surprised to find that his grip was gentle despite how thoroughly his hand enveloped mine.

"And you."

Ipos laughed. "Even Tap's found himself a mate? And one from the celestial plane, unless I'm mistaken?" He looked at me, eyebrows raised.

"Nephilim," I corrected him. "My father is an angel, but I'm demon on my mother's side."

"She's bonded to a hound," Tap added proudly, making me blush. "Ramsey."

"Truly? Well, I'm already impressed. Chosen by a hound *and* you can tolerate him?" He smirked and tilted his head. "You're clearly either mad or brilliant."

"Perhaps both," I said quietly, which only made him throw back his head and laugh.

"What are you doing here?" Seir asked.

"Picking up my exit documents. I've only got a few weeks left at the grounds, and then ..." He shrugged. "My contract is up. I'm not sure I want to retire altogether, but I'm not taking another assignment for a while."

"Reach out when you're done! There are lots of places for you to stay earth-side if you don't want to bunk here." Seir shifted on the balls of his feet like he was anxious to sweep his brother up to the glade.

Ipos grinned, and his own extra sets of sharp canines were revealed. Unlike Seir, he had them on the bottom as well. "Will do. It would be nice to see everyone for longer than an afternoon party." Ipos sighed and glanced over his shoulder. "I should be going, Raxos still holds my leash. For now." His mouth flattened. The brothers embraced again, and he lifted a hand to me. "Very pleased to meet you Phin."

"You too."

"See you soon," he promised before disappearing down the hall.

Seir sighed. "I worry about him."

Tap chuckled and laced his fingers through mine again, then kissed the top of my hand. "You worry about all of us."

He nodded. "I do."

"Come on, Feather, let's go find this administration office so you can get your paperwork."

Seir led the way, explaining how he was only too familiar with Rune's office from his time awaiting release back to Earth when he and Hailon had been separated.

"Always paperwork," I teased.

"But now there'll be less." He squeezed my hand. "Thanks to you."

As we maneuvered the halls, getting several wide-eyed stares as we passed other demons, I couldn't help but wonder what other changes were coming. A Nephilim was being hired as the new archivist, and the stone kin had been contracted to supply the armory for Hell's legions.

It was a whole new world, and I, for the first time in ages, wasn't afraid to be an active part in it.

EPILOGUE
PHIN

I GASPED AS TAP hung the portrait depicting him and his brothers on the wall over the sofa. "You're so talented." It was very clear who everyone was, though I of course hadn't met them all yet. He'd described Orobas and Sitri to me, and they were right there for me to see in delicate strokes of paint.

Ramsey lifted her head from the arm of the sofa. Well done, Watchman. She was back for a few days, her time spent split between my mother and me when she wasn't on some other mission. Hunting down unknown portals had become her new favorite pastime, so she was often gone for weeks before returning to one of us to recharge.

"You flatter me." He stood back, fingers laced through mine, as he stared at it some more. "But I fear I need to make a new one. One that includes all our new members." He pulled me close with a hand around my shoulders.

"I'm sure that can be arranged," I smiled. "I'll sit for you, if you need a model."

His eyes flashed red. "You tempt me, Phin."

I stared back, not blinking. Sooner or later he'd figure out it was a serious offer.

"Come with me?" I asked. "If you're showing me your art, I want to show you mine."

"I'd follow you anywhere, Feather." He smiled, taking my hand as I walked us down the hall to the tattoo room.

While he'd been working on his painting, I'd been plenty busy myself.

Between my new job in Hell and Tap adjusting to not being the only one in charge of watching all the doorways, we'd been rebalancing everything. That included both of us making adequate use of our leisure time, and while I'd dabbled in reading, needlework and even tried my hand at painting, nothing had stuck quite like drawing. It was the only thing that still opened up that quiet blank place in my head, where I could just disappear into the strokes of the quill and float back up a while later to find something beautiful. Except, the desk in the library hadn't worked. I'd had to move a smaller one into the tattoo room for the sparks to really turn into flames.

Lucky for me, Tap was more than accommodating, and some of our most memorable nights had been spent on the cushions after I was done pressing ink into parchment while he decorated his skin.

"What have you been working on, Feather?" he asked, closing the door behind us only most of the way out of habit.

I pushed it the rest of the way shut, his eyebrows raising when the latch clicked into place.

"We should let Ramsey rest."

His tongue swept across his bottom lip. "Am I to assume we will ... not be?" I just smiled and went to my desk, unstacking my labors and spreading them out in the order I wanted. "What's this?"

Tap examined the pages, the borders of which recorded every pattern he'd tattooed himself with, featuring my scroll in the corners. I'd drawn my favorite moments of our time together, some mundane, some sweet, and some very, very explicit. Once I'd assembled them, I realized they were an excellent gauge of where I was in my cycle.

By the time he got to the final one, which was my personal favorite and depicted my recollection of how he'd held me by the throat and made me watch us in the bathroom mirror, he was open-mouthed and sweating.

Tap's control was very close to snapping.

It shouldn't have pleased me so much, but it sent a spike of heat through my veins.

Tap didn't lose control. Ever.

"Feather. This is ..." He grunted and caged me against the back of the desk, his hips against mine as he examined the sheets. "Is there something I should know?" He lowered his head and breathed in deeply as he kissed along my neck. "Have I been missing the signals that badly? I thought we had at least another week."

"I think it's just not as aggressive this time, but I didn't take my tincture yet." He ground me into the desk, his rigid length pressed up against me as his head fell back and he groaned. "I can ... or, we can have a few days to ourselves again. Up to you."

"That should be up to you, Phin, not me." His voice had gravel in it, and his eyes had gone solid ruby.

"Maybe I'll take it tomorrow, then." I watched as the man I loved, the one I craved more than life crumbled.

He took his spectacles off and flung them somewhere across the room before diving toward me, both hands cradling my face as his split tongue coaxed my lips apart. He kissed me like he was suffocating and I was air, like salvation itself was found in my lips. In the end, he got what he needed—I was the one left breathless when he finally pulled away.

His arm swept the pages off the desktop, the whole of them fluttering as they caught the air before slowly falling to the floor.

"I'll fix that later," he promised, and settled me where he wanted me before dropping to his knees.

I was wearing one of the dresses I'd bought in Revalia, and his hands slid up my legs at the same time they pushed them apart. He drew my ankles up over his shoulders, forcing me to lean back on my elbows as his mouth danced along my thigh. My fingers tangled in his hair as heat consumed me, a flush of warmth washing over me from head to toe. Tap latched on to me and sucked, causing every thought to evaporate.

"I love this dress," he muttered, alternating teasing my entrance with his tongue and fingers, sucking, and licking until I was a trembling mess.

In the end, it was his red eyes looking up at me with such devotion that did me in. I came with a rough shout on his fingers and nearly fell off the desk.

He scooped me up and turned me toward the cushions spread out all over the floor. "We're just getting started, beloved."

"Wait," I said on a gasp. "Look at the back."

After setting me down, he stripped off his own clothing a piece at a time while reaching for one of the discarded pieces of parchment. He flipped one over, finding the new symbol I'd created for us.

He reverently traced along the lines. "This is my sigil. But it's not. Not exactly."

"No, it's ... ours," I said, suddenly embarrassed and worried he'd think I defaced his sigil.

"Ours." His smile was slow. "Yes. This is you, here, and this is me ... but they're wrapped together. I can't tell where one stops and the other starts. It's perfect."

Relief washed over me, and then confusion as instead of returning to my side, he went to the cabinet and collected a pot of ink and his enchanted quill.

"What are you doing?"

"Did you think I would see that and not want it on my flesh immediately?" He kissed me hard, then dipped the needle and turned the quill over his heart.

"Wait! There? Are you sure?"

He rumbled a low laugh, the sound making my skin tingle. "I've never been more certain about a tattoo in my life."

He started to draw, and I took the opportunity to return the pleasure he'd given me while his hands were occupied.

"Phin, you ..." He inhaled through his teeth, the quill held safely away from his chest as I licked up his rigid length and then took all of him into my mouth. "Fates. I can't ... concentrate," he groaned as I added my hands and tongue, sliding up and down, finding a rhythm I liked. "You'll kill me," he swore, but gritted his jaw and continued to work the ink into his skin. Every time I glanced up, he was fighting to stay focused, and that only made me increase my efforts. I felt him twitch, and all at once, his hands were pulling me away.

"You're dangerous, Little Feather." He was panting, but the symbol was complete, right there over his heart in black ink.

"Me next," I said.

"Where?" he asked.

"You choose."

His head dropped, and he dragged in a rough breath. He shifted us so that I was on my knees, my front against the cushions, with him behind me. "You should probably find something to hold on to, Feather."

"Why—"

I moaned as he pushed into me from behind, hands braced on the floor under the cushion. It probably wasn't quite what he'd had in mind, but it was the best I could do given the circumstances.

He lowered the quill to my skin right near where my scar was. He would draw a bit, then pause, and check on me in that low voice I couldn't help but melt under.

"You're doing so well for me, Feather," he said, thrusting in and out a few times. Every nerve in my body was buzzing, thoughts unable to form. I realized that at least in part, he was keeping me from feeling any pain from the quill.

After one particularly long pause where he drew in and out of me at an excruciatingly slow pace, he swore.

"I can't ..." I felt him throb inside me and his pace increased to the point we were both gasping. Everything went fuzzy as my release washed over me, Tap only a moment behind. He wrapped himself over my back, and we just breathed together as my heartbeat slowed to a more normal pace. I thought he was rolling away, but instead he reached for the quill again.

"Just a bit more, beloved," he said, and I lay still as he finished placing the pattern on my skin, his body still joined with mine.

Those memories embedded themselves as surely as the ink, a smile locked on my face through the rest of the tattoo, the bath after, and even as we cuddled together on our bed in what had once just been his room for a good night's sleep.

I couldn't wait to draw it.

Want to see the new sparring workshop?
Grab the Bonus Scene Here:

https://BookHip.com/WNBHBRH

What's next?
Book 4 of The Gargoyle Knights Series:
The Gargoyle's Gem — Imogen's story
AND
Book 5 of The Demon Princes Series:
The Demon's Devotion – Ipos's story

Want to be the first to hear breaking news and
other info from L.? Sign up for her newsletter!

http://bit.ly/ALANewsletter

You can also join her reader group to chat
with her and other readers!

https://bit.ly/LilysReaderLounge

Did you like *The Demon's Domain*?
Leave a review on Amazon, Goodreads or Bookbub
to share your thoughts with other readers!

ACKNOWLEDGEMENTS

My GOODNESS Tap and Phin stole my whole heart while making me work for every. Single. Word! Getting to spend a bunch of time at the crossroads was a whole adventure for me. These two people, very alike and yet from very different worlds were so fun to watch as their story unfolded!

Thank you for reading! <3

To my husband who always reads it first, with the most enthusiasm and best ideas and observations. Love you most.

For my Write or Die friends, Shain and Dannie, always and forever! Me and my stories would not be who we are without you both.

Krista for gracefully adjusting schedules around the holidays for my slow progress and managing my extraneous use of commas, em-dashes and ellipses. For Jessica & Stephanie for always making the final product so stinking gorgeous. I couldn't do it without all your help and I mean that!

Beta & ARC readers—I ADORE YOU. Seeing any post with my stuff on it is a humbling, thrilling experience. I couldn't do this without you.

Special thanks always to Caroline & Meri who get first peek, first dibs and always answer my most random DMs. <3

For Kaitlin who makes sure my brain is engaged, events go smoothly and makes all the pretties for me. XOXO

All my admiration to Nya @guardianofshadows, Holly @the-hollyfox and Lana @lana_banana_arts for bringing my characters to life with their incredible art! I'm always ready to start a new round of commissions.

I can't wait for you all to see what's coming! There are more demons to make fall in love and some stone kin I'm dying to help find their mates.

Note: This world is planned to be seven books, one for each brother PLUS a novella for our stone kin friends in-between. I hope you stick with us!

For sneak peeks, discussion and other fun tidbits, make sure you're signed up for my newsletter, & join my reader group.

ABOUT THE AUTHOR

L. Alexander writes Paranormal and Fantasy romance with sweet & spicy cinnamon roll heroes, fated mates, monsters, magic and more. She guarantees a happily ever after no matter what and has a soft spot for broody anime characters.

www.authorlilyalexander.com

@lilyalexanderwrites on Instagram

Lily Alexander on Facebook, TikTok,
BookBub and Goodreads

L. also writes Contemporary Romance
under the name Lily Alexander.